Overseas

Overseas

BEATRIZ WILLIAMS

G. P. Putnam's Sons / New York

PUTNAM

G. P. PUTNAM'S SONS
Publishers Since 1838
Published by the Penguin Group
Penguin Group (USA) Inc., 375 Hudson Street, New York, New York 10014, USA • Penguin Group
(Canada), 90 Eglinton Avenue East, Suite 700, Toronto, Ontario M4P 2Y3, Canada (a division of
Pearson Penguin Canada Inc.) • Penguin Books Ltd, 80 Strand, London WC2R 0RL, England • Penguin
Ireland, 25 St Stephen's Green, Dublin 2, Ireland (a division of Penguin Books Ltd) • Penguin Group
(Australia), 250 Camberwell Road, Camberwell, Victoria 3124, Australia (a division of Pearson
Australia Group Pty Ltd) • Penguin Books India Pvt Ltd, 11 Community Centre, Panchsheel Park,
New Delhi–110 017, India • Penguin Group (NZ), 67 Apollo Drive, Rosedale, North Shore 0632,
New Zealand (a division of Pearson New Zealand Ltd) • Penguin Books (South Africa) (Pty) Ltd,
24 Sturdee Avenue, Rosebank, Johannesburg 2196, South Africa

Penguin Books Ltd, Registered Offices: 80 Strand, London WC2R 0RL, England

Library of Congress Cataloging-in-Publication Data

Williams, Beatriz.
Overseas / Beatriz Williams.
p.   cm.
ISBN 978-0-399-15764-6
1. Women in finance—New York (State)—New York—Fiction.
2. World War, 1939–1945—France—Fiction.   3. Time travel—Fiction.   I. Title.
PS3623.I55643O94   2012   2011047248
813'.6—dc22

Printed in the United States of America
10 9 8 7 6 5 4 3 2 1

Book design by Meighan Cavanaugh

This is a work of fiction. Names, characters, places, and incidents either are the product of the author's
imagination or are used fictitiously, and any resemblance to actual persons, living or dead, businesses,
companies, events, or locales is entirely coincidental.

While the author has made every effort to provide accurate telephone numbers and Internet addresses at
the time of publication, neither the publisher nor the author assumes any responsibility for errors, or for
changes that occur after publication. Further, the publisher does not have any control over and does not
assume any responsibility for author or third-party websites or their content.

To my husband and children,

without whom the rest means nothing.

The rain beat steadily through the night and into the meager dawn.

My raincoat had wilted long ago, and still the bitter spray leapt up against my hands from the nearby cobblestones, drummed out the minutes as the congregation chanted matins in the cathedral across the square.

In some distant corner of my mind, I must have recognized the discomfort. The rest of me hardly noticed. I only huddled there on a wooden bench, under the scanty shelter of a green-striped café awning, and studied the cathedral's west front with trancelike devotion. Inside that soaring space, Captain the Honorable Julian Laurence Spencer Ashford stood with his fellow British Army officers, reciting the psalms and the responses, bowing his head to his Lord. Soon he would rise to his feet and walk through a sandbag-framed door into the dismal wet square between us.

What would I say to him?

A surge of rainfall struck the awning above me and rolled along the cobbles in a wave, flinging itself against the cathedral towers; in that instant, the first low clangs of the bell tolled out across the square to signal the end of services.

I stood up, my heart striking madly against my chest. A few figures began to emerge from the doorway, shrouded by the downpour and the muted light of the early morning hour, and for a second or two I hesitated.

I imagined our meeting, and my limbs went slack under a fresh burst of self-doubt.

But then a new and more horrible idea flashed across my brain.

What if I missed him?

I plunged in panic from under the awning and hurried across the square. I hadn't thought of that. I hadn't thought I could possibly let his familiar figure slip by me, and yet as the bodies appeared, one by one, I realized the British officers all looked alike. All of them dressed in identical khaki trench coats, all wore the same peaked caps, all sported puttees and dark leather shoes. They were like images from a history book, from a war movie. They didn't look anything like the man I knew.

But Julian was there. He had to be. On this day, in this town, in this cathedral, he had attended morning services with another officer and walked back to his billet near the train station. It was a historical fact. I anchored myself to that thought: it gave me courage. I scanned the shifting bodies in front of me, bore down determinedly on a man in khaki and stopped him.

"Excuse me," I said, and cleared my throat. "Excuse me, can you tell me if Captain Julian Ashford attended services this morning?"

He looked astonished, as if a medieval king had leapt off the cathedral façade to address him.

"Please," I said. "It's really important. I have a message for him, an urgent message."

"Yes, he was there," the man said at last. He turned to the doorway. "He was sitting up front; he should be out directly." He looked back at me and opened his mouth as though he wanted to say something more, but hurried away instead.

I stood there, letting the chill rain roll down my body, clenching my fists rhythmically against my coat, waiting. A few French officers came out, and then a cluster of nurses; townspeople, all women; a lone British officer, not Julian. He stopped, consulted his watch, stepped aside.

Into the void walked a tall familiar figure.

Julian. He looked exactly as I remembered, and yet so alien. His luminous face, his broad capable shoulders, the little smile curling the corner of his full mouth, the glance upward into the weeping clouds, the hand reaching up to settle his cap more snugly on his forehead: I knew all those details intimately. I had last seen them only a week ago. But it was all enclosed in his uniform, martial and colorless and nothing like the modern clothes in which my memory dressed him. My brain seemed to split apart, unable to process the two images together.

I realized he was walking away, together with two other officers. "Julian!" I called, but the word came out in a croak; I could hardly hear it myself. "Captain Ashford!" I cried, more loudly. "Captain Ashford!"

He turned at that, searching through the crowd for my voice, brow creased in confusion. His companions turned too, inspecting the faces around them, but Julian found me first, picked me out effortlessly from the shifting throng. He cocked his head and watched me approach, not moving an inch, sizing me up, his skin gleaming with rain in the hazy glow of a nearby arc lamp.

He didn't know me at all.

I'd told myself to expect that, but the sight of his puzzled face still shocked me. It didn't show the smallest bit of recognition. I was a stranger to him.

"Captain Ashford." I tried to ignore the sting of his indifference, tried to ignore his beauty, his magnetism, and the shattering love I felt for him. "Do you have a moment?"

He opened his mouth to say something in reply, some demand for more information, but at the last instant his expression shifted from suspicion to concern. "Madam," he said, "are you quite all right?"

"Yes, I'm fine," I said, but even as the words left my lips, I realized the blood was draining from my face, that my ears were starting to ring and my knees to buckle under me. *Don't faint,* I thought urgently, *don't faint,* but already I was pitching forward.

Directly into his astonished arms.

I.

On the morning I first met Julian Ashford, I woke up panting, roused by the excruciating intensity of a dream I could not fully remember.

At the time, with no reason to believe in anything but the concrete and linear, I put it down to anxiety. I often had nightmares before major business meetings, assuming I was lucky enough to catch any sleep at all. They weren't particularly imaginative. I'd be running late in the morning and find myself stuck in slow motion, as if my arms and legs were made of wire; or else struggling to perform the lead role in a play I'd never rehearsed. Naked, of course.

But this dream was different. It had been submerged not in anxiety, but in a form of panic, so painful it was almost pleasurable. I'd been talking with a person—no, a man. Someone I cared about deeply; someone who cared about me. I'd been trying to explain something important to him, something vital, but he couldn't understand me.

I squeezed my eyes shut, struggling for details, the quick thrust of my heartbeat banging violently into my eardrums. Who was he? Not my father, not a friend or colleague. No one I could identify. The sense of him was already fading, leaving me abandoned, shipwrecked.

I opened my eyes and stared at the ceiling for a moment, and then I threw off the duvet. I showered and dressed and fled to work, but the foreboding persisted, like a vise around my brain, even as I burst free from

the subway stop on Broadway and Wall Street and swept up the tower-
ing sunlit phallus of the Sterling Bates headquarters, where Alicia Boxer
awaited me on the twenty-fifth floor.

An early riser, Alicia; it was her only virtue.

"I mean, what the fuck, Kate?" she demanded, by way of acknowledg-
ing my arrival. "Where the fuck did these revenue numbers come from?
Nineteen percent in year five?"

She sat at the far end of the bank's best conference room, surrounded
by wainscoting and bamboo shades and peaceful low-voltage incandescent light: an elegant contrast to the Modern American Cubicle theme on
the Capital Markets floor downstairs, where I was currently on rotation.
The presentation books for today's meeting lay stacked in front of her on
the mahogany table; her venti holiday-red Starbucks cup perched danger-
ously close to them, scenting the room with vanilla latte.

I eased into the empty chair at her right and summoned my still-reeling
wits. "I think you and Charlie discussed the revenue figures Friday night?
Before you left for the weekend?" I lifted the end of each sentence to make
it sound like a question. You don't do confrontational with Alicia, not if
you don't want to land a pension fund in International Falls, Minnesota,
for your next assignment.

She raised her eyes and glared at me anyway. She had a round babylike
face, so completely at odds with her personality it might have been a private joke between her and God. Pretty, in its way, particularly the arresting
blue of her heavy-lidded eyes, but her current haircut—short and wispy,
aiming presumably for a pixie effect—made that plump florid face look
like Tinkerbell undergoing a severe allergic reaction.

Not that my opinion counted for anything. According to Charlie, she
was sleeping with Paul Banner, head of Capital Markets and my current boss.

"Hmm. Did you forget your makeup today, Kate?" she asked.

On any other morning, this kind of comment—so typically Alicia, tossing her petty kindling atop the impotent inner rage of her subordinates—

would have infuriated me. Today, I could hardly be bothered to shrug. "Your e-mail said to hurry in. And Charlie and I were up late last night, finishing the presentation."

She tried again. "Do you have, like, some powder in your purse? I could loan you some mascara. This is kind of an important pitch, you know." She tapped the stack of presentations. "Southfield Associates is a twenty-billion-dollar fund. A lead steer."

"I've got lip gloss."

"Good. You're not going to find yourself in a room with Julian Laurence again anytime soon. You want to give the right impression."

"Yeah, well, back to the revenue numbers. I had some questions about them myself last night, but Charlie said . . ."

"Charlie is full of shit. You should know that. Year five revenue growth shouldn't be less than twenty-three, twenty-four. ChemoDerma is a *growth* company, Kate. Do you know how much skin serum they sold last year?"

I knew to the last dollar, but the question was obviously rhetorical. "A lot," I said, "but the patent expires . . ."

"Fuck the patent. I want you to redo the spreadsheet with a revenue growth number of twenty-five percent in years four and five. Print out a dozen copies and replace the page in all the books." She rose from her chair.

"But it's not just that page. A couple of charts refer to these projections . . ."

"Replace them all."

I glanced at the clock on the wall. "Um, isn't Southfield supposed to be here by eleven? And Banner has us pre-meeting at ten forty-five."

She ran her tongue along the ridge of her upper lip. "Come on, Kate. Where's that can-do spirit we hired you for? Just find an intern."

She picked up her latte and left the room.

"THANKS FOR SHOWING UP," I growled at Charlie, as he staggered through the conference room door two hours later. I was leaning over my laptop, flipping through the last few slides of the presentation and hoping I hadn't missed any references to the new revenue projections.

"Sorry, dude. My BlackBerry fell under the bed. Did you get them all done?" He nodded at the plasma screen on the wall, which was hooked up to my computer.

"Barely." I clicked back to the title slide and straightened. My back and neck were stiff with tension; I lifted one hand to rub the hardened muscle at the top of my spine.

"You rock." He set two cups on the table. "Peace offering. Peppermint mocha, extra hot, right?"

I looked at the cup. "Thanks," I said, and picked it up, bathing my nose in delicate mint-chocolate steam. The tension eased fractionally. "So where's Banner?"

"He's not here yet?"

"Of course not." The door opened and the intern wobbled in under a stack of presentations. I jumped up and snatched one, flipping to the pages I'd changed. All there. "Thanks, buddy," I said.

"No problem. Just mention me to Banner."

"Yep, sure." I thumped the books on the table, dismissing him, but he didn't leave immediately. He hesitated, hovering between the table and the door; I glanced back just in time to see him turn away with a shaming shake of his head.

I called after him. "Wait. I'm so sorry. What was your name again?"

"Doyle. David Doyle."

"I'll rave, I promise," I told him, flashing a smile.

"Yo, that was awesome," Charlie said, laughing, as David Doyle bolted out the door. "You slayed him."

"Hardly. So where did Banner go?" I repeated. "It's ten minutes to eleven."

"Oh, probably doing the meet-and-greet with Alicia. No way Banner's going to give up any face time with Julian fucking *Laurence*."

"Yeah, well, he *should* be more worried about the actual presentation."

Charlie crashed confidently into a chair and began to swivel. "Kate, nobody around here has even *met* Laurence. Never takes sales calls. Never reads Street research."

"Just the usual jerk, probably. You know these hedge-fund guys." I got up and went to the monitor on the wall, adjusting the display.

"Kate, Laurence is not just *some* hedgie. He's *the* hedgie. Grew Southfield from zero to twenty in, like, seven years. The dude has mythic fucking alpha. The real deal."

I heard the rhythmic squeak of Charlie's office chair, swiveling back and forth, and smiled into the TV monitor. He was a good-looking guy, Charlie. Not that I really noticed anymore, having seen him just about every day of my life for the past two and a half years, often for twenty-four hours straight, sometimes sloppy drunk, and once with horrifyingly explosive stomach flu (his, not mine). Good-looking in a bland way, with regular preppy features and straight thick brown hair, which he wore slicked back like some kind of Gordon Gekko mini-me.

"So what does that make him?" I turned around just in time to catch Charlie checking out my pencil-skirted derrière. "Not just any old jerk, but *the* jerk?"

"Come on, Kate." He pulled a stress ball out of his pocket and began squeezing it with his left hand. "He's a living legend. Timed the post-nine-eleven bounce-back to fucking perfection, made some leveraged bets on financial stocks. Risky shit, but it paid off. They unloaded all of it right at the top. Right at the *top*, dude. Nerves of fucking steel. The guy's a billionaire now." Charlie shook his head. His eyes shone with awe. "Not even thirty-five, and he's cleared the wall. The whole fucking ballpark."

"Impressive."

"Oh, come on. Look at you, all stressing out. Strap on a pair of balls, for once." He switched the ball to his right hand and rolled it around his palm, grinning slyly. "You're a smart girl."

"Thanks." I clicked again to the first of the revised slides and frowned. Twenty-five percent. We were going to get slaughtered.

"No, seriously. Plus you have a major advantage over the rest of us."

"What's that?"

"Your *looks*, Kate." He tossed the ball up in the air and caught it with a deft flick of his hand. "You're the first thing these guys notice when we walk into the room. You should work it."

"Charlie, for God's sake." I said it too sharply. I sensed Charlie's body locking into place, fingers clenched around the ball.

"Oh, dude"—his voice thinned with dawning apprehension—"you're not gonna, like, report me or something?"

"No, no. Jeez, Charlie. It's okay. All fun and games."

His hand slackened; the ball went back in the air. "You seriously don't think you're good-looking, though?" he pressed, relieved, apparently, that he wasn't about to be hauled up in front of a sexual harassment tribunal. One torturous day of our new analyst orientation three years ago had been devoted to gender sensitivity training, as if we hadn't had enough of *that* in college already. Not that most of my colleagues cared much. Anyone who was going to hyperventilate about the crassness of the investment-banking atmosphere did not, ipso facto, have the necessary cojones to kill your career.

"Well, I'm *okay*, I guess," I said cautiously, catching my reflection in the sterile blue glow of the computer screen.

"Dude, give yourself some credit. You rock the whole sexy librarian thing." He leaned back in his chair, propped his oily black shoes on the gleaming mahogany. "I mean, no offense."

"Sexy *librarian*?"

He shrugged. "Some guys love that shit."

"You're so full of it."

"Full of what?" He leaned forward, grinning. "Come on. Full of *what*, Kate?"

The first thing you learn on Wall Street: just play along. "Full of *crap*, Charlie."

"Kate! Did you just *swear*?"

"*Crap* doesn't count."

"Sure it does. It's like *shit* for wusses."

"Deep, Charlie. So Harvard."

"Kidding, Kate. We all love how you elevate the fucking tone around here."

"Any time."

"That prim Wyoming shit . . ."

"Wisconsin." I lifted the cup to my lips.

"Whatever. Just remember what I said, when Laurence . . . Oh, *fuck*." Charlie heaved his feet off the edge of the table, nearly toppling in his chair. "Here they are."

I jerked to attention, with a splash of scalding coffee against the back of my throat. My hand stole up to rip the elastic from the twist at the back of my head, leaving only a skinny tortoiseshell headband to keep my hair in place; not exactly the polished professional, but at least not—*thanks, Charlie*—librarian *manqué*. Had I remembered the lip gloss? I rolled my lips together. Slightly gooey. Check.

Alicia entered first, mouth twitching irrepressibly, jacket unbuttoned to reveal an aggressive bronzed cleavage. Her voice cascaded with false regret. "Kate, *there* you are. I'm afraid I'm going to have to ask you to leave."

The strangest feeling: vertigo, as if the entire broad carpeted floor had fallen away beneath my feet. "Leave?" I demanded, in undertone. "What do you mean, *leave?*"

"I'm so sorry. We had an extra ChemoDerma guy show up."

"What about Charlie?"

"He stays. He's just, you know, a little more *professional.*" She mouthed the last word with relish, hardly bothering to disguise her smile.

I'd had many revenge fantasies about Alicia. My favorite had her going rogue and blowing up the bank in a spectacular career implosion, like Nick Leeson with an industrial-strength push-up bra. Except she didn't work on the trading floor—no math genius, Alicia—and my joy in her demise would be obscured by the fact that most of my 401(k) was held in

Sterling Bates stock. Oh, and I would also be out of a job. Still, her public disgrace had been enjoyable to contemplate in the comfort of my cubicle at three o'clock in the morning: a guilty pleasure for which I usually repented in the light of day.

Not anymore.

I stared at her, only dimly aware of the dark-suited figures streaming through the door, filling the room with affable chuckles. "Okay," I said. I turned to Charlie. "It's all here, ready to go. Watch out for the new revenue numbers."

"Dude," he moaned.

"Don't worry. Alicia's doing all the talking. I'll be in my cube if you need me." I picked up my laptop bag and walked to the door—past Banner, with his craggy overtanned face and emollient smile; past the Chemo-Derma CEO, frowning quizzically; past two or three men who must have been from Southfield. The last one turned his face as I walked by, flashing me a lightning impression of startled eyes and bright extraordinary beauty, but I didn't even pause. I could just hear Banner introducing us: *And these are our hardworking analysts, Charlie Newcombe and Kate Wilson, who put the presentation together for you folks. Um, Katie?*

The door closed behind me, cutting him off.

I WENT DIRECTLY TO MY CUBICLE, as I'd promised Charlie, and kept my phone poised next to me on the desk. I had nothing to do; my laptop was in the conference room two floors above me, delivering the presentation.

I should have been grateful. I had never grown used to meetings like this one, always hovering on the brink of some disaster: six-inch-high spelling errors projecting on the screen, mislabeled graphics, pie charts whose numbers clearly didn't total to 100 percent. Revenue projections pulled out of thin air, neat and pretty and so completely freaking bogus. Ideal target practice for sharp-witted hedgies.

But this wasn't much better, this unnerving idleness, this queasy suspicion that I was missing a deadline or failing in some critical responsibility. I reached out restlessly with one hand and traced the edge of the framed photo on my desktop. Nothing too revealing, just Michelle and Samantha, standing in front of Neuschwanstein at some point during our post-college Eurail trip. Samantha's arm looped around Michelle's shoulders, pulling her off balance; Michelle's fingers stuck up above Samantha's head with the obligatory bunny ears. They were probably hungover. I was pretty sure we'd spent the previous evening at one of the Munich *biergartens*. Or three. A lifetime ago, it seemed; I narrowed my eyes and tried to recall the laughing Kate who had taken that photograph, compare her to the suit-swathed creature I inhabited now. Manhattan Kate, impermeable investment-banker Kate.

Eventually I rose to use the bathroom; not because I needed it, but because it was something to do, however brief. I lingered as long as I could at the black marble sink. I washed my hands with scrupulous care, chased away each tiny droplet under the hurricane draft of the hand dryer, twisted my hair back into its elastic. My face gazed back at me from the mirror, heavy and troubled, unrecognizable.

I picked up my silent BlackBerry from the counter and made my way back through the maze of identical heather-gray cubicles to my own, where I stopped short.

A tall lean man stood there in perfect stillness, resting one hand on the back of my chair. His curling hair gleamed dark gold in the remorseless office lighting; his back, broad and immaculate, bent forward a degree or two toward my desktop.

"I'm sorry," I snapped. "Can I help you with something?"

He straightened and turned to me. "Kate," he whispered.

I flinched in shock. The man was beautiful, unutterably beautiful. His face bore the implausible symmetry of a classical sculpture, almost exotic, with wide vivid eyes that absorbed me greedily. A yellow Sterling Bates visitor's badge hung from the right lapel of his suit jacket, or I might have thought I was hallucinating.

"That is to say, Miss Wilson," he said, in polished cut-glass tones, a plummy voice straight from the Friday night marathon on the classic movie channel. Gielgud, maybe, or Barrymore. He held out his hand. "Julian Laurence."

"Oh," I said, shaking it. "You're British." Of all the asinine things to say. He smiled. "Guilty as charged."

"Shouldn't you be in the meeting?"

"I'm sorry for disturbing you. I only wanted to convey my apologies, for having . . . for the way you were . . ." His voice trailed off, but his gaze, if possible, grew more intense: a strange vibrating stare, as if he were trying to scour the backs of my eyeballs.

"Oh, that's not necessary. Not your fault, I mean. I'm used to getting bumped. It's part of the job description." Was it my imagination, or had the restive murmur of the Capital Markets floor faded to silence? I could sense the heads popping up above the cubicle walls, like prairie dogs. My pulse twitched eagerly in my neck.

"In any case," he said, not taking his eyes from mine, "I'm sorry to have so nearly missed you."

"That boring in there, is it? I guess we should have slipped in a few pictures of celebrities, to keep you guys entertained." I nearly jumped at the spikiness in my own voice. I'd meant it as a joke.

His eyes widened, and a tiny crease formed between them. "Have I offended you? I beg your pardon. I only wanted . . . you see, you took me quite by surprise . . ." He shook his head. "I'm making a muddle of things, aren't I? I *do* beg your pardon."

"There's nothing to forgive." I swallowed, because my mouth was apparently watering, for God's sake.

He parted his lips hesitantly. His right hand curled and flexed at his side, on the outermost edge of my peripheral vision. I wanted to speak, to amaze him with some immortal display of wit, but my brain had frozen into stupidity, not quite able to process that the legendary Julian Laurence stood in full luminescent flesh before me, stammering and begging my pardon, like the shy kid at school who finally works up the courage to confess to his long-standing crush. Not that such a thing had ever happened to me; not that I'd ever met this man in my life.

"It's just this," he said, and a large hand appeared on his shoulder, startling us both.

"There you are," came a gruff voice, belonging presumably to the hand's owner. I tore my eyes away from the noble architecture of Julian Laurence's cheekbones to find a pale dark-featured man, a color-negative of Julian himself, watching me with cool impassivity, dragging his hand back down to cross his arms against his chest.

Julian let out an exasperated breath and cast his eyes upward. "My head of trading, Geoff Warwick," he said. "Geoff, it's Kate Wilson." He spoke with command, putting the slightest emphasis on my last name.

I lifted my well-trained hand, but Geoff Warwick only nodded. "Miss Wilson," he said.

Julian turned back to face me. He looked inquisitive, or else possibly amused, one eyebrow arched, but when my eyes met his, a smile lifted one side of his mouth. A conspiratorial smile, between the two of us: a kind of wink.

"Hadn't we better be getting back to the meeting?" asked Geoff.

"Yes, of course," Julian said, and his smile brightened to iridescence, dazzling the anodyne office air in a current of pure blithe energy. "Kate— Miss Wilson—a very great pleasure." He took my hand again, more a clasp than a shake, and then turned to stride down the aisle with the fluid ease of a natural athlete, drawing the light along with him, Geoff Warwick trotting doglike at his heel.

I stared after them, hardly noticing as the heads swiveled back in my direction and then, one by one, slipped back behind the cubicle walls. I could hear Charlie, of all people, observing in my brain: *Dude, that was fucking weird.*

Amiens

I don't think I remained unconscious long. I became aware of voices, hands; someone was touching my cheek, my forehead; loosening my collar, removing my hat. I seemed to be lying on someone's knee, with a single iron arm supporting my back and the cold rain still dripping miserably on my cheek.

"Who the devil is she, Ashford?" someone demanded, jarringly close.

And then Julian, in a voice so familiar it brought the sting of tears to my eyeballs: "We can sort that out later, Warwick. She's clearly ill."

Warwick. Geoff Warwick. I hadn't recognized the accent.

"Her eyelids are moving."

"Yes, I see. Are you all right, madam? Can you hear me?"

I nodded. "Yes," I scratched out. "Sorry." I dragged open my heavy eyelids, wanting to see his face: there it was, a little blurred, compressed with concern.

"Warwick," he said, glancing upward, "do you think you can disperse this crowd a bit? And see if there's a doctor among them."

"Not likely," said Geoff Warwick, but he moved away and began making commanding noises. I turned my head in his direction, and saw that at least a dozen people stood in a silent awed circle nearby. I struggled upward, but a renewed surge of dizziness and nausea closed my eyes.

"Sorry," I whispered again.

Anxiety clipped his words. "Madam, can I help you? Are you in pain?"

"No. Just tired. Long journey." I tried to smile, but my mouth wouldn't obey.

"Can I help you to your lodgings? Assist you in some way? Warwick!" he said urgently. "Have you found a doctor?"

"Someone's off to fetch one," Warwick said, returning. "How is she?"

"Conscious. Speaking. She seems a bit confused."

"No! I'm all right, really." I struggled to sit up again, with more success.

"Ashford, she's American!" said another voice, behind me. Julian's other companion; I couldn't see his face.

"Yes, I realize that," Julian said. He squinted at me thoughtfully.

"How do you know her?" demanded Warwick.

"I don't know her."

"She knew your name."

"Before God, Warwick, I've never seen her in my life," he insisted. "Madam, where do you stay? You can't return without help."

"I'm not anywhere yet," I said. "I just arrived in town."

A pause. "You must get her out of this rain," said the other voice.

"Yes, of course," Julian said. "Is the Chat open yet, do you think?"

"Not yet." Warwick sounded almost gloating. The chip on his shoulder evidently wasn't a modern development.

Another pause. "Madam, are you able to walk?"

"I . . . yes, of course." I slid off his knee and tested my legs: a bit wobbly, but still capable. Julian's arm remained across my back, supporting me.

"Warwick, you and Hamilton wait here for the doctor," Julian said, over his shoulder. "Tell him to find us in rue des Augustins."

Arthur Hamilton. Florence's brother. I strained to look at him, but his face was hidden under the low dripping peak of his officer's cap.

"Christ, Ashford, you're not taking her to your *billet*!"

"I beg your pardon, madam," Julian said and then turned to Warwick, speaking next to his ear in a stern whisper he evidently thought me too far gone to overhear. "Where the bloody hell else can I take her? It's pouring rain; the cafés aren't open yet. She's no streetwalker, that's clear."

Warwick snorted.

"For God's sake, look at her. You've never seen a prostitute"—Julian spoke the word in such an undertone I could only guess it—"with a face like that."

"You're mad, Ashford. She might be a damned spy, for all we know."

"Rot. Where's your humanity, man?" He turned back to me. "You're quite sure you can walk?"

"Yes," I said, taking a step. Strength was beginning to return, now that the immediate shock of meeting him had receded, but the nausea still lingered.

"I'll help you. Come along; it's not far. The landlady has a parlor, quite private and suitable until you're well enough to continue."

"I . . ." I nearly refused him, but then I remembered this was why I was here: to win his sympathy, to gain his trust. "I'm so sorry to trouble you," I said instead, and the words sounded alien, unlike me.

"Here we are, then," he said, guiding me forward with his arm. "Be decent for once, Warwick," he added, "and see about that doctor. Hamilton, you'll help him, won't you?"

He assisted me across the square and down a side street, not saying anything except for the odd short warning about loose cobbles and sidewalk edges. I stumbled along as if in a dream; or maybe it was a dream. It certainly seemed like one, walking down this street, in this bleak unfamiliar war-ridden French town, with the rain crackling icily down my coat and Julian's right arm encircling me from behind.

"Just around this corner," he said, so close I could smell the faint musk of his shaving soap. I had to dig my fingernails into my hand to keep myself from responding, from leaning into him, from slipping my own arm around his waist.

A door appeared in front of me; Julian opened it and led me into a cramped hallway. *"Madame!"* he called out. *"Madame, s'il vous plaît!* Come along with me," he said, drawing me through a doorway to the left.

A private parlor, he'd called it. Dignified words for such a room; private it might be, but the bare floorboards and sparse furniture and meager coal fire felt inhospitable to the point of grimness. A single electric lamp cast a dim circle of light into the gloom; outside, the storm rattled angrily against a pair of darkly curtained windows.

"Let me have your coat; it's quite soaked through," Julian said, leading me to a squat provincial sofa with decades of morning visits worn into its burgundy upholstery. I unbuttoned obediently and felt his hands on my arms, behind me, drawing the sleeves away. He folded it once, lengthwise, and laid it on the back of the sofa. "Now, do sit down. You must. I'll just find the landlady and have her bring a tray." He disappeared through the doorway.

I dropped into the sagging cushion and tried to gather my wits. A week had passed since I'd arrived in this century, a week of confusion and alienation and hard physical slogging, making my way from the middle of England to war-torn France. I'd had to learn everything from pounds, shillings, and pence to the proper technique for securing a hat with a single long pin; I'd borne all of it under the bruising weight of an impossibly profound grief. And my brain was at last getting used to it all—to the foreignness, of course, but also the unexpected fact that it was so . . . *ordinary*. Strange, without all the modern machines and clothes and conveniences, and yet familiar. Bread tasted like bread. Rain fell as wetly as ever.

Julian was still Julian.

But *young*. Good grief. The physical differences were subtle enough: the hair a shade lighter, the skin more dewy; the face perhaps rounder, less chiseled. The distinction lay more in his expressions, his manner. He wore that unmistakable air of command about him, of course; he'd probably had it since infancy, and the experience of captaining a British infantry company had only intensified the instinct. But here, now, it combined with eagerness, artlessness, less ease and practice. He hadn't quite celebrated his twenty-first birthday, I remembered. I was an older woman to him.

A dangerous line of thought, of course. With unnerving immediacy his golden body rose above mine in the summer twilight, so perfectly authentic that my head bowed before the vision and a heavy weight seemed to press the breath from my chest. I twisted brutally the ring on my finger, forcing my brain to detach, to distract itself with practicalities. No modern expressions, I reminded myself. Tuck in your feet. Posture.

I was going to throw up.

I cast about for a container of some kind, and spied a chipped blue-and-white vase on the windowsill. I staggered over and grasped it just in time.

"My God!" Julian's voice exploded from the doorway in alarm.

I sagged against the window, my throat burning: bile and humiliation.

2.

I disliked Paul Banner for a number of reasons, but primarily because he was always hitting on me.

He wasn't blatant about it. That I could have shut down pretty easily. No, his style was smarmier, sneakier, so I couldn't quite pinpoint just where he'd crossed the line. He'd show up at my desk, for example, and take me out to lunch under the pretext of giving me career advice, but it would still have the nauseating flavor of a date with your lecherous rich uncle. I'd spend the whole time waiting miserably for his hand to show up on my knee, while he probably spent the whole time working up the nerve to do it.

"Katie," he said now, materializing at the edge of my cubicle and taking a long look down the front of my shirt, "let's debrief."

It was just after two o'clock and I was about to crash. I'd had about four hours of sleep the entire weekend, and Charlie had just treated me to an enormous greasy Reuben sandwich—my favorite—from the deli around the corner, to settle accounts over the Alicia incident this morning. It sat in my stomach now in a warm planetary mass, drawing my eyelids downward with the force of its gravitational pull. I could hardly think straight. "Debrief?" I repeated.

"Well, you know, that was kind of an odd situation, back there in the meeting."

I feigned innocence. "How so? By the way, how did everything go?"

"Good. Great. I think they liked me," he said modestly. "Let's grab some coffee. You look like you could use it."

I couldn't argue there. I sighed and reached for my bag. "Charlie," I called over, thinking someone should know where I was going, just in case, "we're just grabbing a quick coffee downstairs."

He looked up from his computer screen and took everything in. One eyebrow elevated. "Sure, dude," he said. "Bring me back the usual."

One of the benefits of working at Sterling Bates, in my book, was the coffee shop next door. According to the office coffee bores—you know, the ones who drone on about Arabica versus Kenyan beans or whatever—Starbucks was crap, but it suited me just fine. It was a place to go when you were sick of the cubicle; at Sterling Bates we used it constantly as our de facto casual meeting space. Any financial journalist wanting an easy scoop, or for that matter any unemployed taxi driver looking for a stock tip, just had to sit in that Starbucks with a newspaper and a latte and keep his ears open.

"So what did you think?" Banner began, taking a drink of cappuccino. In Italy, two summers and a lifetime ago, I'd learned that nobody drank cappuccino after eleven in the morning; the knowledge gave me a pleasant surge of moral confidence.

I settled against the slippery wooden back of my chair and crossed my legs. "I don't know. I wasn't there. What did they make of the revenue projections?"

"They had a few questions." He drummed his fingers against the table and peered outside at the narrow swarming sidewalks. The Sterling Bates headquarters were located only one block down from the New York Stock Exchange, which meant we were among the relatively few people working on Wall Street who actually worked on Wall Street. My folks got a kick out of that.

I sipped at my mocha and waited for him to continue.

"Katie," he said finally, "what are your plans for next year? Business school?"

"I think so. I just sent off the last application on Friday."

"Where did you go to undergrad, again?"

I hesitated. "University of Wisconsin."

"That's right. I remember. We don't usually recruit from there, do we?"

"No," I said. "Not usually."

"Well, I'm glad we made the exception. You've been a remarkably productive asset for us. We'd hate to lose you."

I laughed politely. "Even after this morning?"

"Especially after this morning. Don't think I didn't see how Alicia sandbagged you in there. I've been around here long enough to know a thing or two."

"Hmm." Probably not the right moment to make my *j'accuse* just yet.

His eyes latched onto mine, trying to connect; I raised my coffee cup again as a buffer. "Now, that's what I like about you," he said. "You don't waste your killer instinct on office politics. Unlike most of the jackasses around here. Myself included," he added, with a laugh. "Anyway, you got out of there with poise, Katie. Real poise. Laurence was impressed."

The coffee caught at the back of my throat.

"Very impressed. He was asking me a lot of questions about you at lunch."

"Really." Cough, sputter. "What kind of questions?"

"Just questions. Here's the deal, Katie. I'd like you to take the lead on this thing. Rework the numbers, get something back to them in the next day or two."

"*What?*" I wheezed out, through the coffee droplets. I set down my cup and wiped at my watering eyes, not quite sure I'd heard him properly.

He leaned forward across the table, until I could count the stress lines cutting across his forehead. "We need Southfield in on this deal, Katie," he insisted, pressing his right index finger into the wood veneer. "If Southfield's in, others will follow. Fucking lemmings. You know that."

"No, I get it." I edged back my chair as discreetly as possible. "I'm really flattered. It's just . . . are you sure you want *me* taking the lead? I'm not exactly senior. I wasn't even in the meeting."

"If you're worried about Alicia, I can promise you she won't be a problem."

"No, no," I said swiftly. "I can handle *that*."

He paused for a beat or two, inspecting my expression, and then his face eased into a smug smile. "Relax, Katie. Laurence likes you, and it would be a good high-profile project for you. Pretty straightforward, too. And I'd be one hundred percent behind you."

"Wow," I said. I was beginning to feel like one of those poor schmucks in the *Godfather* movies, being made an offer he couldn't refuse. I ran my finger delicately around the rim of the plastic coffee lid and tried to think of something more to say.

"Good, then." Banner sat back. "Consider yourself the point man. I'll give Laurence a shout to let him know it's coming." He stood and picked up his cup with a wink. "Now, try to go home early and get some beauty sleep."

"So, dude," Charlie said, around one o'clock the next morning, "what's the fucking deal here? Banner's not pimping you, is he?"

I swiveled my chair to face him. "*What?* Oh please. Not that Banner wouldn't try if he could," I admitted, "but I'm not exactly hedgie bait."

"Whatever. I smell a Banner plot." Charlie propped his feet up on his desk and balanced a red editing pen on his knee. He looked tired and pasty under the fluorescent lights, like he'd been hung upside down in a meat locker for the day. "And Alicia's on the fucking warpath, by the way. You'd better watch your ass."

I leaned back in my chair and rubbed my eyes. "That's all I need."

We were sitting in adjoining cubes, coming up with a more sensible revenue model for ChemoDerma. That was the cover story, anyway; at the moment my laptop displayed a long list of Google search results for *Julian Laurence Southfield*.

I'd already read most of them, doing my due diligence on Southfield the last few days, and there wasn't much I didn't already know. How Julian Laurence had started the fund in 2001, bringing together a couple of genius traders and his own impeccable talent for timing markets. Returns had piled up, new investors had piled on, and now Southfield Associates was one of the largest hedge funds in the world.

But for such a dynamic company, it had remarkably little buzz. Here and there a quote appeared, attributed to Julian, usually some dull reflection on market conditions, nothing with any sort of personality.

And that was the strange part. Here was this freakishly handsome man, the young CEO of an explosive hedge fund, an absolute prodigy in every respect: where were the interviews, the *Vanity Fair* cover, the snarky *New York* magazine hit job? Even Page Six returned only one mention from last year, when he had attended some charity function at MoMA: ***Julian Laurence,*** *the elusive founder of mega hedge fund Southfield Associates, made a rare appearance, setting socialites' hearts briefly aflutter until his early departure.*

That was it. Not even a photo of that remarkable face.

I ran my cursor over his name. Why keep such a low profile? He ought to be out enjoying himself, dating supermodels and buying up beachfront property in the Hamptons. He had the world at his feet. He couldn't just be staying in at night.

"So are we supposed to check any of this shit with ChemoDerma?" Charlie was asking. "Because it's pretty weird, messing with the IPO pitch without . . . *shit.*" His feet swung back down to the floor.

I looked down his line of sight and saw Alicia marching toward us in a sleek black pantsuit. There were about a dozen other analysts still in the bullpen, working on various projects, but I knew there wasn't a chance she was hunting down one of them.

It didn't take her long to find me. "Kate, I'd like to . . ." She stopped and ran her eyes up and down my figure. "Is *that* what you're wearing these days?"

My hand went to the strand of faux pearls at my throat, lying atop the wide neck of my charcoal sweater-dress. "I don't have any meetings today."

She narrowed her eyes at me. "Whatever, Kate. I need to talk to you. Is there a conference room free?"

"There should be," I said. "We're not too busy right now."

She followed me into an empty room and shut the door, bracelets clanging against the handle. The floral scent of her perfume closed densely around us. "Just what the living *fuck* do you think you're doing?" she hissed.

"Wow," I said. "I don't know what you mean."

"Stealing my fucking deal, that's what! Cutting me out. Setting Banner against me. And after all I did to make you look good . . ."

My cheeks grew warm. "Excuse me, but what planet are you living on? I had nothing to do with any of that. Banner called me in for a meeting and said he was putting me on the revisions. It wasn't *my* idea. I didn't even have a *choice*."

"Do you think I'm a fucking *idiot*, Kate?" Her voice, building in shrillness, crested on the verge of a shriek.

I raised one fatal eyebrow.

She turned red; her eyes bulged, blue and globular, from beneath their heavy lids. When she spoke, however, her voice had sunk nearly to a whisper. "Oh, you fucking bitch. You fucking *bitch*. You have no idea, no *idea*, no *fucking clue* what I'm going to do to you. If I have to blow up the whole fucking bank, so help me."

She turned and stalked out of the conference room. I stood there, frozen, watching the door ease behind her until it closed at last with a final click.

"MESSENGER IT? ARE YOU KIDDING?" Banner wasn't looking at me as he said this; his thumbs flew away on his BlackBerry, firing off some e-mail.

I folded my arms. "Don't we always messenger these things? Do you want me to e-mail it instead?"

His eyes flashed upward. "No," he said, as if he were stating the obvious. "I want you to deliver it yourself."

I was sitting in the chair in front of Banner's desk, feeling like a kid hauled in to see the principal. As head of Capital Markets, he had one of the plushest offices in the building, full of dark brown furniture and gleaming upholstery, designed to strike clients into acquiescent awe. The lion-footed desk roared Important Antique, or at least a convincing reproduction, and the handsome wing chair in which I was sitting could swallow me whole without a burp.

"Oh," I said. "What about Charlie?"

"*Charlie?* What the fuck?" He began to laugh. "You really don't get it, do you? Look," he said, still chuckling, "here's Laurence's e-mail address. Let him know you're stopping by the office to drop it off. Say you're on your way to the airport for Christmas, and thought you'd hand it off in person."

"But I'm not leaving until tomorrow morning," I said.

"Katie, Katie." He turned back to his phone. "Work with me here."

I straightened in the chair with some effort. "Look," I began, about to make some high-minded protest, like *I'm just not comfortable hanging myself up in the shop window like that.* But then I realized two things. First, arguing with Banner over something like this was akin to the old saying about teaching a pig to sing.

And second—God help me—I *wanted* to see Julian Laurence again.

"Aren't you going to check over the book first?" I asked instead, waving my hand at the printout on his desk.

He didn't look up. "No, I trust you. Look, I've got to get going. Did you write down his e-mail?"

"Yes. Safe in the BlackBerry." I held it up to demonstrate, but he wasn't watching.

"There you go, then. Merry fucking Christmas." He ripped his gaze away from his phone and grinned at me.

I struggled upward from the chair. "You too."

I snatched the presentation from his desk and stalked back to my cubicle, where my laptop bag slumped tiredly against the dividing wall in a bristle of zipper tabs. I stood there a minute, nibbling my lower lip, presentation dangling from my folded arms. Then I tossed the book on the desk and burrowed in the bag for my wallet.

It took some time to find the scrap of paper I sought; it had wedged itself between my University of Wisconsin senior year ID and an ancient loyalty card from the hairdresser next door to my apartment in Madison. I removed it slowly and stared at the image for a long dense moment: a heart, colored in blue-black ink, surrounded by a circle with a slash across the center, like a traffic warning sign.

I'd drawn it on the flight to New York City two and a half years ago, full of apprehension and introspection and a margarita or two from my farewell lunch with Michelle and Samantha. There, cruising above the patchwork farmlands of Pennsylvania, I'd promised myself—in the kind of melodramatic gesture that had once been typical of me—to avoid any kind of romantic involvement until I'd completed the three-year Sterling Bates analyst program. I'd take myself out of the game, keep my life neat and tidy, stay focused on work. Not a single date. Not even a casual flirtation. And I'd kept that vow with near-obsessive scrupulousness.

So what now? Because I wasn't stupid, and for all the orderly window dressing of legitimate business purposes, Banner's scheme had flirtation and more written all over it.

Quickly, before I could second-guess myself, I stuffed the paper back in my wallet and reached for my phone to type a short message: *Hello Julian, heading uptown now, can I drop off the ChemoDerma book on my way? Best, Kate Wilson.*

My fingers hovered uncertainly—should I make the greeting more formal?—but *Dear Mr. Laurence* sounded starchy and *Dear Julian* coyly intimate. I held my breath and hit *send* and tossed the phone on my desk, as if it were a ticking bomb.

I looked over my cubicle. I should probably be gathering up my few things; I wouldn't be back in the office until Monday. I reached for my bag and began putting file folders inside, mostly ChemoDerma material. There would be other meetings, after all. We were flying up to Boston on Tuesday.

My phone buzzed. I counted off three full seconds before snatching it up.

Already gone home for the day. Don't suppose you're on the Upper East? Julian.

My fingers danced over the keypad.

Actually yes, 79th Street.

The response came back just as fast.

I'm at 52 E 74. Could you bring it by?

Me: Of course. Which apt?

Julian: Just the house.

The entire house, his own private rectangle of Manhattan; why not? My fingers began to shake. This was bad. This was monumentally stupid. I should not be doing this.

Okay, be there in half an hour.

Amiens

I felt Julian's arm close around me, thick and steady along my waist. I tried to shrug it off, but my belly heaved up bile again and it was all I could do not to keel forward onto the floor. I felt the sweat pearl out on my temples.

"Sorry," I gasped, pulling away.

"You're ill. You must sit down."

"No, I'm all right, really. Just a little hungry."

"The tray should be along directly. I . . ." He stopped, looking awkward.

I stood there witlessly, staring at the floor, holding an old blue vase full of my own vomit, or what there was of it, considering I hadn't eaten in nearly eighteen hours. "I don't know what you must think of me," I said, sliding the vase behind my skirt.

He cleared his throat. "I think you ought to sit down. Here," he added, snatching the vase, "I'll take that to the scullery."

"Oh, don't . . ." I said, but it was too late. I tottered back to the sofa and sank down with my head in my hands. Everything seemed to be sliding into disaster; worse, I was wasting time, my most precious resource. Think, Kate. *Think.*

The door opened, and Julian walked back in, having disposed of the vase. I straightened and tried to smile, tried to push aside my embarrassment. It was easier than I thought; for one thing, I felt much better now that I'd thrown up.

"The doctor will be here soon," he said.

"Really, it's not necessary. I . . ." I broke off, not quite sure what to say.

"The landlady should be along shortly." He paused and put his hands behind his back, standing there stiffly in the middle of the room, cap fixed to his head. As I watched, the faint shadow of his Adam's apple rose and fell along the line of his throat, so fleeting I might have missed the movement with a single blink.

Something like relief eased through my body at the sight of his nervousness, at the suggestion that, already, I had gained some small power over him. I positioned my hands modestly in my lap. "Thank you so much for your kindness, Captain Ashford," I said, in a dulcet voice, angling my head. His eyes caught for an instant on my exposed throat. "You've been wonderful."

He hesitated. "I beg your pardon, but I'm afraid you have me at a disadvantage. Have we perhaps met?"

I felt my mouth turn up in a half-smile. "Met? Not exactly."

"And yet you know my name."

"Yes, I do."

He stood there expectantly, and I realized he was waiting for me to introduce myself. What was I going to say?

Someone entered the room with a creak of stiff hinges and a heavy tread. I looked to the door and saw a burly woman in a long faded dress and apron, holding a battered tray before her. She did not look amused.

"*Une fille!*" she scolded Julian. I could just make out the words, with my limited high school French. "You have brought a . . . a girl!" Words seemed to fail her. She crashed the tray onto the worn wooden table in the corner and glared at me balefully.

"*Ça suffit, madame,*" he said. "She's ill; the doctor will arrive in a few minutes. Thank you for the tea."

She left, grumbling, wiping her hands on her apron as though to brush away whatever illness I'd carried in with me.

"Now I've got you in trouble with your landlady," I said. "I'm awfully sorry."

"Quite all right. Would you like a bit of tea?"

"I'd love tea. Thank you."

He poured me a cup. "Milk?"

"No, thank you."

"Are you certain? There's no sugar, I'm afraid." He removed the leaves in a practiced gesture and offered me the cup. "Rationing and all that."

"I don't mind." The china stung my cold fingers with divine heat; I raised it quickly to my lips.

"And bread, perhaps?"

"Yes, thank you."

He sawed off a slice from the baguette and handed it to me. I tried to restrain myself, to eat calmly, but the nausea had been replaced by the most ravenous hunger, and I couldn't disguise the eagerness with which I ripped into the bread.

"There now," he said, sitting down in the chair next to the sofa. "Better?"

"I'm sorry. I must seem very mysterious to you."

He inclined his head. "Not at all."

"You want to know who I am, of course. You probably think I'm a spy, or worse." I laughed hollowly. "Worse! I don't see how it could possibly be worse. But I'm not a spy, Captain Ashford." The teacup vibrated in my hands. "I'm . . ."

A knock sounded on the door. "Come in," Julian said, not taking his eyes from mine.

I looked at the doorway. "Hello, Lieutenant Warwick," I said. "Have you brought the doctor?"

He stopped short, stunned. "How the devil does she know my name? Who is she?"

"We haven't got to that, yet," Julian said, and turned to the other man, who'd followed Warwick through the door, right after the slight figure of Arthur Hamilton. *"Vous êtes le medecin?"*

"Oui. C'est la fille, là?"

"Oui." Julian began explaining my symptoms, and the doctor came toward me, eyes narrowed in clinical concern.

"Monsieur, it's nothing," I said, in my halting French. "I'm just tired and hungry."

"You've vomited?" he asked. That, at least, was what I thought he said; he made a brief motion with his hand that seemed to be the universal sign for throwing up.

"Yes, a little," I replied. "It happens when I'm hungry."

He gave me a sharp, wise look. I cast my eyes downward, trying to look modest.

"I will listen to your heart and lungs," he announced, and removed a stethoscope from his black leather bag—a real leather doctor's bag!—and did just that. I sat in my hollow of worn velvet, trying to breathe in a natural rhythm. He listened long and carefully, moving the cool metal of the stethoscope around my torso; he examined my eyes and throat and straightened to skewer Julian with a piercing stare.

"She's as well as can be expected," he said.

"Expected?" Julian asked.

The doctor opened his mouth.

"Because of hunger, isn't it, monsieur?" I said.

He turned back to me with both eyebrows raised and studied my expression. "Yes, hunger. How long has it been since madame has eaten?"

"A day. I've been traveling." I couldn't remember the French word for travel, but I made walking motions with my fingers and the doctor nodded.

"She must eat," he said, turning back to Julian, "and rest."

"Fair enough," said Geoff Warwick, in English. He looked at me. "Where are your friends in this town?"

"Well," I said, "I'm afraid I haven't any. But I'm quite well now. It was only the strain of the journey, just now, and I thank you both very much for your concern. If I may, however, before I leave, have a private word with Captain Ashford?"

They all looked at one another.

"Yes, of course," Julian said. "Perhaps . . . but you must eat . . ." He addressed Warwick. "Why don't I run her over to the Chat for a bit of breakfast? It should be open by now."

"You're *serious*, Ashford? She might be anyone, she might . . ."

"I beg your pardon." I stood up with as much dignity as I could manage: long neck, back straight, shoulders back. "I wouldn't dream of imposing on your kindness. I only wish a short word with Captain Ashford, and I'll be on my way."

"Warwick, you're an ass," Julian said, rising to his feet the instant my bottom had left the sofa cushion. "She's a perfectly well-bred girl, as you can plainly see. The war's imposed difficulties on us all, and I should think *you'd* show a little more humanity, of all people. I'm now going to see that she has a decent breakfast and decent lodging."

"Really, Warwick," said Hamilton. He'd been standing there diffidently, raindrops rolling away from his coat, watching the exchange; his expression wary, perhaps, but sympathetic. "I don't see any reason for suspicion. Ashford's only trying to do the right thing by the poor girl." His accent was stiff, nasal: *pooah gel.*

"Very well," Warwick said to Julian, ignoring me. "Don't forget we're engaged with McGregor and Collins from ten o'clock."

"I shan't be that long, I assure you." Julian turned to the doctor, who still stood there, looking expectant, and addressed some low-voiced question to him.

"Please," I said hastily, reaching for my coat, "I'm not at all destitute . . ."

But Julian had already pressed something into the doctor's hand, and was gathering our coats and ushering us through the door; past Hamilton, who stood back respectfully; past Warwick, who fixed me with a spiteful glare. I returned it in full. I'd worked on Wall Street for three years; I could do the alpha stare.

Plainly, Geoffrey Warwick didn't like me.

But then, he never had.

3.

Julian's townhouse wasn't quite what I was expecting. In the ruthless arithmetic of Manhattan real estate, you bought the finest you could possibly afford; the hierarchy of property aligned neatly with the hierarchy of wealth. A legendary Wall Street investor should inhabit the pinnacle of all: a wide pearl-white mansion just off Fifth Avenue, perhaps, with a ballroom inside and a service entrance below; or else a cavernous floor or two atop some monumental Park Avenue apartment building.

This house was neither. It stood midway between Madison and Park, on a quiet street lined with trees, subdued and anonymous. It looked exactly like its neighbors on either side: twenty-odd feet wide; plain elegant Greek Revival lines; faced half with limestone, half with brick; entrance raised a few steps from street level. The number 52 was carved into the lintel above the front door.

I raised my hand to press the doorbell and paused. I thought I could hear the sound of a piano drifting through the walls, something lilting and complex and faintly melancholy. Chopin? I closed my eyes. When I was young, my father had played a lot of Chopin on the old turntable he'd refused to give up. I hadn't heard it in years; I couldn't even name the piece, but the notes were as familiar to me as my childhood bedroom.

A dark-clad figure approached, shuffling down the sidewalk. I shook off my reverie and pressed my finger against the doorbell. The music cut off.

I heard footsteps, growing louder, and the door opened in a rush of warm air against my cheeks. I was half-expecting to see a butler of some kind, but it was Julian himself, unmistakably and devastatingly Julian, wearing a dark-blue turtleneck sweater over a pair of tan corduroys.

"Hi," I said.

"Hello, there," he answered. "Come on in."

"Oh, that's okay. I just wanted to hand this off to you." I held out a copy of the revised pitch book, bound together by David Doyle half an hour ago.

"Thanks," he said, taking it. "I appreciate your taking the trouble to bring it round." He hesitated.

"Um, well, I'd better get going," I said. "Let me know if you have any questions. I'll be checking my e-mail." I began to turn.

"Wait," he said. "Do you mind coming in a moment, while I look it over?" He unleashed his smile, flattening me. "I should hate to have to interrupt your Christmas with any tedious e-mails."

"Oh, I don't mind *that*. Goes with the territory, right?" I tried to smile back. "But yes, I have a couple of minutes, if you want me to wait."

"If it's not too much trouble."

"Of course not."

He stood back, allowing me past him into the hallway. "Oh," I said, under my breath. I'd expected to find the usual stripped-down bachelor interior, with all the walls knocked out and everything painted in bright stark white. But this was something else entirely. A flight of stairs stretched in front of me, at the end of an entrance hall tiled in worn checkerboard marble. To the right, a broad archway opened to the living room, a spacious high-ceilinged rectangle in which a fire burned invitingly beneath a pale marble mantel, flanked by two plump sofas. The walls, lit by a scattering of lamps, had been painted a warm goldenrod; the abundant trim work a creamy off-white. Books sat everywhere: on shelves, primarily, but also in haphazard stacks, on the floor, on the furniture. It was comfortable. Homelike.

Julian stepped forward hastily and began removing the volumes from one of the sofas. "Sorry," he said, setting them down on the floor. "I don't know how they accumulate like that. They're part rabbit, I think. Please sit down. Can I get you something? Let me take your coat."

He was nervous, I realized. The knowledge hit me like a bludgeon, shocking and rather paralyzing. Julian Laurence, nervous? Around *me*? I felt his hands on my arms, removing my coat; he laid it over the top of the sofa.

"I'm fine," I said. "I didn't mean to drop by like this. It was Banner's suggestion. I hope I haven't inconvenienced you."

"Not at all. Sit. You're sure I can't get you something?"

"No, really. I can only stay a minute."

He smiled, a small faint smile, and picked up the pitch book from a side table. "Then let's get to it, shall we?" he suggested, sitting down on the sofa opposite me. He wore soft old moccasin slippers, curving about his feet with well-worn comfort.

We were quiet for a moment. He bent over the pitch book and began flipping through the pages, leaning against the back of the sofa. I glanced down at the stack of books at my feet and squinted, trying to make out the titles.

"Oh, I see what you've done," he said after a moment or two. "Interesting. So you've broken it down into two scenarios . . ."

"Yes," I said. "The assumptions are in the footnotes."

"But look here," he said. "If sales are going to be growing that much in the best-case scenario . . . Hold on a moment; I'll get my laptop." He rose and padded to the rear of the room, sliding open a pair of pocket doors to reveal what looked like a library, lined with still more bookshelves. I craned my neck to watch him. He went to a desk near the rear window, unplugged a MacBook, and carried it back into the living room. "Do you mind?" he asked.

"No, of course not," I said.

"I was trying to put together a proper model. I don't usually do them anymore, frankly don't find it that useful except as an exercise, but I thought . . . Let me just . . ." His voice drifted off. He frowned into the computer screen, tapping away at his model. He was so deep in concentration I felt, at last, it was safe to study him. I indulged shamelessly, staring at the squared-off tip of his chin, at the elegant line of his nose, at the full arc of his lips, all glowing in the light from the computer screen. His cheeks wore a faint pink stain, starting high on his cheekbones and then fading away into the tiny pinpricks of his beard. I wanted to reach out my hand and touch it.

"Look here a moment." He motioned to me. "This is what I've done."

I got up slowly, almost trancelike, and stepped to the other sofa. He didn't look up. "Look." He pointed at the screen. "Don't you think that's more reasonable? Here, sit down. Hold the book a moment. Now if we look at year four . . ."

I eased myself down next to him on the cushion, trying not to place myself too close, but it was no use. I could feel the slight warmth drifting from his body, smell the clean scent of his skin, hear the faint rush of his breath into the intimacy of the air between us. He was still holding out the presentation; I took it, folding back the previous pages with deliberate care.

"Just a moment," he said, "pardon me," and reached across my lap to the lamp table next to the sofa. He opened a drawer at the top and withdrew a pen. "Now," he went on, taking the book from me and scribbling something into the margin, "I think we need to shift this assumption . . ."

"You're left-handed," I murmured. I thought I said it to myself, but it must have come out aloud.

"No, right," he said absently, and then closed his eyes. "I mean, yes, left."

I forced out a laugh. "I'm confused. Ambidextrous?"

"No. Just some nerve damage a while back. I learned to write with my left hand."

"Oh. I'm sorry," I said, and then added, after a pause, "But wasn't that you playing the piano, when I came up?"

He looked surprised, and then embarrassed. "And here I thought the walls were soundproof. Sorry about that."

"No, it was lovely."

"It was execrable. But to answer your question, it doesn't affect my dexterity so much, or at least not anymore. It's just the grip that's painful." He held up his right hand to demonstrate.

"Wow. How did it happen?"

The color in his cheeks intensified. "Car accident."

"Oh no!" I couldn't help myself. I could almost hear the horrifying crunch of glass and metal. I only just stopped my hand before it reached up to grasp his.

"Oh, it wasn't as bad as that," he said easily, wiggling his fingers. "Still whole, after all."

"You should be more careful," I said.

"You're assuming it was my fault."

"Wasn't it? I can just picture you driving your brand-new Porsche at a hundred miles an hour down the freeway, celebrating your first big bonus."

"Hmm." His expression turned speculative. "And what did *you* do with your first bonus?"

I laughed. "I'm just an analyst, remember? My share of the bonus pool amounts to about a shot-glass-full. I think I went out and got a new pair of shoes, last time, and socked the rest away in the apartment fund."

"Apartment fund?" He seemed amused.

"My roommate's wearing a little thin," I said. "I'd like to buy my own place. Which at this rate will be a hall closet in Washington Heights, but that's why I'm going to business school."

"Business school! You're joking, surely."

"No, I'm serious. Why would I be joking?"

"Because you're too good for this. Come now, you don't really want to be an *investment banker* all your life, do you?"

"Why not?"

"That's the wrong question. Not *why not*, but rather *why*? Why waste your life around chaps like that Banner idiot?" He looked genuinely concerned.

I shifted my gaze downward and fingered the edge of the presentation. "Look, I'm from Wisconsin. Typical suburban environment. I left to make something of myself, and Wall Street seemed the obvious place to start. Where the action was."

"From Wisconsin," he said. "I'd never have guessed Wisconsin."

"Well, we don't *all* sound like we've just stepped off the set of *Fargo*."

"That's not what I meant. I . . ." He checked himself. "In any case, I never went to business school, and it hasn't done me any harm."

"Yes, but you're . . ." I waved my hand at him.

A phone rang, somewhere behind us: the library, probably.

"I'm what?" he pressed.

"Aren't you going to get that?"

"It can wait. Answer the question."

"I can't answer it with a phone ringing in my ears. Will you please?"

He sighed and got up; I heard his footsteps disappear around the back of the sofa and drew a deep breath. I didn't think I could take much more of this. All my high-minded principles had evaporated, just when I needed them most, just when I was tumbling into exactly the sort of situation I'd wanted to avoid. Because Julian Laurence—beautiful, brilliant, leonine Julian—could eat me for breakfast. Could swallow my heart whole and go bounding off with it, never to be seen again. And I doubted I had the willpower to stop him.

The ringing stopped, and the low musical murmur of his voice drifted between the rooms. I rose from the sofa and walked to one of the bookshelves built in on either side of the mantel. The fire had been going for some time. It was small and compact and extremely hot, hissing and popping discreetly in a pile of spent ash. I ran my fingers along the spines of the books. A wide-ranging collection, I thought to myself, smiling; it ran the gamut from Dean Koontz to Winston Churchill to Virgil, in the original Latin. Nothing like a British boarding-school education.

The books were packed in tightly; in fact, no room had been left for anything *but* books. No pictures, no *objets*, no random clutter. Nothing personal, really, unless you considered a man's choice of reading material the most personal thing of all.

"Snooping, I see," came Julian's voice, far too close.

I jumped. "Jeez! You just took a year off my life." I nodded my head to the shelves. "Do you really read Latin?"

"Not a terribly useful skill these days, is it?"

"Not everything has to be useful. I assume you learned it at school?"

"Yes, an old-fashioned education."

Was that a note of strain in his voice? I turned and looked at him. His face had changed, had dimmed somehow, as though he'd gone through and turned off all the unnecessary lights. "Everything all right?" I asked. "The phone call, I mean?"

"Yes, yes. Quite all right." He folded his arms and smiled, somewhat forced. "I've got to fly up to Boston tomorrow, that's all."

"On Christmas Eve?"

"Hard luck, I know."

"Don't you . . ." I swallowed. "Aren't you going anywhere for Christmas?"

He shrugged. "Geoff has me over for Christmas dinner every year. And services, of course."

"Your family isn't . . ."

"Around," he finished for me. "Don't worry. I'm over it, as they say. See anything you like?" He nodded upward, and I followed his eye.

"Oh, wow," I said. "Patrick O'Brian. Are those first editions?"

"I indulge myself." He sounded embarrassed.

"I love O'Brian. Historical fiction in general. My friends were always giving me crap about it in college; everyone else was reading chick lit. *Shopaholic*, that kind of thing. Michelle thinks I was born in the wrong century." I laughed stiffly.

He didn't reply.

I turned around. He looked peculiar, preoccupied. The tiny lines about his eyes had deepened; his mouth compressed in an unyielding line. I tried to think of something to say, but he spoke first.

"Do *you*?" he asked, his voice wound tight.

"Do I what?"

"Think you were born in the wrong century."

I laughed. "Well, not *literally*, I guess. I mean, who wants to die in childbirth? But I do sometimes wish . . ." My voice trailed off.

"Wish what?"

"Well, nothing's a life or death struggle anymore, is it? The era of honor and sacrifice is over." I looked again at the O'Brian novels, lined up in order. "Jack Aubrey's full of human failings—so's Maturin—but they have principles, and they'd give their lives for them. Or for each other. Now it's all about money and status and celebrity. Not that people haven't always cared about those things, but it used to be considered venal, didn't it?" I shrugged. "It's like nobody bothers to grow up anymore. We just want to be kids all our lives. Collecting toys, having fun."

"So what's the remedy?"

"There is no remedy. We are who we are, right? Life moves on. You can't get it back."

"Yes," he said. "Quite. Here you are, off to business school, after all."

"Here *you* are, running a hedge fund."

He smiled at that. "So what would you propose, to win my soul back?"

"I don't know. Not one of those pansy philanthropic foundations, that's for sure. Something more interesting. More skin in the game. Maybe manning your own letter of marque and going after all those Somali pirates, off the African coast."

He began laughing, a rich comfortable sound. "You're priceless. And where would I find a crew reckless enough to go along with me?"

"I'd go in a heartbeat," I said, without thinking.

The smallest pause, and then: "Would you, now?"

Oh, genius, Kate. I cleared my throat and looked back at the bookcase. "Well, except for having to earn a living and all."

"Ah. Hadn't we better get back to work, then?"

I checked my watch. The two sides of my brain struggled: the one that wanted desperately to stay, all night and all week and really all my life, drowning in the light from that beautiful face of his; and the one that wanted to bolt away in mortal fear.

"I'm sorry," I said, "but I've already stayed too long. I've got an early flight from LaGuardia tomorrow morning and, to be honest, I haven't had much sleep the last few days."

I couldn't quite bring myself to meet his eyes, but I felt them penetrating me. "What an ass I am," he said. "You're exhausted, of course."

"A little."

"My fault, I expect, demanding all these rewrites." He ran a hand through his golden hair. "I beg your pardon. Go home and sleep. I'll have a look at these over Christmas and we'll speak again when you're back in the city."

"Thanks."

"I'll just get your coat," he said, moving to the sofa and lifting it from the back. He held it out to me. "Here you are, then."

I let him help me into the coat, a novel experience, and then grabbed my laptop bag and headed numbly for the hallway.

"Look," I heard him say, and I turned at once, nearly burying my nose into his sweater.

"Sorry," I muttered.

"Sorry," he said, at the same time; we smiled awkwardly, stepping apart. "Look, I . . . would it be at all proper . . ." He closed his eyes, and opened them again with a slight rueful tilt to his mouth. "I suppose I'm trying to ask whether I might see a little of you, after Christmas."

"Um, sure." I tucked my hair behind my ear and examined the wall behind his shoulder. "You have my e-mail, right?"

"Yes. I . . ." He stopped. "Will you look at me a moment?"

"What is it?" I asked, dragging my eyes to meet his gaze.

"Christ," I thought I heard him whisper, under his breath, and then, more audibly, "I just want to be clear that it's nothing to do with Chemo-Derma, or any of that rubbish."

"Look here. Don't go around insulting my client, if you think you want to see me again." *Not bad, Wilson. How did you manage that?*

He smiled again, more fully. "ChemoDerma's a lovely, lovely company. I can't stop thinking about it. I shall tuck that charming little pitch book under my pillow tonight."

"Much better."

He reached one crooked finger into the space between us; it hovered for an instant, and brushed along the line of my jaw. "Have a safe flight tomorrow," he said.

"You too."

And then, somehow, I found the strength to turn and walk out.

4.

[via e-mail]

Julian: Kate, at LaGuardia, just boarding now. Pitch book tucked inside my coat, safe and warm. Shall read on the flight. Julian.

Me: What, no private jet? What kind of billionaire hedgehog are you? Kate.

Julian: A disgrace to the name, apparently. Geoff gave me a NetJets share for Christmas last year, but I keep forgetting to use it.

Me: How do you forget to use a private jet?

Julian: Shareholders first. Where are you now?

Me: In a taxi, stuck on the Triborough. Flight's in an hour. I'm getting nervous.

Julian: If you miss the plane, I'll ring up NetJets for you.

Me: Like that wouldn't raise a few eyebrows back home. Here's Kate coming back for Christmas in a Gulfstream. How many carbon offsets would I have to buy?

Julian: Hold on to that thought. I'm supposed to switch my phone off right now.

Me: *[later]* Where are you sitting?

Julian: 8C

Me: Hmm, an aisle guy.

Julian: And you?

Me: Window. 12A. All right, pulling up to the airport. Later.

Julian: Did you make your flight?

Me: Barely. Hold on, they're calling my row.

Julian: Starting to descend now. Boston looking brown and un-Christmaslike.

Me: *[later]* All settled in. So are you overnighting in Boston?

Julian: No. Flying back to NY after the meeting.

Me: And doing what?

Julian: Glass of wine, good book. Pondering the mysteries of that marvelous company of yours. And you?

Me: Family stuff. Dinner, eggnog, carols. You're spending Christmas Eve alone? Aren't you supposed to be having dinner with Geoff?

Julian: That's tomorrow. Don't worry, I'm quite all right. Altogether used to it. Though you're welcome to check in, if you like.

Me: I'll send you so much Christmas cheer your head will spin. What's Geoff like?

Julian: Good chap, rather boring wife, two rambunctious children.

Me: Boring how?

Julian: Conventional. Lives in Greenwich. Shops a great deal. Aspen in January, Nantucket in August. The twins have three nannies.

Me: Yikes. Oops, we're taxiing. Evil eye from flight attendant. Later.

Julian: Rough landing. On way to taxi.

Me: So where is this meeting of yours?

Julian: Harvard.

Me: The endowment fund? How long will you be?

Julian: Don't know. Will let you know when I'm out. Should hate to miss a moment of your Christmas cheer.

Me: Do you still have the presentation with you?

Julian: Next to my heart.

Me: Stop. You had me at hello.

Julian: So there's hope. Just pulling up now. Thinking of you.

Me: *[later]* Landed safely. I'm in the car with Mom and Dad. There's about three feet of snow. Thinking of you too.

Julian: *[much later]* Just left meeting. Glad you got in all right.

Me: Wow. Long meeting. Which shuttle are you taking?

Julian: 8pm.

Me: Maybe you'll see the big guy's sleigh ;-) According to the NORAD Web site he's over the Atlantic right now.

Julian: Shall keep watch. Happy Christmas, Kate.

Me: Merry Christmas. Wish you could see the festive spirit around here. My mom always goes a little overboard. The front yard is a total embarrassment.

Me: *[later]* Checking in, as promised. Lots of merriment here. I think Dad overdid the brandy in the eggnog. His cousin Pete keeps trying to get Mom under the mistletoe. How are you getting along?

Julian: Rather shattered, in fact. Heading for bed.

Me: Good night, then. Are you sure you're okay?

Julian: Right as rain. Good night. Stay away from Cousin Pete.

Me: *[much later the next day]* Julian, just wanted to say Merry Christmas. Kate.

Julian: You too. Off to Geoff's.

Me: Enjoy.

Julian: *[Sunday afternoon]* Dear Kate, I hope your Christmas was happy, without too much frightful knitwear lurking under the tree. I've been thinking, over the past few days, that it might be more prudent to hold off on any personal contact until after the ChemoDerma IPO. It's nothing at all to do with you, on my honor; I only want to forestall the prospect of the ruddy SEC piling on my doorstep at the moment. I do hope you understand, and of course you need not consider yourself bound in any way in the meantime. Let me add, however, that if you should have need of me for any reason, you have only to call, whatever the hour. I shall always pray for your safety and happiness. Yours, Julian.

Me: *[later]* Julian, I was kind of thinking the same thing. Thanks for the heads-up. You phrased it very well. Take care. Kate.

5.

I decided to head home early and go for a run in Central Park. Of course, around here, going home early meant something like eight o'clock, but the long hours were no longer something I resented about life at Sterling Bates. Busy was good.

"Hey, Kate. Free for coffee?" The voice, bright and cheerful like a ray of freaking sunshine, belonged to Alicia. She leaned over the wall of my cubicle, smiling down at me with her small mouth in its large round face. She was growing her hair out, and it hung listlessly in an in-between stage that suited her even less than the pixie cut.

"Actually, I was thinking of going running this evening," I said, trying to sound as cheerful as she did. Rumors had swarmed around Sterling Bates all winter, and everyone was watching breathlessly for my inevitable breakdown. According to Charlie, people were convinced I'd had a one-night stand with Julian Laurence on Paul Banner's orders, and then been turned out the next morning like a whore on the streets, never to hear from him again. Embellishments had evolved into the story over the months—apparently I'd gone in for an abortion in early February and submitted the charge on my expense sheet—but the basic theme hadn't changed, and my only weapon against the gossip was a fierce and unrelenting good mood. Especially with Alicia.

It was the hardest thing I'd ever done.

"Have some coffee first," she insisted. "It'll rev you up."

I bared my teeth in a smile. "Sure. Why not?"

A week after Christmas, I'd received an e-mail from Alicia, apologizing for her rude behavior and asking if we could start fresh. Strangely enough, she seemed to mean it. She'd taken me under her wing, bought me coffee, dragged me to lunch, even brought me out drinking with some of her witchy friends. I'd gone along with her—it was something to do, after all, something to keep my brain from looping back to its preoccupations—until it became an expected habit. I was almost growing to like her.

Going to Starbucks meant taking about ten steps outdoors, from the revolving-door entrance of Sterling Bates to the storefront next to it. On this particular afternoon, they were easy steps to make: it was beautiful outside, that brief period in Manhattan between the fitful bluster of spring and the sticky breathless heat of summer. The warmth of daytime still lingered around us; the sun had only just begun to disappear behind the towers to the west. I drew in the limpid air. The urge to run pulsed through my muscles. Spring fever.

"So has Banner talked to you about the gala thing at MoMA tomorrow night?" Alicia asked, taking a drink of her latte.

"Banner doesn't talk to me much lately."

"Oh yeah." Her mouth twitched. "Well, I spoke to him about it this afternoon, and we agreed you should go."

I wrapped my lips around my straw and drew in my Frappuccino before replying. "Hmm. What is it, exactly?"

"Just a fund-raiser for some big charity. Capital Markets always buys a table, and Banner has his jollies picking which of us should go."

I fell silent. If memory served, last year's gala had been the venue for Julian Laurence's sole appearance in the gossip columns. "I'm not sure I have anything to wear," I said, drawing out my words with care.

"Perfect. We can go shopping. You can ditch after lunch tomorrow; there's not much work anyway right now."

"Well . . ."

"Oh, come on. It'll be fun. You could use a little fun. It's why I made Banner put you on the list."

"No, no. I'm looking forward to it." I pushed out another false smile. "I haven't gotten dressed up like that since the Sigma Nu formal, freshman year."

She shuddered. "Yuck. We are *definitely* going shopping."

"So who else is going?" I asked casually.

"Well, Banner, of course. Me. Two VPs. You. Then a few clients."

"You should ask Charlie. He's been working hard. He deserves a night out."

She tilted her head at me and lifted her latte to her lips. "Yeah," she said thoughtfully, "you're right. He can be, like, your wing man."

"Why would I need a wing man?"

"Come on, Kate. These things are full of rich guys." She winked. "You can totally get laid."

THE GOLDEN WEATHER had beckoned all the runners out tonight, the regulars and the stragglers, but most had started earlier and began to drop off, one by one, as the sky grew purple and twilight wrapped around the horizon. Alicia had been right; the coffee did rev me up. I bounded up the hill toward the main drive and settled into an effortless pace, taking pleasure in the rhythm of my feet striking the pavement, in the feeling of grace that overtook me after the first half-mile or so, deep and meditative.

Of course, meditation was a dangerous thing for me these days. Inevitably I began to think of Julian, and it took effort to turn that around, to force my brain to pursue some piece of busywork: calculating how I was going to pay for business school next fall, for example, or how long my savings would last at various rates of cash burn. Tidy puzzles to solve.

I lasted longer than usual. I ran north, counterclockwise, and had gone around the far end of the park for the steady climb toward Ninety-sixth

Street before my mind began to slip its ropes and wander away. Desperately I tried to haul it back in, but it was no use. Julian's face began to appear before me, that impossibly handsome face; his glowing eyes, his expressive smile. I thought of our e-mail exchange on Christmas Eve, so tender and funny and then so abruptly cold; that last Dear Kate, so exquisitely phrased, with its odd formality at the end, like he'd copied it from one of those old model-letter books. As if I could ever think of calling on him for help. *Hi, Julian. Kate here. Could you write me a recommendation for my summer internship? Thanks a bunch!*

It would have been easier, in a way, if something *had* happened; if there had been anything between us other than a few words, a few intense looks, a sense of dawning understanding. I could be angry with him then. I could wallow in self-righteous bitterness, label him a heartless bastard, throw a few darts at his photograph, and move on. It was infinitely more difficult to have no one to blame. He had behaved impeccably, really. After that graceful good-bye, he hadn't tried to reach me again, not even after the ChemoDerma deal fell apart in February. Humiliating, of course, but better than having the agony drawn out with sporadic impersonal contact. All communication between the two firms had gone instead through Geoff Warwick and Banner.

I'd heard a rumor, a few days ago, that Southfield was winding down its remaining positions, cashing out, and even closing down. Rumors like that were running about Wall Street like frightened rabbits these days. A feeling had seeped into the air, the faint frisson of a market on the point of turning, if you listened to the whispers. Housing market, mortgage-backed securities, write-downs, bank capital ratios. Not stuff you really wanted to think about, but looming there in the background, hard to ignore completely.

Twilight had settled in by the time I crested the hill and began descending through the shadowed woods, green sunk into black. The busy swarm of runners around the Met had thinned out into almost nothing; I heard only a hint of movement from behind, someone pounding against the asphalt like me, breathing hard and steady with the effort of climbing the hill. A bicycle swept by, and another.

The transept approached through the trees on my left, and a man flashed into view between the branches, running hard into the merge with the West Drive. He was big and lean, radiating belligerence. Manhattan was bursting with them: aggressive animals who took out their frustrations on the park loop, creating impromptu competitions that might last fifty yards or five miles. I hung back, not wanting to take up any fresh challenges at the moment, but then changed my mind and drove on. I was in good form. I could handle it. A blowout would do me some good: push myself just a little too hard, crash the barrier.

He reached the merge just before me, but instead of banking left onto the drive, he made a hard right, without even looking. His heavy arm smashed into my shoulder, knocking me sideways into the pavement.

I felt the hard thud of impact with shock. I'd been running fast, and so had he. He still was. He hadn't even slowed down to see if I was okay.

"Watch it, jerk!" I yelled after him, without thinking. I could feel pain begin to gather in my limbs. Definitely needing Band-Aids. Crap. And then I began to shake with rage. "I said *watch* it, jerk!" I yelled again recklessly, as the adrenaline hit my blood.

All this happened in about three seconds. In the next, he turned around.

"What the fuck, bitch!" he shouted. "What the fuck!"

"You knocked me down!"

"You got in my fucking way!"

"Asshole," I muttered, picking myself up.

He rushed me.

I braced myself an instant before the crash, closing my eyes and twisting to spare my soft underbelly. This was going to hurt. This was ambulance time. Stupid, stupid Kate. *Sorry, Mom.*

But the impact, when it came, glanced right off me. I staggered backward a few paces, astonished to find myself still standing up, and opened my eyes.

Two men were rolling on the pavement in front of me. The runner, I remembered. The runner behind me. Or maybe a passing bicyclist. Some freaking hero.

The rolling stopped. One of them straddled the other, throwing punches like a machine, swift and expert. Something dark splattered against my leg. "Oh my God!" I choked out. "Stop it! Somebody help!"

Nobody came. A bicyclist flashed by without stopping; maybe he didn't see us in the shadows, maybe he just thought we were a bunch of drunk teenagers. Maybe he just didn't care.

"Stop it!" I screamed again, louder, frantic. "Stop it! You're killing him!"

Suddenly the man on top jumped off, wiping his right hand on his shorts. The man on the bottom lay still.

"Oh crap," I whispered.

The victor turned to me. "Are you okay?" he asked urgently, holding out his arms.

I couldn't discern his face in the near-darkness, but I knew his voice.

"Oh my God," I said. "Julian?"

"Christ, Kate." His hands were running down my arms, my legs, checking for injuries. "Does anything hurt?"

"Everything hurts," I said, and then my nose crashed against his clavicle, and his arms bound like steel around my body.

We said nothing, only breathing against each other, shuddering, until he pushed me away suddenly, gently.

"You're shaking. You're in shock."

"I'm all right."

"No, you need a blanket. Some kind of . . . hell." He ran his hand through his hair.

"Don't worry. I'm okay. What . . . what are you doing here?"

"Out for a run." His voice was grim.

A groan escaped from the man on the ground. "Let's get going," Julian said.

"And leave him here?"

"He's all right," he said scornfully. "Arsehole." The word sounded especially crude in his cut-glass British voice.

"What if he, like, dies?"

"He's not going to *die*, Kate, I assure you." He met my eyes and drew in a heavy breath. "All right. I'll call 911 and leave a tip."

"We have to stay. We can't just walk away. It's, like, a *crime* scene. Sort of."

His knuckles rested on his hips. I could feel his frown, though I couldn't quite make it out in the gloaming. He looked at the body on the pavement, and then turned back to enclose me in a long silent stare. "Fine. But it's going to get messy. You'll have to give a statement, maybe appear in court. He'll probably sue me, once he knows who I am."

"I'm sorry."

"Don't worry. Not your fault. I can afford a lawyer, for God's sake." He drew out a phone from the pocket of his running shorts and punched the keypad. "I suppose it's the right thing, anyway," he said. "Not that he deserves it, mind you."

I felt my muscles begin to tremble now, breaking past my determination to stay calm. I wrapped my arms around my middle. Julian was talking on the phone, rapid and calm, facing the prone man, but he saw my movement peripherally and his eyes flicked over to me. He reached out his left arm and drew me in. "She seems all right," he was saying, "but she's beginning to go into shock. I'm trying to keep her warm. Yes. All right. Two minutes. Thanks very much."

He slid the phone back into his shorts and put his other arm around me. "They'll be here shortly. Try to breathe slowly."

"Really, I'm okay," I insisted, forcing down a sob. I'd never had hysterics, and I wasn't going to start now, with Julian Laurence holding me in his arms. His thick heather-gray T-shirt felt soft against my face, slightly damp with sweat; his chest radiated with lovely heat. "So how did you happen to be out running just now?" I demanded.

"Ruddy good luck, I suppose," he said.

I turned that over for a few seconds, and then something occurred to me.

"And where did you learn to punch like that?"

"Hmm. University."

"They teach *boxing* at college in England?"

"The sweet science. Feeling better?" His arms began to ease.

"Yes, a little. What if he wakes up?"

"Don't worry," he said darkly, and I shut up. I could hear a siren now, at the outer fringes of my hearing.

"I guess this isn't the right time to talk . . ." I began.

"Hush," he said, running his palms along my back. The siren was getting louder. "We'll talk later."

THE POLICE TOOK ONE LOOK at the situation—my scrapes and bruises, the groaning figure on the pavement, our forthright explanations, Julian's knuckles—and didn't give us much trouble, beyond taking down our statements and names and addresses. They're pretty smart, the NYPD. They can tell the good guys from the bad.

Still, it was late when I got back to my apartment. One of the policemen gave us a ride to the East Side in his cruiser, and dropped me off first.

"You're really all right?" Julian asked, as I put my hand on the door handle.

"Nothing a little Neosporin can't cure," I promised. "Um, thanks, by the way. I've never been rescued before."

"I could have lived without it."

"Of course. Bad joke." I hesitated. "Sorry about the trouble. I mean, I really am."

His voice went soft. "That's not what I meant," he said, and paused. "Take care."

Was that it? *Take care?*

"You too," I said, and got out of the cruiser. It sped off down Seventy-ninth Street and turned right on Lexington, down the five short blocks to Julian's house.

PHONE. PHONE RINGING. I scrabbled at my bedside table for my Black-Berry and pressed the green button. "Hello?"

The ringing kept on going. Must be the landline.

I rolled out of bed and squinted at the clock. Six-thirty in the morning. Who the hell could it be? I couldn't even think straight. Where *was* the phone? Somewhere in the living room, right? We almost never used it.

I found it at last. "Hello?" I mumbled.

"Is this Katherine Wilson?"

"Speaking."

"This is Amy Martinez from the *New York Post.* I understand you were involved in an incident in Central Park last night with Julian Laurence of Southfield Associates?"

The handset slipped from my fingers to crash on the floor.

My thumbs flew. *Julian, the* Post *just called. What should I say? Call me. I don't know your number. Kate. P.S. So, so sorry.*

The phone rang a minute later. "Kate?"

"Julian. I'm so sorry."

"Enough of that rubbish. You've nothing to be sorry for."

"You're right, we should have left him there. I'm so stupid. I didn't think about what it all meant for you."

I heard him sigh. "Kate, it's irrelevant. I can handle a bit of press."

"But you hate publicity."

Silence. "What makes you say that?"

"You're never in the papers. You never give interviews. And now Page Six is calling me and drawing God knows what conclusions . . ."

"Calm down, darling. What did you say to them?"

"Um. I said no comment," I mumbled. "Isn't that what you're supposed to say? I mean, I've never talked to a reporter before . . ."

"What was her name?"

"Amy something. Menendez?"

"Martinez. I'll call her and sort things out. Go back to sleep."

"*Sleep?* I have to go to work. Oh, crap. Work. What should I tell them?"

"Tell them the truth. If they ask."

"Which is?"

He laughed at that point. "Which is that we were running in the park, and some rotter tried to attack you."

"Oh, sure. *That* will shut them all up."

"Look, I don't mind. Tell them whatever you like, whatever sounds right to you. Let me handle Miss Martinez. We've spoken before."

My shoulders slumped. "Okay. Gladly."

"And don't apologize," he warned, just as I opened my mouth to do it.

"Right," I said. "Okay. Thanks."

"Good. How are you feeling?" he asked.

"Sore. You?"

"Right as rain. Now take some aspirin and go to work. I'll handle it."

"All right." I paused. "Thanks, Julian. I mean that."

"Good-bye, Kate. I'll ring you later."

I hung up the phone and stared at it. Aspirin? Who the hell took aspirin anymore?

6.

By lunchtime, the word was out.

Charlie cornered me in one of the unused conference rooms in the far corners of the Capital Markets floor. I hadn't turned on the lights. I was hoping no one would notice me there. "Dude, what the fuck?" he asked under his breath. "You're all over the Internet."

"Oh God. Seriously?"

"Julian Laurence really laid some guy out for you?"

"It was all just a big misunderstanding," I said.

"Some fucking misunderstanding. It's on *Gawker*, dude."

"Gawker? You've got to be *kidding* me!"

"Serious as a fucking heart attack. Links to the Smoking Gun."

"What's that?"

He pulled my laptop over and began typing a new URL. "It's this Web site that posts public documents. Divorce filings and police reports, shit like that. And there! Boo-ya!" He turned the screen so I could see it.

"Wow," I said, impressed. There was last night's police report, every livid detail.

"So is that pretty much how it went down? And why were you out running with Julian Laurence, anyway?"

"I wasn't. He just happened to be there when the guy ran into me."

Charlie's eyebrows lifted. He was no idiot. "Just happened to be there, huh?"

"Yeah. Wild, huh?"

He shook his head. "Full of shit, Kate. Full of shit. I thought we were friends."

"Charlie, I swear to God, I did not go out running with Julian Laurence last night! I was totally shocked when he came up and laid into that jerk."

"Shocked, *shocked,*" he said, like the guy in *Casablanca.*

"Seriously, Charlie. I wouldn't lie to you. Alicia and Banner, maybe, but not you."

He sat down in the chair next to me and swiveled for a moment. "All right. Fine. So do you think it was a coincidence? Or was he following you?"

"I don't know." I turned back to my computer and propped up my chin with one hand.

"It would be some fucking coincidence," he offered.

"Yeah," I said.

"Are you okay? You're not, like, hurt or anything?"

"Oh, *now* you think of my well-being. Once all the gossip is cleared away."

He flashed me a smile. "Hey, priorities! Seriously, though. You're all right?"

"I am totally all right. Just a couple of scrapes." I pointed to my right arm. "Band-Aid stuff."

"Awesome. So have you had lunch yet?"

"Charlie, there's no way I'm poking my nose out of this conference room."

He considered this for a second or two. "I can bring you back something."

"Why are you being so freaking nice?"

"*Fucking* nice," he corrected me. "Because you're famous now, and our celebrity-obsessed cultural imperative makes me, like, want to suck up to you. Reuben, maybe?"

"Too greasy. Maybe something from that soup guy around the corner?"

He stood up. "Done."

"And a Diet Coke?"

"Don't push it. You're not that famous. Oh, fuck *me.* I'm outta here."

He dashed out of the conference room like I'd stung him, brushing past Alicia Boxer with a muttered "Hey, dude."

She frowned at his disappearing figure, and turned back to me with a broad grin. "Wow, Kate! You dark horse, you! Now I know why you jumped at the gala invitation like that." She sat down in the chair Charlie had just left. "So what happened?"

"Oh, it's totally blown out of proportion," I told her. "I was out for a run, and some guy tried to get all macho on me, and Julian sort of punched him."

She tilted her head speculatively. "So you two are, like, together?"

"No, we're just friends."

"Wow." She smiled. "Some friend."

"He's a good guy," I said.

"Hmm." Her lips pursed. "So are we still on for dress shopping today? I can, like, sneak you out the back way if you like."

I opened my mouth to decline, but then an image crossed my mind: me, in some devastating black gown, sweeping through the doorway to an admiring crowd. Which included Julian Laurence.

I stood up. "Let's go."

We were deep inside Barneys before I remembered Charlie and the soup.

"Oh, he can eat it himself," Alicia said. "What about this one?" She held up a long red dress with a V neckline cut down to the navel.

"Um, I was thinking of maybe an empire waist," I said. "It kind of suits me."

She frowned and looked me over. "You have to have a certain kind of body to wear that well, Kate," she said.

Whatever that meant. "Well, I still like it," I insisted.

"O-*kay*," she said. "What about this one?"

"I'll try it." I had just caught sight of something a few racks away and began threading my way warily around the swinging hangers.

My phone rang.

My heart leapt at the sound, but when I took my BlackBerry out of my pocket, the number on the screen wasn't Julian's. I sighed and popped the Bluetooth into my ear. "Hi, Mom," I said. "What's up?"

"Honey, are you all *right*?"

"Oh, Mom, you're not *crying*, are you?"

"Mary Alice called me with the news. What *happened*? Were you . . . *mugged*?" She said it in a hissing kind of whisper, like *raped*.

"It was nothing. Some guy ran into me in the park, and a friend stepped in to help me out."

"Well, who's this *friend*? Mary Alice says he's some kind of . . . *billionaire*." Again, the hissing whisper. For God's sake.

"Mom, he runs a hedge fund, that's all. He's like a client."

"*Like* a client? Or *is* a client?" Mom was invariably at her sharpest when it was least convenient.

"It's hard to explain. Wall Street stuff."

"Oh, honey. How badly were you hurt?"

"Hardly at all. Just a few scrapes."

"But you must have been traumatized!"

"Mom, the police took care of everything . . ."

"Police!"

Oops. "You're making way too much out of this," I said, fingering the dress. It was long and flesh-colored, with a low straight neckline and tiny glittering beads scattered widely over the gauzy skirt: the kind of dress that would drape just so, without looking as if either of us were trying too hard.

"Honey," she said, after a few seconds of stunned silence, "I'm flying out there tonight."

"No! Oh my God, Mom, *don't*! I'm fine, absolutely fine!" Alicia had wandered over and was looking critically at the dress I'd picked out. She lifted it off the rack and held it up to me with a moue of disapproval on her face.

"Honey, you were *mugged*!"

"For the last time, I wasn't mugged. It was just an . . . an altercation. Please don't fly out. Save your money. Think of that retirement in Florida."

Alicia snickered and put the dress back on the rack. I motioned frantically at her to hand it back.

"I don't want to retire to Florida."

"Look, I've got to go. I'm in the middle of Barneys right now. Just don't fly out, okay? I'm totally fine. Physically and mentally."

"I love you, honey."

"Love you. Bye." I hung up the phone and slid it in my bag. "Don't put it back. I'm going to try it on."

"For real? There's a ton of much better stuff."

"I like it."

"All right," she sighed, handing me back the dress. "I'm heading home to get ready, so I'll see you there. Remember, cocktails at seven-thirty. Be late."

"Be late?"

"Only the losers arrive on time."

WELL, CALL ME A LOSER. I took a long bubble bath, I shaved my legs, I exfoliated and masked and moisturized and put on practically invisible new Band-Aids. I even did my toenails. But with all that, with dressing and makeup and hair, with fielding calls from various friends and acquaintances and distant relatives until at last I just turned my phone off, I still found myself pulling up to MoMA in a taxi at seven twenty-nine. I blamed it on the traffic. Park Avenue had been as swift as a motor speedway, which only happens when you're not in a hurry.

There were about eight people there when I walked in, all of them male and over forty. I went directly to the bar. "Champagne, please," I said to the bartender. "Straight up."

He winked. "Coming right up." He whipped out a champagne flute and poured. "So," he said, "what's a gorgeous girl like you doing here so early?"

I took the flute. "Hiding from the press," I answered, drinking deep.

He laughed and refilled my glass.

I wandered over to the silent auction and glanced at the rows of lots and clipboards, ordinary objects describing the extraordinary visual evidence of the lavish world around which I'd hovered these past three years. Lunch and batting practice with Derek Jeter came with a suggested starting bid of $25,000. Lunch and an on-air segment with Brian Williams started at $35,000. I saw plenty of spa visits and weekends in Aspen; a week aboard a private 150-foot yacht, complete with captain, crew, and private chef; a stunning diamond rivière from Harry Winston; a case of 1982 Bordeaux from Sherry-Lehmann with a price tag that made my eyeballs pop out and roll onto the floor. I smiled privately at the sight of a Marquis JetCard—the starter version of a NetJets share—with a starting bid of $95,000.

People were beginning to filter through the room, dressed with painstaking expense. An elegant blond woman in her forties, sporting an endless tangle of fat pearls around her throat, bent over the Brian Williams segment and scribbled in a bid. "Wow," someone said, near my elbow, "you'd never know there was a recession on."

I looked over: a narrow-faced man, chin and hairline receding in tandem, wearing a stiff oversized tuxedo and standing a good six inches too close. "Well, it's not official yet," I pointed out, shifting a step backward.

He smiled and motioned to my hands. "Can I get you another drink?"

I looked at my glass, which was nearly empty. "No, thanks." I smiled back. "I think I'm already past my limit."

"Nothing wrong with that." He grinned. "See anything interesting?"

"Nothing I can afford." I looked over his shoulder, hoping to see someone I knew. Even Banner would make a welcome interruption.

He held out his hand. "Mark Oliver."

I took it lightly, hoping he was one of those people who hated limp handshakes. "Hi, Mark. Kate Wilson." His palm was distinctly moist; I snatched my hand back and wrapped it around the base of my champagne flute.

"Sounds familiar."

"It's a common name. I had two other Kate Wilsons in my graduating class."

"Oh, where did you go to college?"

"Wisconsin." Maybe that would scare him off.

"A Badger! High five." His hand went up.

"Woo-hoo," I said, slapping it. Where the *freaking hell* was Charlie?

"Yeah, I went to Yale myself," he went on, "but I know a couple guys from Wisconsin. My dentist."

"You know," I said, "I think I see someone I know over there. Excuse me."

"Later!" he called after me. "See you around!"

I walked away slowly, hoping someone familiar would materialize before I reached the end of the room. I was stopped twice by waiters bearing hors d'oeuvres, over which I lingered as long as I could, deliberating between coconut shrimp and Thai-chili spring rolls while the crowd accumulated.

"Kate! What's up?"

"Charlie! I am *so* glad to see you. You have to stay right next to me until the dinner starts. It's like a singles freak show over there."

"Harsh, man," he said. "Drink?"

"Champagne. But I'm going with you."

Charlie had his shortcomings, but maneuvering around a bar area wasn't one of them. In less than a minute, he'd secured the drinks and staked us out a prime location that neatly triangulated the bar, the entrance, and the door from which the waiters were streaming with fresh hors d'oeuvres. "Sorry about the soup thing today," I told him, snatching at a skewer of pepper-crusted ahi tuna. "Alicia sort of kidnapped me to go dress shopping."

"No worries. I ate it myself. Mulligatawny, dude. Awesome."

"Well, thanks for the thought, anyway."

"So. Any word from the *man*?"

"The man? Oh, you mean *Julian*? No, he hasn't called. I think he's got some sort of day job. You know, running some money."

"Ouch. Sarc off, man." He took a drink of microbrew. "So are you bummed?"

"Look, Charlie," I said, "I think you're under the mistaken impression, like everyone else in this freaking town, that I've got some kind of *thing* going with Julian Laurence. Which is not the case. Hasn't been, isn't, won't be."

"'Cause I heard he was coming here tonight," Charlie went on placidly.

"Who told you that?"

"Banner. Says Southfield's head trader's wife is on the fund-raiser committee."

Geoff Warwick's wife. It figured. "Banner's full of it."

"*Shit*, Kate. For the last time. Full of *shit*. Yeah, he is, but even a stopped fucking clock is right twice a day." He tipped his beer bottle at me.

"Julian doesn't go out much. I would be shocked to see him here tonight. It's not his thing."

"You seem to know a lot about this guy, considering you don't have a *thing* going." He made quote marks around the word with his fingers.

"Look," I said, exasperated, "why is everyone so obsessed with this? You're all driving me crazy."

He shook his head. "Kate, the guy's a billionaire. A living legend."

"No," I said, "he's just Julian."

"Oh, come on. *Just Julian*. If he weren't rich, you wouldn't be into him."

"I'm *not* into him," I said, not all that convincingly. "And even if I were, it wouldn't be about the money." I tried to smile. "Actually, it's his looks."

"You lie. You so lie."

"You're wrong."

"Am I?" He shrugged. "Dude, it's nothing to be ashamed of. You chicks are lucky. I've only got one shot at getting rich, and that's the hard way. You've got two. You can make it or marry it. So go for it. I'm your fucking cheerleader here. Rock on."

"Oh, please. What are you, Jane Austen? Evolve."

"Kate," he laughed, "life isn't some college feminist studies seminar. It's the real world. Human fucking nature. You can't fight biology."

"I swear to God, Charlie, if he lost every penny of it tomorrow . . ." I stopped.

"So you admit you're into him."

"All right, I kind of like him," I said, in a hushed voice. "And okay, maybe not every *single* penny. A roof over his head would be helpful. But a studio apartment, Charlie. That's all."

"Of course," Charlie said, "that's all talk. There's no way of proving it, short of, like, total fucking catastrophe. Which would give us all a lot more to worry about than getting laid." He tilted the bottle high and drained the last of his beer. "All right, Kate. Come on. Let's work this crowd. It's what we're here for."

"Do me a favor, though. Please don't mention the thing from last night."

He held up his knuckles for a fist bump. "Word of honor, dude."

DINNER WAS called at eight-thirty, with no sign yet of Julian. Sterling Bates occupied two or three tables, sponsored by various divisions, and I recognized a few faces nearby when we sat down at ours. Banner joined us, sitting down directly next to me, and then Alicia, who was already several basis points above the legal limit.

"You look fabulous," said Banner, leaning over my dress to make sure.

"Thanks." I stabbed into my mesclun. "Alicia helped me pick it out."

He turned to her. "Fucking genius, Alicia."

She rolled her eyes and went back to schmoozing the client who sat next to her, a stoop-shouldered man in his middle forties with a thick wedding band on his left hand, which he kept twisting around nervously.

Halfway through the main course, I caught sight of Geoff Warwick past a momentary gap in the crowd. He was about ten tables away, much closer to the podium. Seated next to him was a smug-looking woman with glossy blond hair, presumably the boring wife; she wore a low-cut dress and a spectacular necklace of either emeralds or sapphires. It was hard to tell in the atmospheric lighting.

The seat next to her was empty. Julian's seat.

I watched dully as the speakers ascended the podium, making announcements about the silent auction (it was closing in fifteen minutes) and dancing (after the dinner). Then the speeches started: various muckety-mucks, fund-raisers, donors. The evening's honoree, an aggressive alpha socialite wearing a dress encrusted with Swarovski crystals.

"Excuse me," I said, and rose from the table, taking my clutch with me. I wasn't sure I was coming back.

The bar area wheezed with cigar smoke by now, so I wandered around until I saw a set of open doors leading to a terrace, where the breeze blew in cool and stinking from the Dumpsters out back. The rear elevations of the surrounding buildings rose hideously about me, but I didn't much care; the glamour of the evening was already spoiled for me. What had I been expecting, really? That Julian had received some telepathic communication of my arrival at the gala and shown up to sweep me off my feet? What kind of idiot was I? He was a gentleman; of course he had come to my aid in the park. That didn't mean he had any kind of *thing* for me.

"There you are," said someone behind me, making my heart thud the instant before I realized it was the wrong voice.

I rotated. "Hello. Mike, right?"

"Mark." He beamed me a big grin, apparently encouraged that I'd come within two letters of his first name. "High five," he said, holding up his hand again.

"Sorry. I'm all out."

"That's all right. I brought some champagne," he said hopefully, holding it out.

"Er, thanks." I took the glass and balanced it on the ledge. "I warn you, there's some Dumpsters down below, and I don't think they've been emptied lately."

He shrugged. "That's okay. I have kind of a cold coming on, anyway. Can't smell a thing."

Lovely.

He plunged on into my silence. "So, what brings you out here all alone?"

"The cigar smoke."

"Yeah, it was getting pretty thick, huh? Some assholes from the Sterling Bates derivatives desk."

"Figures," I said, under my breath.

"So would you like to dance? I think they're starting up the music."

"Um, thanks for the offer, Mark. But I think I might head home. I have to go to work in the morning."

"Oh, where do you work?"

"Sterling Bates."

"No shit. Put my foot in it, didn't I?" He paused to crack his knuckles. "So would you like to share a cab?"

"Um," I said, "I actually have a friend . . ."

"Where is he? I'll tell him you're bailing early."

"You know, that's not necessary. I'll just go find him myself." I snatched my clutch from the balustrade, next to the untouched champagne glass. "Have a great evening, Mark."

"Wait." He grabbed my arm.

"Mark," I said, through my teeth, "I have to go to the ladies' room."

"Wait a minute," he repeated, and I could smell his breath now, drenched in Scotch.

I yanked my arm away. "Seriously, Mark. I really have to go."

He grabbed again. "No, wait. You have to listen to me."

"No, I don't."

"What is it with you bitches? You only suck the big swinging dicks, huh? What about mine?"

"Mark," I said fiercely, "I'm going to scream in two seconds. Loud. So you'd better let me go. Now."

He lunged forward. I jerked my knee upward into his groin. "Bitch!" he gasped, doubling over. His arm swung out and thumped my gut.

This was just not my week.

I grabbed the champagne glass and broke it over his head. "There," I said. "Now go fuck yourself, Mark." I swept past him and ran to the doors, straight into the well-tailored chest of Julian Laurence.

"Kate, my God! What's wrong?"

"Oh, *now* you show up. I could have used you five minutes ago."

He looked past me to Mark Oliver's wet groaning figure, flinging champagne droplets over the terrace. He began to laugh. "Oh, I don't know. Looks as though you had the matter well in hand. Poor little bugger."

A smile lifted the edges of my unwilling mouth. "Well," I said, "I'm not totally helpless, you know."

"I know." He took my hand and laced our fingers together. "Come along, then, darling. Let's get out of here."

Amiens

The damp smoky interior of the Chat d'Or bustled with patrons. British officers, mostly, the tidy gloss of their khaki tunics suggesting Staff; some seated together, talking and laughing; some with women, looking self-consciously discreet.

"You're quite sure you're all right?" Julian asked, helping me into a worn ladder-back chair. Not an elegant establishment, the Chat, but despite its mismatched furniture and fuggy atmosphere and plain dark-beamed plaster ceiling, it still clung to a certain provincial respectability. A white linen cloth covered our table in threadbare decency, and the ancient waiters wore black.

I smiled. "Yes. I promise. It was only the shock."

"The shock?"

"Of seeing you at last."

Something important had occurred to me on the way to the café. I'd fought my way to Amiens circa 1916 in a panic, with no further thought than finding Julian and delivering my warning: an absurd failure of imagination. What had I expected, really? That I could blurt out the truth and be believed? That Julian would simply say to himself, *Well, splendid! Awfully good thing that Cassandra came round; I'll just put up here in Amiens for an extra night and thank my lucky stars?*

No, arriving here had been the easy part. The greater challenge, I now realized, lay before me. I had to gain his trust, to convince him somehow that I wasn't insane, wasn't some kind of spy; that my information would save his life. And I had to do it in the next forty-eight hours. So where did that leave me?

Well, for one thing—went my epiphany, as I skidded along the cobbles to the Chat d'Or—Julian Ashford loved me. Not now, exactly. But it lay there, latent, inside him: the predisposition to love me, to adore me, to—this was perhaps the most relevant part—desire me to a degree that muddied ordinary masculine reasoning.

I could awaken that desire, that love. Just a little, just enough so he would heed me; if I were clever about it, confident he *could* love me. *Be yourself*, I thought, watching his mouth, his forehead, the quick movement of his eyes. *Be the Kate he loves.*

"I'm afraid I don't quite understand," he said, returning my gaze with equal thoroughness. "Won't you at least tell me your name?"

"My name is Kate."

"Kate," he said dubiously, stiffly. "Kate . . ."

"Just Kate, for now, if you don't mind."

The waiter arrived, with steaming plates full of coddled eggs and toast and some sort of meat I couldn't identify. A heavenly scent rose up from it, warm and buttery and savory, like nothing else I'd smelled since leaving New York. "I thought it was wartime," I marveled.

He made a self-deprecating movement of his shoulders. "The Chat always manages to find ways around the shortages."

"It looks wonderful." I grasped my cutlery, forgetting everything in the tide of appetite that engulfed me.

Julian watched me eat, his long fingers resting on the handles of his knife and fork. A hum of conversation crowded around us, ebbing and flowing in a timeless human rhythm; someone laughed, a loud braying mule of a laugh, at the table next to ours, and Julian lifted his fork at last. "And your journey?" he inquired, picking over his food. "How long was it, exactly?"

I swallowed a mouthful of silken eggs before replying; it gave me time to produce an answer. "Longer than you can imagine," I said.

"All the way from America, I take it?"

"All the way from America."

"And you came to see me? Me in particular?"

"Yes," I said, with emphasis. "You in particular."

"Hmm." He cut away at his sausage, looking thoughtful, as if he were trying to figure out how to play along. "Perhaps you'd better start at the beginning. How, exactly, do you know me?"

"Everyone knows you, Captain Ashford."

"In America?"

"Yes. We do read newspapers once in a while, from the comfort of our log cabins. Those of us who can read, of course." I raised the brimming fork to my mouth and then drew it out again, lingeringly, the way Lauren Bacall might have done, sending him a look from beneath the narrow brim of my hat. Useful things, hats.

He looked startled, and then a smile began creeping across his face. "And the rest?" he asked.

"Excellent question." I cocked my head thoughtfully. "There's so much to do on the frontiers of civilization. Skin a few grizzlies, I guess. Trade tobacco with the natives. Haven't you read your Cooper?"

"My God." He rested his fork on the side of his plate and beamed. "Who are you?"

"Clearly not a well-bred English girl."

"No, thank God. But there's something else about you; I can't put my finger on it exactly." The faint tinge on his cheeks resolved into patches of eager color.

I felt my own skin warm in response. "Why *thank God*?" I heard myself ask.

"I beg your pardon?"

"What do you have against well-bred English girls?"

"I don't suppose it's the girls in particular. It's the entire circus, the . . ." He narrowed his eyes at me. "That was very well done."

"I've learned from a master."

"Aren't you going to tell me *anything*?" he begged. "Your last name, even?"

"Oh, I certainly can't tell you *that*." I tilted my head, smiling, almost enjoying myself. We were *flirting*. Good grief. "I promise you I'm not a spy, at least."

He dismissed that. "No, of course you're not."

"Not at all," I went on. "I wouldn't know how to begin. I'm a completely unconvincing liar, even after three years on Wall Street."

"Wall Street?" He looked incredulous. "Do you mean stocks and things?"

I laughed, a genuine laugh. "Stocks and things! From you, of all people!" I set down my fork and folded my hands under my chin to look at him. "You may think it's all vulgar and money-grubbing right now, Julian, but I promise you'll change your mind." My voice stumbled. I dropped my gaze down to the graceful white curve of the coffee cup in its saucer next to my plate. "I mean, that you would change your mind, if you had the chance," I finished.

He smiled politely. "I daresay I would," he said, turning back to his breakfast. "But I gather you had a purpose in mind, in seeking me out."

I gathered myself. "Yes, I did. Except I don't think you'd believe me, if I told you. I've been sitting here, trying to think of a way to present it to you, and it just won't work, will it? It's just too . . ." I checked myself at *weird*. Was that in common use yet? Who knew? "Extraordinary," I said, just to be safe.

"You might try me. I'm not quite such a shallow fool as that."

"Shallow fool? You think that's my opinion of you?"

"All that rubbish about empty-headed society girls. About not being capable of comprehending you."

He was leaning forward now, his familiar handsome face drawn into an intent expression, almost anxious, trying to prove himself to me. My Julian, only he didn't know it yet; my own adored Julian, a soldier now, spending most of his days surrounded by mud and blood and sudden random catastrophe. Would that make him more susceptible to accepting my story? Hadn't I read somewhere that belief in the supernatural tended to thrive during wartime? I caught the gleam of his eyes in the dim electric light, their greenishness heightened by the khaki of his tunic, and felt as if I were toppling from an enormous height.

"Tell me," I said softly, wanting to keep his face angled toward mine. "Do you believe in—what would you call it?—second sight? The ability to see the future?"

"A load of rubbish, I suspect," he said, straightening.

I leaned toward him. "Does that mean you really *don't* believe in it, or that you don't *want* to believe in it?"

He picked up his cup and took a drink of coffee. "The second, I suppose."

"Then can't you just trust me? Trust that I might just know what I'm talking about? That I've come all this way, just to try to save you?"

"To save me? From what?" He laughed. "From the war, perhaps? I'm afraid there's not much chance of that."

"Well, no. There's something else. Something . . ." I couldn't finish. I could see from his smile, from the careless tone of his voice, that the spell was broken. He thought I was teasing him now, leading him on: that this was all part of the game.

"Hmm. Fraught with danger, is it?"

I looked down at my empty plate. The scent of eggs and meat still clung to it, and my stomach turned abruptly. "You're going to make this difficult, aren't you?"

He looked blank, as if his tennis opponent had inexplicably withdrawn right after a particularly good volley; then an expression of concern crossed his face. His voice deepened with apprehension. "You're tired, aren't you? You've finished your breakfast; have you thought about getting some rest?"

"I can't. I haven't found anywhere to stay."

"I'll help you."

"You don't need to do that."

"Miss . . . Kate . . . I don't mind. Perhaps my landlady can direct you somewhere."

I opened my mouth to object, to say I was perfectly capable of managing on my own, thank you, but at the last instant I realized what he was offering me: an opportunity, a decorous excuse to further things along, to maintain the elegant fiction that this was all about a disinterested concern for my welfare. Because that was how these things used to be done.

I said instead, "Do you think so? But surely there's nothing available on such short notice."

"I'm certain something can be arranged. Look at you, you're quite done in." His hand reached out impulsively, nearly touching mine, before it recollected itself and retreated, flexing, to the tablecloth next to his plate.

"No, really. I'm fine. It's just the breakfast, making me sleepy."

He motioned at the waiter. "I'm taking you back. You could . . . you could rest in my room, if you like, while I make inquiries. You shouldn't be out like this. My God! You've gone pale as a sheet!"

His alarm was understandable, given the little he knew of me. He was probably afraid of more fainting and vomiting.

"I'd hate to be any trouble," I said.

"Come along," he said, dropping a few coins on the table. "It's no trouble at all."

7.

"Where are we going?" I asked, as Julian led me down the steps.

"Somewhere we can talk," he said. He walked toward one of the black sedans lining the sidewalk outside the building. The driver jumped out and opened the back door, and Julian stood aside to allow me in first.

I sank into the seat and was about to scoot over to make room, when I realized the door had shut and Julian was walking around to the other side.

He settled in next to me and glanced at my bare shoulders. "I forgot to ask if you'd brought a coat," he said apologetically.

"No, I didn't. I'm warm. So where are we going?" I repeated.

"Where would you like to go?"

"Well, I'm kind of dressed up. The options are limited."

I felt him hesitate, his indecision saturating the dark space between us. "Let me take you home, then," he said. "You've got work tomorrow anyway, I expect." He leaned forward and murmured my address to the driver, and we pulled away from the curb.

"So what brings you here tonight?" I asked, threading my fingers together in my lap.

"You. I was trying to reach you all evening."

"Oh!" I remembered. "I forgot to turn my phone back on."

"So I gathered. Then I had an e-mail from your colleague, Mr. Newcombe."

"*Charlie* e-mailed you?"

"About an hour ago. Suggested I put myself in a tuxedo and race to your side."

"Oh my God," I said, my face flooding. "What . . . what did he say?"

"Only that you were looking altogether too ravishing to be there by yourself, and attracting a great deal of unwanted attention."

"I'm sure he put it just that well."

"In so many words." He smiled. "I see he was understating the case, however."

I looked down at my lap, at the fabric falling away in long pale swags from my legs. "That's not fair, you know. Until last night, I hadn't had a word from you in months, and now suddenly you're here with your compliments and your . . . your *tuxedo*." I said this accusingly, as though wearing a tuxedo were some sort of crime. Which it probably should have been, on a man like Julian.

"What else would you have me wear?" he asked.

"That's not what I meant," I said, looking back up. The streetlights flashed across his face as we drove up Madison, casting his noble cheekbones in shadow, exposing briefly the limpid expression in his green-blue eyes. I tried to be objective, simply to applaud the flawless tailoring of his black jacket where it melted against his shoulders, or the way the sharp points of his shirt collar gleamed white against his throat, without falling into a kind of drooling admiration. But it was no use. The formality, the austerity, suited him too well. It made the perfect foil for the lush generosity of his face; it made me want to fling myself headlong into the folds of his lapel.

"Oh, Kate," he said. "When you look at me like that . . . those *eyes* of yours . . ." His eyelids lowered. "I've tried so very *hard* the last few months to stay away from you. To ignore this . . . this hold you have on me. You can't imagine what a challenge it's been. I've been reduced to following you like a lapdog as you run through the park." He raised his eyes to meet mine. "Now you know."

"Oh," I said, taking it in. "But why?"

"Why what?"

"Why stay away?"

"It's rather difficult to explain," he said.

"Well, try me. I mean, it hasn't exactly been easy for me, either. Wondering what I did to turn you off like that, so suddenly. You can't imagine the wild theories going through my head."

He began to laugh, not a jolly laugh. "Nothing so wild as the truth. But let's leave that aside for the moment . . ."

"No. Let's not. I want to know. I think I have a right to know."

"Kate," he said, and his voice went soft again. He reached out and fingered the back of my hand. "Please. I'll tell you, I promise. Just not now. I think . . ." He paused. "I think it might be better if we got to know one another more."

His voice was so charming, so beguiling, that all my objections flew from my head. "But why," I said, trying to marshal at least a little reason, "is that okay now? When it wasn't before?"

"It isn't okay. It's quite wrong. But I've gone past the point of caring anymore. I can't bear to be without you, and I was a perfect idiot to think I could . . ." He checked himself. His hand, which had been running up and down the backs of my fingers, grasped mine and drew it upward, a swift impulsive act, to brush against his lips.

I felt tears start against my eyelashes and drew my hand back down. "Well, I'm glad," I said, voice firm, "because I missed you, too."

"Oh, Kate," he said, turning away, but he kept my hand in his, sliding his thumb along mine and staring out the window.

"Why," I asked, into the tense air between us, "were you trying to find me?"

"Oh, that. I just wanted to let you know that I spoke with Miss Martinez at the *Post*, and the item tomorrow will be fairly innocuous. I asked her to leave your name out of it, but she pointed out that it was already in the public domain, so . . ." He shrugged. "I'm sorry about that."

"No, you did your best. It's no big deal, I guess. It'll blow over. Just a few days of crap from my colleagues, but I can handle that. And thank you," I added. "You didn't need to do that."

"It was the least I could do."

"Julian, you saved me from a serious beating. Maybe worse. And you set yourself up for a ton of unwanted public attention. So I'm the one who should be making things up to you."

"Christ, Kate!" he burst out. "As if *that* matters! My God! What if I hadn't been there last night?"

I returned my gaze to my lap and didn't answer.

We turned right on Seventy-ninth Street and ran off the avenues to my apartment building. "Well," I said, "this is me."

"Yes, it is," he agreed.

The driver got out and held my door open.

"Um, would you like to come in? I mean, not *come in*, come in," I added quickly. "Just to talk."

A smile grew across his face. "Yes, I'd like that," he said, and followed me out of the car. He turned to the driver and said a few low words; the man nodded and got back in.

"What did you tell him?" I demanded. "Because you're not staying over, you know. I'm not *that* easy."

"Of course not." He looked shocked. "He's just going to park down the street."

"Good, then. Now I warn you," I said, as he opened the lobby door for me, "my roommate is a little . . . well, you'll see what I mean. If she's home. Which she's probably not. Hi, Joey."

Joey was on the house phone; his eyebrows went up into his hairline when he saw us. "Good night, Kate," he mouthed meaningfully, as we walked past the desk.

I pressed the elevator call button. The doors opened at once and we stepped inside. "Which floor?" asked Julian.

"Seven."

He reached forward and pressed the button. "So," he observed, as the doors closed, "Joey looked surprised."

"I don't exactly bring home a lot of men."

"Really?"

"None, in fact," I admitted. "I kind of went off dating after college."

"Oh. And why was that?"

"Too many . . . what was that word you used? *Rotters.*"

The doors opened and I led him out of the elevator and down the hall to my apartment door. "We'll see if Brooke is in," I said darkly, as I fit my key into the door and opened it. "Sorry. It's not exactly what you're used to."

"It's fine," he said.

"You haven't even looked inside."

"Well, go on in, then," he urged. "I'm right behind you."

I crossed the threshold, holding my breath, hoping Brooke was running true to form. "Brooke?" I called out. No answer. Thank God.

"She's still out," I told Julian, turning on the entrance lamp. "That little treat will have to wait until later. So, this is it. Typical Manhattan bachelorette pad. Living room, kitchen area, two bedrooms down the hall. Brooke has the master; it's her apartment. Her parents' apartment, I mean. They bought it as her graduation present. I pay rent to her."

He smiled tolerantly at my babbling and walked into the living room, filling the space with his dignity. "And how did you find such a cozy arrangement?"

"Craigslist. Sit down. Can I get you something? Water? Coffee? I have one of those French press thingies; it makes a pretty good cup."

"Coffee, then. But let me help you," he said, and followed me into the tiny kitchen area.

"Oh, that's not necessary," I protested. The sink was still full of Brooke's breakfast dishes. Eggs, from the look of the pan. She hadn't even soaked it, and the remains had dried into an enamel-like hardness. "Sorry about the mess," I said, turning on the water and filling the sink. "I leave way before my roommate does, and I never know what's going to greet me when I come in."

"Darling," he said, "you don't need to apologize for everything."

"Do I? Apologize?" My ears tingled with delight. *Darling* again.

"You do. Now where's this coffee press of yours?"

"Right here," I said, reaching for it.

"No, I'll get it. Just tell me what to do."

He made the coffee and I did the dishes, laughing and getting in each other's way, I in my gown and he in his tuxedo, like some sort of bizarre domestic comedy, and somehow the stiffness between us dissolved into familiarity. "So talk," I said, when we were finally on the sofa, coffee cups in hand. I slipped off my shoes and tucked my feet under my dress.

"About what?" he asked, taking a cautious drink of the coffee. An expression of surprised pleasure crossed his face.

"You see? It's not bad," I said proudly. "A housewarming gift from my brother."

"Tell me about your brother."

"Kyle? Well, he lives back in Wisconsin. He's still in college, senior year. He's a great guy. Very into baseball. He's majoring in accounting."

"You can read *accounting* here?" He laughed.

"Sure you can. We like to take the arts out of liberal arts, here in America."

"Are you close? You and your brother?"

I thought about that for a second. "About average. I mean, I don't spill my guts to him, but I know he'd be there if I needed him. We e-mail a lot. He keeps hoping I'll run into some Yankees hotshot and get an autograph for him."

He smiled, fingered his coffee cup. "And your parents?"

"The usual." I shrugged. "I don't know what to say, really. They're just parents. Dad's in insurance. Mom used to be a teacher. She still subs sometimes, during the cold and flu season, when they're short." I took a drink of coffee. "She likes to read and garden. Pretty typical stuff."

"You're fortunate."

"What about your parents? What were they like?"

"My parents." He looked at me sideways and lifted the cup to his mouth. "I'm not sure I can explain this properly."

"Secret agents, huh? You're the hidden love child of Bond and Money-penny?"

He choked on his coffee. "Bloody hell. Was it that obvious?"

"I took a DNA sample. Look," I said, setting down my coffee cup with an abrupt thrust. "Do you mind if I change?"

"I do," he told me solemnly. "I rather like that frock. But go on. I imagine it's rather more pleasure for me to watch than for you to wear."

"Something like that. I'll be right back."

"I'll be waiting," he said.

I fled down the short hallway to my bedroom. I wanted to change, it was true. The dress wasn't exactly comfortable. But the more pressing imperative was that, after all the champagne and excitement, my bladder was about to explode. I twisted myself into a pretzel, unzipping my dress, and slipped on a bra and my usual evening uniform of tank top and yoga pants and cardigan; then I went to the bathroom and started in surprise at the reflection in the mirror. I looked possessed. My skin glowed with color; my drab gray eyes burned almost silver. I pulled out the pins from my hair and shook it free, and then found an elastic to twist the waving strands out of my face.

He was standing up when I came back, looking at the photographs on the windowsill. "That's me with my best friends," I said. "Michelle and Samantha. We went through Europe the summer after college. I think that was Paris."

"Yes, Paris," he said softly. He turned around and looked at me. "Now I feel rather ridiculous," he complained.

"You can loosen your tie," I pointed out.

"I wasn't brought up to loosen my tie," he said, but he untied the bow anyway and released the top button of his shirt, drawing apart the pointed triangles of his dress collar. He reached into the inner pocket of his jacket and drew out an envelope. "For you."

"What's this?"

"I arrived just before the silent auction closed," he said. "I felt I owed you something more than a simple apology, for my behavior last Christmas."

"You don't owe me anything." I eyed the envelope suspiciously. "And it had better not be that thing with Brian Williams, either, because I don't do live TV."

He laughed. "It's not. Open it."

I took it from him and ran my finger under the flap. "Oh no," I said, feeling the blood drain downward from my face. "Oh, no you don't. You are not, repeat *not*, going to give me a freaking *airplane share*!"

"I already have."

"Julian, the bid was . . . I don't even want to say it! I mean, way, way too much."

"It was a charitable donation," he said.

"That's not the point. You can't just *give* me stuff like this."

"Why not?"

"Because I'm not that kind of girl," I bit out, thrusting the thing back in his hands.

He flinched in horror. "I didn't mean it like *that*! I'm not expecting . . ."

"No, it's not that. I know you're not . . . that it's not . . . But you see," I tried to explain, past the heat building once more under the skin of my face, "it's kind of the elephant in the room, isn't it?"

"Elephant?"

"Oh, please. Who you *are*, Julian. Your . . . um . . . your . . ." I looked down at my fingers, picking anxiously at one another. *Your money. The m-word. Just say it.* But instead I only sighed: "Let's sit down. We might as well get this over with."

"Get *what* over with?"

"This." I sank into the sofa, girding myself. "Ground rule one: you are not allowed to buy me expensive gifts."

"Define expensive." He dropped down next to me and folded his arms.

"Well," I said, "it's kind of like pornography. You know it when you see it. And *this* is definitely too expensive. Way, way, *way*." I peered at his face, which had settled into a pensive frown. "Look, flowers are nice. I love dark chocolate. Maybe even the day spa. But nothing I couldn't afford to buy myself. Nothing I couldn't reciprocate." ·

"But it's *useful*," he protested, holding up the envelope.

"Julian, be serious. I mean, don't you worry . . ."

"What?" he pressed.

"That I'm just a gold digger."

"Of course not."

"Why not?"

"Darling," he said, "believe me, I know the difference. I've had a bloody sign hanging around my neck from the time I was born."

"Well, but maybe I *am* a gold digger." I drew up my legs against my chest. "Because it's part of who you are. Don't you see? I have to prove to *myself* that it isn't true, that I don't care about your millions. Or billions. Whatever it is. Don't tell me!" I held up one hand. "I don't want to know. Look, how do I explain this? I never wanted to be Cinderella. Never wanted to be *that* girl, the one looking for a rich guy to drape her with diamonds. I always wanted to make it on my own, and it scares me that . . . that from the moment I met you, I felt this . . . this connection. And I didn't even *know* you. So maybe it *is* the money. Maybe I really *am* that girl. Charlie said something today . . ."

"Charlie," he said crossly.

"No, but he made me think. Because obviously we can't separate you—Julian—from what you are. You're a very successful man, and I'm a woman, and maybe I'm just *programmed* to respond to that. Millions of years of evolution."

He lifted one of his long angled eyebrows. "And that's all? There's nothing else to like about me?"

"No! No, of course not. You're . . ." I stopped, feeling the blush rise up. "Well, I'm not going to sit here and list it all. But yes. I mean, you don't lack for attractive qualities. Obviously." A pause. "You're gentlemanly, for example. I like that a lot."

"Thank you." He seemed amused.

"Or maybe it's your looks, which makes me even more shallow."

"Kate." He sighed, reached out his hand to touch my fingers. "You're overthinking this."

"Well, I have a tendency to do that."

"Then let me apply a little logic for you. By the very nature of your job, you're in daily contact with any number of wealthy men. One or two of them have surely worked up the courage to ask you out by now. Am I right?"

"One or two," I admitted.

"And did you accept any of them?"

"No."

"Paul Banner, for example. He must be worth a fair amount."

"Oh, *blech*!"

"You see? So please allow me to flatter myself that this sweet blush of yours," he said, brushing my cheek with his finger, "might perhaps be due to some genuine feeling for me. Which I shall do my best to deserve." He paused. "Now, that's a rather cynical expression crossing your face just now. Don't you trust me?"

"Well, no. I really don't know what's going on here, to be honest. Why you disappeared on me, and why you're back. And then why you even began with me at all. You should be out partying with models and actresses, not drinking coffee with nerdy investment bankers."

"Oh, for God's sake. Do you really think so little of me? Of yourself?"

"No. I know my own worth. But it's not the kind of thing that inspires instant attraction, is it? Especially to a man who's spoiled for choice."

He lifted the coffee cup to his lips, covering a smile. "Spoiled for choice, am I?"

"Oh, please. You're like catnip, Julian."

A caustic laugh. "Not if one keeps clear of the cats."

"Well, maybe I'm one of them. How would you know?"

He flashed me a teasing under-look from across the rim of his cup. "Perhaps I've been studying up. Perhaps I know all about you."

My head snapped up. "*What?* Do you?"

The amusement vanished. He regarded me steadily, soberly, faint lines gathering about the corners of his eyes. This time I recognized it, that comprehensive gaze of his: picking apart, one by one, the seams that held me together. "I have," he said, setting down the cup, "been guilty, on rare occasion, of placing myself where I hoped I might perhaps catch a glimpse of you."

"Like last night?"

"A perfect evening for a run; I thought you might feel the same. I never meant to follow you, but it was growing dark . . ." He glanced away. "I was concerned for you."

I watched him for a moment, the side of his face visible in the lamplight: the clean beauty of it, drawn in effortless strokes by some unseen expert hand; the faint blush still staining the skin of his cheek, exactly as I remembered. "I just can't figure you out," I said at last.

He looked back at me, eyes alive. "Can't you?"

"That's why it was so hard, when you cut me off. Because I'd thought better of you. Because when I walked into your house at Christmastime, it all felt so familiar. Like I knew you, knew all about you. Maybe not the details, but the essentials. You were different and interesting and . . . and . . . *right*. It was so *right*." I bent my head into my knees, to block the sight of his face. "And then you just left. You *repudiated* it."

"Kate," he whispered, "I've many faults, God knows, but I never meant to trifle with you. Not the least of my . . . my distress, these past months, was the fear that I'd hurt you. What you must think of me."

I didn't reply.

"Kate, look at me."

"I can't," I said, my voice muffled against my knees. "I can't think clearly when you're looking at me like that. I haven't even gone on a date in three *years*, Julian. I have zero immunity."

"Well, it's been jolly longer than that for me. So if I can be brave, so can you."

I felt his hand on my chin, lifting my head. His face was closer than I expected, aglow as I was, the color high in his cheeks.

"I wish I could promise you I won't hurt you again," he said. "But there are . . . circumstances . . . I can't explain to you, at the moment. And so the only thing I can promise you is that the *feelings* I have for you are very real indeed. I've known them for longer than you realize. And to *those* I can and shall be faithful, without fail. Do you understand me?"

I nodded, mesmerized.

His voice dropped to a whisper. "Oh, look at you, darling. Staring into me with those great silver eyes of yours, reading my soul. I shouldn't be here with you, the most reckless self-indulgence, and yet I can't seem to bloody well *help* it anymore." He stopped and looked down. "And I can't forgive myself for that," he murmured, as if to himself; then he looked back up, holding my eyes, and said fiercely, "But I can at least give *this* to you, Kate: There is no one else for me. There will be no one else."

It was impossible to doubt him, impossible even to look away. I sat there in silence, returning his gaze with bemused fascination. "But you hardly know me," I said at last.

"Yes, I do."

I gestured to myself. "And I'm not exactly trophy material, either. You really should wait with all your fancy promises until you've actually seen the merchandise."

"I believe I've got the general idea." A knowing little smile curled his mouth, not gentlemanly at all. "That damned alluring frock of yours."

I laughed, surprising myself. "You should have seen the one Alicia picked out. Talk about having a sign around your neck."

"And it's such a lovely neck." His right hand lifted, trembling, and fell back into his lap.

"It's all right. I don't mind." I reached out bravely and took his hand and placed it, palm down, between my own. It was broad and capable, lightly callused, with long elegant fingers and neatly trimmed nails. A few downy golden hairs grew up from the back; I whorled them gently with my fingertip. "You must play the piano for me sometime," I told him.

"I shall," he promised.

"Where were you hurt?" I cleared my throat and nudged back the sleeve of his tuxedo, exposing his wrist. He wore simple gold cufflinks. "May I?" I asked, fingering one. He nodded. Carefully I drew the cufflink out of its hole and set it on the coffee table. "I don't want to hurt you," I said, looking back up at his face.

"You won't," he said. "It's long healed."

I drew the sleeve back, almost to his elbow, and took in my breath. A long irregular scar ran the length of his forearm, gouging deeply in the middle. "Oh my God," I said. "What happened?"

"Glass," he said, "from the windshield."

"But it's so . . . jagged!" I ran my finger down the long thick path, lined on either side by white pinpricks from the stitches, and my eyes filled with tears.

"Don't," he said tenderly, reaching up with the other hand to the back of my head, his head bent forward, his forehead nearly touching mine. "It happened so long ago."

I looked back up. "Please don't do this again."

"That's not likely."

"I can't even stand to think about it. Just . . . the pain . . ."

"Well," he admitted, "it bled like the devil."

His left hand still rested on the back of my head, fiddling with the strands of my hair. I lifted the other one to my cheek. He caressed the line of my cheekbone, the length of my jaw; his finger curved around my ear before drawing down the side of my neck, his eyes following the movement, examining every detail of my skin, my shape.

"How terribly *long* I've wanted," he said, "to do just that."

I was splintering inside, absolutely shattered. He held me in the palm of his hand. I let my feet slip back down to the floor and lifted my hand to his face. His brow creased, as if he were under some kind of strain. I ran my fingers along the lines, smoothing them. "It's not fair," I said. "You're so beautiful."

"Well," he told me, looking saddened, "it's yours, for what it is." He turned his head to kiss my palm, and then his hands moved to cradle my face. His thumb brushed against my lips, parting them fractionally, inquiring.

I snapped my mouth shut and pulled away.

"What's wrong?" he demanded.

"Coffee breath," I said, through my clenched lips.

He ducked his head and let out a despairing laugh. "Kate, haven't *I* been drinking the coffee, too?"

"Oh, but it won't affect you at all, will it?" I said bitterly. "You're Julian Laurence, and you're not subject to the same rules as normal human beings. I'm sure *your* breath will be all sweet and limpid, no matter how much coffee is in there, and *I'll* taste like the inside of a Starbucks. A *stale* Starbucks."

"Come here," he said, pulling me into his arms, shaking with laughter. "This is what I adore about you, Kate. There's no one like you. From the first moment . . ." His arms tightened around me. "I want you exactly like this. I want never to let you go." He leaned back against the arm of the sofa, drawing me with him until I rested luxuriously upon the breadth of his chest, the satin weave of his tuxedo jacket cooling my cheek.

"Heaven," I whispered, feeling his fingers travel up and down my spine. We lay there quietly a moment. I could hear his heart beat steadily next to my ear, a strong slow athletic pulse.

The buzzer rang. I jumped up, startled.

"What's that?" Julian asked.

"No idea," I said, checking the clock. Eleven-thirty. "I mean, it's Joey downstairs, but Brooke should have her key. Or maybe he's just trying to warn us . . ." I went over to the intercom and pressed the talk button. "Hello?"

"Kate. It's Joey. You have a visitor." His voice sounded ready to burst.

"Who is it?"

"I've sent her up already. Just giving you the heads-up." I heard him laugh, and then cut off.

Her?

I put my hand on my forehead and slumped against the wall.

Julian got up. "What is it? Your roommate?"

"Worse," I groaned. "It's my mother."

8.

"Hi, Mom," I said, opening the door. "I didn't realize you were coming."

"Honey, I was worried sick! You didn't answer your phone."

"Oh, yeah. I guess it's still turned off." I kissed her cheek and gave her a hug. "Uh, Mom . . ."

It was too late. She was already brushing past me into the living room, and stopped dead.

Julian stepped forward. *Don't worry,* he'd reassured me a second ago. *Mothers love me.* "Good evening, Mrs. Wilson," he said, in that lyric voice of his. "What a very great pleasure."

She just stared at him: at his face, his frame, the immense gravity of his presence; at his tuxedo, with its curving black bow tie hanging guiltily on either side of his unbuttoned collar.

I cleared my throat. "Um, Mom," I said, "this is my friend Julian. Julian Laurence."

"Oh," she said hoarsely.

Julian smiled his radiant smile and held out his hand. "You flew in tonight, I expect?" he inquired.

She placed her hand in his and allowed him to shake it. "Yes," she said. "I was so worried about Kate. I told her, when she moved to New York . . ."

"Mom, I told you I'm fine. It was a completely freak thing."

"I suppose," she said, not taking her eyes off Julian, "I have a lot to thank you for, young man."

I winced. *Young man.* For God's sake.

He shrugged. "It was nothing, I assure you," he said. "Kate's a supremely capable young woman." Then he unfolded his Saturday night special, that wide private beautiful smile, the lady slayer.

Mom was slayed. I watched her face soften and melt, like butter left out in the sun, and turned to roll my eyes at Julian. "Come on, Mom. There's still a little coffee left. Where's your bag?"

"Oh," she said, "that nice young fellow downstairs is bringing it up."

"You mean Joey?"

"Is that his name?"

"You must sit down, Mrs. Wilson," Julian said, motioning her to the sofa. "I imagine you're exhausted. When did your flight arrive?"

"Ten-thirty," she told him.

"I'll just fetch you a cup." He shot me a reproving look.

I folded my arms. "Coffee mugs are in the cabinet to the right of the sink," I called to him, as he disappeared around the corner of the kitchen area.

Mom looked at me with wide eyes. *Wow*, she mouthed.

"Yeah, I know," I mumbled.

The doorbell rang. Joey. I went to the door and opened it.

"Here you go, Kate." He smirked. "Everything okay?"

"Just fine, Joey. Just *fine*. Thanks."

I took the suitcase from him. Mom had finally entered the modern age and bought a black wheelie bag to replace her old hard-sided Samsonite, circa 1962. Like everyone else, she had fastened a rainbow-striped cord around the middle so she could tell it apart on the carousel. I dragged it into the living room, where Julian was presenting my mom with a mug of coffee.

"It was a bit lukewarm," he explained, "so I put it in the microwave. Is it too hot?"

"Oh, just fine. Just . . . just fine." She looked between the two of us, back and forth. "So. Were you two kids having a good time?"

I glared at her full force before replying. "Great. We were at a charity thing in midtown. Julian gave me a ride home."

"And really," he said, checking his watch, "I ought to be going. I daresay you and your mother wouldn't mind a little sleep."

Mom drew a deep breath. "Don't let me chase you away, Julian, if you were planning to *stay over*. I always bed down here, right on the good old sofa sleeper." She patted it for emphasis. "It's very comfortable."

Kill me now.

"You're too kind, Mrs. Wilson," Julian said, only a slight waver in his voice. "But I really must be going. I've got to be at work early tomorrow. Still, I'm delighted to have met you." He smiled at me. "You've raised an extraordinary daughter."

"Really, you don't need to go," she insisted.

"Mom," I said. "He wants to go. I want him to go. It's not what you're thinking."

"Oh." She looked back and forth between us again. "Well, then. It was nice to meet you, Mr. Laurence. I'm glad my little girl has someone to look out for her."

He opened his mouth to make some no doubt sensationally witty reply, but I cut him off with a brisk "I'll walk you to the elevator, Julian."

"Yes, ma'am," he said meekly, and winked at my mother.

She winked right back.

I took Julian by the arm and dragged him to the door. "And no peeking," I threw over my shoulder, as I hauled him out.

The elevator was just around the corner. I pressed the button and turned around to look at him, folding my arms over my chest.

He smiled and reached out and drew me up against him. "Do you really want me to go?" he murmured in my ear.

"At this exact moment, yes," I said, pushing aside the swirling mist that seemed to addle my brain whenever he touched me.

A low little chuckle. "When can I see you again?"

"Call my assistant. She keeps my diary."

"Kate." He chuckled again. "I'll surprise you, then."

The elevator clanged nearer, and I unfolded my arms and wrapped them around his waist. "I can't wait."

The bell dinged. I drew back and looked up to find him watching me intently. He leaned down and brushed my lips with his own. "Neither can I," he said, and stepped into the elevator just as the doors began to close.

"OKAY, MOM." I slammed the door behind me. "That was probably the single most embarrassing moment of my entire life. Forget the day I wet my pants in first grade. Forget the time I screwed up my solo at the jazz choir concert. I mean, Oh. My. God. *Why* did you say that?"

"Say what?" She had risen from the sofa and was now busy cleaning up the rest of the kitchen with her usual air of impeccable moral advantage.

"Oh, you know. *Don't let me chase you away, Julian, if you wanted to* stay over," I said, in falsetto. "I mean, we haven't even had a real *date* yet. We haven't even . . ."

She looked up. "Haven't even what, honey?"

"Kissed," I mumbled.

"Didn't he kiss you good night just now?"

I glared at her. "I thought I told you not to peek."

"Oh, honey," she laughed, "I didn't need to peek to know *that*!"

"Well," I said, "it wasn't a real kiss. So just take that smirk off your face. I mean, for God's sake, you're my *mother*! You're not supposed to sanction *sex*! Under the same *roof*! I mean, *eww*! This room shares a *wall* with mine!"

"Well, in *my* home, I wouldn't. If you bring him for a visit, he'll have his own room. But this is *your* place, honey. You can do what you like."

"And you wouldn't *mind*?"

"I would probably put a pillow over my head," she admitted, giving the counter a last swipe with the sponge and wringing it out over the sink. "But he's awfully good-looking, you know."

"Yes, Mom. I know."

"And he seemed *quite* taken with you."

"Well, I guess I hope so." I dropped onto the sofa and looked up at her. She had left the kitchen area and was wheeling her suitcase from the center of the room to the wall. "He's kind of an amazing guy, Mom."

"He looks it, honey." She paused. "He's the man from the park, right?"

"Um, yeah."

"My goodness," she said, sitting down next to me. "How did you meet him?"

"Business meeting."

"I guess that's how these things work, these days." She straightened her watch, aligning it exactly with the base of her hand. "So is he really . . . what Mary Alice said?"

"Pretty much." I stared at the plain white envelope on the coffee table.

"How do you feel about that?"

"What do you mean, how do I feel?" I snapped. "I've met a lot of rich guys in the past few years. What's the big deal?"

She said nothing. A patient woman, my mother.

I gave in. "All right. Sorry. I know what you meant. Yes, okay, it's weird. But he's not like most of them. He's not flashy. The money's just a fact to him, not—I don't know—some essential part of his ego. Kind of refreshing."

"He has one of those hedge funds, doesn't he?" Almost like she knew what a hedge fund was.

"Yeah. A big one. But six years ago it was nothing. He did it all himself."

"He comes from money, though."

"I'm not sure," I said. "He hasn't told me much about that. But yeah, I think so. How did you know?"

"Oh, honey. You can just tell." She chuckled suddenly.

"What is it?"

"I shouldn't tell you this. You'll kill me."

"What?"

"Well, he kind of reminds me of my father, a little."

"Poppa! Oh, *Mom*! How could you say that? *Poppa?*"

She laughed. "I knew you'd kill me. But it's true. It's his manners, you know. He's very formal. Old-fashioned, I guess. He's been well brought up. Does he open the door for you?"

"Yes," I said.

"Well, there you are. Keep him."

Like it was that easy. "All right, Mom." I patted her knee. "Let's get up and put this bed together. How long are you staying, by the way?"

"I've got a flight back on Sunday morning. It was much cheaper with the Saturday night layover."

We pulled the sleeper out and made up the bed, and then took turns in the bathroom. "I'll leave a note for Brooke on the door, so she doesn't wake you up," I said.

"That roommate of yours." She shook her head.

"I know, I know. Good night." I kissed her on the cheek.

"Good night, honey."

I wrote the note and taped it on the door and got into bed, where I lay awake for a long time, listening to my heart trip restlessly against my ribs, telling myself it was just the coffee.

FRANK, THE MORNING DOORMAN, met me right off the elevator at six-thirty the next day. "You have a visitor," he told me, grinning widely and waggling his eyebrows. "I was about to call up."

My heart jumped into my sinuses. I peered past the front desk into the lobby.

Julian stood there, impossibly radiant, a white paper bag in one hand. I skipped up. "Good morning," I said.

"Good morning." He dropped a glancing kiss on my lips and took my laptop from my shoulder. "I thought I'd drive you to work today."

"But I'm not on your way," I pointed out.

"If you were, it wouldn't be nearly as much fun."

He led me outside, where a sleek dark-green machine perched eagerly by the curb, and opened the passenger door for me. I ducked in and settled myself into the leather, into the cocoon of dials and lights and dormant energy.

The door opened on the other side, and Julian climbed in and threw the engine in gear. "Nice car," I said, grabbing hold of my seat as we thrust forward.

"A recent acquisition. I was rather afraid you might disapprove."

"It beats the 6 train. What's in the bag?"

"Bagels. That doesn't violate the rules, does it?"

"Depends on where you got the bagels." I opened the bag. At least half a dozen shiny plump bagels rested inside, still warm, the yeasty smell rising like heaven into my nose.

"I wasn't sure which flavor you liked," he explained, "so I got them all."

I picked out a blueberry and bit in. "Lovely. Which one would you like?"

"Oh, the blueberry, I suppose."

"Too late. Cinnamon raisin?" I handed it to him.

We rode in silence for a few minutes, pecking at our bagels. He was a quiet driver, working his way through the crawling grid with a minimum of turns and lane changes, anticipating the traffic around him. In a few minutes we were accelerating smoothly onto the FDR, and I tilted my head at last to take him in, to admire his crisp handsome profile etched against the morning sun.

"So how did you sleep?" I asked.

"Dreadfully. I missed you. And you?"

"Pretty well, actually. Very nice dreams."

He glanced sideways at me and smiled. "What about?"

"Sorry. That's between me and my subconscious." I paused. "How did you know I was leaving for work early today?"

"Oh, I didn't." He checked the mirror and eased into the far left lane. "I was going to have Joey ring you up."

"Frank," I corrected him. "Joey's the evening doorman. What if I'd been in bed?"

"I'd have rousted you out, of course. I'm usually in before seven, myself."

I looked at the clock on the dashboard. "Then I'm making you late."

"Geoff can hold down the fort for once."

"When I think of all the trades you'll be missing . . ."

He laughed. "Don't worry about it. The markets will survive without me. I, however, cannot possibly survive without you."

I couldn't think of anything to say to that.

He glanced at me. "Everything all right?"

"Yes," I said. "I just can't quite believe this is happening."

"This?"

"You. Me. *This*. I've never *felt* this way. As though I know you perfectly, but not at all. And then you say ridiculous things like that, when we haven't even . . ."

"Haven't what?"

"You know." I felt the blush climb relentlessly in my cheeks. "Even *kissed*."

A chuckle. "Well, and whose bloody fault is that? *Coffee* breath, for God's sake. Little minx. Anyway, I *did* kiss you last night. And this morning."

"That's not what I mean."

He fell silent for a few seconds, and then the car swerved across three lines of traffic into the exit lane and slammed to a halt. "What are you *doing*?" I yelled, gripping my seat. SUVs and delivery trucks zoomed past us, horns howling in outrage.

"Kissing you," he replied, and he took my face in his large long-fingered hands and bent his lips into mine.

Oh God finally a gentle clasp, warm and lush and generous, cinnamon-raisin and something else, something so indescribably savory *oh God* I wanted more of it, but he held it all in check, the most exquisite self-control: not at all like a first kiss, nothing awkward, perfectly knowing, the tip of his velvet tongue just grazing mine *oh God* the sensation snaking through me like a live current. His hands held my head tenderly in place, his fingertips worked through the fine hair at my temples. An odd sensation began to build behind my eyes and through my torso, as if I were lighter than air, tethered to myself only by the hold of Julian's hands and lips. I slipped my fingers under his suit jacket, clutching at the reality of his flesh through the thin layers of shirt and undershirt. "Kate," he growled into my lips, shifting his body urgently, and I wrapped my other arm around him, nearly climbing out of my seat with a desperate need to connect with him.

He stopped then, breathing hard against the thin skin of my collarbone, his hands still clasping my cheeks, the scent of his hair warm in my nose.

"Wow," I said. I could hear my own pulse, rapid and shocked. "Practice much?"

He raised his head and looked at me, his face only inches away. "Not at all."

"Then you must have really good instincts," I said, running my thumb along the curve of his bottom lip. He closed his eyes and pressed a kiss against it.

The blare of a tractor-trailer horn tore violently through the charged air around us. "Oh my God," I screeched. "We're going to get killed!"

He drew away with a laugh and a last caress to the side of my face. "You asked for a kiss."

"I didn't mean *at that exact second*!" I twisted around to see a wave of vehicles bearing down on us.

"I don't know." His hand went down to the gearshift. "*I* thought it was worth it." With a quick glance in the rearview mirror he released the clutch, sending us hurtling down the shoulder and merging back into traffic as if nothing at all had happened, as if the promising theory between us had not just been transformed into solid fact, as if we were not now different people from the ones who had climbed into the car half an hour ago.

We got off at the Brooklyn Bridge exit and wove through the narrow half-clogged canyons to Wall Street, pulling up in front of the Sterling Bates building with a theatrical roar of the engine. "So what kind of car is this?" I asked.

"Maserati," he said, grinning.

"And I just finished telling my mom you aren't flashy."

A wink. "A chap's got a right to a little fun once in a while, after all." He got out of the car and went around to my side, opening my door while I was still gathering up my things. I started to haul myself upward and found his hand under my elbow.

"Thanks," I said shyly, rearranging myself.

"Of course." He just stood there, studying me. His grin had dimmed into something more wistful than happy.

I realized I was staring at his mouth and cleared my throat. "You know," I said, fingering the strap of my laptop bag, "we haven't gone on a real date yet, either."

"Pick you up at eight, then?"

"Sorry," I said. "My mom doesn't leave until Sunday morning."

"Then she can join us."

I snorted. "Julian, honestly, I don't think even Dante could have imagined anything worse than *that* idea. Try again."

"Sunday afternoon?"

"Um, sorry. Ballet class." I ducked my head, adding sheepishly, "I can't miss another one or they'll kick me out."

"Ballet? I'd no idea. When does it wrap up?"

"Half past six."

"I'll pick you up." His smile widened then, and he reached over to tuck back a strand of hair that had fallen free from my elastic. "Have a good day, darling."

I took my laptop bag from him. "You too," I said, and hurried across the Sterling Bates plaza before he could tempt me into some embarrassing public display. From behind, I heard the distant thoroughbred roar of the Maserati, chasing me into the building.

.   .   .

JULIAN'S KISS BURNED like a neon sign on my lips as I made my way through security and up the elevator to my floor. The financial world is a perfectly evolved mechanism for the rapid transmission of information, and nothing on Wall Street travels faster than salacious gossip; by now just about everyone in the firm, if not the whole freaking city, would know I'd left the MoMA benefit last night in the company of Julian Laurence.

Distracted by a jumble of self-conscious reflections, I'd reached the relative sanctuary of my cubicle and flipped open my laptop before I realized I hadn't even picked up my morning coffee.

Mercifully, the Starbucks line hadn't yet approached its morning zenith. In under six minutes I was swinging back around the corner of my desk, nerves still crackling, and nearly plopped myself into the middle of Alicia Boxer's lap.

"Alicia!" I exclaimed.

She jumped up from my chair. "Oh, Kate! Sorry. I was just looking for a file."

My voice turned to ice. "I keep everything on the server."

"I know." She smiled apologetically. "I couldn't find it, though, so I thought I'd just check your hard drive."

I looked at my laptop screen. "What file are you talking about?"

"The offering memo for that convertible deal we're working on."

"It's on the server. Under Clients."

"Oh, *Clients*," she said, as though it were a revelation. She looked haggard, with bags under her eyes the size and color of prunes, and her hair lying lank below her ears. Considering how wasted she'd been the night before, though, I was amazed just to see her at this hour. "I thought you'd keep it in your personal folder until it was done."

"I finished it yesterday, before I left."

"Wow! You're efficient. How did things go last night, by the way? I heard you left with Julian Laurence. I didn't even see him there."

"We kind of bumped into each other outside."

"Very sly! I like it. Nice Page Six mention, by the way. Popped your cherry, huh? Now you're really someone in this town."

"God forbid," I said. "Do you mind? I've got a lot to do. I'm trying to get out of here by eight tonight."

"Hmm. I smell a hot date. Let me close that window for you." She reached out and clicked, and the blank desktop appeared. "Okay. All yours. Clients folder, you said?"

"Yeah."

"Got it. See you later."

I sat down in my seat, feeling her warmth there with a trace of revulsion. What the hell had that been about? Why was she snooping on my laptop? Looking to feed her gossip habit?

"Charlie," I said, two hours later, when he staggered in and collapsed in the cubicle next to me, "is there some kind of log I can access on the computer, showing me what stuff's been opened lately?"

"Yeah, pretty sure," he said, taking a drink from a coffee cup and closing his eyes in pain, "but you'll have to ask one of the tech guys. You don't have any Advil on you, do you? Mine was fucking expired. Whatever that means."

"I think so." I reached for my bag and dug in. I usually kept a small bottle for emergencies.

"Thanks." He tossed down three gelcaps with another drink of coffee.

"Don't OD," I said, "or if you do, don't sue me."

"Yeah, whatever, dude. So have you seen the *Post*?"

"Not yet."

"Come on, dude. Log on."

I'd been avoiding it all morning; I was trying to convince myself that if I didn't read it, it didn't exist. "All right," I muttered, flipping to the *Post* on my bookmarks list. I clicked on Page Six.

*HEDGE FUND HERO. Gotham's money-managing titans aren't usually known for their chivalry, but Southfield Associates honcho **Julian***

*Laurence gallantly played against type Wednesday night, flashing his knight-errant creds to one lucky damsel in distress. According to police reports posted on The Smoking Gun, the hunky hedgie, who tops many insiders' eligible bachelor lists, came to the aid of 25-year-old investment banker **Kate Wilson** when she was confronted in Central Park while jogging, not far from the site of the infamous 1989 attack that made headlines worldwide. British-born Laurence helped restrain the un-named thug until police arrived to take him in custody, and was back at work the next morning, running his $20 billion fund.*

I let my breath out in relief. "Oh. That's not so bad."

"No shit. You're a boldface now. Congrats."

I handed him the white paper bag over the cubicle wall. "Here. Have a bagel. They're good for hangovers."

"Thanks, dude. Mmm, onion. You rock." He paused to nibble carefully at the bagel. "So have you heard the rumor?"

"Which one?"

"They had a steering committee meeting early this morning. Traders are saying someone's got some massive position we've got to unload."

"How massive?"

"I don't know. But it was enough to call a meeting on a Friday morn-ing." He shut his eyes again and stared up at the ceiling. "Hope it doesn't blow up until after we're gone. I need my last paycheck for fucking b-school tuition."

"What's the trade?" I asked.

"Who knows. Some kind of fucked-up derivative, probably." He paused, drummed his fingertips on his armrest. "I also hear," he went on slowly, "they're all pissing blood about trading volumes with Southfield."

"Southfield?" I frowned. "Where did you hear that?"

"Couple of traders last night. Your boy Laurence have anything to say about it?"

"Why does everyone think Julian tells me his trading secrets?"

"Okay, dude. Calm down. I get it. No shop talk over the pillow."

"There's no *pillow* involved, Charlie. Not all of us are as slutty as you are."

"Wow. Touché." He sounded appreciative.

I pursed my lips and stared at my computer screen. "So are they up or down? Trading volumes, I mean."

"Up, dude. *Way* up." He snickered. "Some fucking coincidence, huh?"

"Go to hell, Charlie."

"Ugh. I'm already fucking *there*, Kate."

I gave him a moment's peace before speaking up. "So, I have a question for you."

"Another one? Shit, Kate. Can't you just figure stuff out on your own this morning? I've got a massive fucking hangover."

"I just want to know why you sent that e-mail to Julian last night."

His grinning skull rolled sideways to take me in. "'Cause I was fucking sick of that lost-puppy look on your face, that's why. I told you, dude. You need to strap on a pair of fucking balls."

Amiens

Someone was in the room with me, rustling conscientiously: the repressed stir of someone trying to be quiet. I opened my eyes. "Julian? Captain Ashford?"

"I'm so sorry. I didn't mean to intrude." He emerged from some corner of the room, looking anxious. "Only adding a bit of coal; it's gone frightfully chilly. How are you feeling?"

I sat up, letting the blanket slide down to my lap. I'd left the lamp on, not wanting to settle too deeply to sleep, and the dim glow made everything look old and weary: the low ceiling, nearly grazing Julian's head; the rusty brown water stain in the corner by the window, creeping lazily over the aging wallpaper; the small cast-iron fireplace with its tarnished scuttle. A small room; though Julian stood politely by the mantel, as far from the bed as he could manage without catching himself on fire, he was no more than eight intimate feet away. "Much better, thank you. I'm sorry to be so much trouble."

"Don't be ridiculous." He paused self-consciously. How handsome and competent he looked, in his well-worn khaki tunic with its large pockets and brass buttons and wide Sam Browne belt, the strict knot at his neck splitting his shirt collar exactly in half. That boyish replica of the face I adored.

I smiled and drew my knees up. "You're feeling awkward, aren't you? Let me guess what you're thinking." I adjusted my tone, took on his supple clipped accent. "Bloody hell, Ashford. How the devil have you gotten yourself in this mess? A strange woman in your bed at three o'clock in the afternoon! Just how the deuce are you planning to get her out and on her way, without being rude?"

His smile spread slow and dazzling across his face, just as it always had. "In fact," he said, "you're not remotely close."

"I'm not?"

"For one thing, I'd never use such language in your presence."

My mouth twitched. "Oh. I beg your pardon."

"And for another thing, it's gone nearly five o'clock."

I glanced at the window. "I'm so sorry."

"You must stop all this apologizing immediately."

"I know, it's a bad habit." I laughed shallowly and turned back to him. "But I *have* put you in a difficult position, haven't I? Did you have time to ask about a room for me? Don't worry if you haven't," I added. "I can find something. I feel much better now, with a little rest."

"The landlady has another room available by this evening," he said. "Some chap going back up the line. You can stay here, of course; I'll move my own things upstairs."

"Thanks. Thank you. You probably think the worst of me already, allowing myself in here without a chaperone."

He laughed. "You don't need a chaperone. You're perfectly capable."

"But the girls you know wouldn't be caught dead here, would they?" I gestured around the room, at his pack resting significantly in the corner.

"No, but you're not like the other girls, are you?"

"Obviously not. I probably curse like a fishwife, by comparison." I smiled repentantly. "Aren't you afraid of my character? Some cheap seductress, maybe?"

He tilted his head, still smiling. "Are you?"

"Of course not. I'm a respectable widow." My voice choked on the word. "But how would you know that? How could you be sure of me?"

"Kate," he said, "it's written on your face. The way you hold your head, just so."

The air between us seemed to slow and thicken. I watched him helplessly, his sturdy figure planted before the fire, hands behind his back, the lamplight casting such deep shadows beneath his cheekbones that he might nearly be thirty, might nearly bridge the gap between himself and the man I knew. "You're so trusting," I whispered.

He shook his head. "Not indiscriminately, in fact."

"Why me, then?"

He seemed to take this seriously. "I suppose," he said, almost to himself, "because it feels almost as though I know you already. That we've met before. I've never . . . But it's absurd, of course. I beg your pardon."

"It's just because of the way I'm talking to you, probably. I started on in like some kind of brazen idiot, assuming things . . ."

"*Have* we met before?"

"Wouldn't you remember? You don't forget faces, and you're never drunk."

His eyes widened. He flung his arms across his ribs and paced the short distance to the window with that leonine grace of his. "How would you know that?"

"I just know things."

"That second sight of yours?" he asked, not looking at me.

"I thought you said it was a load of rubbish."

"I'd always thought so." His fingers spread out along the windowsill, digging into the wood.

"Julian, trust me. Don't be afraid of this."

"I'm not afraid." He turned, meeting my gaze with wide curious eyes. The irises were backlit with emotion, with dawning recognition, the way I'd felt around him all those months ago. "And I do trust you," he added.

"Do you really? I mean really *trust* me? I know that's a stupid question to ask, when you've only just met me, and in the most bizarre circumstances." I set my chin on top of my knees and studied him. "All I can say, in my defense, is that you *can* trust me. I'd never hurt you; never, never."

"Who *are* you?" he breathed.

Silence gathered in the little room. The light from the single electric lamp gasped and shuddered and went out, leaving us in a dusky gloom; then it flickered back on again, just as I reached for the candle on the bedside table.

"Sorry," I said. "It keeps doing that. Come sit down."

He hesitated.

"You don't have to sit next to me," I said. "The chair is just fine."

He walked over and sat down gingerly on the bed, a few feet away. His scent crept toward me, soap and damp wool and smoke, pungent with masculine activity.

"Julian, there's something I know, something I need to tell you."

"What sort of thing?" he asked evenly, guardedly.

"Something that's going to happen. Don't ask how I know it. It's the reason I came here, to warn you."

"How on earth . . ."

"You're not allowed to ask, remember?"

"How can I *not* ask? How can I believe you, if I don't know?"

I reached out to take his unresisting hand and hold it between mine. "Well, that's where the trust comes in." I rubbed his thumb, wondering at the ridged toughness of it, a laborer's thumb. "Look at you. I can see the doubt in your eyes. I don't suppose I can blame you, either; I'm probably not the most credible object you've ever encountered."

"I'm not doubting *you*, Kate. Not your intentions, at least."

I smiled. "That's a relief, anyway. You doubt my information, then? Or . . . or perhaps you think I might be right, and so you don't want to hear it."

"I'm not quite sure, to be honest." His hand began to curl around mine.

"May I tell you, then? And then you can decide the rest for yourself." I drew a slow circle on the back of his hand with my fingertip. "Will you let me, please?"

He nodded.

"Thank you. So here it is: You'll be going on a night patrol, as soon as you're back up the line. Does that sound reasonable?"

A reproachful upward tilt of his mouth. "One doesn't need much second sight to guess *that*. You must know I've run dozens of them."

"So I've gathered." I smiled back. "You and your heroics. But this one will be different, Julian. You won't come back safely to your trenches this time. During that night patrol, something will happen to you, something that will lead to your death."

I saw his face stiffen in the instant before the lamp went out again, leaving us alone in the faded daylight.

"And so I'm asking you, please, *please*, Julian," I said, trying to keep my voice steady and not quite succeeding, "not to go on that patrol."

"How do you know this?" he asked, quite calm.

"I told you not to ask me that."

"How . . ." He bit his lip.

I tightened my hand around his. "Can't you just trust me? Promise me you'll find someone else to lead the patrol?"

His face cleared. "That I can't do. Won't do."

"You won't even consider it?"

"Of course not. What, and let some other man die in my place?" He shook his head. "In any case, every time I put my head up, I run the risk of being killed. It's war."

"But I *know*," I pleaded. "This is *real*, Julian."

"Whether you're telling the truth isn't the point," he said gently, "not that I doubt you. Surely you understand. One doesn't desert one's company. Shirk one's duties, out of fear of death."

"*Fear* of death? Julian, it's an absolute certainty!"

"All the more reason I should go, if the bullet is meant for me."

"In the first place, it's a shell, not a bullet."

"And what about the man who dies in my place? How do I write that letter home to his mother?"

"And what about the letter home to yours?" I asked wildly, feeling desperate now, realizing I'd badly miscalculated. "Please believe me. You will *die*. You *will*, Julian. You can't do that to me." I slid from the bed, onto my knees before him, supplicating. "Please. Please listen to me. What can I say? What can I do?"

He grasped my hands and stood up, tugging at me. "Don't, Kate. Don't. Dear angel, what are you saying? You know I can't do that. If you know me, as you say, then you know I can't decline a patrol, shift the burden elsewhere. Don't ask it of me."

I stared at the roughened khaki wool of his tunic, at a brown stain on the right side, just under his belt, round and ominous. I rose and pulled my hands free. "No," I said dully, "of course not. I don't know what I was thinking. Just telling you, without the rest of it. Of course it wouldn't work."

"The rest of it?"

There was no reading his face, shadowed and inscrutable now in the cold diffuse light from the window. "Look," I said, "I know you're going out with Geoff and Arthur and your colonels tonight. Could you do me one favor, please?"

"Anything," he said softly.

"Could you stop by my room when you're back? Nothing . . . nothing *improper*, I guess, is the word. Just to talk. I have something else to tell you, and it's difficult to explain. You may not believe it at all."

He searched me, so thoroughly I began to flush. I balled my hands into fists, curling the fingernails ruthlessly into my skin. I would not embrace him, could not reach out to take him between my palms. He wasn't *my* Julian.

"Please," I said, into his silence. "If you knew how far I've come, how hard I've fought to find you."

"But why?" he said. "Why? I'm a stranger to you."

"Would it be deeply unfair of me to promise to tell you later?" We were standing so close, there in the failing light; I could hardly breathe, for fear his scent would be the end of me. "When you've come back tonight? Because it's hard to explain on its own."

His right hand rose, grasping, and then fell back. "Kate," he said, "I'll send a message to Warwick and Hamilton, make my excuses. The rain's stopped. We can have dinner. Is that all right?"

"They'll be suspicious. My reputation will be ruined."

"I'll tell them I'm unwell. Exhausted. That I'm keeping to my room."

"I don't have anything suitable to wear," I said.

"That doesn't matter. You look lovely."

"I might be sick again, at some point."

"I'll find you a basin. *Please*, Kate." He lifted his hand again, more confidently, and brushed my elbow. I could hear the coals now, new lumps catching fire at last, hissing with renewed strength to warm the air around us.

I said: "You're impossible to resist, did you know that?"

He grinned, broad and iridescent.

"All right, then, Captain Ashford," I sighed. "It's a date."

9.

Julian stood waiting for me in a shaft of sunlight at the back of the ballet studio, arms folded, with a peculiar smile on his face.

"They're not supposed to let members of the general public inside," I complained, to disguise the way my heart skidded at the unexpected sight of him. I'd been thinking about him constantly over the past two days, and still I wasn't quite prepared for the reality. He stood so tall and broad-shouldered and vital, so radiant with good looks. His extravagant eyes glowed at me.

"I managed to persuade the receptionist to make an exception," he said, stepping forward to drop a kiss on my lips. The other dancers streamed past us, glancing back curiously. Enviously.

"I'll just bet." I sighed. "So how much did you see?"

"Just the last ten minutes." His mouth turned up in that intimate way of his. "Enough to become enchanted with you all over again."

"Oh, please. I'm about the least competent woman in the room. They've all been doing it nonstop since about age three; I only picked it up again last year. I'd forgotten pretty much everything."

He made the smallest shake of his head, still smiling. "You had me mesmerized."

My eyes slipped downward, fastening on the trim white shirt collar showing above the V of his sweater, last button ajar. "Well," I said, "I think I'd better get dressed. Can you wait in the lobby this time, like everyone else?"

"I'll try."

"And no chatting up the receptionist, okay?"

"I wasn't chatting up anybody," he protested.

I thought about this while I was pulling on my yoga pants and hoodie in the changing room. "I think I've found your fatal flaw," I said, as we walked to the elevator a few minutes later.

"Which one?"

"You're smug. You know exactly what kind of effect you have on women, and you don't have any problem using it."

"Is that what you think?"

"Oh, I'm *so* right. Come on. You used it on me. You knew I was a sure thing."

"Not for the reason you think. Anyway, it's hardly a *fatal* flaw." He glanced impatiently at his watch. "Let's just take the stairs. It's only three floors."

We found the stairwell doors and tripped down to street level. "So what reason, then?" I demanded, annoyed he'd admitted it. "Why did you know I was a sure thing?"

He pushed open the door to the building lobby and motioned me through before him. "It's hard to explain. Let me put it this way: when I saw you, in that conference room, I felt as though I already knew you. And it seemed to me that you felt it, too."

"Did it?" I frowned, trying to remember the details of our meeting. I'd been so addle-brained, so distracted by attraction, it was hard to pin down my emotions.

"Well, perhaps I was wrong about that." He shrugged, following me through the revolving doors onto the bustling pitted sidewalk of Eighty-sixth Street. "It only felt natural to me, that you would feel the same attraction I did. It was like something falling into place."

"Oh, is that how it works for guys like you? You just feel this attraction, and the girl follows?"

"You're deliberately misunderstanding me. Where do you want to go, by the way?" We stood on the corner of Eighty-sixth and Lexington, facing west toward the park.

"Well, I guess I should go home and change, right?"

We turned left to walk down Lexington. The pleasant weather had returned after a rainy interlude yesterday, and now the sidewalks were cluttered with people and baby strollers and sudden blinding shafts of sunlight between the cotton-ball clouds.

"You seem to have this idea," he said, picking up the thread of our conversation, "that I'm some sort of . . . of *playboy*, I believe, is the term."

"I didn't say that."

"You accused me of consorting with models and actresses . . ."

"I never accused you! I just thought they were, you know, kind of in your line. As a successful, attractive man, I mean."

"What I'll never understand about the modern era," he said, "is this *fascination* with—what's the word—celebrities, I suppose. Every age has its fixations, of course, but it's as though vanity has suddenly been transformed from a sin to a virtue."

"But we're all vain," I pointed out. "I mean, we all buy into it, don't we?"

He walked along silently for a block or two, eyes fixed somewhere on the sidewalk, a few feet ahead. "Kate," he said finally, "I daresay it's rather a cliché, and in some ways a sort of left-handed compliment, to prattle on about inner beauty. And I don't mean in any way to diminish your own looks, which frankly take my breath away. But I can't imagine feeling this way about a mere pretty face. It's everything else, the . . . the *Kateness* of you."

I tried to speak, but my throat had closed like a vise. We both stopped, and he pulled me into the little recess next to a bodega fruit display. "You always have some fresh surprise for me, Kate. Some new aspect I never suspected. This dancing of yours."

"Oh, come on. I'm honestly not that good."

He shrugged. "You're talking about technical skill," he said, "about which I'm no judge at all. I only saw the way you held yourself, so naturally graceful; or perhaps *poised* is a better word. You possess a certain innate dignity, darling, which expresses itself in ways that fascinate me."

Up until that point, I'd been trying to keep a lid on this infatuation with Julian Laurence. I knew my own weaknesses, my susceptibilities; any romantic illusions had been long ago crushed under the brutally efficient heel of college life. I'd met the first one in the library, as late bloomers do, right after Thanksgiving break: the charming and confident senior of my dreams, handsome, sleepy-eyed. We'd flirted for a week or two before he asked me to the movies with a group of friends—all his, of course—and followed that up with an invitation to watch the Packers game at his house off-campus. Later, I'd realized this was pretty generous wooing, as standards went.

I'd sat on a couch in the living room, surrounded by his roommates, eating stale Tostitos and salsa, sipping from a bottle of Bud Light. When halftime came up, he'd stood and walked down the hall, and his voice had floated out a minute later: *Hey Kate, come to my room, I want to show you something*. I'd heaved upward from the sagging sofa, felt the eyes of his friends shift away, walked down the narrow hallway with its bachelor smells of old beer and old laundry overlaid by the stickiness of a Glade PlugIn. I'd thought, so this is it. Not what you'd dreamed of, maybe, but this is how it's done in the real world, don't be a prude, don't be a coward, get with the program.

Once our clothes were off, I'd blurted—embarrassed, really—that I was a virgin, and he'd said *Oh that's okay, we don't need to go all the way*, and we hadn't, technically. But as I'd cycled through the frozen starry night to my dorm an hour later, my hands still stunned and burning, my flesh strangely raw against the pressure of the bike seat, I knew I was no longer innocent.

He'd asked me over a few more times—I'd never heard the term *booty call*, at that point—until Christmas break arrived and he forgot all about me. Sometime that spring, he'd called up again, out of the blue, because some friend of his had claimed that I was bragging all over the dorm about having had sex with him. I'd stammered my innocence, reeling to recall the melancholy Friday evening I'd confided some part of the story to a trusted friend, and hung up the phone and cried. Not because he'd scolded me unjustly, or because I still cared about him, but because he'd once touched my body so intimately and yet had never known the smallest thing about me: had never understood that, to me, having sex wasn't something to brag about.

And now I stood here with *this* man, with Julian Laurence, in the shadow of a grubby storefront, surrounded by fruit crates and flattened cardboard boxes, powerless again, my eyes cast down to the crumbling gum-blotched pavement. I felt his hand slide into mine, firm and certain, turning me, urging me forward.

"Tell me something," he said. "Why ballet?"

I shifted my throat. "Oh gosh. I don't know. I guess I was looking for something else besides running. You know, cross-training. My friends were into yoga and Pilates and whatever. I was about to sign up. And then I was walking past this ABT poster one morning on the subway, this dancer just *hanging* there in midair, just unbelievably strong and graceful, both at once, and I thought, that's it. That's how I want to be."

"It suits you."

"Well, I danced as a child. Until I was thirteen or so, and it started cutting into the rest of my life. The whole teenager thing. Here's my building."

He waited in the lobby, chatting with Joey, while I raced upstairs and changed into date clothes—silk tank, cardigan, skinny black pants, kitten heels—and loosened my hair from its tidy ballet knot. It swung with an unfamiliar freedom about my shoulders as I came off the elevator; Julian, turning from Joey, seemed to start at the sight, though his voice was casual enough. "You look lovely. All set?"

"All set. Where to?"

"My car's parked across from the house; I thought we'd drive." He stood back politely, allowing me through the revolving door.

"You two have a nice time," Joey called after us.

We started the short walk down Park Avenue just as the lowering sun began to wash the blue out of the sky. The sidewalks were shadowed now, only the rare streak of light finding its way between the buildings, and the fragile spring air had already begun to cool. I felt Julian's hand slip around mine and thought I should say something. "A beautiful evening," I began, but my words were lost in the shriek of a taxi's tires, as it flung around the center median and swerved to the curb next to us.

A man jumped out and started toward us. "Jeez!" I exclaimed, but Julian tugged urgently on my hand, pulling me along the sidewalk.

A voice called up from behind. "Ashford! Ashford, by God!"

"Come on," Julian muttered, pulling me again.

"Ashford!"

I heard footsteps running up behind us. "Ashford! Stop!"

"Does he mean you?" I hissed. My right heel caught on the subway grate, sending me swooping downward. Julian's arm snagged under me just in time.

The man caught up. "Ashford! I never thought . . ."

"Sorry, man," Julian said, in a flawless American accent. "I think you have the wrong guy."

My mouth dropped open.

The man was in his mid-thirties, round-faced, dark hair. He'd sounded British, though it was hard to tell; he was out of breath from running up the sidewalk after us.

"I'm sorry, mate." His eyes swerved back and forth between the two of us, and then settled back on Julian. "You look just like a . . . a chap I used to know. Back in Blighty. I could have sworn . . ."

"Sorry, buddy," Julian said again. "Wrong guy."

"You're sure, mate?" the man said. He peered one last time. "My name's Paulson. Andrew Paulson." He sounded as if he were pleading.

Julian shrugged and shook his head, looking regretful. "Doesn't ring a bell. I must have one of those faces. Sorry."

"Your pardon, then. Good . . . good evening." The man walked away, so downcast I wanted to run after him, but Julian, who hadn't let go of my hand, turned back and practically jerked me along with him.

"Um, wait a second," I said. "That was really weird. Are you going to tell me what was going on?"

"Obviously it was just some idiot, thinking I was his long-lost friend."

"But why did you use that accent?"

"He was British. I thought if I sounded American, he would give up sooner."

"Oh," I said. We were approaching the curb; I looked automatically down the street to check for traffic. We waited for the cars to pass by, and then dashed across against the light.

"Kind of funny, though," I said, as we continued rapidly down the sidewalk. "I mean, he was British. Just like you."

"New York is full of us," he said.

We didn't say anything more. The parking attendant at the garage retrieved the car, and Julian set me inside absently, almost as though he'd forgotten who I was and why I was there. As soon as we pulled out, he reached over with one hand to pull an iPod out of the center console. He plugged it deftly into the port on the dashboard and clicked through the menus until he reached some music. Mozart, from the sound of it.

"So," I said, clearing my throat. "Where to?"

He rubbed his forehead. "I've spoilt the evening, haven't I?"

"Not totally, but it's only eight o'clock. You still have plenty of time to rip it to shreds."

He tapped his finger on the steering wheel and turned right on Park. "Perhaps I should just take you home." He sounded saddened, not angry; it gave me hope.

"Whoa. Wait. Stop. What *happened*, Julian? It's like . . . it's like Christmas all over again! And I swear I won't let you get away with it this time. What's *wrong*?"

"Christ, Kate," he burst out, pounding the steering wheel, "you don't know anything about me. I shouldn't have . . . I'm the most selfish bastard alive, aren't I?"

"Stop it! What does that even *mean*? Julian. Julian, will you listen to me a moment? Pull the car over."

"No. I'm taking you home."

"You're not. I won't leave."

"I don't want you to stay."

"Yes, you do. You *need* me to stay. Julian," I said, more softly, "you *promised*. The other night, you *promised* me you cared. So prove it. Don't let me down, here."

That penetrated. He drove silently down Park, toward midtown. I remained quiet too, not wanting to disturb the truce too soon, letting him work things through in his mind, talk himself off the ledge. Mozart's clarinets wandered nimbly in the stillness between us. Outside the tinted windows of the Maserati, as we waited for the light to change, a forty-something couple propelled a sport-wheeled twin stroller across Fifty-ninth Street, arguing, gesticulating.

I turned to Julian. "Forget the date. You're taking me back to your place, and we're going to talk."

JULIAN DROVE THE CAR BACK to the garage and took my hand to lead me to his front door. The windows were all darkened, except for a glimmer from some distant corner of the first floor. He allowed me in first, closing the door behind us, and punched a few numbers into the alarm keypad.

I turned to face him. "I'm hungry," I announced.

He laughed, unexpectedly. "I expect you are. All right. The kitchen's downstairs."

"Can you make an omelet?" I asked, making my way down the staircase.

"Not well."

The kitchen was at the back, modern and well-fitted, with marble countertops that glowed in the warm incandescence of a dozen recessed lights. It was about eight times as large as the kitchen area in my shared apartment. "Do you even use this thing?" I asked, staring at the spotless stainless-steel gleam of the Wolf range.

"Yes, as a matter of fact," he said, injured. "Porridge and whatnot. I have a housekeeper who comes by a few times a week, while I'm at work. She makes things up for me."

"Wow. Must be nice." I opened up the Sub-Zero and peered inside. A few casserole dishes were stacked in the middle, along with milk and orange juice and ketchup. "Oh good," I said, "she's left us some eggs."

I hunted around and found some fancy artisan cheese and a tomato, closed the door with the heel of my shoe, and began rummaging around the cabinets for a frying pan and a mixing bowl. "You should tell your housekeeper not to leave the tomatoes in the fridge," I said. "It takes away the flavor."

"Look, Kate," he began, "I'm sorry for . . ."

"Nope. Not now. You can't have a reasonable discussion on an empty stomach. Find me some butter, will you? I, sir, am going to make you the best darned omelet you've ever tasted."

"Yes, ma'am," he said humbly. He brought me the butter while I whipped up the eggs into froth and added a splash of water. "You're enjoying this, aren't you?" he observed, watching me pour the mixture into the pan.

"I don't cook much, but I do make a mean omelet. My father taught me. Mom would sleep in on Saturday mornings, and we'd make her breakfast." I looked up and smiled at him. "Good times. Where are your plates?"

He brought over plates and forks, and when the omelets were done I slid them into place. "Here," I said. "Eat it and weep."

We sat down at the counter and began eating companionably, like an old married couple, forks clinking on china. "There," I said, after a few bites, "is that better?"

"Much. This is a jolly good omelet."

"Well, if you ask nicely, maybe I'll make them again sometime." I reached for my glass of water, and his hand caught my arm.

"Is that from the other night?" he asked.

I turned my elbow. Only a single Band-Aid remained, over the worst of the scrape. "It's healing." I shrugged.

His finger ran over the top. "I'm sorry about that. Any other wounds?"

"Bruise or two. I might even show you, if you get lucky tonight."

He let out a single crack of laughter. "*Lucky?* At this point, I'd require divine bloody intervention, wouldn't I?"

We finished eating and put the dishes in the dishwasher. "Now," I said, turning around to face him, "take me back upstairs and we'll talk."

He stood closer than I thought. I felt the warmth of his body, the tickle of his breath on my nose. He studied me, only inches away, his eyes full of some concentrated emotion. His hands reached up and brushed against my ears, not quite cupping my face, the thumbs caressing the very outermost points of my cheekbones. "What a marvelous woman you are," he said.

"It's just an omelet," I said shakily.

Before I could so much as gasp, he bent and picked me up, bearing me upstairs to the library, where he set me on the sofa and knelt on the rug before me.

"Look," I said, "I don't know what happened back there, and I don't care. I don't care if we never go out on a so-called date. That's not important. What's important is that you don't shut me out like that again. Ever. For as long as we're together. If you're done with me, tell me. I won't be a pain about it. But don't go *cold* on me."

"I'm British. It's what we do."

I struggled upright. "Well, we're in America right now. And if you're on my turf, you play by my rules. Oh, Julian," I said, more softly, lifting my hand to smooth his cheek, "you know, you don't need to explain. You lived thirty-three years before you met me, and I'm sure there was plenty of stuff in there you don't want to talk about. That's okay. But don't break up with me because of *that*. Break up with me because you don't care anymore. *That* I can take."

"Kate. *Kate.* You don't know what you're saying. Not *care* about you? Have you been listening to me at all?"

"Men have been known to change their minds."

He lifted both hands and ran them through his hair. "If only you *knew*, Kate. If only I could *make* you understand. My God!" He caught his breath.

"Well, *try*, for God's sake. It's important."

He put his hand on my arm. "Kate, listen. This *thing* in my past. All right, I won't deny it's there. But it's bigger than you could imagine. It's not just *baggage*, or whatever the modern term is. It's essential to who I am."

"And you can't tell me."

"Not for the reason you're thinking. Not because I don't *want* you to know, to share fully in who I am. I want that more than anything."

"Then why not?"

He leaned back on his heels and looked up at the ceiling. "Because it's too great a risk. To you particularly."

"A risk. A *risk*. Well, gosh, Julian. Now you've really got me curious. Did you commit murder or something?"

He flinched.

"Whoa," I breathed.

"No, no," he said hastily. "Not *murder*, for heaven's sake." He ran another agitated hand through his hair. "Look, you promised not to press me on it. Can you just give me time, please? Time to sort things out? It's just so damned complex, and I don't know what the right thing is anymore. Probably there *is* no right thing."

He looked so anxious, so deeply perplexed. I felt a surge of emotion for him, ferocious enough to stop the breath in my lungs. "Why?" I whispered.

"Why what?"

"Why me? You could have anyone. You hardly know me at all."

He smiled then, a tiny wistful smile, tender and intimate. His right thumb reached and stroked along my eyebrow, down the side of my face, around my jaw, feathering my lips. "Kate. I know you far better than you realize. And I never want you to ask that question again. Never again to wonder what I feel for you." He paused briefly, thoughtfully. "Would it help if I said it aloud?"

I found myself nodding.

"You certainly *ought* to hear it, putting up with all my mad behavior as generously as you have." A deprecating shake of his head, and then he went on in a low voice. "Sweetheart, I love you. Of course I do. I love every priceless inch of you. I love you idolatrously, for a thousand reasons, and I shall never stop. Hush," he said, laying his finger on my lips again, "you don't need to say anything. I'm a patient man. Just be easy. Know that it's there, that you needn't doubt me on this, at least."

He bowed his head to settle a silken kiss into the hollow of my throat, holding it there for what seemed an eternity before his mouth began to move up my collarbone, melting it in his wake. I tilted my head back, feeling the prickle of his hair against my cheek. "You . . . are the most baffling man," I managed.

"How so?"

"You just . . . you fell in love with me . . . just like *that*?" My concentration kept lapsing; I struggled to hold on to my thoughts, which I knew were important.

I felt his laugh against the skin of my neck. "Well, look at you, darling. You're love-at-first-sight material."

"Using my own words against me."

"You don't think it's possible?"

"I just can't believe it. That you would feel that way already. That you would *admit* it."

"Well, as they say," he said, nibbling at my earlobe, slipping down to kiss the vale behind it, "faint heart never won fair lady."

I lifted my hand to the back of his head. "I'm going . . . to find out."

"Yes, I expect you shall. What fragrant skin you have, darling; how convenient that the woman one loves should turn out to be so perfectly . . ." He paused to kiss the curve of my jaw.

"Perfectly what?"

"Delectable."

I couldn't take any more. I wrapped my arms about his neck; my face reached toward him, begging for his kiss. I heard him chuckle, deep in his throat, and then at last his lips met mine, hungry and reckless, and I realized he was as desperate as I was. He knelt in front of me, kissing me madly, his warm spread fingers clasping my face, his scent and his taste flooding every pore of me, until all rational thought detached from my skull. My fingers slipped down, almost by themselves, and began to work the buttons on his shirt, trying to discover the precious skin underneath.

He drew away. He put up his hand and trapped my fingers and twisted them around his own. His chest was heaving hard; I could feel it beneath my hand.

"Kate, wait. I don't think . . ."

I looked down. "I'm sorry," I found myself saying, "I just . . . I don't know."

"Let's not be too hasty, shall we?"

"*Hasty?* You're talking to me about *hasty?*"

"Kate, don't be angry."

"Angry? Julian, I'm so full of crazy feelings right now, angry just doesn't have room. Do you want me to stay, or not?"

"My God, Kate. There's nothing I want more," he said, his voice catching, his fingers biting into mine. "Nothing else I can *think* about. But not yet. Not yet, *please.*"

I stared at him. "Okay. Whatever."

"What's wrong?"

"Well, guys don't usually put the brakes on," I said. "Especially after the 'I love you' gambit."

An austere expression settled on his face. "Exactly what do you mean by that?"

"Oh, please, Julian. Let's not have the sex talk right now. I'm not up to it, after everything else."

"The *sex* talk?"

I waved my hand, evading his look. "Going through our quote unquote histories, dredging up all the ghosts. Can we just have the executive summary and move on?"

He went still for a moment, taut as a crossbow, bright color staining his cheekbones. "Come here," he said at last, and sat down next to me on the sofa and gathered me into his lap. "If we do this," he said, the softness of his voice belying the lithe tension in his body, "*when* we do this, it will have nothing to do with what's gone before, for either of us. Nothing. Because I frankly can't bear to think about someone else being with you, and not loving you the way I do. So let's just leave it a blank slate." He kissed my temple. "God knows I don't want you to leave tonight, Kate. I want you to fall asleep next to me, every night of my life. But I'm going to walk you home now, all the same, because I think we'd better not cross that particular Rubicon just yet. Don't you?"

"I . . . I don't know. *Not just yet.* What does that *mean*? Do you . . ."—I swallowed—"do you need me to say it, too?"

"No, darling." His hand brushed along my arm. "Don't worry about that."

"Then I don't understand. I just . . . aren't I . . . don't you *want* me?"

"Oh, for God's sake, Kate," he groaned. "Not *want* you? Bloody Christ."

"Look, you're confusing the hell out of me! If you were in love with me from the beginning, why did you walk away? And if you *do* love me, why won't you just haul me upstairs and *show* me?"

"I left," he said rigidly, "because I thought it was best for you. I didn't realize . . . I thought I was only hurting myself, at that point. But I shan't forsake you again, Kate, I swear it. And as for hauling you upstairs . . . God knows . . ." He shook his head. "It's too important to me, Kate. I won't rush you into something you're not ready for."

"Not *ready* for? Of course I'm *ready*! Trust me, I've never *been* so ready!"

He laughed hollowly. "No, darling. You're not."

"And you think you know what's *best* for me?"

"In this case, I do."

I opened my mouth to cite Beauvoir, chapter and verse, but something stopped me, some unexpected flare of self-insight, or else some realization of what, exactly, he was offering me. So I turned away from him instead, eased myself back against his broad body, squinted up at the ceiling. "You know," I said, after a moment, "no one's ever tried to talk me out of sex before."

"Ah. All those rotters, isn't it?" He was so warm, so gentle; the tension had left him entirely. I felt the steady rise and fall of his chest behind me, the cradling strength of his arms.

"Well, not that many, actually. I wised up before too much damage was done." I paused, letting the unspoken details lie massive and still between us, before going on softly: "But you know, I never realized how . . . just . . . *lame* they were, until now."

He tightened his arms around me. His lips pressed against my hair, reassuring, but his voice was intense. "I could murder them."

"Please don't," I said, half-serious, thinking of the efficient way he had landed punches on my attacker in the park. I sat up. "You promised me you'd play the piano for me sometime."

"Now?"

"Why not?" I twisted in his arms to touch his chin with my finger. "I don't want to leave yet, and you've ruled out sex."

"Kate. And you can't think of anything else to do?"

"Please?"

His eyes rolled upward. "You're discovering your power over me, aren't you? Very well." He stood up, bringing me with him. "Go upstairs. The piano's in the room fronting the street. I'm going to fetch a bit of wine."

"Wine?"

"Stage fright." He stroked my cheek with the back of his hand and smiled at me. "Up with you. I'll be right there."

I skipped up the stairs, turning right at the landing, and found my way down the darkened hall to the room at the front. I was half-expecting it might be his bedroom, but in fact it was more like a study, or perhaps a music room, with a low comfortable English-armed sofa at one end and a grand piano filling the space near the windows. I turned on a lamp and went to the wide window overlooking the street below. What time was it? Not too late, ten-thirty maybe, but it seemed later: the streetlamps cast lurid yellow-orange pools of light on the deserted sidewalk, and the rapid pulse of traffic had settled into the occasional passing taxi and black sedan. I felt a surge of gratitude, to be where I stood, in this tranquil room, with Julian's presence a comforting certainty somewhere nearby.

"Found your way, all right?" came his voice behind me, as though I'd summoned him with my thoughts.

"Mmm, yes," I said, without turning. "I love the room. Very homelike."

I heard his footsteps behind me, creaking the floorboards, and then a glass of red wine appeared in front of me. The warmth of his body hovered over my skin. "Thank you," I said, taking it, and held the glass in my hand for a second or two before lifting it to my lips. "Wow. Delicious."

"What would you like me to play?"

"I don't know. I loved that Chopin you were playing, when I came here at Christmas."

He chuckled, close to my ear. "You seem to be under the misapprehension that I'm some sort of expert musician."

"Aren't you? You're good at everything else."

"I'm passable, but nothing like an expert."

I turned to find his face inches from mine, looking down at me with amusement. "Don't punk out on me, Laurence," I warned.

He smiled and took a drink of wine. "Right-ho. You've asked for it. Have a seat," he said, nodding at the sofa. I went over obediently and sank into the cushion, curling my legs beneath me, wineglass in hand.

Julian stepped to the piano, placing his glass on the edge before pushing off his shoes with his toes and settling his stocking feet on the pedals. "Chopin?" he confirmed, lifting his eyebrow at me.

"Yes, please. A nocturne, maybe. I like those."

He nodded. The piano stood at an angle to me, so I could just see the keyboard and the side of his face glowing in the dusky light from the nearby lamp. "I expect you'll know this one," he said. "The E flat."

He closed his eyes, recalling the music perhaps, and a short silence filled the half-lit room, so dense I thought I could hear the hasty *thump-thump, thump-thump* of my own heart, anticipating him.

Then he looked at his hands, and the first few notes rose upward, poising languorously in midair, warm and flawless, perfectly familiar.

How often had I heard this music? It felt like an old friend, someone we'd both known all our lives, without realizing the shared connection. It hardly seemed like music at all: it stirred the intimate space between us, more like a question, an inquiry. As though he were reaching out tenderly to ask me something, to express the inexpressible.

And I wanted keenly to answer him, to tell him *yes! yes!* but instead I only studied him, enraptured; watched the lines of his face tighten in concentration as he sank into the notes, into the delicate cascades and passionate surges, his eyes following his hands on the keyboard.

He loved this piece. I could see that much. At certain points, points of what might be called suppressed fervor, his eyelids slipped down, sealing an intensity of feeling. *He's sensuous,* slid the thought into my head. *A deeply sensuous man.* The way he kissed me, the way he touched me, the way his fingers traveled knowingly along the piano keys, coaxing out this living music: it was all the same.

His voice echoed in my ear: *If we do this. When we do this.*

He brought the piece to rest on its low final chord, ebbing into the ether. A moment passed of absolute stillness, and then he turned to look at me with a faintly apologetic expression, eyebrow raised in question.

I spoke with effort. "That was amazing. Thank you so much. I . . . wow. I don't know what to say. Play another."

He crossed his eyes comically. "Clearly no judge of music, for which blessing I'm extremely grateful." He paused, and then started something else, restive and vibrant.

"What's that?" I asked, watching his face.

"Beethoven," he answered. "*Appassionata.* First movement."

"Hmm." I listened for a moment, until the melodic line surfaced briefly. "Oh, yeah. I've heard this one."

"I should hope so."

"Where did you learn to play?"

"Endless lessons as a child. My mother used to have me play for her in the evenings, when I was home from school." A little pause. "And I practice a good deal, still. At night, when I can't sleep." He fell silent, working his way through a momentary elaboration, and then asked, "Where did you learn your Chopin?"

"Hmm?" The music wound around us; I couldn't focus on his words. "Oh, my father used to play it on the stereo. He said it was good for the soul."

He smiled, glancing over at me before returning his eyes to the keyboard. "I think I like your father."

"Just an ordinary dad, really."

"Not at all. He raised *you*, didn't he? I imagine," he continued, after a moment, "you grew up feeling as though you didn't quite fit in with your surroundings. That you weren't quite like everyone else you knew. Am I right?"

I shifted on the sofa. "Everybody does at some point. It's part of the human conceit, isn't it, to think we're special somehow."

"And now?"

"I guess I have trouble relating sometimes," I said. "Not that I think I'm better than anyone else; usually the opposite. Not quite cool enough for Manhattan."

He shook his head. "A rose among dandelions."

"Hardly."

He didn't reply, only smiled and went on with the sonata, concentrating fiercely on its intricate pounding final minute, closing his eyes as it drifted into nothing.

"Oh, now you're just showing off," I told him, and he looked up at me and winked. Without asking, he took a drink of wine and started something else, playing as though I weren't there at all.

I must have begun to doze off at some point, because I opened my eyes to see Julian on his heels before me, easing the half-empty wineglass from my fingers. "You're falling asleep," he said softly, reaching out to tuck my hair behind my ear. "Let's get you home."

WE WALKED BACK SLOWLY, hand in hand, to my apartment building, not talking at all. So much had been said today, and our brains were too busy processing it all to think of anything new. It was only when the dark green awning above the lobby entrance loomed ahead that I spoke up.

"So. Should I wait out front in the morning?"

"Actually, I've got to fly up to Boston first thing," he said, a little wryly.

"Oh, no. Not Boston again. I guess this is really good-bye, then." I stopped in the shadows, just outside the glow of light from the lobby, and turned to face him.

He leaned forward, cupping his hand around the curve of my skull, and kissed me, hard. "This is *not* good-bye," he said fiercely.

"Can you blame me? You gave me a pretty good scare tonight."

"I'm sorry," he said, eyes closed, leaning his forehead against mine. The words brushed against my mouth. "Forgive me, darling. I'll make it up to you."

"Not another private jet, I hope. Flowers are okay this time."

"No. I've got something else for you, at the moment." He reached into his jacket pocket and handed me a small folded envelope.

"What's this?" I asked, turning it over.

"Now, don't *freak out*, as you Americans say," he warned. "I don't mean to frighten you off with it."

I looked up at him from under my lashes, and then popped open the envelope to find a set of keys and a piece of paper.

"To the house," he said.

"Whoa."

"Just for emergencies," he said quickly. "If I'm at the office, or out of town, and you need something."

"Oh."

"This one's the knob; the other two are the deadbolts. The alarm code's written on the paper. You needn't ask me first, of course. Borrow a book, if you like."

"Oh," I said again. I risked a glance at his face. His eyes shone down at me, wide and vulnerable. "Julian, thank you. I'm very touched. I mean, you can trust me. I won't, like, invade your privacy, I promise."

As I watched, his expression opened into a smile, and he began to chuckle. He lifted one hand to brush against my cheekbone. "Darling girl, don't you understand? That's *exactly* what I want you to do."

10.

Clouds billowed in overnight, coating the sky like a blanket and turning the balm of the previous day into a broad muggy warning of the summer to come. I trudged through the heavy air from the subway stop on Broadway to the Sterling Bates building on Wall Street, scrolling through my BlackBerry for Julian's latest e-mail. It had been sent while I was swaying down the subway tracks, pressed against the sweaty armpit of some massive guy with a Hitler-style mustache and a cheap suit.

Landing shortly. Boston's in full bloom. Taking you with me next time.

I typed back.

Sounds pretty scandalous. Separate rooms, I hope.

I pushed through the revolving doors and swiped my security pass to activate the lobby turnstile.

It stuck, nearly breaking my ribs.

I swiped again impatiently. Still stuck.

I sighed and turned to the security guard. "Sorry," I said, "I must have demagnetized my pass somehow."

He took the card from me and looked at it. "Just a moment," he said, and reached for the phone.

I stood there, tapping my foot. Julian would be flying back this evening, and we had tentative plans—contingent on my finishing up work on time—to grab a bite somewhere. Or else order in Chinese. Either way, I wanted to clear my desk quickly.

"Yeah. Katherine Wilson," the security guard was repeating into the telephone. He listened for a moment, nodding, and then hung up the phone. "Wait here," he said. "Someone will come down to bring you up."

"Can't you just swipe me through?" I pleaded.

He shrugged. "That's what they said."

I sighed and switched my laptop onto my other shoulder. Minutes passed, as I stood there awkwardly next to the security desk, checking my watch. My BlackBerry buzzed.

Perhaps with a connecting door?

I smiled at the screen.

Honestly, all you men can think about is sex.

"Kate?"

I looked up at Paul Banner.

"Oh my gosh," I said, embarrassed. "I'm so sorry you had to come down. You should have sent one of the interns."

He cleared his throat. "Come along with me, Kate." Not Katie.

I felt a twinge, a warning light flashing on in my brain.

He swiped me through the turnstile with a visitor pass, and I walked with him to the elevator bank. He didn't say anything, just pressed the up arrow and waited next to me. The doors opened, and we went in with about three or four other people, that bulky elevator silence crowding us awkwardly. He reached out and pressed number 18.

Capital Markets was on 23.

I stood there with my palms growing moist and my heart beating *thump thump thump* against the wall of my chest. I felt a strain behind my eyes and blinked hard. *Do not show weakness.*

On Wall Street, when they fired you, even if it was just a layoff and not your fault, someone escorted you up to a room in Human Resources. There, the terms of your severance were announced to you in an arid voice, and you were required to sign a paper renouncing any legal claims on the firm, in exchange for your financial package, which usually amounted to a week of salary for every year you'd worked there, plus 50 percent of the cash portion of last year's bonus, all paid in a lump sum by direct deposit. You then handed in any electronic devices owned by the firm, and a security officer escorted you out of the building. You were not allowed to stop at your desk. You were not allowed to say good-bye to your colleagues.

Talk about the walk of shame.

I wasn't expecting Banner to stay in the room. I'd heard operating managers usually disappeared, leaving the unpleasant bloodletting for the HR representative to oversee. But when we arrived, Banner came right in behind me and motioned me to a seat at a long narrow table, at which Alicia Boxer, along with one or two managing directors, filled a side. A woman in a cherry-red suit presided at the head. She rustled her throat. "I assume you know why you've been called in today," she said.

"Well," I said, "I gather I'm being let go. Isn't that right?"

She looked at me sharply. "You are being dismissed for cause, Ms. Wilson. The firm has, over the weekend, been presented with incontrovertible proof that you have been engaged in an improper, and possibly illegal, information exchange with a well-known counterparty in the financial industry."

I stared at her. "What are you talking about?"

Her eyes fell to the papers in front of her. "After meeting to discuss the matter, the members of the managing committee have decided not to press formal charges. In exchange, you will be required to leave the premises immediately, surrendering all electronic devices and credit cards supplied for your use by Sterling Bates, with no further legal or financial claims on the firm." She looked up at me. "Do you have any questions?"

"I have about a million. I honestly have no idea what you're talking about. I've never passed on material information in my life. I wouldn't even consider it." I looked at Banner. "You know that."

He shifted in his seat and looked down at the table before him. I turned my gaze to Alicia. She quirked me an apologetic smile. Beneath their heavy lids, her eyes shone a triumphant blue.

"Oh," I said. Everything slipped into focus. "My laptop. Friday morning, when you were on my laptop. What did you do, exactly? Plant something?"

"I'm not able to give you any details of our investigation," she said primly. "This is all very unfortunate, Kate. We're all just really, really disappointed."

I looked back at the HR woman. "Where's the evidence? Don't I have any say in this? Can't I defend myself?"

"You're welcome to file a letter of complaint with this department," she said. "If you insist on pursuing legal options, however, I assure you we will prosecute the case aggressively." She put just the faintest emphasis on the word *aggressively.* A little feral snarl. "We are quite sure of our facts," she added.

I took a deep breath. I was going to get out of this with dignity. "Okay, then. Here's my laptop." I unzipped my bag and smiled at Alicia. "No doubt you're familiar with what's inside it." I pushed it across the table. "And here's the BlackBerry," I said, setting it down carefully next to the computer, willing my hands not to shake. It buzzed against the table. New e-mail. Julian, probably. "I don't have any company credit cards or anything."

"Thank you," the HR woman said, sounding relieved. She held out a piece of paper. "If you'll just sign this release, we can close the matter."

I took the paper from her and scanned it. It was all legalese. Even if my brain had been in good working order, which at the moment it wasn't, I probably couldn't have made heads or tails of it. "You know," I said, hesitating, "I think I should have a lawyer look at this first."

"I'm sorry, but I'm afraid I can't let you out of this room until you've signed that paper."

I looked at her, and I looked at Banner and Alicia and the two managing directors. Banner was still staring down at the table. I guessed he knew what was really going on. *Alicia's sleeping with Banner. You didn't know that?* Charlie's voice echoed in my brain, some tidbit of year-old gossip. All fun and games, of course, until the chick hauls you up in front of the sexual harassment tribunal.

Or threatens to.

I hadn't stood a chance, had I?

I turned back to the HR woman and smiled. "Okay," I said, "I'll sign."

I stared at her as I scribbled my name at the bottom, making a show of not even reading it. It was my protest, my way of saying they were full of crap, that this whole meeting was a total farce.

"Thank you," the HR woman said, and she picked up the handset of the phone next to her and dialed two numbers. "Yes, we're ready," she said.

I stood up. "I just want you to know," I said, perfectly composed, "that this woman sitting right there"—I pointed to Alicia—"has just made complete idiots out of all of you. And me, too, I guess. And you'll probably be lucky if she doesn't blow up the whole damned bank some day, maybe even just out of sheer incompetence. Luckily, that's now your problem, not mine."

The door opened, and an armed security guard stood there, waiting for me. I marched out the door and to the elevators, *down down down* to the lobby and out through the turnstiles and the revolving door.

And that was that.

I wasn't going to cry in public. The repressed sobs made my throat ache, made my eyelids stab, but somehow I kept it all in.

I wanted to call up Julian, e-mail Julian, but they had my computer and my BlackBerry now. They were probably going through it all right now, reading all those sweet tender e-mails. The one he'd just sent, the one I hadn't even read yet.

I was still in shock. What was I going to tell my parents? My friends? My life had just been ruined, in ten short minutes. I'd been fired for cause. That meant Tuck would rescind its acceptance. I had no job, no income, a massive black stain against my name in an industry in which reputation counted for everything. I had nothing. How could I face Julian? He'd believe me, of course. He'd know I hadn't done anything wrong. He'd want to take care of me, probably. Provide for me. He'd urge me to move in with him, let him buy me things.

But how could I humble myself that way? How could I accept from him what I couldn't earn myself? And when the flame of his infatuation began to fade, as it inevitably would, where would that leave me?

I rode the 6 train up to Seventy-seventh Street and got off. My apartment was only two blocks away. I walked them slowly, carrying my nearly empty laptop bag, hardly noticing the people and buildings surrounding me. Frank was still on duty in the lobby. He looked at me, amazed. "What's the matter, hon?" he asked. "Come home sick?"

"No. I just got fired." The words hung there, flat and stark. I just got fired. *Fired.*

His mouth dropped open. I walked past the front desk like an automaton and pressed the elevator call button.

"Are you serious, hon? Why? They laying off down there on Wall Street?"

"Something like that," I said.

"I'm so sorry, hon. You okay?"

"Yeah, thanks, Frank."

The elevator door opened.

"Don't worry, hon," Frank called after me, as I stepped inside. "They're always hiring and firing down there. I seen it come and go . . ."

The doors shut, blocking out his voice. I felt the elevator rise with agonizing slowness, clanging at each floor, before coming to rest at mine.

"Brooke?" I called, as I let myself in. No answer. She was either asleep or out. I set my laptop bag on the table and shrugged out of my suit jacket and went to the telephone. The mostly unused telephone. Never really needed it before.

I sat in front of it for a moment, thinking. Julian's number was on my Blackberry, but I'd memorized it anyway. I picked up the handset and stared at the buttons for a long moment, wondering what to say. He was probably in his meeting right now. Good. Voice mail would be easier.

I punched in the numbers. He had a standard greeting turned on; no lyric voice to comfort me. I heard the beep. "Hi Julian," I said softly. "It's me. Kate. Um, I don't know how to say this. I just got fired. Long story. I'm back at the apartment now. They have my BlackBerry and everything, so don't send me any more e-mails. Just call me on this number when you get a chance. Thanks. Um, hope your meeting went well. Bye." I hung up and put my head down on the table.

What were the stages of grief? Denial, anger, acceptance . . . I couldn't remember. I was probably still stuck mostly on denial at this point, but I could feel a little anger, too. That bitch. That puny bitch.

I sat up. What was Charlie's number? I tried to think. In my room somewhere, I still had my Sterling Bates orientation pack, with everyone's phone number and e-mail listed inside. Where was it?

I got up from the chair and went to my room. I kept most of my papers in some file boxes under the bed; I pulled them out and began going through them. There wasn't much. Almost all of my bills were online; even my bank statement came by e-mail now. Sterling Bates had a file box all to itself. I opened it up and saw the glossy blue folder with the elegant corporate logo, and remembered that first day of orientation. I'd felt so grown-up. Salary and bonus and health care and 401(k).

I opened the folder and found the contact list. I checked my own phone numbers first, office and cell; they were still the same, so I assumed Charlie's must be, too. I went back into the living room and picked up the phone and punched in his cell number.

"Hello?" he answered, after the first ring.

"Hi, Charlie. It's Kate."

"*Fuck*, Kate. What the fuck happened?"

"Charlie, can you take this outside? I don't want anyone to overhear you. Just call me back when you get out front, okay?"

"Sure, dude." The phone clicked, and I hung up. It was a cordless phone; I took it with me over to the window and looked out north to Harlem. Don't panic, I told myself. Figure this thing out.

The phone went off a minute later. I answered it almost before the first ring had finished. "Charlie?"

"It's me, dude. So. What the fuck?"

"Here's the deal, Charlie. I don't know what they're telling you, but basically my pass didn't work this morning, and Banner came down to escort me up. He took me to HR, to this room with him and some MDs and *Alicia*, Charlie. Alicia. And they said they had some kind of proof I'd been passing along information. Insider information, I guess. They didn't tell me what it was, and when I asked if I had any way to defend myself, they basically threatened me. So, anyway, here I am. And you know me. There's no freaking way I did anything like that."

"So you think it's Alicia?" he demanded.

"Charlie, I'm sure of it. I caught her on my laptop Friday morning. I thought she was just snooping through my e-mails or something, looking for gossip, but I'll bet you anything she was planting information or evidence or whatever."

"Dude," he said softly.

"Yeah, right?" I sighed.

"So what are you going to do now?"

"I don't know. I wish I could confront Alicia somehow."

"What about Laurence, though?"

"Julian? What about him?"

"He can help you, can't he? He can *crush* them. He can hire the best fucking lawyer in town, get you some bad-ass settlement. You'll be set for life."

"Charlie, I can't ask him to do that! Pay my legal bills? I mean, come on!"

"Why not? He can afford it."

"That's not the point." I rubbed my forehead, as if the friction would somehow jump-start my regular mental function. "What are they saying about it down there?"

"Dude, you don't want to know."

"All right, all right. Look, can you do me a favor or two?"

"Sure thing."

"First of all, try to spread the word for me, okay? Let people know there's another side to the story, that maybe Alicia's had it in for me ever since the ChemoDerma deal, blah blah."

"Yeah, except she's been your BFF the last few months," Charlie said.

"I know, I know. I'm such a freaking idiot."

"*Fucking* idiot, Kate. Jesus. But no worries. I am the master of the rumor mill. I will make sure your story gets out there. Truth to power, dude."

"Thanks, Charlie. One more thing."

"What's that?"

"If you get a chance to do a little snooping at some point . . ."

"Aw, wait a minute, dude. *That's* fucked up."

"No, nothing sneaky or whatever. No office break-ins. Just poke around some of the network files, see if you can find something. This is just all so *fishy.*"

He heaved a sigh. "Okay, fine. I'll get my Hardy Boys on for you. Just don't expect miracles, okay?"

The call waiting beeped.

"Charlie, I'm getting another call. I've got to hop. You can e-mail me on my Yahoo account." I fired him the address.

"Got it. Later, dude."

"Thanks, Charlie." I took a deep breath and pressed the flash button. "Hello?"

"Kate! My God! What's happened?"

"Julian. You got my message?"

"Just now. Are you all right?"

"Fine. I just got, like, *ambushed* by Alicia. She's convinced the managing committee I've been trading insider information. I don't know the details; they wouldn't tell me anything. So I have no idea what I'm supposed to have passed along and to whom. It's all just . . . extremely frustrating . . ." The sobs caught up with me then, choking in my throat. "I'm sorry," I said, "I'm just kind of stressed out here."

"Darling, hang in there. I'm on my way. I'll help you get this sorted out, I promise. I'll hang that little witch out to dry, by God."

"No, no. You don't need to do that. It's my problem."

A short silence. "Kate, don't be ridiculous. This is *our* problem. Because anything that affects you is of the most vital concern to me."

"Stop it, okay? Because I'm having a hard enough time trying to hold myself together at the moment. I really, really don't want to lose it completely."

"Look," he said, "I've got some rather odd news of my own up here. I was thinking seriously of . . . hold on a moment, won't you? I'll be straight back." He put me on hold, probably taking another call. I was still standing by the window, gazing at the thick gray sky and the endless grim towers of apartment buildings and housing projects scattered in front of me. I tapped my fingers against the glass and closed my eyes, willing myself to remain in control. Not to cry. Not to sob.

He clicked back on. "Kate, darling? Are you there?"

"Right here," I said scratchily.

"Kate, my love, I'm going to ask you to do something. Can you trust me?"

"Of course."

"Do you still have the keys I gave you yesterday?"

"Of course. Right in my bag."

"Then I want you to go over to my house and go inside and fetch my spare set of car keys. They're in the middle desk drawer in the library. Take them to the garage and explain to them you're a friend of mine. I'll ring them up and let them know you're coming. Have you ever driven north from the city?"

"No." I was too shocked to say anything more.

"All right, then you'll have to program the navigation system. You're going to drive up to Lyme, to my cottage there. It's in Connecticut, about a half-hour past New Haven. The address is in the GPS; just scroll through the menu until you find it. Kate, are you listening?"

"Yes. Lyme. Address is in the GPS."

"I'll drive down from Boston and meet you there, all right? Can you do that for me?"

"Yes." I cleared my throat and said it louder. "Yes. Meet you in Lyme."

"Good girl. Pack a few things; we may be there for a bit."

"What?" I shook myself. "What do you mean?"

"I'll explain when you arrive. Could you please just trust me, all right? Are you okay to drive?"

"Sure. Yes."

"Are you sure? It's a manual transmission; that's all right?"

"Yeah. Yes. I drove one in high school."

"The traffic shouldn't be too bad, on a Monday morning. It should take you a little more than two hours, if you have a straight shot."

"Two hours. Okay."

"There's plenty of petrol. You can stop on the way, if you get hungry; there's about a dozen bloody McDonald's along the highway. But hurry along, all right? Pack your things and get on the road. I'm just off to hire a car myself."

"All right. I'll be there as soon as I can."

"Darling, we'll sort everything out, I promise. I'll see you soon."

I swallowed. "See you soon."

The phone clicked off. I stood there a moment, frozen, staring north.

It took me a few moments to gather my wits, but then I moved in a frenzy. The longing to see Julian again overpowered everything else. I threw some clothes in my overnight bag, an extra pair of shoes, my travel kit.

I went into the living room and headed blindly for the door. Out of the corner of my eye, I spied the Sterling Bates contact list, still on the table. I grabbed it and shoved it in the front pocket of my overnight bag. Then I took a pencil and scribbled a note for Brooke on the message pad on the kitchen counter. *Brooke, I'm off to spend a few days in Connecticut. E-mail my Yahoo account if anything comes up. Thanks. Kate.*

I slung my laptop bag over my shoulder—it still had my wallet and things in it—and made for the door.

"Where are you going?" demanded Frank, as I hurried through the lobby.

"Away for a few days," I called back, over my shoulder. "Get my head back together."

"Cool. Oh, wait. Package just came for you. I was going to send it up."

I turned around. He held out a small cardboard-wrapped package in the shape of a book. My Amazon order, probably, from a few days ago. I couldn't even remember what it was. Some business book. "Thanks, Frank," I said, tucking it into my laptop bag. "I'll see you soon."

AN HOUR LATER I was soaring past the outer Connecticut suburbs in the taut green Maserati, relishing the eager surge of power every time I touched the accelerator, the obedient snarl of the engine, the way life had been reduced to the elegant simplicity of my body commanding this machine. No phone, no computer. Nobody could reach me, I realized: a strangely liberating feeling, not lonely at all.

The GPS kept me on the freeway until exit 70, just on the other side of the wide gleaming Connecticut River. I made a left at the bottom of the ramp, away from the shoreline, and followed the road northward, past tilting old colonial houses and crumbling stone walls; past fields thick with second-growth forest, filling in the abandoned farmland. Eventually

I turned left, back toward the river, down a succession of winding roads, until I came to a gap in a stone wall with the number 12 painted in white on a small wooden square to the right.

Destination, the GPS voice informed me dispassionately.

I eased through the gap and down the drive, surrounded by oaks and birches in the lush middle green of springtime. The clouds had been breaking up for some time now, and as the Maserati bounced down the narrow gravel road I could feel the sunshine press against the glass, warming the car's interior. I let the window glide down, and a rush of fresh air rolled around my face.

I drove around another bend and a little white two-story clapboard house stood abruptly before me, with a gray Ford Focus parked in the drive outside and Julian sitting on the front step, next to a stone urn frothing with pale impatiens. He leapt to his feet and began walking rapidly toward me, tall and sunlit, irresistible.

I pulled up and jumped out, not even bothering to close the car door, and then I was scrambling in my heels over the rough deep gravel, around the front of the car, pitching myself into his outstretched arms.

II.

Don't cry, I reminded myself sternly, and I didn't. I held myself still, pushing down the sobs, letting Julian draw me to the ground and tuck me into his chest, against the soft thick cotton of his shirt and the steady thud of his heart. His hands drew soothing little circles on my back, and he murmured in my ear. "Hush, now, hush," I thought I heard him say. "It's all right, sweetheart. I'm here."

We sat that way, sprawled together on the gravel, for what seemed like a long time, though it might have been only a few minutes. He went on murmuring into the country stillness, his *Hush, my love, it's all right* stirring the air, answered only by the subdued shimmering chatter of the neighboring birds.

Gradually I became aware of other things. I felt the sun soak through the thin silk of my sleeveless blouse, my work blouse, which I hadn't bothered to change before leaving New York. I looked down at my black pencil skirt, my three-inch calfskin slingbacks, and began to laugh.

His grip loosened. "What is it?"

"I'm not exactly dressed for the country," I said.

"No, you're not. But you look ravishing all the same."

I twisted around to look at him. He was dressed more casually, in a faded blue henley shirt and jeans, barefoot; I'd never imagined him so relaxed. "I didn't know you had a place out here," I said, almost accusingly.

He shrugged. "It never came up."

"But it's not exactly a country estate, is it? I mean, why not a mansion in the Hamptons?"

"Kate," he said reproachfully, "you should know me better than that."
He paused to study me. "Are you disappointed?"

I smiled. "You should know me better than that."

He stood up, drawing me with him. "Then if you're quite recovered,"
he said, "why don't you take off those ridiculous shoes and come inside.
Have you eaten?"

"No." I reached down to draw off my right shoe, and then my left.

"Oh. Well, we'll sort something out. But come along." He pulled me
up the flagstone path to the front door.

It was an old house, a true center-chimney colonial, with lovely worn
wainscoting lining the plaster walls and cabinets built into the corners.
Someone, probably Julian himself, had modernized the kitchen and the
bathrooms, but the original fireplaces were still in place, and the wide chestnut floorboards creaked comfortably beneath our feet. "I had someone in
to furnish it," he explained, waving his hand at the living room, "since I
couldn't spare the time. A local woman. I didn't want one of those over-
decorated showpieces, like Geoff's got."

"I love it," I said. "It's exactly what it should be."

"I'm glad. I want you to feel at home here." He checked his watch.
"There's nothing to eat, however, so I suppose I'll make my way down to
the A&P in the village."

"I'll go with you."

"No, you should rest."

"But you'll get all the wrong things," I protested.

"Kate, I *have* been fending for myself up here for some time."

I shook my head. "Julian, there's no way I'm going to let you cook me
anything. You were way too impressed by that omelet yesterday. And if
I'm going to do the cooking, I should pick out the food."

"Make me a list."

"You're seriously going to do the grocery shopping?" The idea of Julian
Laurence sniffing cantaloupe and checking expiration dates was completely absurd.

"What do you need?"

I went into the kitchen and took inventory. The refrigerator didn't hold much, just basic condiments; the pantry was a little better, with a wide assortment of canned goods and cereal and a few jars of dried herbs and spices. "Spam?" I demanded, holding up a package. "You have a billion dollars, and you keep *Spam* in your pantry?"

He snatched it away. "It's a perfectly good product," he said defensively. "You can make any number of dishes with it."

"Not on my watch." I tapped my finger against the door molding. "Do you have a Weber grill?"

He looked blank.

"Shoot. Okay. Let's just stick to the basics. Eggs, milk, cheese, tomato, maybe some bagged salad, fruit, a steak or something for dinner . . ."

He sighed. "Hold that thought. I'll fetch a pen and paper."

HE LEFT IN THE RENTAL CAR, and I stared after him until the last flash of metallic paint had long disappeared into the foliage. I'd forgotten to ask him why we were here in the first place. Why Lyme? It wasn't like I'd been banned from Manhattan, after all, just that corner of it occupied by the Sterling Bates headquarters. It felt almost like we'd gone into hiding, like fugitives, as though we were concealed here, deep in the Connecticut woods, surrounded by an impenetrable layer of trees and birds and rambling stone walls.

I hauled my suitcase and my laptop bag out of the Maserati and carried them into the house. I wasn't sure where to leave them. The subject of sleeping arrangements was so far untouched. I felt a curl of divine nervousness wind through my midsection at the thought, at the sudden mental image it conjured: white sheets and warm naked skin and intimacy. Well, why not? It must be why he'd asked me here. A sanctuary, a love nest.

The phone rang from the direction of the kitchen, making me jump.

I hesitated for a second. It was Julian's house. I probably shouldn't answer it. But what if it was Julian himself, wanting to ask me whether I liked skim milk or 2 percent? He knew I didn't have a cell phone anymore.

I hurried in the direction of the ring, and found the telephone on a small desk next to the wall. My hand hovered for a second or two, and then I picked it up.

"Hello?" I said, and then added quickly, "Laurence residence."

Silence. A hint of someone's breathing.

"Hello?" I tried again. "Julian, is that you?"

A pause, and then a male voice asked hesitantly, "Is Mr. Laurence available?"

"Um, no. He's stepped out for a moment. May I tell him you called?"

"No message," the caller said, and hung up.

A half-hour later I heard the crackle of gravel from the driveway and went outside. Julian was unloading groceries from the car. I reached in and grabbed a few bags. "Stop it," he said. "That's my job."

"I could use the exercise. I haven't been running in days."

"That's not the point," he said, but I was already walking up the path.

We took the groceries inside and began unloading. "Oh, someone called while you were out," I said.

He stopped and turned to me. "Did you answer it?"

"Yes. I thought it might be you." I felt the weight of his stare, and reached into the bag for the orange juice. "Um, is that okay? I didn't mean to, like, overstep."

He exhaled, and I realized he'd been holding his breath. "No. Of course not. I mean, no, answering the phone isn't overstepping at all."

"No crazy ex-girlfriends or anything?" I prodded, only half teasing.

A snort. "No." He set the grapes in the fruit drawer of the fridge. "Did he say who was calling?"

"No," I said. "I asked, but he said there was no message."

"American or British?"

"American."

"Did you give him your name?"

"No. Why?"

He cleared his throat. "Given the circumstances, you might not want to give out that information."

"What circumstances?"

"Kate," he said, "there might be questions asked, if word of this . . . this incident today leaks out. Our names are already connected; if someone puts two and two together and realizes you're staying at my house . . ."

"Worried about your reputation?" I inquired coldly.

"No. I'm worried about yours. And your safety."

"My safety?" I set down the loaf of bread I was holding. "What do you mean, *safety*?"

"Nothing. Just that, taking everything into account, we should err on the side of prudence."

"Is that why I'm here? You're worried about my *safety*?"

He tried to smile. "That, and other things."

"What other things?" My stomach growled.

"Hungry?"

"Don't change the subject."

"Have a sandwich," he said, reaching into the last bag and tossing me a ham and cheese hoagie, fresh from the deli counter. "We'll talk about it later."

JULIAN SPENT THE AFTERNOON on his laptop and BlackBerry, working. I'd forgotten about that, strangely enough. The private Julian was, to me, almost irreconcilable with the public version. *The dude has mythic fucking alpha,* Charlie had said, all those months ago, in the Sterling Bates conference room, meaning, in Wall Street shorthand, the rare and godlike ability to beat the market, year after year. *Alpha:* Julian was drenched in it.

I tried not to eavesdrop—poking determinedly through the books in the living room, plunking out a few notes on the baby grand in the corner—but I could still hear the commanding tone of his voice through the door of the library on the other side of the entry hall: the brusque way he issued orders, the evident passion with which he approached his work. He wasn't even thirty-five years old. Where had he acquired that confidence, that experience, that ease of command?

Eventually I went outside to the back garden, which had an unexpected and glorious view of the river, glimmering in the falling light; there I perched atop one of the ancient fieldstone walls crisscrossing the meadow and watched the sun slip down against the hills on the other side of the water.

"Glass of sherry?" came Julian's voice, over my shoulder.

"Sherry?"

"Very nice before dinner, I've found. Try it." He handed me a small ornate glass.

"Must be a British thing." I took a tiny sip, letting the sweet intensity spread luxuriously over my tongue. I dipped down for another.

"I brought you a sweater. It's getting chilly." He laid it over my shoulders, light and warm.

"Thanks," I said. It smelled like him, like the scent of his soap: clean and warm and outdoorsy, like sunshine on grass.

He clambered over the wall to sit next to me. "You've discovered my favorite spot already."

"It's beautiful. How long have you had this place?"

He shrugged. "A few years."

"Do you make it up often?"

"Not as often as I like. I enjoy the peace."

"Doesn't it get a little lonely?" I took a drink of the sherry to cover my anxiousness for his reply.

He chuckled and bent to kiss my shoulder. "Sweetheart. Yes, it does. Achingly so, at times. I've had Geoff and Carla up once or twice, but I expect she found it a bit rustic. One of the boys picked up a tick in the woods over there." He nodded in the direction of a copse of birch. "She nearly called nine-one-one."

I laughed. "That's why they call it Lyme disease, right?"

"I shall have to check you over very *thoroughly* for the little buggers," he said solemnly. "Every evening."

"If you must. And I suppose I'll have to do the same for you."

His low laugh rustled the air again; I felt his hand cover mine on the wall. "So tell me what happened today," he said, "if you can speak rationally yet."

I stroked my fingers along the tiny diamond-like ridges of the sherry glass. The firing seemed like a distant memory already. "Kind of like a scene from a movie, really. They'd shut out my security pass, so Banner escorted me upstairs like a . . . like a stormtrooper or something, and there was Alicia, looking smug. The HR woman handled it. Said they had evidence I'd been quote unquote engaged in an illegal information exchange with a—how did they put it?—a counterparty in the financial industry. I have to assume it was Alicia who manufactured it. Motive and opportunity." I took another drink and stared down at the darkened grass.

"Can't we find out?"

"Yeah, well, they shut that down pretty quickly. I asked if there was any way to defend myself, and she said they would pursue aggressive legal remedies if I tried. Aggressive, she said. Like she meant it."

He sprang from the wall and turned to face me. "They bullied you, in other words."

"You could say that."

"Kate," he said, taking my chin in his hand and looking me in the eye, "they haven't *seen* aggressive legal remedies. You and I are going into the house, and I'm going to call up my lawyer. And by the time I'm through, they'll be on their knees, begging your pardon. And as for that scheming harpy of yours . . ."

"Stop. Stop." I set my glass on the wall and took hold of his forearm and stared straight back. "That's exactly what you're *not* going to do. You're not going to run up millions of dollars in legal fees to get me back a job I never even liked. You're not going to expose yourself and your firm to the publicity it would cause. We're just going to let it drop for now."

"The *hell* I will," he began, but I laid my finger on his mouth.

"Please," I whispered. "Look, there's no need to get the legal broadsides firing yet. That would only scare them into destroying whatever evidence might be hanging around. I asked Charlie to do a little snooping for me. See what's going on. Like who this counterparty is supposed to be, and what kind of information I'm supposed to have given them. If I can find out exactly what Alicia was doing, maybe I can nail her."

"Not you," he insisted. "We."

"No. Not a chance. *You* are on the sidelines here, Laurence. You are not going to go all Terminator on me again."

"Again?"

"In the park. You were *whaling* on that guy. I'm not sure you wouldn't have killed him if I hadn't said something. It was seriously spooky."

"Kate," he said, "I would never hurt you."

"I know." Twilight was falling now, casting his face in blue shadow, stark and beautiful. I placed my hand on his cheek, felt the subtle rasp of his day-old whiskers under my palm. "So I've been thinking."

"Hmm. About what?"

"We're not here because of the firing, are we?"

He hesitated. "No, not really. Though I think it's doing you good, being away."

"I like it here. But don't change the subject. You said something, on the phone, about some news. Odd news. So is everything okay?"

He sat back down on the stone wall and drew me under his arm. "It's nothing to be all that worried about. More an excess of caution, really." He paused, reaching up to finger a lock of my hair. "How shall I put this? There's a bit of a question about my—and by extension, your—personal safety."

"What? What do you mean?" I demanded. "Someone wants to hurt you?"

"No. Not exactly. Look, as I said, it's a little hard to explain."

"I'm a smart girl."

"Yes, you are," he said darkly, almost as though that weren't a good thing. "All right, here it is: in early January I decided to start winding down the fund."

"Oh. I think I'd heard that rumor."

"Yes, well, I wanted to tell you before, but I couldn't put you in that position, since you were working in an investment bank. Anyway, we recently broke the news in a letter to our investors, with cash-out planned for the end of the summer, and a few of them haven't reacted well. End of story."

"End of story? Are you kidding? Who? What's the threat?"

He shook his head. "I'm not going to tell you. We're just going to lie a bit low for a little while."

"But why *we*? Not that I'm not delighted to be here with you, but why would this disgruntled investor hunt *me* down?"

I felt his kiss along my hairline. His voice was endlessly tender. "Because you're important to me. We've been publicly linked, and you never know. I didn't want to take any chances."

"A pretty slim chance."

"The only acceptable chance, with you," he said, "is none at all. So I'm going to keep you right here until things blow over."

"Wait a minute. How long is that?"

"I don't know. A month or two, perhaps."

I struggled up. "A *month* or two? Are you crazy? I can't just disappear like that! I mean, I only brought a change of clothes."

"There's a shopping mall up the freeway a bit."

"I'm not going to buy myself a new *wardrobe*..." His mouth began to open. "And neither are you!" I snapped.

"Kate, calm down..."

"You might have told me, you know. I'm going to have to go back in the city . . ."

"No," he said sharply. "I'll pick up whatever you need; just give me your key."

"What? So *you* get to leave and I don't? What the hell is going on here? You've, like, *kidnapped* me?" I scrambled back over the other side of the wall and began to stomp back to the house.

"Kate, it's not like that . . . Oh, bloody *hell*, Kate. You make it so damned difficult to take care of you . . ."

I spun around into his chest. I hadn't realized he was following so closely. "That's because I don't *need* taking care of. I don't *need* saving. I'm not, like, your *mistress*. Actually, I don't even know *what* I am!"

"You're the woman I love."

I closed my eyes. "Julian, you know you can't mean that. It's wonderful to hear, and it's all very romantic, and it makes me want to have mind-bending all-night sex with you, but you've known me for, like, two weeks, if you subtract the five-month freak-out you treated me to."

His mouth dropped open, speechless at last.

"So let's just leave *love* out of it for now, okay? Because I'm already *hooked*. You don't need to go setting me up for complete and total heartbreak."

And I turned and marched back into the house.

I COULDN'T REALLY stay mad at him for long. In the first place, here we were, alone together in a romantic old house, and unless I wanted to commit grand theft auto in his hundred-thousand-dollar car, I had few options for a self-righteous exit, stage left.

In the second place, well, he was Julian. It was no use trying to nurse resentment when his every touch triggered a primordial flood of oxytocin throughout my starved body.

So I went to the kitchen instead and started making dinner. Julian came in a moment later, standing hesitantly in the doorway as I banged around the pots and pans like a demented housewife. "Can I help?" he asked.

"That depends. Do you know how to boil water?"

"Very funny," he told me, and went to fill the pot.

I made chicken and pasta and salad, and we ate it quietly with a bottle of wine at the table in the kitchen. Julian was clearly thinking things over. His brow had compressed into serious lines, as if he were trying to derive some complex quadratic equation. Solve me for x and y.

Eventually, as the wine kicked in, we started exchanging a little conversation. Small talk, mostly. Things began to thaw out. "So, mystery man," I said, picking over the salad leaves, "do you think you can bear to tell me something about yourself? Maybe some childhood stories? You can change the names and dates to protect the innocent."

He smiled. "Really, it was a fairly ordinary childhood, at least for my crowd. We lived primarily in London; my father was somewhat active in politics. During recesses we went out to our house in the country. Southfield, you see."

"How clever of you."

"Yes, I'm startlingly original. In any case, I suppose you could say my parents raised me in a fairly old-fashioned way." He slanted me a playful look. "A mischievous child, I'm compelled to admit. The despair of my long-suffering nanny."

"Really? Mischievous how?"

"Oh, the usual rubbish. Frogs in the cupboards. Scientific experiments gone awry. Pranks on unsuspecting houseguests. It's just possible I may, at one point, have cost my father the chance of a cabinet position. I'm merely speculating, of course. I was only eight years old at the time."

I was laughing. "I can't imagine what . . ."

"And I shan't tell you. In any case, boarding school at age ten, then on to university." He took a sip of wine. "Then I joined the army."

I nearly choked on my arugula. "The *army*? Seriously? Why?"

He shrugged. "It seemed like the thing to do at the time. Adventure, excitement. I learned a great deal about leadership. And decision making: you can't dither on about your options in the middle of a . . . a training exercise."

"Wow." I chewed and swallowed, taking my time. "Were you in Iraq?"

"No, not Iraq. That was after my time."

"So that Terminator thing in the park. Your warrior instincts at work, I guess. Hmm. It's all clicking into place now. Why didn't you tell me before?"

"You didn't ask."

"I didn't *know* to ask. Do you have any good stories? Pinned down under fire or whatever?"

He smiled wryly. "A few, here and there. I'll try to think of some for you. In any case, I left the army after a bit, moved to New York, and started Southfield."

"Obviously that's the short version."

"The details are rather dull."

"Why Wall Street?"

"Friend of a friend."

"And you were wildly successful, just like that."

"I have good instincts. And I got lucky."

I shook my head in amazement. "You're obviously one of those really sick individuals who does everything well. Just my luck."

"Rubbish. I certainly don't do everything well. I only pursue what I'm good at."

"Which is everything."

He aimed his eyes upward in exasperation. "Must I sit here and enumerate my many shortcomings for you? I can't cook, as you've perhaps noticed. I can't sing a bloody note. Never get my Christmas cards out in time. I shall probably forget your birthday at least once, unless you're so good as to remind me. Am subject to hay fever in early spring. Rather uneasy around snakes . . ."

I grinned. "You're scared of snakes? You mean like Indiana Jones?"

"I did *not* say I was scared. *Uneasy*, Kate." He paused and folded his arms. "Not particularly keen on stinging insects, either."

"So I'll have to kill my own spiders?"

"No, spiders are quite all right. Just wasps and things. Owing to an unfortunate incident in my childhood. Too inquisitive for my own good."

"Well," I said, trying to keep my face straight, "I guess I can live with that."

We did the dishes together, even laughing as we tried to figure out how to work the garbage disposal. When the kitchen was tidy, and the dishwasher hummed industriously, Julian hung up his towel and turned to me.

"I'm sorry, Kate. I didn't mean to turn autocratic on you, back in the garden. Another of my faults, and rather more serious, is a tendency to want to order things around me. To a somewhat arrogant belief in my own capacities." He frowned, and finished, more softly: "I won't make you stay if you'd rather not."

I reached out to hook his fingertips with mine. "Julian, don't be ridiculous. Of course I want to stay. It's like living out a fantasy, being up here with you. Which is exactly why I can't just bury myself for the summer. I've just lost my job. My whole career, in fact. And if I don't try to get things back together soon, I'm afraid I'll just get swallowed up by you. Be sucked completely into your world."

"I'd never do that."

"You couldn't help it. I *have* to have some other life. I can't just become your dependent out here. I'd turn into one of those complacent little Stepford women, like Geoff's wife."

"No, you wouldn't," he said. "You're not like her at all."

"But maybe I would be. It would be too much like winning the lottery, and they say lottery winners are about the unhappiest people on the planet."

He laughed grimly. "Believe me, I'm no lottery win."

A smile crept onto my lips. I reached up and stroked the side of his cheek. "Believe me," I said, "you are."

His hand wandered up and covered mine; the other arm wrapped around my waist and eased me against him.

"So what next?" I whispered into his chest.

He moved up and down under my cheek in a deep sigh. "To be perfectly honest, I've got some work to finish up before tomorrow. I have to drive back into the city first thing. Just for the day. Consult with Geoff about a few matters, wrap up some loose ends here and there."

"You're *leaving* me here? By myself?" I drew back and looked at him, aghast.

"Just for the day," he said. "I'll leave at break of dawn and be back by dinnertime. There's a Range Rover for you in the garage, probably more suitable for the country roads than that hired piece of rubbish. You won't be stuck in the house."

"Hmm," I said.

"I can drop by your apartment, pick you up a few more things."

"And I'm not allowed to go with you?"

"Wouldn't you be happier here?" His tone turned persuasive, almost wheedling. "You've had a difficult time. You can relax. There's some sort of spa, I think, across the river; you could go there, pamper yourself."

"Do I have a choice?"

He bent his head to kiss me. "Of course you do."

But I could tell from his voice that I didn't, really.

"You put me in your *guest* room?" I demanded.

Julian sat up straight, disoriented, sleep clinging to his face in the dim glow from a nearby nightlight. "Kate?" he mumbled.

"Your *guest* room?"

"What *time* is it?"

"Two o'clock in the morning."

"Christ, Kate." He threw himself backward into the pillows. "What else was I supposed to do? Bring you in with me?"

"Well, *yes.*"

"Well, you were asleep," he yawned. "I couldn't exactly ask. I thought I was being a gentleman."

"Do me a favor next time," I said, hands on hips, "and don't be a gentleman. Do you know how freaked out I was, a moment ago?"

"I left a note."

"Well, it took me a little while to find it. Although I admit it was a very nice note," I added contritely.

"Look," he said, sounding grumpy, "come to bed, then. Only stop talking, for goodness' sake."

"So, a morning person."

"Kate," he said, from the depths of his pillow, "I held you for two hours on that damned library sofa. I held you until my arms cramped. I tried to wake you, and all I had for my trouble was a stream of *decidedly* unladylike language. So at last, giving up, I nobly tucked you into the spare bedroom and went to bed. I thought I was being kind."

"My skirt's all creased. It's going to have to go to the dry cleaners."

His arm lifted from the covers and pointed to a door in the corner. "Basket's in the bathroom."

I paused. "Can I borrow a T-shirt?" I hadn't thought about pajamas when I packed. Oddly enough.

The pointing finger shifted. "Top drawer on the right."

I went to the chest of drawers and pulled out a soft white undershirt, then stepped with as much dignity as I could summon to the bathroom, where I changed clothes and, after a second's reflection, rubbed some toothpaste onto my teeth. His shirt smelled faintly of himself, of that clean soapy smell I loved already.

I took a deep breath and slipped out of the bathroom. In the subdued glow of the nightlight, the large room seemed modest: a plain original fireplace settled into one wall, flanked by low well-stocked bookshelves, and a few pieces of simple dark furniture served the necessary functions. The bed was perhaps queen-size, four carved posts, clean white bedding. Unbearably inviting.

"Come to bed, Kate," Julian murmured.

I set my knee cautiously on the mattress. He lifted the covers and patted with his hand.

If I couldn't trust him, I couldn't trust anyone, I decided.

I crawled in and felt his arms close around me. "There you are," he said against my cheek, and I lay awake for some time, listening to his breathing settle back into a steady rhythm, feeling the heaviness of his arm across my waist, wondering if my heart would actually burst.

12.

I woke up to a flood of May sunshine tumbling through the window. For a moment I thought I was back in my bedroom in Wisconsin, where the window faced east and roused me at sunrise every morning. Then I saw the whiteness of the sheets and pillows, the dark antique furniture, the empty pillow next to mine.

I sat up. "Julian?" I called out.

No answer.

So I looked for the note. Julian would certainly have written me one before he left for New York. *Sweet dreams, beloved* had been the simple message, in spidery black italic handwriting, resting on the plump down pillow in the guest room last night. Surely a night spent in his arms, however virtuous, rated even better.

I checked all over the bed, finding nothing and getting unreasonably frantic, before I thought to look on the nightstand. There it lay, a folded ecru sheet. I snatched it and leaned back into the pillow; a set of car keys fell into my lap. The Range Rover.

Darling girl, your frightful snoring awoke me early this morning, so I took the opportunity to make a timely start for the drive to Manhattan. Everything here is yours. Shall return with all possible speed. XX

He'd pay for that.

I jumped out of bed, charged with energy, and padded to the bathroom. It was simple and white and new, awash with morning light, with a large deep tub against the wall and a separate shower cubicle. Julian had brought up my suitcase and laptop bag, both unopened; I took out my travel kit and brushed my teeth and took a long hot shower.

I hadn't been thinking clearly when I packed yesterday. I frowned at the contents of my suitcase: three tank tops, one sweater, my favorite yoga pants, two pairs of underpants, and four pairs of socks. I'd either have to go shopping or have Julian bring something up from my apartment.

Shopping. Definitely.

I got dressed and went downstairs and made a bowl of cereal in the kitchen. He'd left another note on the marble countertop, with the password to his desktop computer and the house alarm code. *Missing you already,* he'd added at the end.

I took my cereal to the library and turned on the computer, chewing thoughtfully as it booted up. I was going to have to let my parents know what had happened before they called into work and started panicking. How to begin? *Dear Mom and Dad, I just got fired from Sterling Bates for insider trading. Have moved to Connecticut to live in sin with Julian Laurence. Have a great day! Love, Kate.*

They'd be delighted.

Eventually I managed to compose something that resembled the truth and moved on to a more straightforward activity: researching the shopping opportunities within a twenty-mile radius of Lyme.

But before I left, I reached for Julian's phone and called his cell number.

He answered immediately. "Good morning, darling. Sleep well?"

"I just want you to know you're going to pay, and pay dearly, for that snoring remark."

"They were the most elegant little snores. Really quite charming."

"Okay. Not helping."

He laughed.

"So here's what I'm going to do," I went on. "I'm going to seduce you tonight."

"*Are* you, now?"

"You don't stand a chance, Laurence. Not a chance."

"You think not?"

"Because I, for one, will shove a stake through my heart before I spend another night in your bed without making love to you. I realize you find me utterly resistible . . ."

"Just because I spent years in army discipline, darling, learning to endure unimaginable extremities of physical hardship . . ."

". . . but even *you* won't be able to withstand what I have in store tonight . . ."

". . . doesn't mean I'm not aching for you in the most acute way . . ."

". . . because I am going to run my tongue over every inch of your body, *every delicious inch,* until you beg for mercy . . ."

I paused for effect, but he had nothing to say. Until, at last, a subdued "Go on."

"No," I said, "on second thought, I'm going to leave the rest to your imagination. So hurry home." And I hung up.

THERE WAS REALLY NOTHING like retail therapy for a girl with a train-wrecked career and a near-paralytic case of sexual frustration.

It occurred to me, as I swung the car into a parking space at a nearby upscale outlet mall, that someone who'd just lost her job really shouldn't be out spending money like this, but I pushed it aside. I'd made decent coin for the last three years, had saved all my bonuses, and kept my expenses low. Why not tap a bit into my savings for a little well-deserved catharsis? The thought carried me into J. Crew and beyond on a wave of self-righteousness. I bought shorts and tank tops and sundresses and sandals, running clothes and a bikini and a collection of lacy underwear to make Julian's eyes pop out.

It was only when I walked back through Julian's front door, tapped in the alarm code, and stared at all the loot that my mood began to sag.

I left the bags in the hall and went into the library to sit in front of the computer. The room faced north, probably to protect the books from the sun, and it was cool and dark and serene inside, with a large wood-stacked fireplace suggesting cozy winter evenings. Very much Julian's room: I could almost feel him in it.

I clicked the computer into wakefulness. No reply yet from my parents—they checked their e-mail about once a day, if that—but there was a message from Brooke, of all people. *the doorman said some guy came looking for u today, he didn't leave a name. b careful honey cause that could b trouble, take it from 1 who knows. xoxo b.*

I felt a chill at the back of my neck. Would Alicia stop at getting me fired, or would she take it to the SEC now? Oh my God. What if they arrested me? My fingers poised above the keyboard, ready to send Julian a frantic e-mail, but I checked myself. E-mail trails could be followed. What if they investigated Julian, too, knowing the connection between us?

I sat back in the chair and stared at the ceiling. Maybe Charlie had something for me. Where was his number? My laptop bag, right? I went upstairs to Julian's bedroom and found the bag next to the chest of drawers. I opened the zipper. There was the Sterling Bates contact list, right at the top, and the Amazon book that had arrived before I left.

Only it wasn't from Amazon, I noticed. Same kind of packaging, obviously a book, but no Amazon logo. The Pearl Fisher bookshop in Newport, Rhode Island, it said on the return label. Maybe the book had been listed by a dealer, not Amazon itself. Sometimes I hit the order button without reading too closely.

I shrugged and opened the packaging.

It must have been a mistake. I didn't recognize the book at all. It was used, a bit dated-looking, but in good condition. A history book. I turned it over and read the title.

And the Lamps Went Out: Julian Ashford and the Lost Generation, 1895–1916, by Richard G. Hollander. Below it, the sepia photograph of a broadshouldered man in a British army officer's uniform stared up sternly at me.

With Julian Laurence's face.

His great-uncle, I thought immediately. Or a cousin. Family resemblances could be so strong. He'd probably sent it himself, too modest to tell me face-to-face about his famous relative, but wanting me to know the family history.

I opened the book with ice-cold fingers, trying to ignore the strange high-pitched ringing in my ears, and read the inside flap.

Of all the tragic losses of the First World War, none rocked the British nation more deeply than the death of Captain the Hon. Julian Laurence Spencer Ashford, M.C., only son of Liberal cabinet minister and Asquith intimate Viscount Chesterton, during a night patrol along the Western Front in March of 1916. He represented all that was then held dear by the British public: his golden good looks, his stacks of academic prizes at Eton and Cambridge, his celebrated athletic achievements, his acts of heroism on the battlefield had all become legend even before his death was finally confirmed by special dispatch (his body was never actually recovered). Shortly afterward, his poem "Overseas" was published in the Times *by his grieving fiancée, the future writer and peace activist Florence Hamilton, and would be committed to memory by generations of British schoolchildren over the ensuing decades.*

But who was Julian Ashford, and why should his death, and those of his peers, matter so much today? In this groundbreaking work, drawing from unprecedented access to the papers of both Ashford and Hamilton, Dr. Hollander explores the man's life and connections, his intimate thoughts, his war record, and the chain of events leading to his death on the battlefield, all in an attempt to understand the meaning of his loss. How would Britain and the world be different today if he had lived? And how might those other lost soldier-poets, the cream of a golden age of British manhood, have altered the dismal course of the twentieth century?

Dr. Richard G. Hollander, emeritus professor of history at Harvard University, has published numerous books and articles on the subject of the First World War and its far-reaching effects . . .

I closed the book and set it down carefully on the bed.

We lived primarily in London; my father was somewhat active in politics . . .

Then I joined the army. It seemed like the thing to do at the time. Adventure, excitement . . .

No, not Iraq. That was after my time . . .

The scar. The man on the sidewalk, calling frantically: *Ashford, by God!*

His body was never actually recovered . . .

My muscles began to tremble. I got up and walked around the room, trying to think calmly. A logical explanation surely existed. Captain Julian Ashford had died on the Western Front in 1916; I'd already known this. It was one of those minor historical factoids you learned in high school and promptly forgot. Hadn't "Overseas" been one of the poems on my AP Lit exam? Compare and contrast with "Dulce et Decorum Est"? So of course, *of course,* I could not have spent last night sleeping in the arms of its composer. That was just *ridiculous.*

His great grand-nephew, maybe. But not him.

I mean, we'd had *phone sex* this morning. For God's sake.

My gaze, traveling randomly through the room, trying to distract itself, landed on the leaf of notepaper lying next to the bed, where I'd tossed it this morning. I could see, from several feet away, the elegant black scribble of Julian's handwriting. His rather unusual handwriting. Some might call it old-fashioned.

I walked over, very slowly, and bent down to pick it up. Then I sat on the bed and took Dr. Hollander's book and flipped through the pages until I came to the photograph section in the middle. I tried not to look at the faces. I didn't really want to know what this Florence Hamilton woman had looked like. Beautiful, no doubt. There must have been twenty glossy white pages covered with prints: portraits, snapshots, newspaper clippings. All the varied physical detritus of a famous life.

On the last page, I found what I'd hoped for: a copy of a letter. My eyes dropped to the caption. *Note sent to Lady Chesterton by Ashford, March 25, 1916, before going on patrol. Ashford's last known correspondence.*

My fingers shook. It was difficult to hold the notepaper steady next to the page, but I managed it. I looked back and forth meticulously, between the nimble scrawl of my note and the writing on Lady Chesterton's letter.

At first I was relieved. The two looked similar, but not identical; the older script seemed less refined, clumsier, like that of a twelve-year-old.

But the more I stared, the more uneasy I became. Both sets of writing had the same weight, the same brushstrokes, the same pressure of ink on paper. And both slanted the same way, an odd not-quite-right way.

As if the writers were both left-handed.

And certain letters—the *f,* the *y,* the capital *I*—looked exactly alike.

As if the writer of my note were a grown-up version of the one in the book. Or, perhaps, someone who had spent some years writing with his left hand, instead of someone still learning to do so after, for example, a serious injury to his right arm.

I dropped the book and the note and ran to the bathroom, where I vomited thoroughly into the toilet.

13.

I was sitting on the stone wall, in the same place I'd occupied yesterday evening, when he returned from New York.

The weather had turned chillier tonight. I wore one of my new pairs of jeans and Julian's cashmere sweater, the same one he'd put over my shoulders yesterday. I sat breathing in the scent of him, watching the sunset glow on the horizon, wishing I could turn back the clock twenty-four hours.

I heard the Maserati pull up the driveway, heard the last little rev of its athletic engine before he switched it off. Heard the car door slam, and his footsteps crunching in the gravel to the front door. It was a clear night, and the sound traveled perfectly well through the empty country air.

He must have gone through the house for a minute or two, looking for me. I just sat there, imagining him walking from room to room, floorboards creaking under his polished shoes, calling my name in his plummy voice, with its odd nostalgic accent. Its aristocratic accent.

Eventually I heard the French door open, a hundred or so feet behind me, and I closed my eyes, feeling the stir in the stillness as he approached me.

"There you are." His arms went around me from behind; I felt his chin rest lightly on my head. "Sorry about the time. I drove as quickly as I could. The traffic through Fairfield County was atrocious."

"Mmm." I tried to say more, but my voice wouldn't work.

"I missed you terribly," he said, pressing a kiss against my temple, the way I loved. "Shall we go inside and have some dinner?"

Still I couldn't speak, couldn't move. I only absorbed him, all the sensations of him: his arms, his breath, his lips, his warmth, the sound of his voice, the smell of his skin.

"Oh, darling," he said, "are you cross with me? I was only joking about the snoring, you know. You'd have rolled those lovely eyes of yours, if I'd told you what I really did. How long I lay there, listening to the sound of your breathing, wishing I'd the courage to wake you."

I turned my head, just an inch or two, so he could hear me. "I wish you had," I said hoarsely.

He groaned, tightening his arms around me. "Darling, I couldn't . . . we *can't* . . ."

I interrupted him. "Tell me," I said, and cleared my voice of the strange obstruction there, "tell me about Florence Hamilton."

He went still.

A bird sang out from the nearby trees, full-throated and eloquent.

"Ah." He said it flatly, everything contained in that one brief sound.

I let the silence spin. I didn't want to rush him.

"Where did you hear that name?" he asked finally, almost casually.

"A package arrived at my apartment just before I left," I said, and I pulled the book from my lap and put it into the hands in front of me.

"Ah," he said again.

"I kept thinking it must be a strange coincidence, that this must be an ancestor of yours. But then I saw your note, and the handwriting looked . . . not exactly the same, but obviously . . ." I heard my voice break.

"That's my clever girl," he said. His arms still encircled me, warm and tender; I could smell the faint musky hint of leather clinging to him from the long car ride. His thumbs brushed against the cover of the book. "How much did you read?"

"Just the inside flaps. I couldn't bear to read more."

He set the book, with exquisite care, on the stone wall, and then he climbed over it and knelt in the grass before me. "Only tell me one thing," he whispered, taking my shaking hands. "Does it matter?"

The tears leaked out. "Matter? Of course it matters! It's who you *are*, Julian! You're . . . I read about you in high school, I wrote an *essay* on that poem . . . I can't even begin to understand this! Swallow me whole? My

God! You were just a mere colossus before, a billionaire hedgie, nothing at all. Now you're *Julian Ashford*! I mean, how can Julian Ashford be *here*? Be in *love* with me? It's just *impossible*!"

"It's not impossible." His eyes burned earnestly at mine. "It's the most essential truth of my life."

"No. Don't. You were *engaged,* Julian. How can I possibly compare with Florence Hamilton? I've *read* about her. She's an *icon.* The *Times* ran an article, just a few weeks ago . . ."

"We'll speak of her later, if you like," he said, "but you should know she was never my fiancée. Except, perhaps, in her own mind."

"Whatever," I said despairingly. I tried to rise, but the snug grip of his hands held me in place.

"Is that all you're worried about? My feelings for you?"

"Of course not. That's nothing, compared to . . . to the rest of it. How and why. What you've endured. This new Julian I don't even know."

"But you *do* know me. *I* haven't changed." His thumbs rubbed urgently against the bones of my hands. "Look at me, sweetheart. It's just *me*. I'm exactly the same man; you *know* me."

"This is not happening. This is really not happening." I looked down at our hands, clasped together. At *his* hands. Hands that had lobbed a grenade, pulled the trigger of an Enfield rifle, scribbled a canonical poem into an infantry officer's notebook.

Julian Ashford's hands.

"Are you all right?" he asked, after a moment.

"I'm better than I was. At three o'clock this afternoon I was throwing up."

"I'm sorry, Kate." He bent his head and kissed my cold fingers. "If you knew how it's troubled me, *tormented* me, wondering whether I should tell you. How I should tell you. Knowing what an ass I am, pursuing you at all."

"It didn't take much pursuit, did it?" I raised my eyes back to his. "So don't be sorry. It's not your fault."

"I tried to stay away. I should have stayed away."

"I was miserable without you."

"And this is any better?"

"I'll get used to it. Give me time." My voice caught on the last word.

"All the time in the world."

"I will get used to it. I have to get used to it," I went on, squinting my eyes shut. "I don't have a choice anymore."

"Yes, you do. I'd understand."

"Oh please. That's not *helping*." I took my hands from his and rubbed my fingers against my temples, hoping it would help my brain to expand, to wrap around this thing.

"I mean it, Kate," he said. "You don't have to stay, if it's all too much."

I opened my eyes again. His face wavered before me, through the unshed tears, his wide forehead creased with earnest lines and his green-blue eyes reflecting the light from the house. "Yes, I do. That's the whole point, isn't it? I'm long past being able to walk away from you. Whatever and whoever you are."

His own eyes closed, and then he rose and turned around to prop himself against the stone wall next to me. His long legs stretched out to the grass, the quadriceps curving with latent strength under the fine dark wool of his suit trousers; I could sense the radiant heat of his arm behind me on the cool wall, not quite touching my back. "I suppose you have questions."

"About a million. But I don't even know what to ask. I don't even know how to believe it. Even now, feeling you next to me, real and warm and solid and . . . and *real*, I keep thinking to myself, it can't be true, it just can't be. Because only last night, only this morning, we lay there together . . ." I couldn't say it. The memory was too precious.

"Can we go into the house? Talk it all over, with a bottle of wine?"

It sounded so prosaic, but what else was there to do?

I nodded, and he drew me to my feet and took my hand. We walked silently to the house, everything shifting and recalculating between us, my brain spinning. Somehow, I hadn't thought he would acknowledge it. Somehow, against all probability, I'd thought he would have some laughing explanation, even if it wasn't true, and we both knew it wasn't true; somehow I'd just been hoping it would all go away, and we could be Kate and Julian again.

He led me to the sofa in the library and made me sit down; he returned a moment later with a decanter of red wine and two glasses. "Lafite, '82," he said, pouring me a glass. "I've been saving it for a special occasion."

"Like telling your girlfriend you're a war hero from 1916?"

He grinned at me. "Ah, your sense of humor's come back," he said, setting the bottle on the coffee table and sitting beside me. "A good sign. Though in fact I decanted it this morning before I left." He let his nose hover over the glass.

"You were planning on telling me tonight anyway?"

"No." His smile turned sheepish. "Only carried away by the sight of you on my pillow at daybreak." He held his glass forward, and I clinked it.

"I have no idea what we're toasting," I said.

"To the truth, I suppose. You know, it's rather a relief for me. Particularly since you seem to be taking it so well."

"That's just because I'm still in shock. I'll probably go into hysterics later." I took a long drink of wine. "Oh my God," I gasped, staring down at the glass. The dense fruit rose up gracefully to envelop my brain.

"Oh, that *is* handsome," he agreed, swirling his glass and taking another sip. "So. First question, please."

"*How,* I guess. I mean, I just stop right there. *How?* How can you be sitting here next to me? Some weird physics thing? The fountain of eternal youth? Or, like"—I ducked, embarrassed to say the word—"magic?"

"Actually, I still haven't figured that part out. I heard a shell screaming overhead, thought my number was up, and the next thing I knew I was waking up in a French hospital. A *modern* French hospital, near Amiens."

"So . . ." I took another drink of wine, deeper this time. "So you traveled through time." My brain zoomed out, hearing the words from a distance, and marveled at their matter-of-fact tone. As though we were discussing the Yankees game. *So, a walk-off home run. So, time travel.*

He looked surprised, as though he'd never considered another possibility. "Yes. I suppose that's what you'd call it. Apparently someone had found me in a field, with my ears oozing blood, and called an ambulance."

"Who?"

"I don't know. The chap disappeared. But a letter arrived at the hospital the next day, addressed to me, typewritten, with instructions not to speak to anybody about my past. Included in the envelope were the keys to a locker at Amiens railway station. When I opened it a week later, it held a knapsack with clothes, money, papers: everything I needed, more or less, to start a new life."

"Like it was planned, somehow. Weird." I stopped for a brief sarcastic laugh. "Now there's an inadequate word. *Weird.*"

He fingered the rim of his wineglass. "I was in shock for a while. As you'd expect. It's the most supremely disorienting experience you could imagine. At first I thought I was dreaming, or dead; then I was only glad to be alive. And then I started thinking about things, other things. Everything I'd left behind. What might lie ahead in the future."

"And you moved to New York."

"Yes. Mucked about Wall Street for a bit, and eventually started Southfield."

"You've adjusted pretty well." I stopped and shook my head.

"What is it?"

"I can't believe I'm having this conversation. This is insane. Am I dreaming? You really are Julian Ashford? *The* Julian Ashford?"

"I am, I'm afraid."

"*Corpses half-unearthed.* What was it? *Jaws wide in silent shriek.* That was you?"

"Ah. You know the poem, then?"

"Oh, *please,* Julian." I cocked my head, taking him in. "And all this time, you were *alive?* Running a *hedge fund* in New York City?"

"I had to do something."

I smiled. A giggle escaped me, and another. He looked at me strangely for a moment, until his own lips started to tug upward. I leaned forward, still laughing, and pressed my head into my forearms. "I'm sorry," I said. "It's like some kind of weird satire, in a way. Running a hedge fund. I mean, what's Rupert Brooke doing, do you think? Surfing in Baja?"

He shook his head and chuckled. "Brooke's an ass."

"You *knew* him?" I sat back again, facing him, one knee on the sofa.

"We were at Cambridge together, briefly." He reached out with one hand, touching mine, feathering his fingers on the ridge of my knuckles.

"Of course you were," I breathed. "You knew everybody, didn't you? You were probably friends with, like, Churchill."

"Well, he was older, of course. But we were acquainted."

"What was he like?"

"More or less as you'd imagine. Tenacious. Opinionated. Ruddy good company at a dull dinner." He began to massage the tips of my fingers, sending shivers up the length of my arm to gather pleasurably in my scalp. "That was rather gratifying, you know," he went on, a wry smile crossing his lips. "Finding out he'd gone on to save the free world and all that."

As you might have done.

He looked remarkably at ease now, relieved, as he said, that everything was in the open at last. His broad shoulders settled into the sofa, veiled by his white dress shirt; his collar still fit stiff and neat against the pale gold of his corded neck, though he'd loosened his blue necktie; his firm jaw angled upward, as if the memories he sought had drifted upward to the plaster ceiling. The lamplight gathered like a nimbus around his head, pulled in by the irresistible gravity of him.

I had the strangest sensation, then, of the entire world opening up before me. That, far from being terrifying, this shocking revelation of his was a *good* thing, an illuminating thing. That, sitting here on this sofa with this dazzling man, radiant and powerful as a young prince, I had been entrusted, for no particular virtue of mine, with a precious gift it would take me years to fully unwrap.

"Tell me everything," I said, leaning in toward him. "I want to know everything." I looked down at his hand, caressing mine, and slid my fingers under his sleeve. "Tell me what really happened to your arm."

"Shrapnel."

"Well, obviously shrapnel," I said, trying to sound worldly. I set down my wineglass and slipped his cufflinks free and rolled up his sleeve, just as I had before, not so many days ago. "It's so jagged," I said, tracing the scar with one weightless fingertip.

"A glancing wound, really. I was lucky. I'd only been in the trenches a week; it was rather humiliating to be sent back down the line so quickly."

"Humiliating. When you could have been killed. Or . . . or lost your arm completely."

"Shrapnel's nasty stuff," he admitted, looking down at the scar. "They stitched me up pretty well. Wanted to keep me in hospital, but I hated to be away so long."

"So you made them send you back. With nerve damage and everything."

"It wasn't that serious, really. Looks worse."

I looked at his face for a moment, trying to erase the horrifying image from my head: Julian hurt, bleeding, his arm torn open. His teeth ground shut, confining the agony. "Thank God," I said, "thank God this . . . this *thing* happened. Brought you safely here, before something else could get you."

His mouth flattened. "Do you think so?"

"My God! Of course! You're sitting here with me, instead of buried in France somewhere. One of those white headstones. I'd never have known you."

"Perhaps that would have been better."

"No. *No.*" I shook my head and squeezed his hand. Hard, so my fingernails left tiny crescents in his skin. "Don't start that. I won't let you slide back into some survivor guilt funk."

"*Survivor* guilt?"

"You know, feeling guilty because you're alive, when everyone else . . ."

He pulled his hand from mine and leaned against the back of the sofa. "Kate," he said, "we're not discussing an abstract psychiatric condition. I'd abandoned everyone who needed me."

"Not by *choice*, Julian!"

He stared into the empty fireplace. "I haven't even had the heart to look up my old company. Who was killed. Who spent the rest of his life in shell shock."

Killed. Shell shock. I heard the alien words in my ear, felt his withdrawal in the air between us. I turned and leaned back against his chest; lifted his heavy arm and placed it around me, entwining my fingers firmly around his hand. His ribs rose and fell steadily behind me, and I soaked it all in: his warmth, his vitality. The mere fact, the mere miracle, that he was alive at all.

"Did you have shell shock?" I asked at last.

His shoulder moved beneath my ear. "Not really. Just the odd nightmare. Taking fright at certain noises, which is rather a nuisance."

"What was it like? What were *you* like?"

A little laugh. "Muddy. Dirty. And the smell! My God, that charnel-house smell! I still remember it, the rot of a million dead bodies, soaked into the earth around us. You can't imagine. It's not possible to describe it. And long stretches of boredom, of mindless administrative duties, of interminable waiting. Then everything in a panic, or else going on some sort of patrol and balancing on the knife edge of life and death. Thrilling. Horrifying. Ennobling. Soul-destroying."

I closed my brimming eyes. "Well, that clears it all up," I observed, stroking his finger joints patiently. "So was it hard? Shooting at people?"

"If you're asking whether I actually killed anyone . . ."

"I guess I am. But you don't have to answer."

"I have," he said simply.

"Does that bother you?"

He took his time to answer me. "Not exactly. Not really. Perhaps abstractly, or rather unconsciously, but not in a rational moral sense. After all, they were trying to kill us." He paused. "Does it bother *you*?"

"No. If I saw someone trying to hurt you, I'd want to pick up a gun and kill him myself."

"That's my line, darling. I'm supposed to come to *your* defense."

"It's a two-way street in this century," I said. "But you'd probably be much better at it than me. You've established that pretty well, so far. In the park, I mean." I let out a laugh, remembering. "That poor guy. He had no idea what he was up against." Another laugh, a small disbelieving shake of my head. "A First World War infantry captain, for God's sake. You just never know who you're going to run into in that freaking city."

His lips touched the tip of my ear in a fragile kiss. "I did tell you I had a complicated past."

"Yet, strangely enough, I never figured time travel." I said it lightly, but the words seemed to take on weight, rotating slowly between us.

"So you've accepted it?" he asked, after a moment, his voice quite low.

"Accepted it? Julian, I . . . I mean, I *have* to, don't I? You're here, aren't you? You're not a hallucination. You can't be lying; it's just too massive and complicated and unnecessary to lie about. Or maybe I'm dreaming the whole thing, but it doesn't feel like a dream, either." I paused. "And you know something? It just fits, somehow, bizarrely. You were just so different; I couldn't figure you out. It was like one of those 3-D movies, before you put the glasses on: the images blurring, not quite matching up. And now I'm wearing the glasses, and you're leaping out at me, a thousand times more clear and real and vivid than before. You make *sense,* now."

"And it doesn't frighten you?"

The breath left my body in a rush: part laugh, part gasp. "Frighten me? Julian, it *terrifies* me. If I sit here and close my eyes and think *he was born a hundred years ago, he dropped through some wormhole or whatever,* it just . . .

sounds so . . . *unreal.* It *is* unreal. Not just that you're here, but you are who you are. You're a *historical figure.* I don't know how to begin to deal with that. If you let go of me, I'd be shaking."

His arm pulled me in; his head bent down against mine. "Kate, sweetheart, it's only *me,* there's no need . . ."

I interrupted him. "And then I open my eyes, and you're real again, and I *know* you; you're the most familiar person on earth to me." I turned my face to his, until our cheeks nearly touched. "And I think about how you held me last night, and how I felt then. How I feel now."

"Tell me."

"Cherished. Safe. And the fear goes away, until it—until this, *you*— seems almost . . . normal." I shook my head, not quite believing in my own belief. My eyes fastened on the pool of wine in my glass, red-dark and still; I reached out one finger to circle the stem. "So, okay. I'll buy it. You're Julian Ashford. Which is really, if I think about it objectively, pretty cool."

"Cool?" He began to laugh, shaking my torso. "That's the best you can come up with? *Cool?*"

"I'm sorry," I said, laughing too. "That was pathetic. How's this: you're Julian Ashford, and it's remarkable. Miraculous. The most wonderful thing I've ever known, and I am just so *grateful* for it. You're Julian Ashford, and you're *alive,* thank God, thank *God,* sitting here right next to me, and . . ." I paused, my voice dwindling into nothing.

"And?"

"And you're *mine.*" The last word wavered upward as it came out.

"Kate," he said, gathering me close, dipping his head back down, "I'm yours. Believe *that,* at least."

The warmth of his cheek spread into mine, linking us, and all at once I *did* believe it. I understood everything. What had been enigma resolved into clarity, into the keen marrow-deep certainty that I existed to give Julian Ashford's uprooted soul a home in this modern world. That his happiness had been placed between my palms, a divine mysterious charge. That he *was* mine. That I was his.

I lifted my hand and rested it against the other side of his face, holding him in place. "So what do you think, anyway?" I asked.

"About what?"

"Modern life. Sex, drugs, rock and roll. Technology." I paused. "Career women."

"Well, it's not as if you *invented* them all, darling. When I was a boy, it seemed every week some new machine or discovery was announced. All sorts of upheaval, social and technological. A fascinating time to be alive. I read magazines, books. H. G. Wells, that sort of thing. And music!" He chuckled. "My parents were appalled at us. Ragtime. All the new dances."

I twisted to look at him. "Oh, no. *No*. Tell me you didn't do the *turkey trot*!"

He cast his eyes to the ceiling.

"Get *out*! You *did*! Oh, that is freaking *hilarious*!" I leaned backward on the sofa, laughing from deep in my chest. "The turkey trot! Will you show me?"

"Absolutely not." But his mouth edged upward.

Eventually my laughter settled down and I eyed him a moment, smiling. "But you weren't that naughty, were you? Not compared to today."

"No, I suppose not."

"Especially the girls, I guess. The ones in your crowd." I reached out to grasp the bowl of my wineglass and lift it to my lips. "No more blushing virgins today."

"No, not that many."

"Does it bother you?"

He took a moment to choose his words. "Kate, I can't blame you for belonging to a different world. My own wasn't perfect. I don't suppose human beings have ever figured out how to order these things very well." He lifted one hand to rub his temple. "I'm jealous," he admitted, "but I'll try to be modern about it."

"And you? Did you . . . was there anyone?"

He knew what I meant. "Yes. One," he said. "During the war."

"And not since? With all the willing women thrown your way?"

"Not since."

"And how long is that, exactly?"

He paused. "Twelve years," he said reluctantly.

"For real?" I drew away, so I could turn around and look at him.

"Why are you so astonished? You know I don't go out."

"But you have *needs*, don't you? I mean, you're a man."

"I deal with it."

"Oh," I said. "Well, at least you can't play the virgin card with me."

His face relaxed. "No, I can't."

I considered for a moment. "Most men would have kicked up their heels. Taken advantage. Enjoyed themselves."

"I couldn't do that."

"Why not?"

He frowned at me. "Because I couldn't go to bed with a woman without telling her the truth. It wouldn't be fair. And I never found the right sort of woman for that."

"What do you mean, the right sort of woman?"

"Fishing for a compliment, are you?"

"No. I really want to know. Because you didn't actually *tell* me the truth, did you? I found out on my own." I paused for a drink of wine, feeling a blush coming on. "Which is fine. You've been understanding about my . . . about where I'm coming from, and I can do the same. The guest bed was actually pretty comfortable."

"Darling, you've got it all wrong."

"I must," I said rapidly, "seem pretty slutty to you. Throwing myself at you. That . . . that stuff on the phone today."

"I didn't mind that at all."

"I just want you to know it's been years for me, too. Since college. Because it turns out you were right. Sex *is* a big deal. It was too big a deal for me. So it always turned out to be a disaster, and I wish . . ."

"Wish what?"

"Wish I'd know you then, I guess. You would have been much kinder."

"*Kinder?*"

"When it ended. When you were over me."

He gazed at me for a moment; then he took my glass from me and, together with his own, set it on the coffee table. He placed one hand on either side of my hips and leaned in close to my ear. "Tell me," he said, "what do I have to do to convince you of my sincerity?"

I felt myself grin. "Well, we could start with mind-bending all-night sex."

His laugh tickled my neck. "Kate, Kate. You're killing me."

"Why not, though? Don't you believe *me*? Or is it the moral thing? No sex before marriage?" The word darted from its mental crevice before I could trap it.

He looked at me a long time, his green eyes soft and glowing, until I could feel each distinct cell of my flushed skin as it scraped against my clothes. "When I saw you in that conference room," he said at last, in his low coaxing voice, "all I could think was *there she is!* I've found her at last. I meant to woo you properly, Kate. To marry you. I'd forgotten, for the moment, in the *elation* of having found you, that I was a freak of nature. That to ask you to stay, to be mine, meant forcing you to share it all with me, and who knew what might lie ahead for me? I couldn't ask that of you."

"And so you pushed me away." I felt the beat of my heart, trotting eagerly to some unknown destination behind my breast, and raised my hands to the curving angle of his cheekbones, to that beautiful face of his, filled just now with an expression of deep longing, of passion held just in check. I held him there for a moment, letting my eyelids drift downward to better collect the sensation of his skin, warm and intimate, against my palms. "What changed your mind?"

He answered without hesitation, in a hard flat voice. "When I saw that man attack you in the park. I'd never felt anything like it. Not during the worst moments of the war."

My hands slipped down his jaw, his throat; I loosened the knot of his necktie and drew it free.

He closed his eyes. "I'm the most selfish being alive, wanting you to stay."

"No, you're not." Delicately I unfastened the top button of his shirt, and then the next. "You're lonely." I dipped my lips into the hollow of his throat and felt him tremble. So large and so capable a man, and yet I could make him tremble. "You need this. You need *me*."

"I haven't the strength to do the right thing anymore. I don't even know what the right thing is."

"This is the right thing." I tasted his skin.

"This *can't* be right."

"It is, in my century. The century you're living in now."

"You haven't thought it through."

"I don't need to think it through." I nibbled along, trying to keep my wits, trying to find just the right words to convince him. "It's not the kind of thing you think through. I mean, who reads the full prospectus, line by line, before buying the offering?" I felt him quiver under my lips. "You are who you are. It's the *essence* of you that matters to me. The man inside, the man I adore. The rest of it is just details."

"Details, that I was born over a century ago? Details, that I'll always be hiding things, keeping secrets, from our closest friends? What if it happens again, without warning? Think of all the ways, Kate, in which this complicates your life."

I drew back, searching his face. "It was always going to complicate my life, Julian."

"Don't remind me," he said bitterly. "I should have told you before. I should have stayed away from you, before you could be hurt."

"Impossible. Because it was already too late, from the very first meeting."

"And in ten years, twenty years, when you're tired of hiding my secrets?"

I pushed that aside. "I'd never see your past as anything other than a gift, Julian, because it's what brought you to me. It's what makes you so particularly *you*, like no one else in the world."

"Someone else may find out."

"We'll manage."

"Kate, it's an impossible burden . . ."

"Well, I'm not going to let you go on bearing it alone! I'm *here* now, Julian. You did this. You bound me to you, and what I learned today doesn't change that at all. So deal with it, okay? Take me upstairs. I need"— tears, for some reason, began to seep around my eyes again—"I need that reality. I need—I can't explain it—I'm reeling with all this, just barely hanging on, and I need you to take me in your arms and just . . . *please* . . . just *unite* us . . ." I seized his hands, knitted my fingers through his, tried to communicate.

"Kate, oh sweetheart, *don't.* I can't resist that, I can't . . ."

"Don't, then. *Don't* resist it. I wouldn't ask, wouldn't beg, if it were just sex. You *know* that. You *know* what I'm asking for."

His eyes shut tightly. "I know, darling, I want it too, I want it passionately, you can't *conceive* . . ."

I pulled on his hands, trying to draw him up with me.

"No. Wait." He stopped me, heaving a deep breath. "Even if it *were* all right, there's still another thing."

"*Other* thing." I leaned against the sofa back and stared up at the ceiling in despair. "There's *more*? What now? Freaking *vampires*?"

He let out an amused noise. "No, a little more down-to-earth than that."

"Oh, no," I groaned. "Please, not the moral scruples. I'm already a ruined woman, Julian. I don't have any virtue to preserve. Neither do you, technically."

"Well, there's that, too," he said, "but I've already conceded that point, weak flesh-made man that I am. No, it's a more practical concern."

I waited. He remained silent, staring at his hands, looking awkward. "Well?" I demanded at last.

"Kate," he said, "I'm no expert on any of this, but I do know that when two people, when a man and a woman . . ." He broke off, and then tried again. "Kate, have you thought about the possibility . . ."

I began to giggle. "Julian, you Edwardian, are you trying to ask me about *birth control*?"

His cheeks flooded with color.

"Julian," I said, "I'm on the Pill. So just take me upstairs, already. For God's *sake*."

"Kate, I . . ."

I stood up and held out my hand. "Julian Laurence. Julian Ashford, I mean. Whoever you are. I really don't care anymore. Come upstairs with me *now*, or you can just find yourself another girlfriend."

"Girlfriend." He shook his head, staring at me intently.

And at last he made his decision: he stood up, bent down and slung me over one shoulder with a single effortless heave. "Fine, then. On your own head be it," he growled, and carried me into the darkened hallway and up the stairs, two at a time.

Amiens

So," Julian said, "I've treated you to a handsome dinner. I've been sporting company, with all your tantalizing revelations. And now I think I've quite earned the honor of your confidence. Who, exactly, are you, Kate from America? Can I at least have your last name?"

"That," I said, "will certainly have to wait for later." I stepped gingerly around a puddle, left over from the day's rain, gleaming silver in the moonlight. "You're not going to believe me. And even if you do, it's going to wipe that charming smile off your face. You'll storm off in a huff, or else run screaming to the nearest police station."

"Look here, Kate. This is altogether too much mystery for a straightforward chap like myself; I shall go barking mad in a moment. Would you simply come *out* with it? Careful," he added, offering his arm to help me navigate a rain-filled gutter. "Public works in a shocking state, aren't they? *C'est la guerre,* I suppose."

I felt the scratchy wool of his coat under my hand and leapt over the obstacle. I did not, however, give up his arm afterward; nor did he draw it away.

"Tell me about your husband," he said.

"My husband."

"You did say you were a widow, I believe?"

"Yes." I felt an ache collect at the back of my throat. "You know, I think

I'd rather not talk about that, at the moment. If you don't mind. It's still very new."

His voice fell into contrition. "I'm so terribly sorry. How wretchedly dull of me. Forgive me; army life can be so coarsening."

"Forgiven. It was a natural question. And I *will* tell you about him, later." I paused. "I loved him deeply."

"A very lucky chap, I believe."

Our feet clacked companionably on the damp cobbles. I looked down and watched the tips of my sturdy shoes disappearing and reappearing next to his larger ones. From around the corner ahead of us, the sound of anxious laughter rippled through the dank evening air, cracking the un-natural wartime stillness: other lives, other histories, all returned to dust by the time I'd been born. I spoke up suddenly. "All right, then, Ashford. You asked for it. Here it is. I'll just say it. You leave Amiens on Thursday, right?"

"Yes, as I said."

"You'll be going back up the line to Albert, and then wait for your turn in the front-line trenches. You'll have a meeting with Major Haggard, dur-ing which you'll lay plans for a night raid on Saturday, at 0200 hours, on the German front line, in order to gather prisoners for interrogation and intelligence gathering. I can tell you now, if you lead that raid as planned, you won't return to your trench."

"Yes, I realize you have an uncanny ability to predict the future, Kate," he said impatiently, "and I'll be curious to see if it all turns out as you say, but *why*? How do you know this, or think you know it?"

"No, wait," I said, "there's more. And I have to tell you, so you'll be-lieve what comes next. Julian, I know how and when this war's going to end. I know how the next one's going to start. I know . . . I know Florence Hamilton will marry a man named Richard Crawford in 1921, and bear him three children, Robin and Arthur and Sophia, and Robin will go on to become an MP for Hatherleigh in the 1950s, before involving himself in a Communist spy scandal a few years after his election."

He came to a stop, frozen there on the wet cobbles, like a military memorial in some village square. "Good God," he mumbled.

"Next year," I continued, "the Bolsheviks will start a revolution in Russia, turning it into a Communist dictatorship, and in 1929 the world stock markets will crash, the first disaster in a decade of financial depression. In 1969, men will land on the moon and walk on its surface."

"Good God," he repeated.

"What else? Oh, here's a good one: Great Britain will elect its first female prime minister in 1979. And your Prince of Wales will inherit the throne in—oh, I don't know the year—the thirties somewhere, and abdicate soon after in order to marry an American divorcée. I'm sorry, I'm having difficulty being chronological about this. The point is, Julian, I'm about to tell you something extraordinary. Something . . . something you'll never believe. But I can prove it. I've brought proof. Julian, listen to me: I was born in the year 1983."

He turned and stared at me, as if I were some kind of ghost.

"I was born in 1983," I said, "and I can tell you just about anything and everything that's happened in the world until 2008, when I traveled back here, to you. Only a week ago, in my time. Only a week since I was surfing the Internet, drinking a latte. A nice hot freshly . . . freshly brewed . . . *latte*." My voice cracked.

"You were born in 1983," he said, still staring.

"I know, I know. I felt the same way, when I . . . when the same thing happened to me. When someone told me about this." I seized his hands in mine and took a step nearer, close enough to feel the sweet wine-laced warmth of his breath on my face, to bind him to me before he fell apart. "But please, Julian," I whispered, "try to push past the *how* of it. The impossibility of it. Just take the leap, try to understand . . ."

"But that's marvelous!" he burst out, squeezing my hands. "Bloody marvelous! My God! Like the chap in the book! So you're from the future? It's really possible?"

My mouth opened and closed. I felt a single raindrop strike my hairline, at just that instant, with memorable conviction. "You *believe* me? Just like that?"

"It makes perfect sense. You're so completely different, so utterly original. Of course. I should have seen it! Second sight, indeed." He laughed. "Tell me everything. Tell me . . . tell me about Mars. Have you been to Mars?"

I took him in: the extravagant mad grin, the eyes wide and glittering in the faint light of a nearby window. "Are you *insane*? You're not, like, freaked out?"

"Well, it's extraordinary, of course. But I should have thought they'd find a way, a hundred years from now . . ." He shook his head. "Have you told anyone else? Where else have you been? Or *when* else, I suppose!" He laughed again. "How absolutely jolly well marvelous!"

I couldn't help it; I began to laugh with him. "Julian Ashford," I gasped, between giggles, "you never cease to amaze me. Here I was, expecting this great dramatic scene, with you running off screaming and me begging and pleading . . . hours of explanation, of trying to prove it to you . . ."

I found myself talking into his chest; he'd thrown his arms about me in sheer exuberance and began swinging me in reckless circles around him.

"Tell me everything, everything! I've so many questions, I don't know where to start. Do you have your machine with you somewhere? Might I see it?"

"I must say," I remarked, trying to extricate myself before I suffocated, "you're taking it much better than I did. I was throwing up at this point."

He drew back and peered at me. "Really, you've the most exceptionally weak digestion. Is that common in the future?"

"Well," I said dryly, "let's just say you have that effect on me. Look, can we go somewhere and talk? I think it's starting to rain again."

"Sweet Kate." He smiled, squeezed my hands, kissed each one. "Divine miraculous Kate, I'd like that more than anything in the world."

We raced back, hand in hand, through the mounting drizzle, to the tall narrow house on rue des Augustins. As Julian fumbled with the latch-key, I thought I saw a dark-coated figure hovering by the street lamp; but then the door thrust open and Julian urged me inside, and the image disappeared.

14.

I knew, even before I became conscious of my own name, that I lay alone in the bed.

"Julian," I said soundlessly, a breath of air, but no reply came.

I struggled upward. The shades had been drawn down, but I could see from the rampant light spilling around the edges that the morning was already far along. He'd let me sleep in. I turned my head to the clock on the nightstand. My brain felt drowsy, drugged; it took me several seconds to decipher the meaning of the numbers and hands. Ten forty-five? That was late, wasn't it? Where was Julian?

Julian. I flopped back into the pillows and closed my eyes. The whole of last night began tumbling through my brain, a waterfall of impressions. The thoroughness of it. His hands and lips on my body, everywhere, wondering and worshipful and urgent; mine on his. The soft glow of his skin in the lamplight. Whispers, laughter, cries of delight; my name on his breath, spoken like a benediction. The unbearable sensation of joining, as though I had finally become whole after a lifetime of emptiness.

Julian, my lover now: gentle, fierce, ardent. Where was he?

I forced my legs to swing downward toward the floor. My muscles felt pulverized. I looked at my nakedness in wonder; had it all really happened? To this humble body? I rose upward and walked, unsteadily, to the bathroom, where a few gutted candles still remained from a midnight picnic in the bathtub. Julian must have cleared the rest of it away this morning.

When I returned, I saw the note on the pillow next to mine. *Yours*, it said simply, in Julian's beautiful scrawl, a line drawn underneath for emphasis. A single word, expressing everything.

I looked around for a robe of some kind, but saw nothing. My clothes still lay scattered disreputably about the floor, so I pulled one of the sheets free from the disarray on the bed and wrapped it around me, under my arms.

I thought I knew where to find him, and went down the stairs to the library to find I was right: there he sat at the desk, laptop open, Bluetooth in his ear, speaking in a low, decisive voice. He felt the whisper of my entry and looked up.

I smiled shyly.

He held out his arm and I went to him, holding up the sheet with one hand. "Geoff, I've got to go," he said, into the headset. "I'll call back later."

"Much later," I said in his other ear.

He pushed back his chair and tossed the Bluetooth on the desk and eased me into his lap. "There you are, my love. I was afraid you'd sleep all day." He nuzzled a kiss into my neck. "How do you feel?"

"Mmm. Like I've been run through a laundry wringer," I said, "but otherwise heavenly."

"A laundry wringer?" He chuckled beneath me. "Aren't those a bit before your time?"

"You're sounding smug this morning, for a man who hardly slept at all."

"Ah, well, that's precisely why I'm smug, darling. That, and I've got the most beautiful woman in the world wrapped in a bedsheet in my arms." He bent his head and kissed my swollen lips tenderly. "Although I believe I was promised all-night sex, and you were quite finished by three o'clock; is that really fair?"

"We could try again tonight."

"At least you delivered handily on the mind-bending part," he continued, sliding downward from my mouth to my throat. "I'm still trying to gather my wits."

"No regrets, then?"

He laughed against my skin and raised his head. "Do you have to ask?" His thumb brushed the corner of my mouth. "Passionate Kate," he murmured.

"I missed you, when I woke up." I covered his thumb with my hand and kissed it. "Did you have to leave?"

He shrugged in the general direction of the laptop. "Things are busy. We've been trying to unwind a few positions."

"Can't Geoff manage it?"

"It's my fund. I can't just abandon things at the moment."

"What will you do when it's all finished up?"

"Since you brought it up," he said, "I was thinking of taking an extended honeymoon."

"Oh." I tucked my forehead into the side of his neck.

His hand began to describe little spirals into the bare skin of my back. "Where would you like to go, my love? Anywhere in the world. Shameless luxury, adoring husband. An offer you can't refuse. So long, of course, as you haven't any ambitions to be a viscountess one day; I'm afraid all that belongs to my cousin Humphrey's miserable heirs now." He tweaked my nose with his other hand. "Lady Chesterton."

"Julian, are you *proposing* to me?"

"I'm an honorable chap, Kate. Having thoroughly debauched you last night, from your eyelashes down to your delectable toes, I thought it was the least I could do. Better late than never, as you Americans say."

"And this is it? No traditional setup? I'm kind of disappointed." I was still blushing too madly to look him in the face; I started drawing tiny hearts into the hollow of his throat, to distract myself.

"Well, in all candor, sweetheart, I haven't bought the ring yet. And I thought you'd try to fob me off in a direct approach; the ambush strategy seems to be far more effective with you."

I made a face. "My parents would freak, you know."

"And here I had the vanity to consider myself a reasonably eligible match."

"It's not that. Mom's already in love with you." I let my hand slip down and fingered the edge of the sheet. "It's just I think they were hoping I would have some sort of career first." I sighed. "I sure showed them, didn't I?"

His thumb trickled along the length of my upper arm and back again. "Have you told them yet? About your job?" he asked, more seriously.

"I e-mailed them." I glanced at the desktop computer, sitting behind his laptop, and frowned. I'd wanted to forget all my real-world troubles for a little longer. "I wonder if they've read it yet." I looked back at Julian. "And don't think you can just rescue me from the wreckage, Prince Charming, and sweep me away to your fairy castle."

"Why not? Why bother with that bloody old firm? Or the markets at all? We'll find something else to do. A world awaits us. Perfect freedom."

"You were swearing revenge the other day."

"Oh, I still want revenge," he said grimly. He nodded at the computer. "Yesterday I instructed Geoff to cut off all our relationships with Sterling Bates—trading, banking, clearing. And I put in a call to my lawyer and explained things briefly; we're going to conference him at one o'clock, you and I."

I straightened. "What? I thought I told you not to do that!"

"He won't initiate anything without your instructions. It's only to review your options. Lay the case in front of him." His voice softened. "Darling, you know you won't be happy until it's cleared up. And my sole object in life now, Kate, is your happiness."

"Lawyers are expensive," I said, trying to ignore the spreading glow those last words gave me.

"Kate, Kate. You have lovely principles, darling, and I admire them extremely. But this is absurd. How can there be any question of financial accounts between us, after last night?"

"*Especially* after last night! It's like taking your money in exchange for . . . *that*. As though it gives me some kind of *demand* on you!"

"*Demand* on me?" He looked astonished. "My God, Kate, of course you have a *demand* on me. On all of me. You seem to have some"—he shook his head—"*demented* notion that love exists in some sort of higher plane, free of the muck and mire of human obligation."

"It does," I said. "It should."

"Bollocks. That's just words, and any man who thinks that, who tells you he loves you with that in mind, is nothing more than a vile seducer." His voice pitched low and intense. "Darling, look at me. When *I* tell you I love you, it means this: That I am your servant. That these two hands"—he held them up before me, and then cupped my face—"labor for you alone. That you have a *demand* on me, an eternal one, which has everything to do with the incalculable favor, the immeasurable *honor*, you granted me last night, in taking me into your heart and your bed."

I couldn't say anything for a moment. His eyes, his wide green-blue eyes, illuminated into brilliancy by the shaft of sunlight tumbling through the window, held me dangling in midair, ready to splinter. "Well, technically," I whispered at last, "it was *your* bed, you know."

He shook his head. "*Our* bed. Understand that, Kate. Everything I have, everything I am, is yours. Ah, don't cry, sweetheart."

"I'll try," I said, but a tear rolled out of each eye anyway, and he brushed them away with his thumbs.

"Happy ones, I hope," he said.

I nodded. "It frightens me, though. How you can be so certain."

"Aren't you?"

"Yes. *Yes!* I wish I knew how to tell you, how to express it." I reached out and traced the round velvet curve of his bottom lip with my forefinger. "So very, perfectly certain."

"Then why won't you allow it of me?"

"Because . . . I don't know . . . because I didn't know men thought that way. Because I can't imagine myself worthy of you, of that beautiful soul of yours."

"Hmm," he said meditatively. His thumbs brushed again along my cheekbones.

"What is it?"

"I am reminded," he said, "that, in earlier years, my beloved may have met with a dodgy inconstant character or two. Some damned *fools*"—he almost hissed the word—"who didn't know how to value her. Who perhaps broke that sweet heart I prize so dearly."

"No." I aimed my gaze at his chin. "No. Not really. They never . . . I mean, it was never a question of love or anything. I just . . . I didn't read the rulebook before playing the game. My bad."

"I see." He tucked my hair behind one ear, laid the waves gently along the line of my back. "Kate. *Please* look at me, sweetheart. Don't be shy of me. Let me see your eyes."

I dragged them upward.

"Beautiful," he said, smiling mildly. "Now, since it apparently falls to me to restore my Kate's faith in male fidelity, tell me: How would I go about that? How would an old-fashioned chap like me convince a cynical modern girl that he can be trusted with her love?"

"Julian." I sighed, linked my hands behind his neck. "I can't even *think* straight when you look at me like that. *Talk* to me like that."

"Damned filthy blackguards," he muttered, "treating *my* Kate like . . ."

"Shh." I put one finger on his lips. "Okay, I'm going to try to express myself here. Which does not come as easily to me as it does to you, so bear with me."

He kissed my finger and captured it in his hand. "Take your time."

I studied the top button of his shirt. "All right. First of all, last night was the most *beautiful* of my life." I felt my face growing hot, but plunged on anyway, because he deserved whatever eloquence I could muster at the moment. "Also the most pleasurable, by which I mean complete freaking *ecstasy*, as you maybe noticed, so I think we can safely say any lingering bad memories from my past have been thoroughly erased. Truly a blank slate. And finally," I said, lifting my eyes at last, because he deserved that too, "I have never felt this way about anybody, Julian, not ever. Not even remotely close. You stand so . . . so *high* above any man I've ever met, so honorable and brilliant and charming and . . . and intense—no, please listen—and funny and *sexy*, oh my God, the most amazing lover, that picnic, how did you *learn* all that . . . I've run out of words, and there's so much more I adore about you. I can't . . . I tried, last night . . . I hope I *showed* you how much. When . . . when . . ." I felt the tears well up again, damn it, at the sight of his earnest enraptured face. "I'm sorry. I'm terrible at this. But I have to say it anyway." My voice reduced to a sandpaper whisper; I put my hands on his chest, just below his collarbone, securing myself, and pushed out the words in a rush. "When we . . . that moment, Julian, when we first came together, fitting each other so perfectly . . . well, that was . . ." *Say it, trust him.* ". . . that was *sacred* to me. I want you to know that. And I hope . . . that maybe . . . it meant the same to you."

His glittering eyes studied me for some time, and then with excruciating slowness he brought my face to his and kissed me, each movement of his lips so deliberate it left a wholly separate place in my memory.

I struggled upward, on my knees in the wide deep chair, straddling him; I put my hands around the back of his head and deepened the kiss, frantic for him, for every possible point of physical contact between us. The sheet slipped downward, and suddenly his need was as passionate as mine; we tumbled to the floor, past reason.

"TELL ME," HE SAID, some time later, trailing his fingers through my hair, "about this pill of yours."

I cleared my throat. "Well, my dear sir, it is ingested orally, once daily, during the four weeks of a human female's reproductive cycle . . ."

"Darling, I'm not a complete caveman. I have some idea of how it works. But would it be too indelicate to ask *why* you were already taking it? When . . ." He stopped.

"When I wasn't having any sex?" I twisted in his arms and rested my chin in my hands on the broad plane of his naked chest. We were lying together on the library rug, a plush thick Oriental weave, no doubt priceless. The white sheet coiled around us in an elaborate knot. Julian was staring up at the ceiling, a scarlet blush coloring his cheeks: whether from our recent vigorous exercise or general male embarrassment, I wasn't quite sure. "Well, without getting into the icky details, it sort of smooths out the rough edges of that part of my life. Especially since I travel a lot for work. Or did."

"I see." His eyes squinted shut. Menstruation evidently wasn't high on his list of conversation topics, for some reason. "And it's reliable? Effective?"

"Don't worry. Over ninety-nine percent, when taken as directed."

"Which means?"

"Every morning, same time, never miss a day. Oh, crap!" I cried, jumping up. "Just a minute." My legs tangled in the sheet, tripping me up as I staggered out of the library and raced up the stairs to my travel kit in the bathroom.

He was there in the bedroom when I came out. "It's all right, isn't it?" he asked anxiously.

"Fine. Only an hour off from yesterday." I tilted my head. He'd put his chinos back on, but not his shirt; obviously he'd come up in a hurry. "Um, relax. It's okay. Not pregnant."

"You're sure?"

"A little jumpy, aren't we?" I folded my arms. "Not that I want a baby just now, either, but it's not like the *world* coming to an end. You did just vow eternal love, right?"

"I'm sorry." His lips aimed a smile at me; he sat down on the bed and reached out his arm to draw me in between his legs. "I haven't any experience with these things. It's just I understand you modern women aren't at all eager for babies straightaway, and I should hate to cause you any distress."

"I like babies." I smiled. "Someday."

"Mine, perhaps?" His eyebrow arched.

"Julian. Of *course* yours. *You*," I said, my brain leaving that thought behind, "are about the most beautiful man ever created. Look at you." I ran my fingers admiringly along the neat taut line of his shoulders.

He rolled his eyes. "Your experience is clearly limited, my love, for which I'm very thankful. And now I think I'd better head back downstairs, before these"—he kissed each breast worshipfully—"lure me in again."

"Oh, all right." I ruffled his hair, not quite able to tell him I was feeling a bit saddle-sore myself. "I should probably shower and dress, anyway. I'll be downstairs to make some lunch in a bit. And make the bed, too, I guess," I added, with a wistful glance at the tangle of linens.

"I could help with that," he offered, looking guilty.

"Actually, Julian," I said, over my shoulder, as I walked back into the bathroom, "that would probably be counterproductive."

I BROUGHT MY SANDWICH into the library so I could check my e-mail on the desktop computer. Julian was outside at the moment, turkey and Swiss in hand, barking into his headset, and I thought I'd take my chance while I could get it.

The inbox was full today. My parents had weighed in, full of indignation and concern over the firing, with oddly nothing to say about my sojourn with Julian; Michelle and Samantha, exactly the opposite. I replied to each one, as noncommittal as possible. What could I really tell them, after all? I glanced out the library window, which looked over the garden, and smiled at the sight of Julian pacing along the grass, snatching bites of his sandwich, talking apparently into the air.

And suddenly, without warning, I saw it. Saw him pacing, instead, along the duckboard of a muddy trench, wearing a belted khaki uniform and puttees, his cap pulled down low on his forehead, German shells screaming overhead. So terribly, piercingly real; I thought I could taste his very death in my mouth. The breath fled my body, leaving a hollow vacuum inside me.

Then it all shifted back to normal, and Julian stood in the warm May sunshine, surrounded by green meadow grass and the first wildflowers of summer. Safe. Here. Now. *Mine.*

I turned back to the computer, shaking. A new message had appeared at the top of my inbox. It was from Charlie, his personal e-mail account.

> Hey dude, where are you? Tried your apt about fifty times, just got your freaky roommate. What is with that poor bitch? Anyway things are jumping here, wild rumors flying. I checked the network files and saw nothing weird, but did some bitching with the traders over a few beers last night and found out Alicia is doing the dirty with some guy in Compliance. Sounds fishy to me, no way she's found true love with the back office. NOT ONLY THAT. I found out who your alleged counterparty is supposed to be. Southfield. So go ask your new boyfriend what's up. Will try to get more. This is some fucked-up shit.

I stared at the screen for a moment, reading the message over a few times. I looked out the window again. I couldn't see Julian anymore, and an instant later I heard the French door in the kitchen open and close. "Kate?" he called.

"In the library," I called back.

"We've got that call with my lawyer in about fifteen minutes. What is it?" he asked, seeing the look on my face.

"Um, nothing. I mean, something. I don't know. It's kind of weird." He gave me a quizzical look. "Just got an e-mail from Charlie, as a matter of fact. He—I don't know, it might not be true, traders are so full of it . . ."

"What *is* it, Kate?"

202 / BEATRIZ WILLIAMS

"Well, I guess they're saying the counterparty, I mean the supposed counterparty in my so-called information exchange, was Southfield."

"*My* firm? Oh, that's rot," he said. "None of my traders would think of doing that. I'd have their heads, even if it weren't you on the other end."

"It *wasn't* me."

"You know what I mean."

The phone rang in the kitchen. "That's odd," Julian said, starting out the doorway. "I assumed he would call my cell number."

I followed him into the hall and down to the kitchen. He picked it up. "Daniel?" he asked. "I thought you . . ." Silence. I folded my arms and leaned against the doorway, watching Julian's face turn from vague irritation, to surprise, to concern.

"I see," he said. "No warning at all? . . . Yes, odd, certainly . . . Yes, I'd be happy to. May I have your number? Just a moment, please." He motioned to me; I leapt for the notepad and pen and handed them to him. "Yes . . . yes . . . Thanks very much . . . If I might ask, how did you find this number? Ah, I see . . . yes, very good. Good-bye, then."

He stood for a moment, staring down at the numbers scribbled on the notepad, tapping the pen against them.

"Well?" I asked. "What was that all about?"

"Nothing, really," he said, not looking up.

"I thought you were finished with keeping things from me."

He looked up. "What's that?"

"Look," I said, "if it's really nothing, fine. I trust you. But if it's something, do you mind telling me? Because I've gotten pretty *involved* at this point. If there's something wrong in your life, I'd like to know about it. Maybe even help. If that's okay with you."

"Forgive me, sweetheart. Of course I trust you. It's just I'm frankly so used to secrecy . . ." He shook his head. "I don't quite know where to start."

"Does it have to do with the reason we're here? The disgruntled investors? The meetings in Boston?"

"Ah. Yes. You've a good memory."

"Julian, I can put a few things together." I frowned at him, doing just that. "Your meetings were at Harvard, weren't they? But not the endowment fund. The professor, right? The one who wrote your biography. Hollander. He knows all about you, doesn't he? So this is all starting to make sense. You go to visit him, and come out in a panic . . ."

He glared at me. "I don't panic, Kate. I never panic. I only act on information."

"So I'm right?"

"You're too bloody clever, is what you are." He ran an exasperated hand through his hair and tossed the pen onto the counter. "All right, then. Here it is. I came across Hollander's book in, oh, ninety-seven or ninety-eight, in a bookstore in Park Slope. I was at rather an all-time low at that point; quite in despair. I'd no one to talk to. I'd found a quiet job in the Goldman back office, kept my head down, saw nobody, was ready to leap off the Brooklyn Bridge."

I made a little sound at the back of my throat. I wanted to go to him, to comfort him, but he'd spoken so matter-of-factly, without any emotion at all, and I couldn't quite bridge the distance. He was in full stiff-upper-lip mode.

"So I thought I'd take a chance. I sent him an e-mail, telling him I'd read his book, was terribly interested in the subject, could we have a meeting. His reply arrived almost immediately. I took a day's leave from work and flew up to see him." Julian turned around and leaned back against the kitchen counter, staring at the floor. "He knew who I was at once, of course. He was astonished, delighted. I suppose any historian would feel that way, to see his subject walk in through his office door one morning. He accepted the fact of my existence with astonishing sangfroid; my world had always seemed so real, it was only later that the significance of it struck him at all."

"Yeah, I've had a few professors like that." I tried to smile.

"So he helped me. We talked a great deal, became friends. I nearly moved up to Boston, just for the company, but I was also becoming more interested in my work at Goldman. The slippery slope that eventually led down to starting up Southfield. In any case, he's kept my secret, and in return I've helped him with his work, offering the contents of my memory for his examination. In the past few years things have been perhaps a touch less warm. He wasn't pleased about Southfield. Ruddy old Marxist," he said, with an affectionate little smile.

"So what happened?" I asked. "You met with him at Christmas, and then cut me off. You met with him two days ago, and fled here. And now this phone call. So I'm guessing the problem is not with some disgruntled Southfield investor, right? A wee white lie?"

He flinched. "I hated telling you that."

"Sorry. I didn't mean to push any buttons. I know you gentlemanly types have your codes." I took a few steps toward him and touched his elbow. "In fact, they're beginning to grow on me."

His arm reached around me. "I was only trying to protect you," he said softly.

"I know. I'm not mad." I slipped my arms about his waist, felt the yield of his flesh, accepting me. "So tell me what happened at Christmas."

His hand began to stroke my hair. "Someone had approached him about me, about the historical Julian Ashford. He'd read the biography, was particularly curious about Ashford's final days, could he have a look at the primary materials?"

"What primary materials?"

"Oh, letters. My service notebook, that sort of thing. Hollander had facsimiles of all of them, from the current Ashfords. Hollander refused the request, of course, not knowing the chap from Adam. That was the day you came to see me at the house."

"When you had that phone call." I nodded against the side of his chest.

"So Hollander tried to fob him off, and the chap took a different tack. Said he'd heard about this Laurence chap at Southfield, saw his picture in the *Times*, didn't Hollander think he had a strong resemblance to Ashford?"

"Do you mean he *knows?*"

"I don't know. He pressed Hollander quite hard. Offered him money, and then made a threat or two. He had . . . he had an odd piece of information he'd come across. A bit of trivia, about my last days in France, which we're not sure how he could possibly know. But he did. It was enough to send Hollander dialing my number the instant he'd hung up the phone. He had the impression, you see, that this anonymous chap was an interested party."

"I'm not sure I follow you."

I felt the heave of his sigh. "Kate, there are any number of people who have, quite legally and properly, benefited from my presumed death. The current Lord Chesterton, God bless him. Various political characters, for more complicated reasons." He paused. "Some would argue, if they didn't know any better, that Flora Hamilton's children might never have been born, if I'd lived through the war. Which is rubbish."

"Her children?"

"She married soon after the war. Three children; one of them began in politics; you'll know his name. Bit of a rabble-rouser. His son's carried on the family tradition."

"And all these people would be unhappy to find you alive today?"

"It hardly seems credible, does it? No one could possibly believe it's really Julian Ashford, vintage 1895. But we don't know what else to think. People hear things; they react irrationally. That's what I'm afraid of." I felt his face burrow into my hair. "That someone might threaten you, because of me."

"Why on earth would someone do that?"

"To make sure I don't reveal myself, for one thing."

"But you'd never do that."

"And how could this mysterious fellow of ours be certain of such a thing?"

I thought this over. "Do you think he's the one who sent me the book?"

"Possibly," Julian said, in an even tone. "I'd certainly like to find out. Do you still have the packaging?"

"Yes. It came from a bookstore in Rhode Island. I forget the name. It's upstairs, in my bag."

"Then let's ring them up." He paused, and his tone slipped lower. "Or visit. We could sail over in my boat. There's a lovely hotel in Newport. Owner's a client of ours."

"Mmm." I fingered his shirt. "But what's the update today? The phone call?"

"I met with him, with Hollander, two days ago, as you know. His offices had been ransacked, and a copy of the *Post* left on his desk, with that Page Six item folded back."

"Oh my God," I said. My brain pivoted dizzily around this piece of information. I glanced at the French doors leading to the garden, almost expecting to see some menacing face pressed against the glass.

"Yes. Now do you understand why I wanted you up here? It's not so far-fetched as you think. Clearly the man's serious. Knows something, or thinks he knows."

"But what about security? How did this guy get in? Weren't there cameras?"

He shrugged. "Hollander left the door unlocked, of course. Stepped out to deliver a lecture. He says the cameras showed nothing useful, just the usual scrum of students entering and leaving the building. And now that phone call comes in"—he nodded at the telephone—"from a colleague of Hollander's. Apparently the old chap's gone missing."

"Missing!"

"Well, not missing exactly. He sent an e-mail to this colleague, saying he'd gone on an unexpected research trip, which isn't unusual for him; but he left my name and this number, which *was* odd. So the colleague, quite properly, wanted to know what's going on. So should I, for that matter."

"You don't . . . I mean, are we in *danger*?" I only just got the word out.

His other arm came up, compressing me. His voice was vehement. "Of course not. Nobody knows about this house, other than Geoff. I've taken the greatest pains to keep it secret; the deed's in the name of an obscure holding company of ours. The perimeter's alarmed, and the house itself. You're perfectly safe here, darling, I promise. I shan't let anyone touch you."

"Hollander has the number. The area code . . ."

"It's unlisted. Even if our menacing fellow gets hold of it, he can't trace us easily. Look, Hollander's done this before, taken himself off without a word, all quite routine. You mustn't worry. I'll try his cell after the conference with my lawyer. Speaking of which"—he frowned, peeling his arm away for a look at his watch—"where is the chap?"

As if in response, Julian's cell phone rang.

"Chin up, darling," he said, and picked up the phone. "Laurence here. Yes, Daniel? Yes, thanks for calling. Hold on a minute; we're going into the library. I'll put you on the speaker."

Julian motioned me forward, and I led the way into the library, feeling numb. He had a conference phone on a tripod table near the window; he rummaged through his desk drawer for a cord and hooked up his Black-Berry. "Daniel?" he asked, into the speaker.

"Right here," came the lawyer's voice, and Julian pulled a chair over for me. "How's the country air, Laurence?"

"Fine, fine. I've got Miss Wilson here, Daniel."

"Ms. Wilson. Hello. Daniel Newton. I understand you've been thrown to the wolves by those assholes at Sterling Bates."

"Um, it's Kate. Yes, I guess that's about it," I said. A mass persisted at the back of my head, heavy and menacing. I glanced upward at Julian, settling himself with swift competent movements into the chair next to me, straddling it backward, running a hand through the dark wheat of his hair. I couldn't imagine anyone piercing that resolve, deflecting the juggernaut force of him.

"Watch your language, Daniel," Julian warned. "She's got a bit more breeding than those women *you* consort with."

A large laugh exploded from the conference phone. "Ha, ha, ha!" Daniel barked, genuine unself-conscious *ha*'s, each one individually pronounced. "Sounds like you've met your match at last, Laurence. Ha, ha, ha. So, Kate. Tell me what happened. I'm itching for a fight with these . . . these fine gentlemen at your venerable firm. Ex-firm."

I smiled. I found myself liking Daniel Newton. I imagined him at his desk in Manhattan, as a large full-bellied bear of a man, with a printed silk handkerchief in his breast pocket and an old-fashioned gold clip securing his tie to his handmade shirt. The weight in my brain began to ease. "Well, I'll tell you what happened on my end, Daniel," I said, "though I can't tell you what happened on theirs, since they weren't exactly forthcoming."

"Better and better," he said.

I told him what I could, from the earliest fracas with Alicia over the ChemoDerma deal, to her strange behavior over the following months, to the laptop incident, to the rumors about trading volume with Southfield, to the actual firing. I threw in what Charlie had learned for good measure. Daniel listened as only a lawyer could: intently and without interruption, except to ask a few clarifying questions.

"Well, Kate," he said, "if that's everything, I think we've got a pretty good fu . . . a pretty good case here. I'd recommend we start by filing a complaint, demanding to see your personnel records, and more specifically the evidence they've got against you. It's an absolute freaking crime you weren't allowed to see it in the meeting, but they were counting on your inexperience, I guess. You said you signed something? What was it?"

"Yes, I did," I said, "but I don't really know exactly what it said. Some kind of release. I know, I know, it was stupid. Go ahead and give me the lawyer lecture. But I was too mad to care at that point, and they were making these threats, they weren't going to let me leave the room and I just wanted to get out of there . . ."

"Please understand, Daniel," Julian broke in, with a voice so cold and deadly I nearly jumped from my chair, "I want these bastards hung out to dry. I want *prosecutions*."

"Oh, I'm just as pissed as you are," Daniel said. "But it's up to Kate, right?"

"Let's take it slow, okay?" I begged. "I have some friends asking a few questions around work. I'd kind of like to see how that pans out before going all legal on them."

There was a little silence from the speaker. "Well, Kate, I'll hold off a bit if you like. But we can't wait too long. And just looking over my notes, I have a pretty good guess about what happened. Clearly this Boxer woman was using Kate's e-mail to send information to one of your guys, Laurence . . ."

"Wait just a moment, Daniel . . ."

". . . knowing Kate's already been linked to you," Daniel went on, disregarding him. "I'm assuming, Kate, this wasn't the first time you left your laptop unattended?"

"No," I said. "I mean, I had no reason to think . . ."

"You're a nice girl, Kate," he said brusquely, "so you never even dreamed anyone would fu . . . would screw with your e-mail, right? Probably she created another account, just to make sure you wouldn't find the evidence if you looked in your Sent file. That's what I'm guessing. Shame you had to surrender the laptop. She was probably counting on that. Anyway, that explains the increased trading volumes going to Sterling Bates."

"Damn it all," Julian burst out. "I can't believe one of my traders would do that."

"Happens all the time. Every guy has his weak spot, and this Boxer feline is just one of those who knows how to find 'em. Anyway, it's actually good news. Means that Southfield has a record of what went on. We may be able to track something down from that. So *your* homework, Laurence, is to find out which of your guys had contact with Boxer. Thinking it was Kate, here, mind you."

"Bloody hell," Julian said, sitting back in his chair and staring at me.

"Kate," Daniel continued, "I'll get that complaint prepared, so it's ready to go when you're ready to strike."

"Yes. That's fine. Thank you, Daniel."

"Pleasure. Don't worry, hon. We'll get these ass . . . these fine folks for you. Laurence? That all?"

"That's all, Daniel. Thanks very much." Julian leaned forward and punched the off button. He looked back at me.

"Don't say you're sorry," I said. "It's got nothing to do with you."

"Kate, it was one of my traders. My God!" He jumped up from his chair and paced across the floor. "I'm going to call up Geoff straightaway . . ."

I cleared my throat. "I don't mean to overstep here . . ."

He turned around. "I've already told you, Kate. It's not possible. Say what you're thinking."

"Well, I don't know Geoff as well as you do. He has your trust, so I'm sure he's a good guy. Just the outsider's perspective here. Squash it if it's way off base. But maybe you should suspect everyone, just as a precaution?"

He fixed me with a penetrating stare. "Are you saying *Geoff* might be the mole?"

"No! I'm not saying anything. Like I said, I don't know him. You do. But maybe we should eliminate him first of all. In fact, let's do it right now, so you can call him up and get started."

Julian didn't reply at first. He stood, arms folded, looking out the window at the back garden, with his eyebrows drawn in firm and close. The pale diffuse light floated through the glass against his face, gilding it like an angel's.

"What is it?" I prodded.

"I suppose I'm trying to work out how to explain something to you." He tapped one finger against his forearm.

"Explain what?"

"Why it can't be Geoff who did this. Look, Kate, do you remember the man in the taxi, on Park Avenue? The one who recognized me?"

"Yes," I said. It was one of those details I'd pushed to the back of my mind, knowing it was significant somehow, but not having the mind space to deal with it at the moment. "Are you trying to say you *knew* him? That he's, like, *one of you?*"

"It appears so," he said, and turned back to face me. "In fact, it *is* so."

"There's *others?*" I felt a wave of queasiness cross my body. "But I thought you said you were *alone*, you had nobody!"

"I thought I was," he said, "and then I was sitting on the subway one morning in 1998 and found myself staring into the face of one Geoffrey Warwick."

"Geoff?"

"He was one of my lieutenants in France. One of my friends at Cambridge. And according to the British National Archive, he was killed on the first day of the Somme, in July 1916."

15.

I jumped up from my chair. "Are you saying *Geoff*'s from your time, too? *Geoff*?" I tried to bring up his face, his voice. I'd only seen him twice. "But he's American, isn't he? He *sounded* American."

Julian leaned back against one of the built-in bookshelves surrounding the window frame. "Geoff adjusted to the change a little more quickly than I did," he said. "He took it as a God-given deliverance, and made an early decision to make the most of things. He hadn't left much of worth behind him, you see: parents both dead, no strong ties. The papers he'd been given identified him as an American, so he took on an accent, moved here, and began working as an investment analyst."

"Why Wall Street?" I asked.

"His father was a City stockbroker; he was supposed to take over the business."

"Oh." I swallowed, trying to take it all in. "But that's amazing! How did it all happen? It's like you're ghosts or something. Or someone's zapping you with a time machine. And you've never found out where all this is coming from?"

"No. Never. Well, Geoff's never really looked. He likes his life here. He brought me into the firm he worked for, and then encouraged me to start Southfield after I'd had some success managing portfolios. He met Carla around the same time, married her . . ."

"Does *she* know?" Somehow it was hard to imagine the immaculate Mrs. Warwick in possession of that kind of information.

"Carla?" Julian laughed. "No."

"How does he keep it from her? Surely she'd have noticed something being a bit off, here and there, over the years. No family, no childhood friends. Except you."

He shrugged. "She's not the most curious woman."

"Wow," I said. "Wow."

"Are you all right?"

"Maybe I should sit down." I lowered myself cautiously onto the sofa. Julian crossed the room and had his arm around me by the time I'd hit the seat cushion.

"I'm sorry. All these shocks, all at once."

"No! I mean, I should be used to it by now. And don't say you're sorry. My God, I'm *glad* you weren't alone, all this time. It's just so amazing, that's all. A whole First World War reunion going on in New York City, and no one knows." I shook my head. "So who was that man on Park Avenue, then?"

He laughed dryly. "Andrew Paulson. Poor chap, though of course he ought to have known better than to be so indiscreet. I've put Geoff to work, tracking him down."

"And what will you do when you find him?"

"Help him out, of course. If he needs it. A job at the firm, something like that. Or simply commiseration." He spoke offhandedly, but I could discern the thread of emotion in his voice.

"Who was he?" I asked, lacing my fingers into his.

"Oh, an old rock, Paulson. One of my sergeants when I was just starting out with a second lieutenant's commission. Taught me a thing or two about keeping my head down and so on." His voice drifted off, and I sat there for a moment, letting him recollect in silence, feeling his breath warm my hair. "So you see, beloved"—he gathered himself at last and went on—"I trust Geoffrey Warwick quite without reserve."

I gave his hand a reassuring squeeze. "All right. Geoff's off the suspect list. So what do we do next?"

"*I,*" he said, with just the faintest emphasis on the word, "am going to have a long conversation with Geoff, go over the trading records with him, narrow the list. It shouldn't be too difficult."

I sighed resignedly. "I guess that means you'll be back in the city tomorrow."

"I'm afraid so."

"How long will you be gone?"

"Just the day, I promise. I shan't leave you alone overnight, not with all this unresolved. Which reminds me." He rose up from the sofa to approach his desk. His laptop bag was propped up next to it, on the floor. He picked it up and rummaged through. "I brought this back for you," he said, and tossed me a box. "So you can keep in touch when I'm away."

I looked at the box, and then up at him. "A BlackBerry?" I cried in delight.

"Yours to keep."

"You won't ask for it back, if things don't work out?" I teased, opening the flap.

"Does that mean you're actually accepting it?"

"Here's the deal. I'll let it pass, as long as the monthly bill goes to me."

He shook his head sadly. "I see my eloquent words of this morning had no effect on you whatsoever."

I pulled the BlackBerry from its box. "The truth is, I'm so glad to have one back, I'd take it from Alicia Boxer herself, if she offered."

"Oh, thanks bloody much."

"There's a reason they call it the CrackBerry." I stroked it lovingly against my cheek. "Did you have it hooked up already?"

"Yes, I bloody did. And if that's all the thanks I'm getting . . ."

I bounded over to him in two long strides and flung my arms about his neck. "Darling, thoughtful Julian. Thank you so, so much." I kissed him with abandon, and found myself hoisted up by the bottom with my legs dangling around his hips. I pulled back and smiled. "Is that better?"

"Remind me," he murmured, "to bring you gifts more often."

"Remind me not to let you."

. . .

I KNEW IT WAS A DREAM, a nightmare, but still I couldn't break free into consciousness. I kicked upward toward the surface, thrusting with all my might, until my lungs burst with a scream that wouldn't release. Someone called to me: distant, urgent.

And then I emerged, sweating, with Julian's arms around me and his voice murmuring in my ear. "Sweetheart, wake up. Kate, it's all right."

I turned blindly into his chest. "You're here," I said, between heaving gasps of air. "You're still here."

"Of course I'm here. Shh. Of course I'm here."

He held me against his body, enfolding me with himself, and gradually the panic died down. I concentrated on breathing slowly, on grasping at the solid physical details around me, anchoring me to reality: the sheets, the faint glow from the nightlight, the cool air entering my nose. Julian's skin pressed into mine.

"Better?" he asked, after a minute.

"Yes," I said.

A low chuckle rumbled from his throat. "Your first nightmare already. Is it all so very dreadful?"

I snorted into his chest. "Terrible. A severe case of endorphin overload. I may not live through the night."

"Rubbish," he said. "*My* endorphins are jolly well singing in my ears, and I'm not moaning on about it."

"Oh, I don't know." I snaked my hand along his side and administered a sharp tickle. "I definitely heard moaning."

"Look here. *Stop* that. Stop it, I say. *Kate!*" He doubled over and tried to roll away without falling off the bed.

I began laughing. "Oh my God. You're *ticklish*. Come back here."

"I am *not* . . . Kate, you're *rubbish* . . . stop that *at once*!" His frantic hands manacled mine at last; he flipped me onto my back and held my wrists above my head. "Minx," he muttered, kissing me. "You'll pay for that."

"You're just . . . *full* of lovely . . . secrets . . . aren't you?" I giggled around his kisses.

"Mmm." His body began to transform, to mold itself to mine; his lips edged downward, damp and scorching, along my throat and breasts. He drawled: "But not nearly as many as you, sweetheart."

What is it, really, that makes a man a good lover? *Beloved, I'll do my best, but I'm rather a novice at all this,* he'd said last night, fumbling with the hooks of my bra, and yet he'd gone on as if he possessed the secret map to my body: discovering hidden points of sensitivity I never knew existed, touching my flesh with a preternatural sensual attunement, delivering himself to me with every stroke. He allowed no hiding under sheets, no closed eyes, no defense whatsoever. It was like falling backward into a pit of extraordinary depth, trusting him to catch me; the most exquisite, excruciating vulnerability, made bearable only by the certainty that he felt it, too.

We lay afterward in tranquility, in wordless communion, hardly able to move; I on my side, one leg buried between his, studying the pattern our woven fingers made against his chest. I could feel his other hand tangle through my hair. His flushed skin seemed to melt downward through mine, layer by layer. "So," I heard myself say, dreamlike, "are you absolutely sure you haven't had any lovers in twelve years?"

"Let me think a moment." A dramatic pause, and then: "Yes. Yes, quite sure."

"Hmm."

"Kate!" His head tilted upward. "You're *doubting* me?"

"I'm just saying, you seem to know your way around. How to please me."

"Well, for heaven's sake, I *want* to please you. I want to maintain you in a state of perfect drunken bliss. A dizzy hormonal stupor. Anything at all, you see, to entice you to soldier on with a lonely benighted chap who can't"—he kissed the tip of my nose—"*quite* seem to see his way without you anymore."

"Idiot." I curled a lock of his hair tenderly around my finger.

He drew his hand along the curve of my waist, his smile deepening as he went. "Besides, it seems to me, since *my* pleasure is more or less a foregone conclusion, the main object of the exercise ought to be *your* pleasure."

"Hmm. I never thought of it that way."

"A rather elusive creature, I've heard. Fascinating sort of quarry."

"Wait a minute. You're *hunting down* my orgasms?"

His laughter burst out like a rifle salute. "Kate. You damned magnificent creature." He rolled onto his back, bringing me with him. "Yes, my darling. That's exactly what I'd like to do, on and on until the end of my life."

"Well, you're off to a flying start, I have to admit."

He said nothing to that, only tucked my hair behind one ear with a shadowed smile. His eyes had lost all color in the dimness, depthless and unreadable. "So do you mind telling me about it?" he asked at last. "Your dream?"

I folded my arms across his chest and rested my chin. "It's stupid. Just an anxiety dream. I get them every so often. Kind of ridiculous, since you're the war hero; I should be soothing away *your* nightmares."

"What are you anxious about?"

"I don't know. I usually only have them before a big meeting, some sort of performance." I touched his lower lip. "I had one the night before we met."

"You were nervous?"

"Oh my God. Was I *nervous*? Do you have any idea how intimidating you are?"

"I am? I thought I was rather a nice chap, actually."

I shook my head, incredulous, and slid back down to rest against his side. "Julian, you have kind of a hard-ass reputation, in a business setting. No offense."

"Oh." I could hear the bafflement in his voice. "And I'm still giving you anxiety dreams?"

"I don't know. Maybe. It's my subconscious, remember?"

"So I've managed to convince your conscious mind, but your subconscious still thinks I'm a bounder?"

I laughed. "Hold on. *I'm* the overanalyzer in this relationship, okay? Look, it's no big deal." I closed my eyes, forcing out the details. "I think it was like the one I had the night before our meeting. I can't really recall it exactly. Just kind of panicky, trying to explain something to someone. Someone dear to me. You, maybe? And that person, that man, drifting slowly away from me, not understanding, and the panic sort of paralyzing me."

"Explain what, exactly?"

"I don't know. Something important. Something vital. Life or death." I opened my eyes to Julian's face, taut and intent beneath the shadows, and tried to push away the feeling of dread that insinuated itself into my brain as I spoke. "But it's like we're speaking two different languages, and the harder I try, the further away he floats. Bizarre, huh?"

He tucked my head under his chin and began to stroke my hair. "Kate," he said hoarsely, "Kate."

"Don't," I said, into the hollow of his throat. "It's just my silly neurotic brain. Nothing to do with you. I *trust* you."

He said nothing for a long time, only went on caressing my hair: long regular strokes to the very tips, letting the strands slip away from his fingertips to rest on my back and shoulders. I let my eyelids sink downward, savoring the tickle-soft sensation. Eventually I felt his voice stir the air above my head. "I won't drift away, Kate. I won't *fail* you." He said it fiercely, as if he were trying to convince himself.

"I know that," I said, more to comfort him than myself, and stretched luxuriously against the solid mass of his body. "You're so hard on yourself." I yawned. I was beginning to feel drowsy again, despite the clinging uneasiness.

"Am I?"

"Way too hard." I put my arm across his chest and closed my eyes. "I don't need you to be perfect, you know. I just need you to be *you*. To be"—my brain was beginning to float—"to be mine."

He made a noise of some kind; I couldn't quite tell whether it was a chuckle or a groan. "Yours always, darling. Now go to sleep. No more nightmares. You're safe, now. I'm here," he said somewhere near my ear. It was the last thing I heard before drifting off, hoping sleep would dissolve the knot of foreboding in my belly.

HE WASN'T THERE, THOUGH, when I woke up. My new BlackBerry sat on the pillow in his place, with an e-mail at the top of my inbox.

> Beloved, I must be mad, to tear myself from your side like this. Sleep late and enjoy yourself. I left the Rover for you. Go find some alluring frock and meet me at the Lyme Inn at 8pm. XX

16.

[via e-mail]

Me: I thought of a whole list of questions for you while I was using up all the hot water in the shower.

Julian: A bewitching image, that.

Me: So join me next time. First question: what do you miss most? Besides family and friends, I mean.

Julian: Foxhunting.

Me: Seriously?

Julian: Yes.

Me: You murderer. The poor fox.

Julian: The fox is a rural menace. You modern city-dwellers have the most idiotic romantic notions about wildlife.

Me: Were you good at it?

Julian: Yes.

Me: Will you teach me how to ride?

Julian: If you're a very, very good girl.

Me: I can be very good. Second question: Did you wear spats?

Julian: On occasion.

Me: What exactly are spats, anyway?

Julian: http://en.wikipedia.org/wiki/Spats

Me: LOL I would so pay to see you in those.

Julian: In what coin?

Me: Your favorite.

Julian: A tempting offer indeed, beloved.

Me: I thought you Edwardians were supposed to be sexually repressed.

Julian: Myth.

Me: Mmm. Last question, then you can get back to work: What exactly went on between you and this Hamilton chick? The book is not all that clear.

Julian: Stop reading that rubbish. I'll tell you whatever you want to know when I'm home.

Me: Hurry back. I'm pining for you.

Julian: Hurrying. Trust me.

I stared at the BlackBerry screen for a moment longer, and then glanced over at Professor Hollander's biography, which sat next to me on the library sofa, bookmarked with a piece of paper from the notepad in the kitchen. Julian's face, so familiar and yet so foreign, looked up at me with the grim detachment of a soldier in a portrait studio. The strangeness of it rolled over me again: I'm having an e-mail exchange with Captain Julian Ashford, iconic war poet, author of "Overseas." About foxhunting and spats.

Julian Ashford, my lover.

I'd spotted the book this morning, after showering. It had slipped under the bed, dislodged from the nightstand at some point; the corner peeked out seductively from the shadows. I'd ignored it at first, making the bed and fluffing the pillows with great concentration, but eventually I couldn't resist. I'd picked it up, carried it down to the library, and traced my thumbs over the dust cover for a moment or two.

It was somehow easier than I'd expected. The book was a biography, after all, and Julian didn't exactly leap out in full living color from the thicket of passive constructions and vague rambling sentences. He stayed, thankfully, at arm's length, a distant historical figure: no shocking revelations, no hint of abuse or dysfunction or obscure Oedipal motivations. Just, it seemed, a relentless desire to distinguish himself in everything he did, as if he couldn't bear anything less than perfection. At Eton he won every prize in sight, academic and athletic, and led the school's Officer

Training Corps as color sergeant. He went up to Cambridge in 1913, reading mathematics and plunging himself into a whirlwind of editorships and debating societies and athletics, until the outbreak of war the following year redirected that energy into obtaining a lieutenant's commission in the Royal Welch Fusiliers. He'd departed for the front a few months later.

Where had it come from? Parental pressure, or inner drive? Both, I supposed. An only son, with enormous natural gifts, being raised to take his place among the pantheon: he'd no doubt felt the weight of outsize expectations all his life. And to his credit, he'd risen to accept that burden. Had borne it with grace and a certain easy-going humility.

All this made good skimming, insightful and even endearing. More irritating was the regular appearance of Florence Hamilton's name. Flora, Julian had called her, with unthinking intimacy. I'd tried to skip over those pages, but it wasn't quite possible to avoid them all. My eyeballs kept dragging on certain words, certain passages. Such as on page 302:

> *Though Hamilton's diary is curiously and uncharacteristically mute on the subject, it is evident that their relationship reached some point of climax during this last leave. Her next letter to Ashford, sent on February 12, is riddled with allusions to this event, whatever it was: "I had not imagined such joy could exist between two living beings," she writes rapturously, "and can only hope that you felt it as I did. Your words, as ever, were so circumspect; how this hateful war has changed you!" His reply, unfortunately, does not survive.*

I could imagine what it said, though. He'd admitted it himself. *Yes. One. During the war.* Point of climax, indeed.

I'd flipped to the photo section at that point. This was more fun: there was Julian as a perfectly angelic baby, as a mischievous towheaded toddler on some sort of Swiss holiday with his parents; performing his color-sergeant duties at Eton, in a top hat at Ascot with Winston freaking

Churchill. Another photo, captioned *June 1913: At Henley with Hamilton and her brother Arthur, after having stroked the eights to victory against Oxford,* showed him impossibly boyish and handsome, in laughing conversation with an extremely pretty young woman, dressed in white. She was dainty, elegant, rising barely to his shoulder; she looked like an exquisite china doll. She had her hand on his arm; his head bent attentively in her direction. Another man stood on Julian's other side, watching them both with an amused expression. Florence's brother. It looked like he approved.

That was when I'd slammed the book shut and started e-mailing Julian.

Beloved. I could still see the word on the BlackBerry screen when I closed my eyes, and I knew he meant it. He belonged wholly to me now. Florence Hamilton had died long ago; even in his own disjointed lifetime, he hadn't seen her in twelve years. So why did it kill me to see them together in that old photograph, that vanished sepia world of theirs? Because she was of his time? His class? The subject of his famous poem? The woman he should have married, if by some miracle he'd survived the war?

I looked at the book again, and then I looked at my watch. Noon. Plenty of time.

I grabbed my bag and the keys to the Range Rover and headed out the door.

THE DRIVE TO NEWPORT took less than an hour, past the reedy green Connecticut shoreline and right up along the coast of Rhode Island, where Long Island Sound opened up into the broad Atlantic Ocean. A beautiful day: the midday sun glittered brilliantly on the fidgety water, and a chaste blue sky set off the extraordinary whites of the sails plying the harbor. I found myself wishing Julian were here with me, that we were coming up for some romantic weekend at one of the old hotels in town.

I felt my mood lifting as I followed the GPS instructions, weaving my way down the narrow streets with something like euphoria at the prospect of doing something more productive than shopping or twiddling my thumbs in Julian's library all day.

The surge of exhilaration carried me right along the main commercial street in town. I found a parking space readily—it was only a Thursday, and Newport was nothing if not a weekend town—and walked the half-block or so to the shop in a quick swinging stride. THE PEARL FISHER, read the oval wooden signboard, in carved faux-antique letters painted with gold, and underneath it, BOOKS BOUGHT AND SOLD. It wavered uncertainly in the salty breeze gusting from the water, making a seaman-like creak. I paused to dig in my bag for the book and heard my phone ring.

"Hi, there," I said. "You'll never guess where I am."

A brief silence. "Tell me."

"Newport. It's so pretty here. You're right, we should really come up together some weekend."

"You're in *Newport*? Why the devil?"

"The bookstore, the one that sent the biography. I thought I'd make myself useful. I'm standing outside right now. Can I pick you up anything?"

"Good God. The *bookshop*? You're joking. By yourself?"

"*Yes*, by myself. What do you mean? I'm a big girl."

"What a bloody reckless *idiotic* thing to do! Why didn't you wait for me? What if the chap's a regular there? He'll follow you back."

"Oh *please*."

"Do you think I'm *joking*? Couldn't you at least have *told* me first?"

"What, I have to ask your *permission*?"

"You're not taking this at all seriously, are you? I'm trying to *protect* you, Kate. As I've told you before. In fact, I thought I was quite clear about the danger you're . . ."

"Are you *mad* at me?" I demanded. "Because if you are, well, tough, okay? You encouraged me to go out, remember?"

"Not to bloody *Newport*, Kate!"

"So shopping and getting my nails done is okay, but doing something useful is bad and dangerous? I'm not allowed to cross state lines or some-thing? Or is it about taking your car and . . ."

"The *car* is not the bloody point. Good God. The car's yours. It's your life I'm more concerned with."

"My *life*? Are you *nuts*? No one's going to off me in a bookstore in Newport, Rhode Island, okay?"

He paused, a good long space of silence. "Look," he said finally, his voice wound tight as new rope, "I've got rather a lot on my plate here, at the moment. I wish you'd told me, that's all. Can you let me know when you're finished?"

"I'll send an e-mail," I told him. "Don't want to bother you."

"Now *you're* angry."

"Of course I'm angry. You're taking this way too far."

"I'm not, actually. So let me know you're all right, please?"

"I will." I bit my lip. "Good-bye."

"Good-bye, darling. I . . ."

He was probably going to say *I love you*, but I cut him off, too annoyed to hear it at the moment. What was *that* all about? I could just understand his reluctance to let me go into Manhattan, if this whole business with the Harvard professor and the office ransacker was really something to worry about, but getting all worked up over a quick trip into Newport? To a *bookstore*? Did he think I needed a freaking *chaperone*?

I thrust energetically through the door of the bookstore and pasted on a blank cheerful expression. The shop was empty, other than the rows and stacks of books and a single clerk at the raised wooden counter, reading a copy of *The Kite Runner*. He looked up at the sound of the tinkling entry bell. A young guy, I thought. Twenty-one, twenty-two. Goatee. An ironic goatee, or was he playing it straight?

"Hi." I forced away my irritated thoughts and tried to focus on the mission at hand. *Be cheerful. Make him want to help you.* "I, um, received this book as a present a few days ago. A biography." I held it up helpfully. "It was mailed from your shop here. But I didn't see a card with it or anything, so I was wondering if you could tell me who sent it?"

He frowned. "Someone sent it from *here?*" he asked, as though the idea of an actual paying customer beggared belief.

"That's what the return label said. It was sent to Katherine Wilson, on Seventy-ninth Street in New York City. Maybe you have it on the computer."

"Can I see the book?"

I handed it to him.

"Used, right?" He flipped through it. "Don't recognize it. I guess I can look it up."

He sat down and turned to the computer, punched in a few words. I tapped my finger on the counter and felt a knot of anticipation tighten in my center. "Oh, it was a *telephone* order," the clerk said, as though that explained everything.

"A telephone order. Can you give me the name?"

"No name. Paid by credit card, but we don't save that information. Security."

"You seriously don't have any information on the sender?"

"Yeah, that is kind of weird." He peered at the screen. "Just the telephone number. Must have forgotten to enter the rest. Gina's kind of absentminded sometimes." He rolled his eyes, just to let me know that he, himself, was sharp as a tack.

"Can I have the phone number, then?"

"Sorry. I'm not allowed give out personal details." He looked back down at me and smiled apologetically.

I paused for just an instant. "Really? Oh, that's so disappointing. I really wanted to be able to thank him." I leaned into the counter, letting the tops of my breasts plump out against the wooden surface, and smiled up winsomely. "Are you sure I can't just peek? Just to see if I can recognize the number?"

"Well," he told my cleavage, slowly, "I guess that's okay. If you don't write it down."

"Oh my God. Of course not. I just want to see if it's someone I know." I gripped my handbag under the counter, thinking of the BlackBerry inside, as though Julian could somehow channel himself through it and witness the scene.

The clerk turned the screen in my direction and pointed. "Right there."

9175553232. I imprinted it on my brain.

"Thank you so much," I said. My mind was already racing. 917 was the Manhattan cell phone prefix.

"My pleasure. Really."

I straightened and held my hand out. "Um, my book?"

"Oh, yeah." He shoved it back at me. "Sorry."

I took hold of the book, but he didn't let go. "Anything else I can do for you?" he asked, rubbing the bottom of his goatee with his hand.

"Oh, no thanks. You've been great." I started to turn.

"Um," he went on, "are you in town for a while? Maybe we can grab a coffee or something?"

"I'm so sorry," I said, dimming my smile several notches, "but I'm here with my boyfriend."

"Maybe next time."

"Yeah, maybe. Thanks again."

I hurried out of the store, letting the door close behind me with a wild jingling of bells, and started up the street. When I got to the corner I took my phone out and punched the number in.

It went immediately to voice mail. The standard greeting, a woman's neutral automated voice. *The number you have called 9-1-7-5-5-5-3-2-3-2 is not available at this time. Please leave a message at the tone, or remain on the line for more options.*

I opened my mouth to leave some provocative message, but hung up instead at the last second. It might be better if the guy didn't know I was onto him yet.

When I got back to the Range Rover, I sat silently for a moment in the hot stale air, chewing my lip, before beginning my message to Julian. *In and out. It's a Manhattan cell phone. They didn't have a name. Do you recognize? 917-555-3232. Sorry I snapped. I'm a little touchy about my independence. A modern woman thing. You'll have to get used to it.* My fingers hovered over the keypad. *You can still cuddle me after nightmares, though. See you tonight.* A bit cheesy, but that wouldn't bother Julian a bit.

I sent the message and started the engine. I hadn't turned the radio off, and it startled me, bursting out the climactic frenzy of a baroque horn concerto. A growl leapt from my stomach in response; it was nearly lunchtime, after all. Maybe I should look around for a café before leaving town. On the other hand, I didn't want to run into the bookstore clerk on his lunch break, which was just the kind of awkward coincidence to which I was regularly prone.

My BlackBerry buzzed. Julian must have been waiting for the message.

But it wasn't Julian. It was an e-mail from Charlie, startlingly brief: *Do you have a phone number yet? C.* I replied immediately with my new cell number, and it rang a moment later.

"Dude, where are you?" he demanded.

"Um, in Connecticut," I said cagily.

"Where in Connecticut? With Laurence, right?"

"Um, yeah," I said, "but don't tell anyone, okay?"

"Yeah, I'm not sure how much longer you can keep *that* secret. Have you heard?"

"About what?"

"Southfield just filed a complaint with the SEC about Sterling Bates."

"What?" I nearly dropped the phone into the steering wheel.

"Oh yeah! It's all over the wires, dude. I hear it names *names.*"

"Oh my God! He *promised*!"

"Promised what?"

"Not to go all legal on me!"

"Yeah, well, he must be out for serious revenge, 'cause I hear it's bad."

"Can you e-mail me the details?"

"I'll try, dude."

"I've got to go. Thanks, buddy." I slammed the phone down on the console just as it buzzed again.

Don't recognize the number. Will try to curb autocratic tendencies in future. Arms always ready to ease your nightmares. XX

I put the car into gear, tossed the BlackBerry into the passenger seat, and whipped out of the parking lot with a squeal of the Range Rover's high-performance tires.

JULIAN CALLED ME AT SIX O'CLOCK, from the road. "I've got a lot to tell you, darling," he said grimly, "and I couldn't really speak about it until I left."

"You're not driving, are you?"

"Yes, exit eleven. Ridiculous traffic."

"Pull over first. Do you know how dangerous it is, driving on the phone? It's worse than driving drunk."

"I've got the Bluetooth in," he protested. "Both hands on the wheel."

"That doesn't actually help. Call me back from the next rest stop." I hung up the phone.

It rang again a few minutes later. "You're bossy, did you know that?"

"Where are you?"

"The rest stop before exit thirteen."

"What's the price for a gallon of regular?"

"Three dollars and ninety-six cents. You insult me."

"Julian," I said, "do you have *any* idea what it would do to me if something happened to you?"

He hesitated. "All right. Fair enough. No more driving on the phone."

"Thank you. Now that's out of the way, what the *hell* do you think you're doing?"

"I take it you've heard the news?"

"You could have at least told me."

"It's not about you," he said. "Geoff did some digging overnight and uncovered a massive problem: This Boxer woman of yours, this vengeful little *she-wolf,* could have brought down *my firm.*" I heard a thump, like he was pounding the steering wheel. "You were right; Daniel was right. It was one of my traders."

His outrage was so palpable, my own began to fizzle. "Well, I'm sorry about that," I said brusquely, "but couldn't you at least have *told* me? I heard it from *Charlie*!"

"I've been closeted with Geoff and Daniel since noon. And don't be sorry, for God's sake. It's what I deserve, for being so arrogant as to think I was invulnerable."

"Charlie said you named names," I said. "Mine, I suppose?"

"No," he said, "the trader admitted he knew it wasn't you. So we only named Alicia."

"But my name will get dragged into it."

A pause. "It might."

"I can't believe this."

"Could you just try to look at it from my perspective? We had to act; it's complicated, but the damage she's done . . ."

"Fine. Okay. I get it. Just let me know next time, okay? It's very annoying to hear about your latest exploits from third parties."

"I'm sorry. I had the devil of a time getting out of the city. I'll have to go back in tomorrow."

"You should have just stayed, then." The words snapped out before I could stop them, squatting brutally in the cell-phone ether.

He didn't reply immediately. I heard his breath rustle against the mouthpiece once, twice. His voice, when he spoke, was nearly inaudible. "I hope you don't really mean that."

I thought for just an instant about the prospect of spending the night alone in his bed. "Not that I'd want you to," I conceded, "but it's a lot of driving for you."

"That's nothing, compared to the alternative."

"Can't I just come back into the city with you?"

"No. Look, can we finish this later? I'm desperate for the sight of you, and since you won't let me drive . . ."

"I'm sorry. All right." I paused. "Do you still want me to meet you at the inn for dinner?"

"I'd be devastated if you didn't." And he hung up.

17.

I drove into the parking lot of the Lyme Inn two hours later, and found to my surprise that it was empty. No green Maserati; no other cars at all, in fact.

I eased out of the Range Rover, feeling distinctly out of place in the black chiffon dress I'd picked out that afternoon from the Saks outlet. My hair flowed loose over my shoulders; another odd sensation, since I usually twisted it back on my head whenever I went out. A tiny silver barrette now held the waves back from my face.

I reached the front entrance and nudged the door open. A dark candlelit interior unwound around me, the fading daylight gathered about the windows. It had the feel of a rabbit warren, with doors and hallways and rooms branching off the entrance corridor and the lazy scent of wood smoke lingering in the air. A maitre d' hovered by the desk. "Hello," I said, pitching my voice low. "I'm joining Mr. Laurence. Has he arrived yet?"

"Good evening, Miss Wilson. Not yet, but if you'd like to follow me?"

I trailed behind him down the hall and to the left, peering around me and finding none of the other tables occupied. The maitre d' led me leftward into a small paneled room, where a single table sat before a dancing hearth.

"If you'd like to be seated?" he prompted.

I dropped obediently into the chair he offered me, too embarrassed to say anything. "A glass of champagne?" he inquired.

"Apparently so, thanks," I said, and he exited swiftly, returning almost before I could gather my thoughts, with a tray on which two glasses bubbled delicately.

Julian arrived about ten minutes later, coming up so silently I had only an instant's warning before his warm hands clasped my shoulders, and his head bent down to press a kiss right where my clavicle merged into my throat.

"I expect you're spitting mad at me," he said.

I let out a small laugh. "No, not *spitting* mad. Not anymore." I covered his hand with mine and turned to look up at him. "You're all dressed up!" I accused, taking in his tuxedo, his crisp white shirt-points, his newly shaven face glowing in the firelight.

He smiled and shrugged. "I took a moment to clean up. I'm so sorry for being late, darling; I had a great many things to look after." He lifted my hand and kissed it ardently. "My God, look at you! You're ravishing! Not at all sporting of you, darling, when I've been aching for you all this endless beastly day."

"Good effort, Ashford."

His shoulders fell in a sigh. "Look, shall we talk first, then? Clear the air?"

I opened my mouth to make some polite dismissal, but realized it would be a mistake. "Yes, I guess we should."

He reached over and took his chair and drew it next to mine. "Sweetheart," he said, sitting down, "I was rather an ass this morning when you called me up from Newport. I'm sorry about that. I'd been sitting down with Geoff and Daniel, realizing the full magnitude of things, and I wasn't in the best of moods." He took my hands and stared at them. "You see, this is all rather new to me."

"This?"

He looked up. "Having you in my life. To worry over, to protect."

"Julian, I'm a grown woman, not your firstborn child."

A rueful laugh. "You're probably thinking I'm some sort of ghastly Victorian ogre, eager to repress you and all that."

"No, of course not." I ran my thumb along his. "But I think you *are* a man of your own world, Julian, and . . . and that's wonderful, most of the time. And you're *not* domineering. I realize that. You aren't trying to control me; you're just worrying over me, and that's a big difference. An *essential* difference."

"Thank you," he said eagerly, "thank you for understanding that."

I held up my hand. "Hold on. But you're also used to getting your way, and telling people what to do, and you can't just *do* that with me. I won't let you cross that line, from protective to controlling. And you can't make decisions that affect me, like filing that complaint, without giving me a heads-up."

"Fair enough. But isn't that really what I was asking of you this morning?"

"Well, not *quite*. I mean, I was only driving to Newport."

"Don't be disingenuous. Visiting that bookstore was a great deal more."

"Honestly, I never thought it constituted a risk. I would have asked you about it if I did. Look, if it means so much to you, I promise I'll call you when I go out. Check in every so often, so you don't have to worry." I looked down at his hands, and without warning an erotic image spread across my brain: those same fingers caressing me intimately last night, agile and curious.

"Kate?"

"Um. Yes. I'll call you next time. I promise."

"I'd appreciate that. I won't be away often, but when I must . . . darling, you're so infinitely precious, I can't help worrying. I . . . ."

A waiter arrived, bearing tiny bowls of fragrant soup. Julian rose smoothly and adjusted his chair while the man set down the dishes.

When he left, Julian lifted his champagne glass and clinked mine. "Is it all right, then?"

I tilted the glass to my lips and studied him. "Julian, the last thing I want to do is waste time being mad at you. Let's just recognize we come from different places and try to respect that, okay?"

He smiled. "I suppose I can manage that all right. I *have* been living in your world for most of my adult life. I do know what's expected of me as a modern man."

I tasted the soup. *Crab*, reported my mouth to my brain, but the information ricocheted harmlessly away. "I don't want you to change who you are, Julian. It's just . . . I hope you understand who *I* am. I'm not . . ." I swirled the soup with my spoon, until a tiny eddy formed in the center. "I'm not like the girls you admired in your own time . . ."

"Oh, Lord. Are we talking about Flora Hamilton again?"

"Julian, you don't need to diminish it for my benefit." I cleared my throat, forcing my voice into an objective tone. "I realized, reading about your last leave . . ."

He put down his spoon and spoke fiercely. "That bloody book. Yes, let's clear up *this* little matter straightaway. Since it's causing you so much distress."

"You don't need to. She was your first love; I understand. She's just a little intimidating, that's all." The soup eddy deepened, drawing tiny bits of crabmeat and chives into its vortex.

"Kate, listen to me. I was never in love with Flora. Not really. Our mothers were friends. We knew each other all through childhood, she and her brother and I. All quite close. It was perfectly apparent to both of us that the families hoped we'd marry one day, and we joked about it. But I should imagine I spent more time with Arthur than with her. We went to school together; he was a good friend."

I glanced up. "Oh, come on. There's more to it than that. I saw that picture of you at Henley. She had her hand on your arm, and you were eating her up."

"I thought you said you didn't care."

"I didn't say I didn't *care*, just that you didn't owe me any explanation."

"Well, here it is, anyway. Flora was very pretty, very flirtatious. I may, at some point in my misguided youth, have rather fancied her. A crush, I believe, is the modern term. We corresponded while I was at university.

She was the sort of girl who liked to think herself quite special indeed, not at all like the other girls; she became involved in one cause and another, taking up suffragism one month and socialism the next. At one point she had grand plans to try for a place at one of the women's colleges at Cambridge, but found the Greek and Latin preparation too much for her."

"Greek? You had to know *Greek*? To go to *college*?"

He waved his hand impatiently. "In any case, she was violently patriotic in the first year of the war, waving her flag as I left for the front and joining the nurses' auxiliary and so on, and then violently pacifistic ever after. We began to quarrel in our letters, and when I came home on my last leave, she insisted on meeting me, on having me to stay with her family at their house in Hampshire." He took a drink of champagne and set the glass next to the pointed tip of his knife, turning the base just so. The bubbles rose upward in long fine threads, undulating hypnotically; he watched them for some time before he continued. "We were up the entire night talking, arguing, until I was half dead with exhaustion and general annoyance. I said something cross, I don't remember what, and she flung herself at me, begging forgiveness and all that, and I found myself kissing her. I put a stop to it directly, of course, but she went on and on about her supposed love for me, and perhaps I should have been more emphatic, more unequivocal in rejecting her . . ." His voice drifted; he looked up and met my eyes. "I left the next morning, determined never to see her again, and was astonished to receive her letter after I was back in billets two days later. She had the most extraordinary ability to interpret events to her own liking. I wrote back firmly, telling her in as gentlemanly a fashion as I could that things were not quite as she remembered them. She didn't reply for some time, and then . . ."

"That was about the time you went on your last patrol, wasn't it?"

"Yes," he said, "and it astounded me, later, to see what she'd manufactured for herself out of that thin raw material. Her war memoirs were a shocking fabrication; I hope you don't plan on reading them. They brought her fame, of course, and I don't suppose it does me any actual harm. And she lost her brother, you know, less than a year after my own supposed death. Blown to pieces by a German shell, apparently. A terrible blow for her; they were quite close. So it would be churlish of me to hold grudges."

"You never loved her?"

"Darling, by the time I left for the front, Flora Hamilton was beginning to represent all I most disliked about my world. And to compare the . . . the *fleeting* feelings I had for her with those I bear for you . . ."

"But you wrote the poem for her."

"Ah, yes," he said. "The poem."

"Your everlasting fame comes from a . . . a love sonnet to another woman," I said, hiding my expression behind the soup spoon.

He spoke slowly. "It's generally supposed that I was referring to England. To the love of king and country as redemption for war's evil."

". . . And her beauty
Glowing through the rain, like minnows flashing silver
From some shaded summer pool; or else the moon,
Radiant behind a veil of streaming cloud . . ."

I quoted, into my soup. "Excuse me, but no man is that patriotic."

"You've memorized it?"

"I told you, I wrote an essay on it in high school." I looked up at him and smiled, a little ruefully. "I had to compare you to Wilfred Owen."

"How did I come out, in your estimation?"

"I think I stumped for Owen," I admitted. "I thought 'Overseas' sentimental, especially laid next to those froth-filled lungs of Owen's. But you were writing during the first part of the war, before the Somme, and he wrote at the end. That was the point of the essay, you see . . ." My voice dwindled. "But I *liked* yours the most. I thought it was the most hopeful, the most redeeming, especially that bit at the end about defeating eternity. Poor Owen's just miserable. There's no compromise, nothing to soften the blow. Nothing to hope for."

"Well," Julian said meditatively, "the war itself was bleak and horrible. Either you saw a higher purpose in it, or you didn't."

"Did you?"

He considered. "I suppose so. Partly because I was doing my duty, not just to my country but to the men I commanded. And partly because I was a silly young ass, after all, just out of university, thinking myself jolly splendid in my uniform. It suited that rather barbaric streak to my nature. Going from the quite rigid civilization of my earlier life, its petty proprieties, its various hypocrisies, to going without washing for a week at a time. Up all night, running raids and repairing wire and that sort of thing."

"Weren't you scared? Horrified?"

"Well, yes. Of course. Shell fire particularly; most nerve-racking, that. Incessant bloody noise. And the beastly snipers taking potshots at all hours. But you see, I was one of those lucky chaps that could stand it, more or less."

"I'm not sure I buy that. I don't see how it couldn't affect you."

He ran one finger along the stem of his glass. "Look, I didn't say it didn't affect me. But I don't brood about it. I don't know why; perhaps because I never fought a major action, only damned little raids and patrols. Perhaps because I'd been stalking deer and shooting birds all my life; I hadn't any illusions about what happens when one fires a gun and hits something. Or perhaps because it was all overshadowed by what came after. Really, Kate, what do you want me to say? That I'm wounded inside and I need you to heal me?" He said it lightly, teasingly, but I caught a faint note of warning in his voice.

I leaned forward, unimpressed. "So why did you write the poetry, if you didn't need to get things off your chest?"

"Kate, *everybody* wrote poetry. My formal education, you understand, consisted largely of memorizing endless sections of verse, epic and otherwise. I could jolly well recite you every bloody word Milton ever wrote. Virgil, in Latin. The entirety of *Henry V.* 'Once more unto the breach' and all that. So it was more or less inevitable that my fellow officers and I, finding ourselves in the middle of an historic European war, well-larded with long stretches of interminable boredom, were moved to cram our service notebooks with all sorts of derivative rubbish." He paused to drain his champagne, an uncharacteristically gluttonous act, and fiddled the empty glass between his finger and thumb. "I suppose, in my case, I wrote to keep my intellect from surrendering completely to the sordidness around me."

"To the distant sweetheart."

"Yes. True enough, but those words suit you far better than her. I think of you when I remember them."

"*Now* you do, maybe, but not in 1916." I finished my soup and replaced the spoon on the saucer. "So if Florence wasn't the one, who was?"

"The one?"

"The one you slept with, during the war."

"Look," he said roughly, "didn't we agree to keep this a blank slate? I won't ask you any pointed questions about your lovers, and you won't ask me about mine."

"I'm sorry."

An expression of shock struck his face. "Oh, *hell*, darling. I didn't mean that. Tonight of all nights. Come here. Don't be shy; we're alone." His long arms reached out to lift me bodily into his lap. "I should be shot, sweetheart," he said. "That was vulgar of me, vulgar and boorish and ill-bred. Forgive me. Oh, darling, don't be hurt. Don't. If you knew how I revere you . . ."

"*This* is what I meant, before," I said bitterly. "Deep down, you want the kind of girl you used to know. Aristocrats, with perfect manners and deportment and *virtue* . . ."

"Restless, shallow girls, mere useless tinsel, without a hint of genuine originality, and without an ounce of *real* virtue, *real* nobility: *your* nobility, Kate."

"Nobility!" I turned my head, feeling his shirt-point press into my cheek. "I'm from *Wisconsin*, Julian. My dad's in insurance. I don't have so much as a drop of blue blood."

"I don't mean your *blood*, sweetheart," he said. "God knows that means nothing to me anymore. I mean your soul. Your heart."

"How can you know that?"

I felt a light pressure on the top of my head: his kiss. "I just do."

"Tell me something," I said, after a moment, when his body had poured enough comfort into me, "if you don't mind my asking. If it's not a violation of the blank-slate agreement. Why only one? When you could have had anyone?"

"You overestimate my powers of seduction, Kate."

I snorted. "Julian. Your powers of seduction could light up the entire borough of Manhattan whenever the grid craps out again. Believe me, I know."

"You're a trifle biased, sweetheart."

"Well, that's kind of a circular argument. I'm biased because of your powers of seduction, after all. But you're avoiding the question. Not that you have to answer it."

"I'll answer it," he said, wrapping his fingers around mine. "In the first place, it wasn't quite so straightforward a matter back then, for a callow young chap just out of school. Willing females not so easy to come by, you see; at least of the amateur variety. Have you read anything about my father?"

"Lord Chesterton? Not much. He was in politics, I know. One of those Eminent Victorian types."

Julian smiled. "Yes. Rather into politics. He and my mother had a love match, you know, which was not altogether unheard of at the time, but not quite the usual thing."

"Oh, I'm so glad for you."

"Yes, when you look at some of the other families, we were really quite happy. And instead of taking me to a brothel for my fourteenth birthday—as did the fathers of several of my friends, to my certain knowledge—mine sat me down for a long talk and obtained my promise that I shouldn't set out to seduce any woman unless I'd made her my wife.

Because, upon meeting my mother one day, in the midst of a providential June downpour, he found himself wishing he'd done the same."

"Oh." I swallowed. "That's about the *sweetest* thing I've ever heard."

"Which is why," Julian went on, as if he hadn't heard me, as if it were all part of some speech he'd planned, which I began to realize it was, "I've asked you to join me here tonight, Kate." He slipped out from beneath me, placing me on the chair, and went down on his knee before me.

At once, his words receded in my ears, as if they were coming from the end of a long narrow tunnel. *Don't faint,* I told myself sternly.

He gathered my fingers between his own and spoke slowly, deliberately, in that lush persuasive voice of his. "It's why I'm asking you, my beloved, to do me the very great honor of accepting this humble hand as your own; to take this grateful man as your husband. Will you marry me, Kate?"

I squeezed my eyes shut, because the sight of this beautiful man, this heart-shattering Julian, kneeling at my feet, proposing to me in this sweet ridiculous way, like no man had done to any woman in about a century, caused quarts of adrenaline to shoot through my veins with staggering effect. I didn't know what to say, or do. I found myself slipping off the chair, onto my knees next to him. "Oh, Julian, you don't have to do this. Stand up. Don't kneel at me. *I* should be kneeling."

"Only say yes, Kate. Say yes, and I'll stand. Say yes."

"All right. Yes. *Yes!* But you don't need to do this. You don't . . ."

I couldn't say any more, because he'd risen, pulling me up with him, and lifted me from the ground for a champagne-drenched kiss.

"Thank you," he said at last, setting me down on the floor. "You've made me the happiest of men."

HE DROVE ME BACK HOME in the Range Rover later that night, loopy and confused still, and led me upstairs to a bedroom overflowing with roses and candles.

I gaped about, stupefied. "When did you do *this?*"

He drew his arms around me from behind. "The innkeeper's a friend of mine."

"Obviously you figured I was a sure thing."

"I had my hopes. You hadn't shown too much resistance to the idea before."

"Well, I was afraid you might ask eventually, but . . ." I turned in his arms. "You really don't need to do this, Julian. I told you, I'm already a ruined woman."

"You are nothing of the kind, and every moment I've spent in your arms these past two nights, I've been aching to put this right. Kate, you must understand, I would never, *never* have brought you here, *lured* you here, if I hadn't the most honorable of intentions." He smiled. "I promised my father, didn't I? And as long as you're willing, as long as you'll have me, I simply can't wait any longer to have at least the *promise* of marriage between us, when we lie together."

"I see. You want me to make an honest man of you?"

"If you'll have me," he repeated seriously. "I know it seems soon to you, darling. And I realize there's a great deal to consider. Who I am, and all that comes with it . . ."

"That's the least of my worries, in fact."

He frowned. "What are your worries, then?"

"That you're rushing into marriage before you know me well enough. That this mad infatuation of yours . . ."

"Mad infatuation." He pulled me into his chest and spoke with quiet assurance into my hair. "Kate, *really*. You know better. *I've* known, from the very beginning, that we simply fit together. Don't you feel it? As though something between us is in perfect tune somehow. Beyond this *mad infatuation*, Kate, this . . . this *passion*, this desire to carry you off to bed, make you cry out again with that lovely feral howl of yours . . ."

"Julian, good *grief* . . ."

"Don't you feel it too? I'm not putting it eloquently, perhaps, but surely you know what I mean? That we simply *understand* one another? And that we therefore, in plain straightforward logic, belong with each other, and no one else?"

"I feel it."

"Thank God. I should hate to think I've been hallucinating it all this time. Here, I have something for you." He put his hand in his pocket and drew out a box.

"Oh no. *When* did you have time to go ring shopping?"

"There's a marvelous jeweler on Lyme Street, in the middle of the village. As good as any in Manhattan."

"Just my luck."

"So I called ahead, described what I wanted, had them put a few pieces out for me." He opened the box. "If you don't like it, of course, we'll go back tomorrow. I tried to find something in your taste. Something simple and elegant."

I'd been filled with foreboding, half-expecting some ten-carat monstrosity, but it was only a slender band of diamonds in a platinum setting, the three square center stones slightly larger than the rest. "Oh," I breathed, without thinking, "it's perfect!"

"Thank God. You've no idea . . ." He took the ring out of the box and eased it onto my trembling finger and folded his hand around it. "I knew you wouldn't want something flashy, but at least the stones are without flaw . . ."

"Stop. I don't care. It's perfect." I put up my hand to caress his cheek, and the diamonds on my finger caught the light with an unfamiliar glint. "You darling man, you could have bought the whole store for me . . ."

"I wanted to."

". . . and instead you brought back what *I* would want. And it's perfect, and I love it. And I'll marry you, Julian. Of course I will. With only one condition," I added, when his lips were a breath away from mine.

He stopped and made an inarticulate noise. "I should have known," he groaned. "It was all going so well."

"Just this," I said. "Six months. We wait six months before setting a date."

"Six *months*? Before setting a *date*?"

"Because it *is* all too soon, and you know it. I need six months to sort my own life out, career and everything, so I won't just lose myself in being your wife. Julian Laurence's wife, I mean, which is different from being *your* wife, from being Kate Ashford." The name emerged so naturally, so beautifully, it was almost as though I'd heard it before.

He examined me for a few seconds, concentrating, the candlelight shifting across his face from all angles. "Fair enough, then. I see your point."

"And I need six months to be sure you really want me. If you still feel this way by Christmastime, we'll start making plans. And if not," I continued, "and I'll be able to *tell*, Julian Ashford, so don't be noble and *pretend* you're still in love with me, then we walk away from it."

"And in the meantime, you'll wear the ring? We'll be properly engaged?"

"Yes, if you like."

"*If I like.*" He brought his hands up behind my head. "Beautiful Kate, beloved Kate. Look at you, so fine and loyal. That sweet trust of yours; I shan't ever betray it, I swear. I shall protect you, fight for you, with every last breath in my body."

"Julian, it's two thousand and eight. Good luck on that."

"Look, darling, I'm in the middle of a *speech*, here. I'd appreciate your breathless attention."

I curled my arms around his waist. "I'm sorry. Please go ahead. I love your speeches. It's like being in the middle of a Trollope novel."

His thumbs brushed my cheekbones. "Minx. You're mocking me. And yet I mean all of it, you know. Unredeemed old-fashioned bloke that I am."

"I know you do."

"I *would* fight for you, Kate. I'd kill for you. Die for you, if I had to. *Six months.*" He shook his head. "As if six more months could alter me." His face came close to mine, until our foreheads were almost touching, and he spoke to me in the fiercest whisper. "Every possible vow, darling, I've made you in my heart. I'm already your husband—didn't you know that?"

"If it makes you feel better, while you're busy debauching me night after night . . ."

"It does," he said, and then there were no more words, at least coherent ones; I felt only his lips, his hands, his golden body slanting over mine in the candlelight: union and ecstasy and, at last, the warm tangle of a deeply contented sleep.

IN THE MORNING, WHEN I WOKE, he had already left for Manhattan, but a large silk-lined box sat on the nightstand beside me. Inside lay a king's ransom of jewelry: ropes of diamonds, bracelets, earrings, rings, glittering in all colors; and a note, written in elegant black ink on an ecru card: *Humor me.*

Amiens

The dream reared up suddenly, in the midst of a deep velvet sleep. The same as ever, except it had taken on even greater intensity now; it filled me with something beyond panic. An end-of-the-world feeling, an Armageddon. The man couldn't hear me, couldn't understand me. He smiled at me, confused, and as I spoke more loudly, more urgently, he backed away, still smiling, into a blackness so absolute it seemed to swallow him. "Stop!" I screamed at him. "Stop! Come back! Don't leave me!"

Something patted my hand, called my name.

"Come back! Don't leave me!" I screamed again.

"Kate! Kate!" I felt my hand being gripped, hard; the voice called in my ear now. Julian's voice.

I sat straight up, banging my nose against something hard. "Julian!" I exclaimed, flinging myself into his chest. "You came back!"

But it was all wrong. The chest felt scratchy, woolen; the arms around me stiff and formal. A hard leather strap lay beneath my cheek.

"Kate," he said awkwardly. "Are you quite all right?"

Oh no. Not Julian. Julian, but not Julian. Not *mine*. I pulled back, humiliated, all the light snuffed out of my heart.

"Oh, I'm so sorry. I . . . it was a nightmare . . ."

"Your nose . . ." he said, peering at it.

I put my hand up. I didn't feel much pain, only an aching numbness. "I think it's okay. Did I bang it on you? I'm sorry. What time is it?"

"Seven o'clock in the morning."

"Oh. Oh, I'm so sorry. I woke you up. I woke the whole house up, probably."

"No, I was already up. I've a round of early meetings. I was just passing by your room, and heard . . ." He cleared his throat and placed a small object on the nightstand. "Your key. I had to lock it from the outside last night, and then it wouldn't fit under the door afterward."

"Oh. I suppose I fell asleep, didn't I?"

A smile rolled across his lips. "My fault. Keeping you up so late." A classic British understatement: We'd talked until two in the morning—about the future, about the past, about politics and war and literature and Mao and opera and 9/11—until I must have drifted off, for my last confused memory of the night had something to do with being tucked into bed with a possible kiss brushing against my forehead. I looked back at the key on the nightstand and saw a row of hairpins lined up next to it, in perfect order.

"Now that's what I like about you old-fashioned types," I said, reaching one hand to gather my tumbled hair on my back. "Perfect gentlemen."

"Except for giving you nightmares, apparently." He wore his uniform, neat and immaculate despite its overall shabbiness from the endless winter hours spent in muddy trenches; his peaked officer's cap hung courteously from one hand. I hadn't grown used to that yet: to the sight of Captain Ashford, soldier, trench dweller. "Are you all right, then?" he asked, more seriously, setting his cap on the bed and then snatching it up again.

"Oh, yes." The air seemed frigid, now that he'd pulled away. I tugged the wool blanket back up to my shoulders, letting my hair fall away in loose waves around my head. "Just a little cold."

He nodded to the small wrought-iron grate. "Your fire's out. No kindling, of course, dash it. I'll send up the char on my way out; she ought to be in by now."

"Thank you. I'm . . . well, I'm not very good with fires."

"Quite exceptionally useless. Central heating in every home, I expect?"

"Pretty much. How . . . how long do your meetings run?"

"All day, I'm afraid," he replied.

I wrapped the blanket around my shoulders and rose from the bed. He turned away, toward the fireplace. "And then?" I asked, flipping the switch on the electric lamp. It flickered indecisively, and then held.

"And then I thought perhaps, if it isn't inconvenient . . ."

"Inconvenient?"

He turned to face me, his face reddened in the glow from the lamp. "Perhaps I might see a little more of you."

"Captain Ashford," I whispered, "I'd like that very much."

"I've so much more I'd like to ask you," he said hastily.

I reached out to touch his hand. "I'd love to tell you."

"It was so good of you, last night, to sit up with me so late . . ."

"But I didn't convince you, did I?"

"Of course not." He smiled. "But I had rather an idea, after I left. Shells, you see, are all a matter of chance, of timing. I shall simply change the scheduled start of the raid to 0215. That should satisfy Fate this time."

"But then something else might find you."

"Something else might always find me." His hand worked its way around mine: those familiar fingers, coarse and callused now, strong and beloved.

"How do you stand it? How do you bear it? How did any of you bear it?"

"Well, one doesn't mind so much for oneself."

"But others, Julian. The ones who care about you." I squeezed his fingers, felt them curl in response. "Please don't go. I know it only hurts you to hear that, because you can't refuse your duty. I understand, I really do. But I can't help myself. I have to try. I can't just hope that a . . . a *timing* adjustment will keep you safe. I can't take a single chance you'll be out there that night. It's too important."

"Why," he asked wonderingly, "does it mean so much to you?"

I reached out to touch the corner of his mouth. "Who can look at you, Julian, who can *know* you, and not understand the answer to that question?"

His lips just parted, exhaling against my skin. His fingers tightened around mine; I sensed the other hand rise and fall back.

"You'll be late for your meetings," I told him. "But find me when you get back. I have one more arrow left in my quiver for you."

His head bent down; he kissed my hand. "I'm at your mercy," he told me, and donned his cap and left the room.

18.

"Tell me something," I said, late one afternoon at the end of August, when we lay entwined and peaceful on the grass outside, listening to the cicadas shimmer the humid summer air.

"Hmm," he allowed, playing with a curl of my hair. "What is it?"

"Why do I always wake up alone?"

He hesitated, so briefly I might have imagined it. "Because, lazy child, you've a fondness for lying in, whilst *I* am obliged to work for a living."

"Well," I said, picking up his hand and threading my fingers through his, "*that* was a lame answer. Dig deeper, Ashford."

"You're too jolly persistent, you modern girls. Can't a chap have a little peace?"

"Not in this century."

He sighed and squeezed my hand. "Stand to."

"Is that an army thing?"

"Most offensives, at least in the early part of the war," he said dispassionately, as though he were a history professor delivering a lecture, "were launched at dawn, for various reasons. So each morning, when we were in the frontline trenches, we were required to stand to, to make ourselves ready for the enemy's possible approach. Fix bayonets and all that. Rather a tense moment, if you understand me."

"And you did this every morning?"

"Every morning, as the sun rose over the German trenches," he said. "Waiting and waiting, peering into the mist with our periscopes, not making a sound. Nothing ever happened, of course, or hardly ever. But it's the sort of thing that sticks with a chap. Even after all these years."

"I'm sorry."

"Don't be," he said. "It's a small price to pay."

"To pay for what?"

"For being here. For you."

I turned in his arms until I faced his side. He was staring up at the pale hazy sky, his eyebrows drawn together in concentration. I propped up my head and ran my finger along the side of his cheek and down to the corner of his mouth, enjoying the sight of him, of his strong well-built face and his eyes reflecting the blue above. "Listen to you," I said. "Compartmentalizing."

"On the couch again, am I?"

"Mmm. This busy brain of yours. Everything locked away neatly in its own little box. The childhood box." I pressed my finger against the side of his forehead. "The alpha hedgie box." I moved my finger. "The Kate box."

"A cracking big box, that."

"It's my favorite." I drew a circle around the spot and bent down to impress it with a kiss. "And the war box, of course." My finger moved again. "Long months of stress and trauma, all packed away under the vigilant watch of that amazing self-control of yours."

"And you think it will all explode into the open one day?" He sounded amused.

"I don't know. I guess not. Your way of dealing with it seems to be working. Throwing your energy into other things. Southfield did that for you, I think. Gave you something to obsess over, all those years."

"And now I have you."

"You're *obsessed* with me?"

"I take that to mean you're not obsessed with *me*?" An injured air.

I laughed. "*Obsessed* sounds unhealthy. This"—I kissed him—"is very healthy. Except I think you just artfully changed the subject on me."

"We compartmentalizing types are famous for that."

"I just worry I'm wrong, that it affects you more than I realize, and you're just being all British about it. So if you could just sometimes let the

Kate box know what the war box is thinking"—I moved my finger from one to the other—"or even *feeling*, God forbid, it might help."

"See here. I must take exception to that. The Kate box is absolutely crammed with feelings; spilling out the sides, in fact. I'm good about *that*, aren't I?"

"Yes, you are. It's a lovely box. A loving, tender box; I'm proud to belong there."

"I've put into it," he said softly, "all the best in me."

I bent my forehead into his chest. "Which is plenty," I said. "But the war box, on the other hand . . ."

"Look, must you be off coveting the contents of other boxes? They're not nearly so nice as yours. Nor a fraction as important to me."

"Stubborn. I'll have it all out of you eventually, you know."

"Mmm. I'm sure you shall." He lifted my chin up and kissed me. "You've an entire lifetime for the job."

I felt the soft nibble of his lips, and the prickle of ripe grass beneath me, and the warm sun soaking my flesh, and I gave up. "So I'll never have the pleasure of waking in your arms?" I asked wistfully, running my finger along his upper lip.

"If only you'd wake up sooner, my love. But you're always dead asleep."

"That's because I've been up half the night, answering your insatiable demands. With you trying to make up for twelve years of celibacy in one short summer. I don't know how you manage, actually."

A tiny smile lifted my fingertip. "Sleep appears a complete waste of time, at the moment," he said, and gathered me up for a proper kissing.

I couldn't resist him; I never could. We'd been living in the cottage all summer, and still all he had to do was look at me with that particular expression in his eyes—or any expression at all, really—and my insides melted like wax under flame. He knew it, too. He knew exactly his effect on me, and, being a quick learner, had already grown adept at using it to distract me from certain topics of conversation.

Not that I minded. I was deliriously, rapturously in love. The summer was passing by in a haze of wonder: days spent swimming and sunbathing at the beaches, sailing Julian's nimble cutter on Long Island Sound, prowling the shops and sights of the nearby towns. We might go running or sculling on the river first thing, before the air grew too hot, and then Julian would disappear into the library for a couple of hours to conference with his lawyers or his traders; after that, the time was ours. We'd find somewhere to go, something to do. Mini golf, once, at which Captain the so-called Honorable Julian Ashford had played a shockingly dirty game: distracting my swing, knocking my ball with his own like it was a croquet match, and then making the critical mistake of trying to kiss his way out of trouble afterward.

Of course, there were other days: the days he left at dawn to drive into Manhattan, once or perhaps twice a week. I kept myself determinedly occupied then. I went to work in the garden, I read book after book, I sent cheerfully reassuring e-mails to my puzzled friends and family (*Just taking the summer off! It's amazing! Country air! Beach!*) and posted smiling photos on my long-dormant Facebook page. I baked my own bread, traded my own modest portfolio, ran errands. Each month, when I mailed off the rent check to my roommate, I marveled at the barefoot fullness of my life: at how, without accomplishing anything newsworthy, without going farther afield than Newport, I felt more charged with connection to the surrounding world than I ever had in those cyclonic years on Wall Street.

And yet no matter what I did, however much I managed to amuse and occupy and even enjoy myself, I missed Julian. It was like having some essential organ in my body absent itself without warning. We e-mailed, of course, and he always called me at least once or twice, between meetings, but it did little to fill the gap. I tried not to count the minutes until eight o'clock—the earliest possible hour I could expect him—or to hang around the front door, waiting for the sound of his car in the driveway. But I knew when he arrived, all the same. I could feel him, his sunshine entering the house, and all the dull ache of missing him was cured, all our dissected parts safely reassembled. "There you are, beloved," he'd smile, reaching for me, and I'd step into his embrace to be hoisted in the air, or kissed breathless, or waltzed about the room.

And the evenings! Sometimes we went out to dinner or the movies, but mostly we stayed in. Julian might play the piano, Chopin or Beethoven or Mozart, which I loved, but also ragtime and old music hall songs with raunchy lyrics, made all the more hilarious because Julian—as he'd warned me—had no singing voice at all. Some nights he downloaded old recordings into his iPod and showed me how to waltz, to polka, to do the turkey trot and the bunny hop and the grizzly bear until we collapsed, laughing, on the living room floor. Other nights I made him instruct me in the fundamentals of fencing, boxing, cricket, rugby; then I'd enlighten him on various aspects of American football, with a particular emphasis on the history and hagiography of the Green Bay Packers. Or else I sang for him, or he settled me on the sofa and recited bits from Shakespeare or Homer or Wordsworth, or some ridiculous doggerel he'd picked up in a pub somewhere, his expressive voice shifting effortlessly from high art to low, never missing a word. I could have listened to it all night.

I never did, of course. As the summer wandered on, we craved each other with an immediacy that grew rather than lessened, nakedly carnal, as if through the tactility of physical union we could somehow seize control of this capricious mystery that had brought us together. I often wondered whether Julian felt it even more than I did. He was always touching me, holding me, drawing me into himself: eager, compulsive gestures that seemed to bring him relief rather than joy. There were times he possessed me with a peculiar gentle ferocity I didn't fully understand: when the vile traffic on the interstate had kept him away until after sunset, perhaps, or when I hadn't been quite within earshot when he came home, and he'd had to go looking for me. An edge of panic would lever his voice, and his arms would greet me with an instant of crushing strength, before softening to cradle me. He would kiss me, vibrating, scintillating with need, and I'd melt myself into him, letting him know it was all right, that I understood; he'd carry me upstairs and make love to me with the most exquisite care imaginable, and the more delicate his touch the more desperately I knew he wanted me. *Let go,* I'd urged him, in the early days, marveling at his restraint. *I won't break.* Later, as I began to have an inkling of what was going through his mind, I whispered instead that I was okay, that I was safe, that I wasn't going anywhere, I'd be here for him always, always.

He'd lie atop me for the longest time afterward, a precious crushing burden, not saying anything, his head dropped down next to mine, his hands buried in my hair, his eyelids pressed shut: looking asleep, though I knew he wasn't. "Happy or sad?" I'd asked him once, running my finger languidly up and down his spine, and he'd murmured, "*Happy,* you silly thing." Because of course he knew that was what I wanted to hear.

But whatever the mood, we had always had the night afterward, the luxury of falling asleep together, skin on skin: an uncanny sensation of merging, of blending into each other, seamless and indivisible against an arbitrary universe. And if sometimes I stirred in the dark hours to find his arms wound around me in a suffocating hold, I learned it was a simple matter to turn and kiss him awake until the shadows fled, and he was my own teasing laughing Julian again, whispering naughty Latin in my ear until I fell back asleep.

Yet every morning I woke up alone in our bed. On the days he went into Manhattan, it was understandable. He wanted to be there and back by the end of the day, so naturally he had to leave with the first hint of dawn. Other mornings, I would try to wake up earlier, to catch him before he slipped away, but I never succeeded. He never needed as much sleep as I did.

He was kissing me now, his warm lazy kisses, stirring the embers, and it took all my strength to pull back my lips and place my hand on his chest. "Please. Wake me up tomorrow morning. Just once."

"I can't. You look so peaceful. I've thought about it, believe me, but I can't quite bring myself to do it."

"Well, what if the house were on fire?"

"If it were an emergency, of course."

"Well, I consider this an emergency."

He laughed against my skin. "An emergency, that you've never had the privilege of experiencing my dulcet breath in the morning?"

"The immortal Julian Ashford does not get morning breath."

"*Au contraire*, Mrs. Ashford." He liked to call me that from time to time, just to see the alarmed expression on my face. Or else Lady Chesterton, when he *really* wanted to freak me out. "You have the strangest notions about me."

"Please, Julian. I promise I'll make it worth your while."

That stopped him. "How, exactly?"

I leaned to murmur into his ear. "I'll make you breakfast."

"Breakfast?" He brightened. This was even better than he'd expected.

"Oh, yes. Yummy eggs." I kissed him on the corner of his jawbone, "and bacon," nibbling down his neck, "and sausage," into the hollow of his throat, "and toast, *hot* toast, dripping with butter."

He closed his eyes. "Siren. But I can't do it tomorrow. I've got to be in the city."

"Again? You've already gone in twice this week."

"I'm sorry, love." He rolled on his side and brushed my hair over my ear. "You know how I hate to leave you. It's just this SEC rubbish, God rot them all. The fund's all cash, ready to dissolve. And I pity the poor buggers who aren't, just now."

"No, I understand. I don't mean to be clingy." I shuddered. "It's just you've got me *trapped* up here. I'm getting antsy."

"I know, and I'm sorry," he said again. "We should be wrapped up in a month with these filthy bureaucrats, and then I'll take you away somewhere. God knows I've been anxious enough, with you here by yourself . . ."

"Only during the day. Totally safe." I pulled his face down for a kiss. "So where are we going?"

"Anywhere you like. The farther the better. We could sail around the world, wallow in the Tahitian sands. I'll buy you an island. A Spanish castle."

"Sounds very fortresslike." Julian's protective streak had expanded into a six-lane freeway since we'd become engaged. He'd quietly hired a private security firm to keep an eye on the cottage when he was away in Manhattan, and he tended to get worried if I didn't check in every few hours with what he called my saucy e-mails. It was starting to feel just the tiniest bit oppressive.

"Or an Italian palazzo," he added quickly, "or a lake in Switzerland."

"Flashing your money around again, are you?"

"*Our* money," he said, "Mrs. Ashford."

"Not yet. Not officially."

"As far as I'm concerned," he insisted. "And a few more of the legal bits are wrapping up as we speak. Daniel's dropping off those papers at the office this afternoon."

"Oh, not *that* again."

"I want you taken care of, darling, should anything happen to me. And since you're not legally my wife yet . . ."

"Nothing will happen to you," I said fiercely. "Don't even suggest it."

"Darling, a man in my position . . ."

"I hope this obsession with your mortality is just a relic of the whole war experience thing," I interrupted, "and not because of something you're not telling me."

"It's not just mortality. What if this *thing* happens to me again? Takes me away from you?"

I lifted my hand to stroke along his cheekbone. "Then all the money in the world won't help me."

"Don't say that."

"Well, honestly, Julian. If you're going to bring up the subject of your last will and testament. It's hard enough knowing you spent a year and a half on the Western Front, the *Western Front*, with artillery shells and machine guns pelting you day and night. Stand to at dawn, for God's sake."

"That's all over, darling."

"Yes, exactly. So no more worries. Or I call up Daniel and make sure you're in line to inherit my priceless collection of official state tourist spoons, should I get plowed over by a bike messenger on my next trip to Manhattan. Whenever *that* might be."

"Tourist spoons?" he asked, eyebrow raised.

"Yes. Those of us who weren't brought up on English country estates took normal vacations every year. You know, spending two weeks in the stinking rear seat of the family station wagon with my kid brother and an Igloo cooler, visiting the world's longest toothpick or whatever in Pete's Armpit, Arizona. And buying the spoon in the visitor center afterward. What?"

He'd rolled onto the grass beside me, shaking with laughter.

"I take it you haven't seen the movie *Vacation?*"

"No," he gasped out.

"Yeah, well, that was me."

"Well," he said, recovering himself and turning on his side to beam me a sweetly idiotic smile, "all the more reason to sweep you away to some private resort in the Cook Islands, servants waiting on you hand and foot."

"As long as *you're* waiting on me hand and foot," I said generously, "I really don't need the servants."

"My dear Lady Chesterton," he said, in his best toffee-nosed accent, "I shall be happy to oblige you."

"What about"—between kisses—"a sheep station in Australia?"

"Or a llama farm in Peru?" He pulled aside the thin straps of my sundress to nibble the flesh beneath.

"Or a . . . a . . ." My words began to stumble. "A salmon hatchery in Norway?"

"Mmm," he said, working the dress down to my waist. "Perhaps a Malaysian rubber plantation?"

"One of those ice fishing huts . . . in Minnesota," I said breathlessly, as my head fell back in the grass. "Thermal . . . sleeping bag . . . good for cuddling."

"Ah, I like the way your mind works." His hands slid behind my back, unhooking me deftly. "But why stop there? I can think of a weather station in Antarctica . . ." His head bent down again, just as his phone rang from somewhere in the grass nearby.

"Ignore it," he growled into my skin.

I began to laugh, nearly dislodging him. "You know I can't."

"*I* can, and it's my own bloody phone."

"Julian, *please*. I can't stand it!"

He sat up. "We're going to have to cure you of this bizarre sensitivity to ringing phones. Perhaps I'll set you up in a roomful." He reached reluctantly for the BlackBerry and held it up to his ear. "Laurence," he barked, not taking his eyes from me.

I stretched my arms luxuriously above my head and watched him back, just for the pure pleasure of taking in his beauty, now so dear and familiar and perfectly expressive of *him*, his essence. His tawny-gold hair glinted in the light, tousled by my own hands, and I marveled for the millionth time that this was mine, all mine: mine to love and worship. I inhaled deeply, letting the scent of sun-baked grass fill my head, hot and summerlike; the tips of my fingers began to tingle, and I sat up to ease them under his T-shirt.

His hand reached up to caress the top of my head, but I sensed his attention was shifting. The phone call had taken on intensity, something about bloody bastards and emergency meetings and insolvency. His face furrowed into annoyance. "Look, you know how things are. I'll be down first thing tomorrow, can't it . . . Christ, Warwick, they can't *do* that . . . Bloody fucking hell."

I started; I'd never heard that word from him before.

He felt my surprise, and his hand moved reassuringly in my hair. "All right, then," he said angrily. "Yes, straightaway, damn it."

He tossed the phone in the grass, but the face that turned to me was anything but tender. "Darling, something's come up."

"I gathered."

"A bit of trouble with one of the banks," he went on, "and bloody

Treasury's called an emergency meeting to see about solvency. The damned idiots."

"*Solvency*? Someone's blowing up? Who?"

"Darling, it's privileged. You know I can't put you in that position."

There was no point in arguing with Julian's sense of integrity. "And you have to go tonight?" I asked, in a small voice. He hadn't spent a single night away from me, not since I'd driven up here in May.

"Yes," he replied, scowling. "I've half a mind to take you with me . . ."

"Yes!" I exclaimed. "Please! I'd be very good, Julian. I'd seriously play along. I'd stay at your house, I wouldn't put a foot outside without letting you know. I'd keep the alarm on and everything. Totally safe."

"Kate, don't tempt me. Our address in New York is public; nobody knows us here. You're much better off staying. I'll call the security to keep watch."

"Like a guard dog. Like I'm some kind of Mafia wife."

"Darling, I'm sorry. It's for your own protection."

"But there's nothing to worry about! Hollander turned up safe and sound from his research trip, just as you said he would. We haven't heard anything else from the mystery man; he's probably moved on to a new conspiracy theory by now. You've got me in hiding for no reason at all."

"Just because we haven't heard from the fellow doesn't mean the threat's disappeared. It's *real*, Kate. I assure you."

"Oh, come on. How can you be certain?"

Julian took my chin in his hand. His head bent toward mine, the brow set in a single rigid line above his eyes. "Can you not simply trust me on this, Kate?"

"Why?" I narrowed my eyes, trying to fathom the meaning in his expression. "Is there something you're not telling me? Something to do with the SEC investigation? The lawsuits?"

"I've told you everything I can." His thumb brushed along my lip. "Look, this isn't some sort of whim, Kate. I'd like nothing more than to bring you along; I'm a mere soulless husk of a chap without you, as you know perfectly well. And besides," he added, straightening, his voice taking on a teasing note, "it might encourage you to relax your unreasonable obstinacy over that damned bit of plastic."

I pushed his hand away. "Excuse me, Ashford, but do I look like the kind of girl who would flash her rich boyfriend's credit card up and down Madison Avenue?"

"It's *your* card, darling. That's the point."

"On your account, so what's the difference? Anyway, it's just for emergencies, remember? That was the deal, the only reason I let it stay in my wallet to begin with." I winced, thinking of my name, KATHERINE E WILSON, embossed confidently against the glossy black.

He groaned. "You're impossible. You plunder every corner of my shabby soul, inhabit my every thought. And then you recoil at the sight of a credit card."

"Julian, I don't want to go into the city to *shop*," I said dryly. "Just see a few of my friends. Figure out what I'm going to do with myself. Maybe try to fit in a ballet class. Go out to dinner with you and then drag you upstairs to your bedroom."

"*Our* bedroom."

"No, *your* bedroom. How can it be ours if I haven't even *seen* it yet?" I slid my hands back under his shirt. "Don't you want to break it in?"

The next instant, I lay on my back in the grass with his face bent over mine. "Oh, we'll break it in," he promised. "Just not tonight."

"Julian, that's not *fair . . .*" I began, but I never got a chance to finish.

HE LEFT AN HOUR LATER in the dark-green Maserati, with his overnight bag in the seat beside him. "Security's going to be watching all night," he said, "and making regular patrols during the day. E-mail me. No, better call: it should give me an excuse to duck out." He met my eyes for a moment, and then reached out and pulled me close. "Have you any idea, darling girl, how difficult it is to drive away from you like this? Like having one's heart pulled out from the roots."

"I still don't understand why they need you," I said. His body still shimmered with exertion, glowed like the sun against my cheek and arms and belly.

"There are reasons. It's the last thing I want to involve myself in, particularly now. You know that, darling. But I can't very well refuse a direct request."

"So you're off to save the entire global banking system?" I tried to smile.

"Hardly."

"You know what really annoys me?" I pulled back. "You're going to be in the middle of things, and I'm stuck out here on the farm. And I was there, too, just a few months ago. Feeling important. Like I was doing something that mattered."

"Kate, you're bloody well important to *me*," he said, drawing me back in. "*This* matters."

"Yeah, well, Tuck started classes two weeks ago, so it looks like you're the only one who gets to bask in the glory of my importance for now."

He held me still. "Are you unhappy?"

"Oh my God! Julian, of course I'm *happy*. It's been the most wonderful summer of my life. It's just I've always been an independent person. I've never let myself take the easy road to anything. And now I suddenly have this perfect life, and I didn't have to do anything. I didn't *earn* you." I reached up my hands to cup the back of his head. "You came out of the blue, my missing half. In love with me."

His hands shifted, solid weights along the sides of my waist. "And that isn't enough for you?"

"*Enough?* It's too *much*, Julian. Too easy, not to be earning my own living. Paying my own way." I shot him a sarcastic look. "Except on my back, I guess."

He grinned at that. "Not *exclusively* on your back, by any means."

"Ha freaking ha."

"I *have* urged honorable marriage as an alternative. Say the word, and I'll whisk you down to City Hall and end all this rubbish about dependency."

"But then it's just the same thing under another name, isn't it?"

He drew my head into his chest. "Kate, *please.*"

"Sorry." I rubbed my forehead against his shirt, absorbing him. "I think this is called a culture clash."

"There's a difference between giving and sharing, darling. I'm not *giving* you anything. You're a part of me. It's all just *yours.*"

"Hmm. I guess I'll ponder that for a while." I leaned back and broke into a smile. "Look at you. That's the same expression you wear when you're studying a stock chart."

"You're far more bloody complex than a stock chart. It's not as though you *enjoyed* working at Sterling Bates, after all."

I shook my head and went up on my toes to kiss him. "Don't worry, I'll figure things out. My own fault, actually. I've been kicking back the past three months, enjoying myself, instead of getting serious about the whole career thing."

"You're allowed a respite, darling."

"Not a permanent one."

"Look," he said, still looking worried, "if you'd like to invite Michelle or Samantha up, or your brother, your parents again . . ."

I ground my lip under my teeth. I loved my parents, of course, but I'd hardly yet recovered from the awkwardness of their first visit, nearly two months ago. Julian, the honorable nitwit, had called up my father before proposing last May, asking for his consent—*consent*, mind you, not blessing—to marry me. Dad, probably feeling a little like poor old Mr. Bennet, hadn't dared to refuse him, but he and Mom had insisted on hopping a plane two weeks later to check out the situation firsthand.

Julian had been perfectly charming, of course: the complete host, attentive and conversational, treating them with filial respect and me with his usual open easy affection. We'd gone sailing and sightseeing and out to dinner at one of the famous local inns, and on the last evening Dad and

Julian had worked the brand-new Weber grill, Heinies in hand, discussing steak and baseball. "What are you thinking, honey?" Mom had asked, noticing me staring at them through the French doors from the kitchen.

Oh, if only Churchill could see him now.

"Just that it's great to see them getting along so well."

"Oh, your father's come completely around. Thinks the world of Julian now. I told him so," she'd added, with a little sigh. "I didn't think they made men like that anymore."

It had been on the tip of my tongue to say *Actually, they don't,* and then I'd realized I couldn't tell her, couldn't *ever* tell her that essential truth. It was Julian's secret to reveal, if and when he chose. And though I'd never been deeply intimate with my mother—maybe once a week on the phone, visits every few months—that jagged epiphany had cut me with an unexpected sharpness, one that hadn't dulled over the long dreamlike weeks since.

"I'm sure they'd be delighted to come back," I said now, reluctantly. "Or Michelle and Samantha. But that's not the real problem at the moment. I want to come to the city with you, and you won't let me."

"I'm not *forbidding* you." He looked scandalized. "Just *asking* you."

"Bringing extreme moral pressure to bear."

"Beloved, if one hair on your head were hurt because of me, and my wretched past, I'd never forgive myself. It's why I stayed away from you, until my willpower ran dry." His voice took on an agonized edge. "It's my *weakness* that's put you in danger."

I took his face in my hands. "Julian. Don't be ridiculous. *I* chose this. I chose *you.* So whatever happens to me is *my* fault, not yours." I pushed out a smile, linked my fingers behind his neck. "So get going. Save the world. Do what you have to do. Only think about what I said, okay? Please? Because you can't just cover me in bubble wrap forever. I won't let you."

He kissed me tenderly, then hard; then he climbed into the car and drove off. I stood waving in the driveway until he went around the bend and disappeared from sight.

Time to give Charlie a call. Because enough was really enough.

19.

"So this is, like, a jailbreak? Is he going to be totally pissed?"

I rolled my eyes and took a drink of coffee, just to show how relaxed I was. "Don't be stupid, Charlie. He's not holding me *prisoner* up there."

We were sitting in a sidewalk café on Broadway and 116th Street, near the Columbia campus, where Charlie was settling into his student digs before the start of his first quarter of business school. The smell of summertime Manhattan saturated the air, strange and familiar, exhaust and hot pavement and sour human: a world apart from the dense green living scent of the Connecticut backwoods.

"So why the secrecy? I'm kind of spooked, dude. He could blackball me if he finds out."

"He'd never do that. Not his style at all."

"You think not? Dude, have you no *idea* what's been going on at Sterling Bates the last three months? Your man has balls of spun fucking steel."

"That was different. That was about Alicia."

"Dude, it's like he's trying to take the whole fucking bank down. It's messed up. He must really have a thing for you."

"He's not trying to take the bank down, Charlie. They're handling that part by themselves."

"Well, someone at Southfield has it in for them. The shit I've heard . . ." He shook his head and drained his coffee.

I frowned. "Like what?"

"Like that huge position, the one I told you about, before you bit it last May, was mostly fed to them by Southfield." He leaned forward. "And it's total shit. Like, it's still sitting on the books. They can't unload it. All fucking leveraged and shit. Bad news."

"Wait a minute. What kind of securities are we talking about?"

"I don't know. Some kind of CDO. I'm guessing mortgages."

"So maybe that was Alicia's deal," I said slowly. "She got one of our traders to buy up their stuff in exchange for Southfield agreeing to set me up . . ."

"*Laurence* set you up?"

"No, one of his traders did." I snorted. "One mystery solved."

"And Laurence didn't tell you?"

"I didn't ask. I just assumed she was blackmailing the guy. That's her usual MO. Jeez, no wonder they fired me. They must've thought I was trying to blow up the bank."

"Well, I hear they're meeting at headquarters right now."

"Who?"

"*All* the swinging dicks. Treasury. The Fed. Bank CEOs. Trying to save the sinking fucking ship."

My mouth dropped open. "*That's* the big meeting? Saving *Sterling Bates*?"

"Why? What?"

"Nothing." I shifted in my chair, feeling its hardness through the thin cotton jersey of my sundress. Was *this* why Julian was so paranoid about my safety?

"So Laurence's in it too, huh? And he didn't even tell you?"

I jumped to Julian's defense. "He couldn't, idiot. It's not public."

"Yeah, well, *I* heard about it," Charlie said. "So someone's not keeping the secret very well."

"Well, it's not Julian. He'd never put me in that position."

Charlie sat back and looked at me curiously. "What does that mean?" he asked. "You're not getting back in the game, are you?"

"Of course I am. I'm not *retired*, Charlie. I have ambitions."

"Seriously. Wow." His head tilted. "Well, you're set now, right? You could get any job you want."

"Oh please. I'll have to reapply to Tuck . . ."

He laughed aloud. "What the fuck are you talking about? You don't need *business school* anymore, dude. You're Laurence's chick; you're fuck-ing hired."

"I'm not going to have Julian pull strings for me!"

"You won't have to. Everyone knows who you are. Everyone wants an in with him." Charlie shrugged. "You could do whatever the fuck you want now. If he lets you."

An unexpected breeze ruffled the wisps of hair at my temples, punctu-ating his words, and I thought, incredulous, *He's right.* I'd been drowsing away in Connecticut all summer, living so simply, basking in the vibrant glow of Julian's love. I hadn't even thought about how something so per-sonal could affect me professionally; it hadn't even occurred to me that *of course* everyone on the Street would be begging to hire Julian Laurence's fiancée. I *could* do whatever I wanted, which really meant I couldn't do anything anymore.

Not on my own merit. Not as Kate Wilson.

Nothing would ever be the same, would it? I'd never be normal again. Never be just *myself* again. My brain ground slowly to a halt, trying to process this information. "You know," I said numbly, looking down at my BlackBerry on the table, "I should probably check in now."

"Check *in*? Dude, so this *is* a jailbreak."

"It's not like that. He's just protective."

"Fucking paranoid."

"Well, put yourself in his place. He's got money; someone could, like, kidnap me. I'm just lucky he hasn't posted a bodyguard on me."

"How do you know he hasn't?"

"Be serious. He'd tell me. Ask me first."

Charlie laughed and sat back in his chair, stretching out his legs. "Well, he will *now*, if he finds out where you are."

I shot him an annoyed look and picked up my BlackBerry. *Just checking in. Miss you. When are you coming home?* I was about to press Send when a twinge of curiosity stopped my finger. *I hear from Charlie you're meeting about SB. True, false, no comment?*

The reply flashed back.

No comment. Strongly suspect I miss you more.

Charlie's voice cut through the happy haze. "Look at that love-struck smile. You've got it bad, dude. What did he say?"

"None of your beeswax, *dude.*"

The phone buzzed again. I looked down.

What else does Charlie say?

I typed rapidly, chuckling.

That I must have it bad for you, because I've got a big stupid grin on my face.

Oh *wait.* Oh *crap.*

The phone rang.

"Where exactly *are* you, Kate?" asked a crisp British voice, deceptively mild.

A taxi honked, ten feet away. I cleared my throat. "Um, Broadway and One hundred and sixteenth. I just have things to take care of, and I was going a little nuts by myself up there. I thought I might surprise you."

"I'm surprised." Still way too mild.

"Julian, it's all right. Charlie's with me. We're at a coffeehouse, hundreds of people in view. Totally, totally safe. More safe than Lyme, where no one can hear me scream."

Silence.

"Julian, please say something. Don't be mad."

"I'm not mad. I'm thinking."

"Look, I just didn't want you to worry. It isn't as though . . ." I glanced at Charlie and checked myself.

Julian seemed to read my mind. "Hmm. Is Charlie still there?"

I looked across the table. "Yes."

"Put him on."

I held the phone out to Charlie. "He wants to talk to you."

Charlie turned white. "*Fuck*, dude," he hissed. "What do I say?"

"Come on, Charlie." I smiled. "Strap on a pair of balls, for once."

He glared at me evilly and took the phone. "Um, sir?" he asked. He listened closely for a few seconds. "Um, no, not yet . . . Nope, no plans . . . Yeah, I could do that . . . No problem . . . Like glue, I swear . . . Every hour . . . Eight o'clock, yeah . . . Okay, bye."

He handed the phone back. I put it to my ear, but Julian had already hung up.

"Well?" I demanded.

He folded his arms with a grin. "I think the big guy just hired you a bodyguard for the day."

"So what was that about eight o'clock?" I remembered to ask Charlie half an hour later, as we were rattling down the subway to Seventy-ninth Street to catch the crosstown bus to my apartment.

"Not sure, but I think that's on a need-to-know basis only," Charlie said.

"And you don't think I need to know?"

"Dude, I answer only to Laurence now," he said. "So are you guys, like, engaged or whatever?" He nodded at my left hand where it gripped the pole.

"Kind of," I said, switching hands.

"Jeez. Not much bling for a billionaire. You should have held out on him."

"Not my style."

He nodded sagely. "That's probably why he's so into you."

The train slammed into the Seventy-ninth Street station, and we got out. My phone buzzed as soon as the cell signal hit.

Would you like to stay here tonight?

Well, that was something. "Hold on a sec, Charlie," I said, and sat down on the bench to reply.

Of course. Where else?

"Come on, dude," Charlie said. "The bus doesn't care who your boy-friend is."

I followed him up the stairs to the M79 bus stop on Broadway, where the next e-mail came in.

Did you bring your key?

The bus roared up and pitched to a stop; we climbed on and sat down.

Me: Yes. I told you, I was going to surprise you.
Julian: Then make yourself at home. Charlie's supposed to stay with you
    until I can get back. Where are you now?
Me: The M79, crossing the park.
Julian: Please inform Charlie you are not to board any further damned
    BUSES. Call Allegra at once and arrange for a car.
Me: Aye aye captain.
Julian: Will you be serious. She's also making dinner reservations for
    8pm at Per Se. Will try to make it there myself, otherwise take Charlie.
Me: Will you be home tonight?
Julian: Not sure. Going back in now. Please be safe, beloved. You've my
    life in your hands. XX

"Love sucks, huh?" Charlie said.

"No, it doesn't." I slipped the phone into my bag. "It's wonderful. You should try it sometime."

A grin flashed across his mouth. "I've got to admit, it's working for you. Look at you, dude. All glowy and shit. Like, you are getting some sweet-ass lovin' up there."

"Okay, *thanks,* Charlie. That'll do."

He snorted. "You are, right? Man oh man. Dude's a fucking stud."

FRANK WAS ON THE HOUSE PHONE when I waltzed through the lobby of my apartment building, and he just about dropped the receiver. "Hold on a moment, please," he said to the person on the other end. "Kate! Long time no see!"

"Hi, Frank. Just came by to pick up a few things. Is Brooke around?"

"Haven't seen her leave. You still got your key?"

"Oh, yeah. Of course. See you later."

He looked as if he wanted to say something more, but then gave a little shrug. "Let me know if you need something," he said, and put the phone back to his ear.

No sign of Brooke in the living room, though her bedroom door was tightly closed. Sleeping it off, probably. I looked around, thinking about the last time I'd stood here, and everything that had happened since. "Wow," I mumbled to myself, tossing the keys in the basket.

"Do you mind if I turn on your TV?" Charlie asked.

"Suit yourself. I'll just go get my things," I said, and went into my bedroom.

I'd left in a hurry. A few drawers were still askew, as though someone had slammed them shut in haste. The file boxes with my papers inside were still on top of the bed; how had I been so careless?

I frowned and went over. Strange. They looked as though they'd been rifled through.

I tried to remember exactly what I'd done that afternoon. It had passed in such a blur of activity and emotion, and everything overshadowed by what had come after, but still. I knew I hadn't gone through my student loan records, or my college transcripts, or my few old handwritten letters.

But clearly *someone* had.

Swiftly I stuffed the papers back in the file boxes and went to straighten the drawers of my bureau. I paused. A note had been taped to the mirror above, the scrawled handwriting barely legible. *Doctor called re missed appt.*

Doctor's appointment? How had I missed a doctor's appointment?

Oh yeah. Because my calendar was in my old BlackBerry. Oh well. Re-schedule that. It would be just about time to renew my Pill prescription . . .

Oh. Holy. Crap.

My fingers went cold. I sat down, trying to stop my brain from spin-ning. How long had it been? How the *freaking hell* long?

I'd left my overnight bag in the hall, with my travel kit inside. I walked back out in a daze to the living room, where Charlie was standing in front of the TV, watching CNBC. "Dude," he said, not looking up, "the cam-eras are already camped outside. They had a shot of your guy a second ago, walking in."

"Oh, really?" I picked up my bag and took it back into the bedroom and unzipped it. My travel kit sat at the bottom, under the bit of lacy underwear I'd packed, just in case.

I opened it up and began sifting, thorough and methodical. Yes, there it was. My round pink pill case. I always got the twenty-one-day pack, because I found it annoying to take the blank pills the other seven days, knowing they were just placeholders.

Except it was so easy to forget about starting the next pack that way. You just kind of . . . forgot. Got out of the habit. Especially when you were so dizzy in love, your brain wasn't always functioning properly, anyway.

Okay, stay calm. When was my last period? Not that long ago, right?

The second week of August. I knew exactly, because it had ended with such perfect timing, the day before we sailed to Newport for the long-promised weekend away. I'd been free to indulge a sense of delicious naughtiness as Julian had slipped the key into the hotel room door, even though I bore his ring on my finger, even though by August we were so wholly knit with one another that a marriage ceremony seemed a superfluous formality. Julian had booked us the most luxurious suite in the building, with champagne and chocolate truffles and ripe red strawberries cooling on the nightstand; he'd swung me into his arms and begun kissing me almost before the door had closed.

Yet my clearest memory of those few days came not from any particular encounter—the intensity of emotion blurred the details for me, in recollection—but during a tranquil hour late Saturday afternoon, as the honeyed sunlight slanted through the window onto Julian's sleeping face.

I'd hardly ever seen him sleep. We drifted off together every night, and he always woke before I did, stealing away at dawn with one of his tender notes left behind on the pillow. So I'd watched him that afternoon with minute fascination. He'd slept on his stomach, an expression of utmost peace relaxing his features; his naked back, crossed by a white sheet just above the curve of his buttocks, rose and fell with the slow patient rhythm of his breathing. On his right forearm, lying palm-down alongside his face, I could just discern the erratic line of his scar as it trailed through the pale fine hair, glinting in the sun.

Thank you, I'd prayed in wonder. *Thank you so very much. I'll take good care of him, I promise.*

Eventually I'd risen, reminded by our location of the dangling question of the mysterious book sender's identity. Julian hadn't ever pressed me on it, and after trying the phone number a few times and getting nothing but voice mail, I'd given up and moved on to far more agreeable activities. But it was still saved on my BlackBerry, and with Julian dozing peacefully away on the bed, I'd slipped away to the sitting room and tried again. It rang once, and then someone answered.

"Warwick," he'd said gruffly.

I'd hung up.

Later that night, I'd settled into Julian's arms and asked quietly, "Why didn't you tell me it was Geoff Warwick who sent the book?"

He hadn't answered at first, only stroked my arm the way he often did. Finally, after a long interval of silence, he'd kissed my temple and said, "Because he's my closest friend, and I want you two to get along."

"You should give me more credit."

He'd let out a little snort. "To be perfectly honest, once I knew it wasn't someone dangerous, it didn't matter anymore. I more or less forgot about the whole thing." He'd dropped his lips against the round ball of my bare shoulder. "Are you angry?"

"Sort of. Though I guess it's ancient history now, isn't it?" I'd turned in his arms and faced him. "But tell me next time, okay?"

He'd kissed my nose. "Okay."

We'd gone to sleep, and left the next morning to sail back to Lyme.

Where I had *not* started a new month of pills.

I sat down on the bed now, staring at the empty case in my hand. No need to panic. Let's see, statistics. Wasn't there only one chance in ten per month, even without contraceptives? Or was it one in three? Holy crap. I put my hand on my belly. Surely not. And oh my God. Julian would kill me. Or no, he wouldn't. He would probably be delighted at the excuse to haul me before the altar, posthaste. But I wouldn't forgive myself, for trapping him like that.

How the hell had I forgotten? Just *forgotten?* Just like that? All freaking *month?* Me, so organized and methodical? Were my brains that scrambled? The thought had never once entered my head: *Gosh, Kate, have we been taking our pills lately?* Never once. Almost like I'd *wanted* to get pregnant. As if I'd been in the grip of some sort of brazen subconscious urge.

No. Impossible.

My fingers began to shake. What was today? August twenty-ninth, right? How many days was that? I tried to count and gave up. Enough that the deed, if it *was* done, was already done. So just wait. Forget about it for a week, until I could find out for sure. Too much other stuff to worry about.

I stood up and began to throw things into my overnight bag. Some shoes I'd missed. My favorite headscarf for bad hair days. A few shirts.

Jeans. Then I zipped up the bag, shoved the file boxes back under the bed, and walked back out to the living room.

"Dude, this is wild," Charlie said, still staring at the TV screen. "Bartiromo's out there, trying to interview people. They keep showing the clip of Laurence walking into the building. Look, there it is again."

I squinted at the screen and saw Julian, his dark blond hair gleaming in the TV lights, dressed in a navy suit and red Hermès tie, striding confidently into the revolving doors with a brief wave to the phalanx of reporters screaming questions at him. Terribly photogenic. No wonder they kept replaying it.

"What are they saying?" I forced myself to ask. To even care.

"The big question is whether they let it fail or not." Charlie folded his arms.

"Fail?" That penetrated the mist. "*Fail? For real?*" I'd tossed the concept around before, of course, but without truly believing it. Without thinking Sterling Bates, the august and admired Sterling Bates, would actually and for real blow up. It was unthinkable. Had Alicia really done that? Had one thoughtless petty vengeful bitch brought down *Sterling Bates?*

"Yeah, that's what they're saying," Charlie said. "Gasparino was on a second ago, talking about Southfield—well, not naming it, just saying 'certain hedge funds'—and the rumors that it had, you know, put Sterling Bates in the crapper with those bad assets. The whole SEC complaint they filed in May, all that shit. He was like, 'and there's Julian Laurence, head of Southfield Associates, walking into the building, wonder what that's about . . .'" Charlie shook his head. "Don't let him off the hook, dude. Get the full story. Work your wiles. This is, like, historic."

Historic. My spine felt cold. "Okay." I cleared my throat. "I have all my stuff here. Should we bail?"

Charlie looked over at me. "What's that? Oh, yeah, sure," he said, picking up the remote and switching off the TV. "Where are we going?"

"I guess we'll just head over to Julian's house, if that's okay."

"Sure. I'm just the bodyguard. Can I, like, take your bag?"

We walked down Lexington, weaving through the swarm of sidewalk traffic, until we reached Seventy-fourth Street and Julian's townhouse. I reached into my bag for the key and couldn't find it. "Hold on," I said, taking the bag from Charlie and setting it down on the stoop. "It's here somewhere. Probably at the bottom." I began to rummage, looking for the envelope he'd given me all those months ago.

"Hey, dude," Charlie said quietly, "I hate to, like, feed the paranoia or anything, but there *is* a guy hanging out at the corner over there. He just kind of looked over here."

"What?" I exclaimed, straightening.

"See? Corner of Park."

I glanced over in time to see a male figure disappear around the corner of the apartment building at the end of the block. "Are you sure, Charlie? He just left."

"Dude, he was standing there watching us, I swear it."

"Well, he's gone now."

"Do you want me to go check?"

"You're taking this bodyguard stuff pretty seriously, aren't you?"

"Yeah, well, I don't want the big guy coming after me if you get 'napped. He'd fucking kill me, right?"

"Look, the man took off, so don't worry about it. Here's the key. I've got the alarm code."

We went inside, to the warm woodsy-plaster smell of an old house left empty all summer. I looked down the hall. It was all exactly as I remembered it. I'd stood right here last Christmas, when Julian had asked to see more of me, and stroked his finger along my jaw. I covered the skin with my hand.

"Nice place," Charlie said. "Good work, Wilson."

"Yeah, thanks." I went to the living room to look out the window at the street corner.

A man stood there, leaning against the apartment building, talking intently on his cell phone and staring at Julian's front door.

20.

I holed up obediently with Charlie all day, except for one brief trip for some basic groceries, watching CNBC on the computer and trying to figure out what was happening. No new information was coming out of the meeting, so the screen was full of endless replays of Julian walking into the Sterling Bates building and various market insiders speculating on what might be taking place inside.

As dinnertime approached, I sent Julian a message. *Are you coming home tonight? What's going on? Your picture's been on CNBC all day today.*

He fired back quickly. *Won't make dinner tonight. Will certainly be home for a few hours' sleep. Don't wait up.*

I looked up at Charlie. "I think he's tired. And maybe cranky."

"Your problem," he yawned, "not mine. Dude, is this okay for Per Se?"

I looked at him. He was wearing a respectable button-down shirt and khakis, but no tie. "Don't know. Never been there. Maybe you could borrow a tie from upstairs."

He frowned. "Would that be okay?"

"If he's mad, it's on me, okay?" I got up and went upstairs, taking my overnight bag with me. I knew Julian's bedroom must be in the rear, because I'd already visited the piano room at the front. Remembering, I felt the color rise in my cheeks.

I thumped my bag down the hall and opened the door. I was right. This was definitely his room. Dark spare furniture, white bedding. I stuck my bag in the corner and looked for Julian's closet. Only one door, other than the entry: I opened it, and saw it led down a short hall, lined on both sides with paneled wardrobe doors, to the bathroom. He wouldn't mind, would he? I wasn't going to snoop. Just find a tie.

Of course he wouldn't mind. He'd want me to. I could hear his voice in my head, impatient: *Kate, for goodness' sake, it's your home now.*

I opened one door and saw, to my surprise, it was completely empty. I frowned and tried the one next to it: also empty. Another one, fitted with drawers this time. Empty. The whole side, nothing but hanger rails and drawers and empty space, smelling of paint and sawn wood, never used.

I turned around and opened a door on the other side of the hall to find a row of dark suits, neatly organized. I touched one, ran my hand along the sloping shoulder, felt the smooth tight weave under my fingertips. A faint scent of cedar drifted past my nose. I bent my lips down to the navy wool for just an instant and pressed the door shut.

The next section was fitted with drawers, no ties in sight; but in the third closet Julian's dress shirts and a tie caddy dangled from a pair of gleaming stainless-steel rails. Thank God. I selected a tie at random and shut the door quickly and stared for a long moment at the opposite wall, the wall of empty closets.

Waiting for an occupant.

THE CAR ARRIVED at seven forty-five on the nose, a discreet black sedan just like the one in which we'd gone home after the benefit, just like all the black cars I'd taken home from Sterling Bates at three o'clock in the morning for the past three years.

"Laurence party," I said to the maitre d' when we arrived.

"Yes, of course, Miss Wilson," he said. "If you'll follow me."

We went past all the tables and through a doorway to a private room. There, gathered around the table, sat my father and mother, my brother and Michelle.

I stopped, stunned. "Oh my God! What are you *doing* here?"

They were all around me in a second, laughing and hugging and explaining.

"That sweet young man of yours," Mom said in my ear, surrounding me with the familiar scent of Joy perfume. "He flew us out in his *private plane* this afternoon!"

"What? *What* private plane? The *NetJets* share? Oh, he didn't. Oh no."

"Oh my God, Kate, it was so cool!" burst out the normally unflappable Michelle, grabbing my arm. "Champagne and everything. So awesome."

"But when did he . . . when did he *plan* this?" I asked, bewildered, as we began sitting down at the table.

"He called us all this morning," my mother said, "asking if we could come out to New York today and stay with you, because he was going to be tied up in meetings and didn't want you to get bored." Her eyes glowed.

"I'm like, *jeez*, Kate," Michelle whispered in my ear. "What did you *do* to this guy? Where did you, like, *find* him?"

"Did he ask Samantha, too?"

"Yeah, but she couldn't come. Work. I guess Julian offered to speak to her boss, but she was too embarrassed."

I put my head in my hands. "Could you guys excuse me for just a second?" I got up and stood outside the door for a moment, trying to bring myself under control before I took out my BlackBerry to call Julian.

His phone rang several times, and then he came on. "Darling? Sorry, I had to duck out before I could answer."

"Julian, you . . . you . . . I can't even talk. This is just so over the top. Oh my God."

"Hush. Did everyone make it?"

"You didn't need to do this."

"Yes, I did. There's plenty of spare bedrooms upstairs, and I want them all safely filled until we head back to Connecticut."

I sniffed. "This is about the nicest thing anyone's ever done for me."

"Darling, I haven't even begun." He chuckled.

"So how are things going?"

"You'd not believe your ears. I can't say more. Darling, I've got to go. Enjoy yourself tonight. I'll try not to wake you when I get home."

"If you don't wake me," I said, "I'll never forgive you."

He laughed and hung up.

"ALL RIGHT, MISSY," said Michelle, closing the door behind us two days later, "it's time to spill."

"Spill what?" I tripped down the steps to the sidewalk and turned right toward Park Avenue.

"You know. I've finally got you to myself. No eavesdropping parents. So talk."

I made a defeated little grunt. It was eleven o'clock at night, and my parents had gone to bed in one of the spare rooms upstairs; my brother had met up with a college buddy of his somewhere downtown. Julian was still in meetings, and had been all day. So rather than sit restlessly around the living room, waiting for him to return, Michelle and I had decided to skip out for a quick coffee.

"I don't know what to say. It's hard to know where to start." We started crossing Park Avenue, heading toward the nearest Starbucks on Lexington and Seventy-eighth.

"Because it was kind of surreal for us, back home. Oh, Kate's seeing this hedge fund guy, she's on Gawker, she's moved with him to Connecticut, she's, like, *engaged*. I mean, you've known him for maybe a few months."

"Since December, actually."

"You know what I mean. Don't get me wrong, he seems great. Flying us out here was so, just, amazing. But, honey . . ." Her voice trailed off. Michelle was deeply practical, always the voice of reason in our trio. She'd been the one to negotiate the lease when we went off-campus our senior year. She'd always remembered to bring the map when we went out at night in some new European city during our summer abroad. And she'd been the one to pick up the pieces and force me to move on after my college heartbreaks.

"I know how it looks," I said, turning left onto Lexington. "And it's true, I'm dizzy in love with him. My toes still curl when he walks into the room."

"Good in bed, huh?" She was not one for beating around the bush.

"Oh, jeez, Michelle."

"Awesome. So he's fantastic in the sack. He's got the romantic gesture thing down. He's rich as hell. You're dizzy in love." She shook her head. "Kate, will you put your fucking head on, please?"

"What? Isn't that all *good*?"

"Come on, Kate. I know you. You're not *vixen* enough for a guy like that."

"Julian is nothing like the other men I've dated," I said. "You have no idea, Michelle."

"Oh, for God's sake. Look at the guy. You'll be in his shadow all your life. Women will be flinging themselves at him. He's human. Do the math."

"You don't think I can hold him? You don't think he could resist?"

She hesitated. "I'm just saying . . ."

"Look, could you do me the favor of meeting him first? I wish I could tell you . . ." I took a deep breath. "Just trust me, okay? Here we are."

We walked in. The store bustled with people, despite the late hour; luckily the line was in ebb mode rather than flow.

"And what about the money thing?" she pointed out, in a hushed voice.

"What about it?" I muttered back. The man behind us in line was standing just a little too close, as if he were trying to listen in on our conversation. Or was I letting Julian's paranoia get to me?

We stepped up to the counter before she had a chance to answer. "What're you having?" I asked.

"I don't know. Vanilla latte, I guess. Grande."

"I'll have the same," I told the barista, and then something fluttered at the back of my head. "Um, decaf," I added.

"Since when do you order decaf?" she asked.

"It's late, Michelle. I'd be up all night."

"I thought that was the point."

"With my luck he won't be back until three in the morning again." I handed the cashier a ten-dollar bill and put the change in the tip box. I turned to the pickup counter and nearly ran into the man behind me, who was even closer than I thought. Blood rushed to my cheeks. How much had he heard?

I pulled Michelle with me, squinting at the man as he ordered his coffee. He had an unmistakable weird-guy aura around him, not that it was all that uncommon in a city like New York. He was dressed more or less normally for the Upper East Side, with a navy blue polo shirt over dark khakis and a baseball cap pulled down low on his forehead, but there was something about the way he stood, the way he ducked his head. Lonely furtive movements, like a closet child-porn freak. I couldn't see his face well, but the hair wisped dark and curling from under his baseball cap.

The lattes came up; we grabbed them and found a table that had just been vacated. I pulled out my BlackBerry and set it on the surface next to my coffee before shooting a glance back at the weirdo. He was getting his coffee from the counter; he didn't even look in our direction. My gut began to unclench, surprising me: I hadn't realized I'd become so tense.

"I'm sorry for being such a downer," Michelle was saying, watching me with that creased expression she wore when her mind was full of reservations.

"Well, stop worrying, okay? I know what I'm doing."

"Kate, it's in his genes, okay? He's the top dog. Leader of the pack. Men like that don't stay with one woman, not unless she has more fucking balls than he does. It's the only language they understand. Control."

"You don't have to be morally deficient to be successful, for God's sake."

"But he's a strong man, isn't he? Likes to have things his own way?"

"Strong and selfish are not the same thing."

She shot me a pointed look. "You can't have one without the other, can you?"

I set my latte down with a thump. "You never give me credit, do you? Just because I'm not an ass-kicker, like ass-kicking is some kind of virtue. Like everything reduces to power games. Like we're not *grown-ups* here."

"Look, I didn't mean . . ."

"Do you have any *idea* how many doors I had to crash to get into Sterling Bates from a state school? What I've been through since? So don't sit there and tell me I can't stick up for myself."

"Whoa. Slow down. I'm not saying you're *timid*, sweetie. I'm just, like, suggesting you take a break from the alpha males. Find yourself a nice poet somewhere. Try to . . . what, you're *laughing* now?"

"Nothing. Just . . . poetry."

"Whatever. I realize in your eyes he's Mr. Perfect. I'm just *saying*, that's all."

My BlackBerry buzzed. "He's not perfect," I told her, picking up the phone.

Finished up at last. In your arms in ten minutes. XX

I slipped the phone into my handbag. "They're finally done. Can we finish these on the way back?"

"Sure." She stood up.

We went to the door with lattes in hand and walked back out into the mild September night. The lights had just changed, and a raft of taxis streamed down Lexington, looking for fares back downtown. I glanced over my shoulder just in time to see Weirdo Man emerge from the Starbucks and turn down Lexington after us.

"So tell me more about his faults," Michelle was saying. "Is he, like, flatulent? A nose picker? Does he sit there tickling his balls while he watches TV?"

I tried to laugh. "Michelle, stop! Okay, first of all, he doesn't watch TV."

"No TV? No Sunday HBO? Are you freaking *serious*?"

"We find other stuff to do." We paused on the corner, checking for traffic. I used the opportunity to look casually backward again, but there were several other people on the sidewalk and I couldn't pick him out.

"Well, what about the rest of it?" she prodded. "Because this is a whole different world for you. Won't you have responsibilities? Charity stuff? Ladies who lunch? Tweed Chanel suits? You know that's not for you."

"He'd never push me into that."

"Seriously, though. What happens when you get married and have a baby or two and wake up one day to find you're just Mrs. Julian Laurence, the billionaire's wife? Where's *Kate* going to be? Can you honestly say that's all you want from life?"

I opened my mouth to answer her and found I had nothing to say.

I mean, what could I tell her? *Julian's a great guy, but I'm worried his trench warfare experience left some scars he just won't show me?* Of course not. I couldn't tell her any of that, just as I hadn't been able to tell my mother. I couldn't even tell her the good things, like how this precious secret of ours had bonded me with Julian so closely it felt, at times, as if we shared the same mind, even if parts of it were frustratingly closed off to me; that it had braided us together in a way that made laughable the very idea of his disloyalty, or mine.

And that realization stopped me cold. I'd always been able to tell my girlfriends nearly everything, far more than I'd ever told my mother. But now that barrier had thudded down again, thick and impenetrable. I couldn't talk to anyone. This secret, which had drawn me so close to Julian, had simultaneously distanced me from everyone else in my life.

So when Michelle made a perfectly valid point, that Mrs. Julian Laurence might well sink Kate Wilson into total oblivion, I couldn't really reply. For one thing, I was deeply afraid she was right.

And equally afraid there wasn't much I could do about it.

I frowned and glanced behind me.

"What's that?" asked Michelle.

"Nothing," I said. "Just a guy. He was kind of hovering in the Starbucks line, and I think he's behind us now. Don't *look*!"

Her head stopped in mid-swivel. "You think we're being *followed*?"

"No, no. I'm just being stupid. Julian gets worried, you know, because he's a bit of a target."

"A target! Like the Mafia or something?" she asked eagerly.

"No," I laughed, "just, you know, because of the money thing. He thinks someone might kidnap me or whatever."

"Jesus. I never even thought of that." We stopped on the corner of Park, and she made a casual look backward, like she was just checking out one of the grand apartment buildings. "There *is* a guy there," she said. "Don't know if he's following us or whatever, but I think he's watching."

"Shoot," I said, trying to decide what to do. Go straight back home? Or try to lose him? There were plenty of people around, plenty of doormen in the buildings nearby. We weren't in danger, exactly. This *was* Park Avenue.

"Okay," I said finally, "let's just walk back to the house. Act normal." I slipped my hand into my pocket and fingered my phone.

We crossed Park and walked down the two blocks to Julian's street. I didn't look back, but I could sense him there—unless it was just my neurotic imagination—ten, fifteen yards back, matching our pace, dodging in front of taxis to keep up.

We turned onto Seventy-fourth Street. Julian's house was only a few doors away, and as we started down I saw a black sedan pull up outside it. The rear door opened almost before the car had stopped, and Julian's familiar figure sprang out. "Thank God," I said, hurrying my steps, pulling Michelle along.

"Welcome back," I called out, as he crossed the sidewalk to the steps.

He looked over and saw us. His face, in the pale yellow glow of a nearby streetlamp, broke into a wide exhausted smile. He set down his laptop bag and opened his arms just in time to receive my hurtling body. "Hello, beloved," he said, in a husky whisper delivered directly to my left ear.

Then his arms loosened and he looked up.

"Ah," he said, and I could sense the smile in his voice, "you must be the famous Michelle." I stepped back, and he reached out his hand to her. "Julian Laurence. Delighted to meet you at last." ·

She rose to the occasion. You could always count on Michelle for that. She shifted her latte to her left side and shook his hand firmly and said, without the smallest bit of self-consciousness, "Hi, Julian. Great to meet you. And thanks so much for having us all out. It's been great seeing Kate look so happy."

His eyes moved back to my face, and the corner of his lip lifted intimately. "I certainly hope so," he said. "That's all that matters."

"Very happy," I said. I hadn't seen him since he'd driven away from the cottage three days ago, except for the half-remembered sensation of his body curling around mine for a few hours' sleep. "How did everything go? Did you save the world?"

The smile disappeared. "Not exactly, but we've at least hammered something out. I'll tell you all about it in the morning." He looked back at Michelle and twinkled. "I trust you're not going to ring up your broker with that information, hmm?"

"Don't have one. Kate's the finance guru. I majored in anthropology." She nodded at me. "So is your stalker still around?"

I glanced to the corner and saw a male figure hovering there. "Michelle, don't," I warned, but it was too late.

"Stalker? What's this?" Julian's body coiled in readiness, like a snake's.

"Yeah, some weirdo at Starbucks was following us back." She swiveled. "Look, he's still there. Ducking back around the corner."

"Wait! Julian, I . . ."

He'd already taken off, a sprinter out of the blocks, exploding down the sidewalk.

"Oh my God," Michelle said. "Do we follow him?"

"No," I said sharply, "wait here," though my every nerve strained to go after him.

"*Shit*, he's fast. I've never seen a guy move like that in a *suit*. Like freaking Superman."

"He's pretty active." I stared intently at the corner around which he'd just disappeared, remembering all our hours spent running and swimming, rowing and hiking and sailing.

"He's not going to get hurt, is he?"

"Actually, I'm more concerned for the other guy." I looked down at his laptop bag on the steps next to us and picked it up.

We waited a big longer. Nothing: no sound, no sight of them.

"Okay, if he's not back in another thirty seconds, I think we should go check it out," Michelle said.

But Julian appeared back around the corner almost as she spoke, walking quickly, straightening his suit jacket. Alone.

"What happened?" I called out.

"He ran off. Disappeared."

"Seriously?" I asked. "He dodged *you?*"

Julian shrugged. "He had a good head start, and then he went 'round the corner of Sixty-sixth and vanished, more or less." He ran a hand through his hair. "I wouldn't worry, though. He didn't seem that threatening. I doubt he'll be bothering you again."

I frowned. This was not like Julian at all. "Okay," I said slowly, "if you say so."

"Come along." He took my hand. "Let's get inside. Michelle? Everything all right?"

She shook her head clear. "Yeah. Just way more drama than I'm used to, that's all."

Me too, Michelle. Me too. The words rose up uninvited into my thoughts, followed closely by: *And I guess I'd better get used to it.*

WE WENT UP THE STEPS and into the house. Julian ducked into the library to put away his laptop bag, and I took the latte cups down to the kitchen to throw away. When I came back, Julian and Michelle were standing in front of the living room bookshelf, trying to find her something to take upstairs.

"Latin?" she was saying. "You have books in Latin?"

He laughed. "That's more or less what Kate said, the first time she stood here."

"Yeah. I'll bet. And wow," she added, fingering another title. "*Fanny Hill*, huh? Lucky Kate." She pulled it out. "I think I'll take this one, if you don't mind. Haven't read it since college."

I lifted my eyebrow at Julian; he winked back.

"Look," Michelle said, "I'm super tired, and you two probably have a lot to chat about, so I'll just discreetly head upstairs. Good night, sweetie." She gave me a hug and a kiss on my cheek. "Good night, Julian. Nice meeting you."

"I like her," he said, as her footsteps tripped up the stairway.

"Well, she thinks you're going to break my heart."

He looked down at me bemusedly, and I saw the weariness in his eyes.

"Oh, look at you." I put my hands to his cheeks. "I'm so sorry. You're exhausted."

"A little." He eased his arms around my waist and turned his head to kiss my palm. "It's been a rough few days, and not just this debacle downtown."

"What can I do for you? Food? Bath? Bed?"

"I've eaten, more or less, but the other two sound ridiculously inviting."

I smiled. "I'm at your service. Come along." I slipped out of his arms and took him by the hand, up the stairs and down the hall to the bedroom.

"Take off your suit," I ordered, over my shoulder. "I'll run your bath."

"You're an angel."

I turned on the faucets to the bathtub and poured in some vanilla bath oil. The steam began to rise, humid and fragrant, from the water; I turned to see him standing there, fiddling with his cufflinks, his suit jacket and trousers already put away.

"Let me do that," I said.

He held out his arms, one by one, and I pried the cufflinks from their holes and set them down on the counter. His hands looked pale, as though the fluorescent office lights had somehow leached away the summer tan from his skin over the past few days. I began unbuttoning his shirt, trying to keep my fingers steady, to stay dispassionate; to remind myself that he was tired, that he was human; that it was my turn, now, to make the necessary sacrifice.

The last button came apart. I reached up and pulled the shirt from his shoulders, and then grasped the bottom of his white cotton undershirt with my fingertips. He lifted his arms obligingly, the better for me to ease it up over his chest and head. His skin shone like honeyed alabaster in the gentle glow, dusted with fine blond hair.

"Okay," I said, "I think you'd better do the rest yourself, or this bath water is going to go to waste."

"Kate," he said, taking my hand, "join me."

I looked at the bathtub. It was one of those old-fashioned roll-top models, perfect for a single Edwardian male, not so much for an adventurous modern couple. "Is there room?"

"We'll make room," he said, pulling impatiently at my camisole. "I can't bear to be away from you any longer."

He settled into the bathtub and reached for me, his arms enclosing me, my back melting into the muscles of his abdomen: the sweet osmosis of reunion. I felt his breath brush against my ear, and I closed my eyes and tucked my head against his collarbone. "This is insane," I sighed. "It's only been a few days. What if you have to fly to Hong Kong or something?"

"I'd take you with me." He bent his head to nuzzle my cheek.

I sat quietly, listening to the sound of his breathing, of the vanilla-scented water lapping around us. "Thanks again, by the way," I said at last. "For bringing out my family to babysit me. You blew them away. And me."

"You give me far too much credit. Allegra made all the arrangements; I only issued the invitations."

"You did way more than that."

He didn't answer for a moment, and then: "I'm glad it made you happy."

"*You* make me happy. I'm sitting here, right now, feeling you next to me at last, and I'm just . . . happy. Just *happy*. This is all I want in life."

"All?" His fingers entwined with mine; I felt his thumb press my ring.

"You," I said. "Just you."

"You have me, Kate."

"Yes, finally." I pulled his gleaming arms closer. "I've been craving you. Your touch. Not to sound melodramatic or anything; I've just been spoiled all summer, having you within reach most of the time."

"Mmm." Another moment of quiet communion, until he broke the stillness in a low full voice. "Do you know what kept me going, in the middle of those damned sessions, bank officials droning on pointlessly?"

"I can't imagine."

He bowed his head next to mine and let his breath warm the skin of my face, my neck. "I started off by picturing you at your very height, beloved. When your cheeks are flushed scarlet and your eyes burn up at me, begging me to send you over the edge. And I wonder how much longer I can hold out, how much longer I can keep you teetering on the brink, without simply disintegrating altogether."

"Oh, great. With the fate of Wall Street hanging in the balance." I closed my eyes. Steam curled into my nostrils, vanilla and Julian, delicate alluring alchemy.

"Or else when you've taken charge of things," he went on, drawing his wet hands upward. "And your head's tilted back, and that midnight hair of yours tumbles down your shoulders, and your pale breasts dance before my eyes, and I'm half mad with the sight of you, the feel of you."

"Julian." I covered his hands with mine.

"But that proved far too stimulating," he conceded, brushing his thumbs against my breasts. "And so I thought of you afterward, sprawled across my chest, your skin glowing against mine like a moonbeam. And the way you look up at me, at last, with your limpid eyes and your enchanting smile. Or else with some cheeky remark, perhaps, to keep me properly in line. And I wonder whether such happiness is even *right*. Whether I'm not tempting the gods into some unholy vengeance, knowing such bliss."

"Only you," I said weakly, "only *you* could worry about that. All that's going through *my* mind at that moment is how much time you're going to need to recharge."

"That's *all*?" He reached down under the water and pinched my backside. "I'm expiring with love for you, little minx, and you're only thinking about your next ruddy *orgasm*?"

"Well," I giggled, squirming to avoid his nipping fingers, "you do it . . . so *well* . . . *Julian*! All *right*! Yes, I do . . . on *occasion* . . . reflect on the metaphysical profundity . . . *Julian*! I'm serious. You know that. You know I'm . . . that I . . ."

"You what?" He stilled his fingers, eased his arms back around me.

"You know how I feel."

"Mmm." His lips buried themselves in my hair, and I placed my arms over his. In the quiet, I could discern the faint creaking of the floorboards above us, the trickle of water through pipes: Michelle, I guessed, getting ready for bed.

"Charlie tells me you had an uneasy moment the other day," Julian said at last.

I shifted against him. "Oh, that. Just a guy hanging around outside yesterday, when we got to the house. Maybe the same guy as tonight. Same build."

"Mmm," he said again.

"And there was something else. When I got to my apartment, it looked like Brooke had gone through my things, and I was kind of thinking . . ."

"Gone through your things? What do you mean?" His voice sharpened.

"Well, my papers. Drawers. Not that I have anything top secret lying around. But with all this going on with Sterling Bates, and both of us involved in it . . ."

A beat of silence. I felt the slow spooling of tension in the muscles beneath me. "Darling," he said, "why don't you ring up Allegra tomorrow and give her the details. We'll have a moving van there straightaway."

"Yikes."

"Lest you forget, Mrs. Ashford," he said, "*this* is your home now. Our home."

"I know. I'm just getting used to the idea."

"We could always find something else, you know. If you're not comfortable here. An apartment, perhaps, if you'd rather. Grand or small, anything you like."

I smiled at the thread of anxiety in his voice. "I love this house, Julian. It's perfect. It's home. It's just a big change for me, that's all."

He pressed my ring again. "Does it bother you?"

"Well, strangely enough, it was easier when you were back in Connecticut. As Julian Ashford, I mean. It all makes more sense coming from the real you. This, on the other hand, is more intimidating." I waved my hand.

"This?"

"Your Manhattan life. Julian Laurence, head of Southfield. Crusher of evil business adversaries. Endless loops of you on CNBC."

He began laughing. "Kate, for goodness' sake. We're the same man."

"No, you're not," I insisted. "When you're talking on the phone with one of your traders or whatever, you're all ruthless and commanding. Which is sexy, I won't deny it, but . . . Excuse me, would you stop laughing for a moment?"

"Darling," he said, picking up my hand and kissing the inside of my wrist, "what would you have me do? Whisper sweet nothings in the poor chap's ear?"

"I'm not saying that. I'm just saying I don't see that side of you. You don't *show* me . . ."

"That's because I'm *in love* with you. Besides, if I but *tried* to talk to you that way, minx, you'd let me have it." He paused and covered my other hand with his own, drawing them both inward. "Sweetheart, I know what you're trying to say. You haven't been living with this as long as I have; it's not natural to you. But you're overanalyzing again. Whatever I am, darling, Laurence or Ashford or whatever the ruddy hell, you're always at the absolute center of me. Don't waste an instant worrying about any of *that*."

I wiggled my toes, catching the emphasis. "So what *should* I be worrying about?"

He hesitated.

"Look, Ashford. I can tell when something's on your mind by now. So spill it, please, so we can move on to the welcome-home sex."

"Nothing like candor, is there?"

"You love my candor. Now talk."

His body shifted, straightening against the back of the tub. "Kate, I've been doing a great deal of thinking during these interminable meetings. I think it's time for a change of strategy."

"Strategy?" I trailed my fingers through the cooling bath water, watching the ripples spread out and ricochet from the walls of the tub. "What do you mean?"

"You were right to come into the city. I've been a coward, an ostrich, hiding both our heads in the country soil and hoping it would all go away. I haven't learned the lessons of my own war, you see. I've been busy digging in, instead of taking the battle to the enemy and ending the conflict entirely."

"Sorry, I don't quite follow military logic. What exactly are we talking about?"

"I mean it's time to flush out whoever it is that's threatening us."

"Threatening us? Is someone actually *threatening* us? Like that guy tonight? Because you didn't seem worried . . ."

"Because I don't think that's related."

"Related to *what*? To my stuff being searched? To all these vague premonitions of yours? I mean, what's going *on*? What aren't you telling me?"

He didn't reply at first. "Look, Kate," he said finally, "you'll have to take a bit of a leap of faith here. There *is* a danger, a real one. I honestly can't tell you what it is. I don't even properly know myself. But it's there, Kate, whatever it is, and I think it's time to stop hiding from it."

I was silent.

"What are you thinking?" he pressed me.

"Julian, I trust you. If you think there's something out there, fine. Hire a bodyguard. Do whatever it takes so you can rest easy at night, and we can live our lives." I stopped. "Just what do you mean by flushing it out?"

He drew in a deep breath; I felt myself rise and fall on his chest. "I mean go out. In public. Charity balls, opening nights, that sort of thing. Allegra can arrange it all; she's quite efficient. Make a bit of a splash."

"What?" I sat up and turned to face him, sloshing water over the sides of the tub. "Are you *kidding*?"

"It may, I hope, provoke our chap to act. And we'll be prepared for it."

"Julian, I don't do that stuff. I'm terrible at it. Look at what happened at MoMA. I broke a *champagne* glass over a guy's *head*. And I wasn't even drunk."

"I'll be by your side every second," he said. "It's September, and the social calendar is full of all sorts of rubbish. You might even enjoy yourself."

"No, no, no. Way out of my sphere. What, prance around in designer dresses and be your *arm candy*? Are you *nuts*?"

He frowned at me. "I thought you *wanted* to spend some time in the city."

"I didn't mean I wanted you to turn me into some kind of *socialite*! I was thinking more along the lines of a *career*!"

"Doing *what*?"

"I don't know! Something!" I stood up and snatched a towel. "I mean, why don't you just dye my hair blond and stick me in Greenwich with *Geoff's wife*?"

"What the devil? Who said anything about bloody *Greenwich*?"

I stepped out of the tub and wrapped the towel around me. "But that's what would happen, right? Pretty soon I'd be out in the 'burbs, having babies and doing tennis lunches at the club with the other hedgie wives. Gossip and . . . and *handbags*. This is exactly, *exactly* what I've been afraid of all along!"

"Oh, for goodness' sake, Kate." He dropped his head back against the rim of the tub and glared at the ceiling. "We're talking about a few months here. And you haven't the faintest interest in handbags."

"Yes, I do. I like handbags. A little. That's the problem. It would be too easy to just . . . be that girl. Get all shallow and complacent."

"You're being absurd. You'd never do that. You're not *like* those women. You're a completely different animal. It's why I love you."

"Then why try to turn me into one of them?"

He stood up, letting the water drip magnificently from his body for a moment before dragging a towel off the rack and draping it around his midsection. An athlete's body, an active man's body, flat smooth muscles flexing effortlessly under his glowing skin, making it hard to concentrate on quarrelling with him. "For the last time," he said through his teeth, stepping out of the tub, "I'm not doing anything of the kind. It's nothing to do with you becoming a damned socialite. It's about finding out who's going to ruin our lives and stopping him before he has the chance."

"*Who* wants to ruin our lives? *Why?*"

"I don't know! That's what I'm trying to find out! If you'll let me!" He grabbed a hand towel and rubbed his hair furiously with it.

I stared at him. "You really *are* paranoid."

He turned to face me. "Yes, I am," he said, his voice breaking. "I'm wild with worry for you. You've no idea. Keeping you safe is the first thing I think about in the morning, and the last thought in my head as I go to sleep."

"Well, stop wasting your time. I'm fine. You should be more worried about yourself. You're more of a target than I am."

"That may be true, but *you're* the one . . ." He stopped.

"What are you *talking* about? What's going *on*?"

"Damn it." He turned from me and struck his fist on the counter. "I *wish* I knew more. I've been racking my brains, trying to remember . . ."

"Remember what?"

"Details, *clues*, Kate. I can't explain. I only know someone wishes us ill. Someone's going to have a go at us. At *you*. It may be the chap harassing Hollander. Or something to do with this mess with the banks. I don't *know*, damn it all. I never found out." His head bowed, overburdened; his hands gripped the pale marble edge of the counter. "But it's *there*, Kate. It's coming. I need you to believe that."

He was so obviously distressed. I felt my anger melt into compassion. "Look," I said, stepping near him, "stop thinking you can control everything in life. You can't. I could get run over by a bus tomorrow. So could you. But the odds are pretty narrow on that, so why spoil the time we have, worrying about all the things that could go wrong?"

He stared at our mingled reflections in the mirror. "Kate, won't you please try this with me? I give you my word, it's only for a short while. You don't have to join all these ruddy clubs and committees and things. I'll take care of all the donations and arrangements; you'll just come along with me and amuse yourself."

"Arm candy."

"Well, you can't help being beautiful," he coaxed, turning around. "I know you don't enjoy these things, but I'll be with you. You like going out with me, don't you?"

"Except for all the women trying to seduce you away from me, yes."

He laughed and reached for me. "The only woman I've eyes for," he said, next to my ear, sensing my imminent capitulation, "the only woman with even the faintest power to seduce me, is your own lovely self. I shall be fighting my way through your hordes of admirers, trying to reach your side."

"Cue the crickets chirping."

"We shall pose for photographs," he said, moving one hand to untuck my towel, "and drink rivers of champagne. Then we'll pick your reward from the auction . . ."

"Nice try, Ashford, but no dice."

My towel dropped to the floor.

". . . and make shallow brilliant conversation with a few select guests . . ."

"And if one of these super-skinny social types gets catty with me?"

"Get catty back," he advised, swinging me up into his arms and carrying me out of the bathroom.

"I was kind of hoping you'd, like, ruin her husband or something."

"Oh, that goes without saying." He tossed me onto the bed and crawled after me like a hungry golden panther.

"Rrrrr." I looped my arms about his neck. "So kiss me already."

"I thought you'd never ask," he growled back.

"THERE'S JUST ONE THING," Julian said, some time later, just as sleep began to drift over me in my warm cocoon of white sheets and male skin.

"What's that?" I said drowsily, skimming my fingers over the long ragged scar on his right arm.

"I'm afraid, my darling"—he kissed the tip of my nose—"you'll be obliged to go shopping."

Amiens

By five o'clock that afternoon, the rain had paused and a genuine beam of sunlight struggled out between the clouds. I smiled at it, feeling unexpectedly lighthearted, and drew the straw market basket more firmly into my elbow. I'd gone shopping, scouring the scantily shelved shops of Amiens to gather together a simple picnic: bread and cheese and what looked to be a pretty decent pâté, with wine for him and Perrier water—Perrier, God bless them!—for me. Yes, a picnic. Julian loved picnics.

So distracted was I, cheerful face upturned to the mottled sky, that Geoffrey Warwick's outstretched hand seemed to emerge from thin air when it grasped my upper arm and brought my momentum to a staggered halt.

"Oww!" I exclaimed, trying to pull away. "What do you think you're doing?"

He replied quietly. "I might very well ask the same thing of you."

"Lieutenant Warwick." I encircled his wrist with my fingers and removed it. "If you're trying to intimidate me, I should warn you: I'm not like the shrinking violets you're used to. I can run a mile in six minutes, and I know a self-defense move that would lay you flat on your back in less time than it would take me to scream rape." That last part was technically a bluff; I'd learned the maneuver in theory during freshman orientation, but I'd never tried it out on a real live six-foot attacker.

"Do you really think," he said, voice still low, "do you really *imagine* you can insert yourself into his life like this? Brazen, unprincipled woman. Have you any idea of the pain you're causing?"

"If you mean Arthur Hamilton," I said, "I believe I do. Of course I do. And I'm sorry for that, very sorry, more than you can possibly know. But you've no idea, do you, what really lies between them, between Julian and Florence . . ."

He started, a sharp backward motion of his head. "What do you know of Miss Hamilton?"

"I know everything. And it's not what you think. Julian doesn't . . ."

He lifted his right hand in a reflexive motion, as if warding away a blow. His face had grown pale under the shadow of his cap. "I don't give a tinker's damn about that. It's not my concern. My concern is for my friends, one of them walking headlong into his own ruin . . ."

"Ruin!"

"And the other utterly broken, refusing to think the worst of a man upon whose fidelity he stakes his faith in humanity itself . . ."

"*Ruin* Julian! You think I'm trying to *ruin* him? I'm here to *save* him, you jackass, and from you most of all! Ruin him. For God's sake." I nearly spat the last words; I wanted to strike him. My hand twitched with violence, until I had to fist it behind my back.

He flinched. "Who the devil are you?"

"You don't deserve to know that, Geoffrey Warwick."

"I demand to know it."

"By what right?"

His eyes narrowed into severity. "No one," he said coldly, "no one is more devoted to Captain Ashford's well-being than I am."

I shook my head and opened my mouth to speak, and at that moment the light shifted around a passing cloud, catching the man's eyes from under the brim of his dun-colored cap. Brown, a light speckled brown, nearly hazel and bristling with sincerity. What had Julian told me about him? Not all that much. The son of a City stockbroker, worlds away socially from Julian's ancient family. They'd struck up a friendship at Eton, gone on to Cambridge together. A great deal must lie behind that bare history, of course: Julian bravely extending his hand across the great chasm of class and adolescent social pressure dividing them, Geoff probably fiercely loyal as a result. A new world for the City boy, full of careless unstable aristocrats like the Hamiltons, shades of *Brideshead* in there somewhere. And here I came, out of the blue, disturbing the balance. Clearly not in the Florence Hamilton mold, clearly not an aristocrat, clearly not worthy of Julian in Geoffrey's eyes. I thought about the Greenwich estate, the trophy wife, the relentless ambition. Geoff was a striver, a gold digger in his way; perhaps his instinct to protect Julian from me contained more than a little self-hatred.

Perhaps the key to saving Julian lay right here, before me.

"Look," I said, softening my voice, "let's talk a moment. I mean, I think we both have Julian's best interests at heart here . . ."

"I doubt that extremely."

"You really are stubborn, aren't you?" I said. I set down the basket, which was getting heavy, and crossed my arms. "Look, whether you believe it or not, I love Julian Ashford. Not for his money or his position, God knows, but for himself. For all his wonderful qualities, all those reasons I'm sure you appreciate, too. Wait." I held up my hand. "Just hear me out, please. You're aware I know a lot about your past; well, as it happens, I know certain things about the future too. Things that will happen to us, all of us, that will cause harm to Julian, whom we both love. And my whole purpose here is to save him from that. So . . ."

"What rot!" he burst out, tugging off his hat to run his hand over his hair. "What bloody vicious *nonsense.* Some sort of Gypsy witch, are you?"

"Now, you see, I'm more enlightened than you are," I struggled for composure, "so I'm not actually offended by that."

"What I understand," Geoff said, replacing his hat, calming his voice, "is that you believe yourself to be saving Captain Ashford from *me.* From me, of all people, when I'd defend him with my last breath. I ought to kick you to the gutter, where you belong . . ."

"He'd never forgive you."

His eyes drilled into mine. "Women like you . . ."

"Okay, enough. There's only so much of this I can take, even for *his* sake. So fine. Let's agree not to like each other; I don't see any way out of that. But can we please, *please* set that aside, and put Julian's interests first?"

"Captain Ashford's best interests lie in your immediate withdrawal from his life."

"No!" I pointed my finger at his chest. "Julian's interests lie in your hands. Because *you're* the one who's going to betray him. *You.*"

He started backward, agape, his hard leather shoes slipping against the still-damp paving stones.

"Yes, I've got your attention now, haven't I? This ridiculous hatred you bear me, Geoffrey Warwick, this bigoted *jealousy* of yours, will mean Julian's death and your own. So you'd better get over it, before you ruin us all." I picked up the basket and settled it back into my elbow and gave him a last hard look. "Just let him be *happy*, for God's sake."

I turned around and marched back down the street, toward rue des Augustins.

21.

Blue. A blue line. Sharp, vivid, unequivocal. *Here I am, Mommy!*

The wand dropped from my shaking fingers. I stared at it, there on the bathroom floor, an earthquake compressed into white plastic.

"Darling," Julian called from the bedroom, "are you almost ready? The car's waiting."

"Um, yeah," I called back. "Just putting on my lipstick." I leaned down and grabbed the damning evidence and shook it back and forth. As if that would change the result. Make it less . . . *blue.*

"Can I help?" he asked, his voice coming nearer.

"No! Just finishing up. Hold on." I grabbed a tissue and wrapped it around the wand and stuck it in the back of my drawer.

I checked my face in the mirror. The hairdresser had departed ten minutes ago, leaving my hair pinned atop my head in a pert cascade. I'd done my makeup myself, as always: a bit heavier than I liked, but I'd seen the results from my first effort in the Sunday Pulse section of the *Post*, and quickly grasped that if the camera added ten pounds of fat, it also took away the equivalent amount of makeup. I'd looked like a college student. And not in a good way.

"Darling," Julian prodded, right on the other side of the door.

I turned at once and yanked it open. "Sorry. Too much, do you think?"

"Yes. But you look stunning anyway." He wasn't much of a makeup man, Julian.

"Sorry," I repeated. "Have to look the part."

"What do you think?" He lifted both hands. "Diamonds or rubies?"

"You pick."

He held each one carefully up to my neck. "Rubies," he decided.

"Nothing says *notice me* like a fortune in sparkly red jewels," I sighed, turning around for him to fasten them around my neck.

"When we return home tonight," he said, his fingers cool and dexterous against my nape, "I want you to wear these, and nothing else."

It had taken Julian a day of pleading and seduction and completely bogus threats to get me to wear any of the jewelry he'd had brought down from the safe in Connecticut; in the end, he'd called in Michelle and Samantha one weekend as reinforcements. Traitors. He'd won them over in no time, with his damned relentless charisma and his private planes and his funding of a shopping spree to end all shopping sprees. They'd transformed into his willing accomplices, sneaking things past me to the sales staff, coming home with armloads of shoes in my size, making me try on gown after gown. Their eyes had glazed over with perpetual glee, as if every pleasure center in their respective brains were being pummeled by an outsized hammer.

I turned around. His face was so close I could smell his freshly brushed teeth. "Mmm, minty," I said, without thinking, and leaned forward to kiss him.

"Stop that," he murmured, bringing his hands up to the back of my neck. "We haven't time," and his mouth curved lingeringly around mine. "Seductress," he said at last, pulling away. "Now I've ruined your lipstick."

I rubbed the evidence from his lips with my fingers. "It's your fault, walking in here with that face of yours. How's my dress?'

"Like it should be ripped from your body."

"So you like it?" I twirled. The pearl-gray layers floated around me, draping my figure with ridiculous suggestiveness. I had to admit, these couture designers knew what they were doing.

"I despise it. Every man in the building is going to be thinking the same thing I am." He looked downward and frowned.

"It's called a push-up bra, Julian," I said helpfully.

"Bloody hell," he muttered.

"Well, this was all your idea, remember? I'm just following orders."

"Revenge is more like it. Very well, then." He held out his arm. "Shall we, Mrs. Ashford?"

"Why, thank you, Captain Ashford." I took his arm and snagged my bejeweled clutch from atop the chest of drawers. "If I may say so," I added, allowing myself to be led from the room, "you look pretty delectable yourself."

"Just the same old tuxedo," he said.

"But you wear it so well."

We made it to the bottom of the stairs, where Eric, my bulky new bodyguard, stood waiting for us like a two-legged Doberman pinscher. Julian let my arm slip away until he was holding my fingers. "Christ, Kate," he exclaimed, "you're like ice!"

"Nerves."

Julian wrapped his hand around mine and gave Eric a nod, signaling him to lead on through the front door and down the steps to the black sedan perched by the curb.

It was like I had two brains: one was flirting happily with Julian, as if everything were perfectly normal, and the other one was busy calculating just how far along I must be. I'd waited an extra week or so, hoping against hope, before taking the test, and even then I'd still been bizarrely surprised at the sight of the blue line. I mean, I couldn't be *pregnant*, for God's sake. We weren't *trying* to get pregnant. It was just one single stupid month. Other couples tried for years for a baby. And for us? Boom? Just like that? Knocked up? No way. Not possible.

I felt sweat break out, sudden and damning, all over my body. And was that *nausea*? Please not. Please, just *nervous* nausea, not *pregnant* nausea.

"Are you all right?" Julian asked suddenly, looking at my face.

"Just nervous." I laughed. "I can't seem to get used to this stuff."

"It should be easier tonight, love. Even you've been looking forward to this one." The car eased around the corner of Fifth Avenue and onto the Sixty-sixth Street park transept, heading for Lincoln Center.

"I know. I should feel lucky. And you, the opera lover! Right up your alley."

"It's not a proper opera on opening night anymore," he said. "A bit of *Traviata*, a bit of *Manon*. Final scene of *Capriccio*. It's become an event now."

"Isn't that the point? For us, I mean?"

"Yes." He sighed dramatically. "But I grieve for the art."

"We can go to others."

"Oh, yes," he said. "When all this is over, when it's all back to normal . . ."

I looked out the window at the stone walls of the transept blurring past us. "Can we really put the cat back in the bag, though? You're the savior of Wall Street now, which pretty much counts as the entire known universe in this town. And there's your ridiculously photogenic face." I reached for his hand. "You're like a perfect storm."

He frowned and turned his own gaze out the window, as uncomfortable with that reality as I was. The past few weeks had taken on a surreal quality. I'd woken up the morning after Julian's return from the Sterling Bates negotiations to find my lover was a hero. There, in that roomful of bankers, he'd stepped forward to keep the house of cards from tumbling down. With Southfield essentially dissolved, he'd committed almost the entirety of his personal equity capital to a new firm that would establish and operate auctions for the illiquid securities dragging the Sterling Bates balance sheet into bankruptcy; then he persuaded—browbeat, cajoled, whatever—others to do the same. In exchange, he'd demanded the resignation of key Sterling Bates executives, a selloff and reorganization of the bank's various divisions to raise capital, and the implementation of new and rigorous risk-management protocols.

Of course, it had taken days for Julian's role in the whole debacle to trickle out; it began as a whisper, from those who'd been in the meetings, and the legend had grown almost by itself, an open secret in the notoriously gossipy financial community. Even now, there had been no feature in *The Wall Street Journal*, no interview on CNBC. But everyone knew.

Why? I'd demanded. Why take command like that, bring attention to yourself? Your cover could be blown, just like that.

Because it had to be done, he'd answered simply.

Because, in Julian's world, that was what people did. They stepped forward. They did their duty, without excuses. They made the necessary sacrifice.

I looked at him now, at his clean pensive profile, cast in blue shadow by the fading late-afternoon light, and all my tension dissolved. I reached out and placed my hand on his opposite cheek, and turned his face toward mine. "Julian," I said, "darling," and his eyes widened, because I hardly ever used endearments. "Forget what I said before. I'm *honored* to be your arm candy."

His smile spread slowly, warm and intimate and mine alone. "Sweetheart, the honor is all mine."

The car burst free of the park and crossed Central Park West onto Sixty-seventh Street. "By the by," he said, his tone a bit forced, "you'll see Geoff Warwick and his wife there tonight."

"Oh," I said. "Can't we just avoid them?"

"I'm afraid not. We have seats in the same box."

"We're going to be sitting in the same *box*?"

"I've shared it for years with him. I know it's awkward, darling, but I'm sure we can all manage to be civil. For Carla's sake, if nothing else."

"Since when have you been so careful of Carla's feelings?" I said. Geoff I despised, of course, but Carla was even worse, in her way. She'd no doubt treat me with exactly the kind of falsely enthusiastic familiarity I hated most.

"Darling, be generous." His hand worked its way into mine.

"I'm just not good at that kind of thing. Social niceties. Being friendly with someone you don't like."

"Think of it as a game," he said. "I've told him to make himself civil."

I returned the pressure of his fingers. "I don't know why he never liked me. I mean, I'm a nice enough person, aren't I?"

"It's not you," he said. "He's a good man; he's just protective of me. Always was. Considered me a credulous chap in school, always too willing to make new friends. More or less appointed himself my watchdog." I glanced at him sharply; his voice had taken on a strained note.

"Look," I said, "I know it's unfair to you. I'll try to be good, I promise. After all, it's kind of bitten him back, hasn't it?"

"How so?"

"Because." I leaned over to kiss him. "Without that book, I might never have lured you in."

He returned my kiss. "I daresay we would have managed eventually. But here we are." He pulled his mouth away, brushed my lips with his thumb. "Are you ready?"

I glanced outside. Red carpet. Photographers. What had happened to my life? "Okay," I said, taking a deep breath, "let's get it done."

"I'll be right here beside you."

The car door swung open, and a minor explosion of flashbulbs hit my eyes. I stepped out of the car as gracefully as I could, taking the driver's hand for balance. Eric appeared imposingly at my left side, and Julian at the other an instant later. I felt his fingers slip around mine and smiled serenely. Back straight. Shoulders back.

We walked along slowly, striking an obliging pose when a photographer screamed at us, trying to look gracious and relaxed. No one asked us for an impromptu interview, thank goodness; that had happened at a movie premiere last week and I'd stood there like an idiot while Julian dazzled the reporter, some heavily made-up girl from E! who probably didn't know a hedge fund from a hedge trimmer. Again, it was his good looks that had snagged her attention. She'd probably thought he was actually in the movie. Michelle, practically bouncing in her seat, had shown me the You-Tube clip the next day:

Manhattan power couple Julian Laurence and Kate Wilson showed up at the Purgatory *premiere in New York City and showed Hollywood*

A-listers a thing or two about glamour! The billionaire hedge fund manager, credited by many with a leading role in the well-publicized rescue of mega-bank Sterling Bates earlier this month, showed off his beautiful investment-banker fiancée to the delighted crowd, and had this to say about the film's controversial subject matter: [cue eloquent rubbish from Julian, who hadn't even known what the movie was about]. *And note to Hollywood stylists: those stunning diamonds around Kate's neck weren't on loan from Harry Winston! Laurence reportedly gave her the two-million-dollar necklace as an engagement present. Lucky Kate!*

And there I stood at Julian's side, looking like a stunned deer (*What do you mean? You're totally gorgeous!* exclaimed loyal Michelle), while he flashed his lady slayer into the cameras and kissed my hand, to an explosion of paparazzi flashbulbs. That picture had made it into an obscure corner of *Us Weekly* a few days later.

We made it through Lincoln Plaza and into the lobby of the opera house, where Julian snagged me a glass of champagne from a passing waiter. I was about to take a long drink, and stopped myself just in time. "Thanks." I wet my lips gingerly.

"You were magnificent," he said, next to my ear. "Come along, let's find our seats."

We weren't in the center box—this being Manhattan, there were plenty of men far richer even than Julian—but not far from it. When we ducked inside, though, I found myself wishing we'd waited longer in the shifting power crowd: Geoff Warwick sat in a red velvet chair, arms folded, glancing up at my entrance with his usual contempt. His wife was missing; instead, a young man sat with him, studying the program.

Julian stopped dead. "Geoff," he said, after an endless second or two, "good evening. Arthur? What brings you here?"

Both men stood up. I took a deep breath. "Geoff. I'm so pleased to see you. Where's Carla?"

"Stomach flu. Good evening," he said reluctantly, shaking my offered hand.

The other man smiled with great warmth. "I'm to fill in for her tonight," he said. I shot a lightning glance at Julian. The newcomer spoke with an unmistakable English accent. "Hello, Julian," he went on, shaking Julian's hand.

"Arthur," Julian said, in a carefully controlled voice, "how are you? Darling, this is Arthur *Haverton*, our client relations manager. Arthur, my fiancée, Kate Wilson."

Arthur smiled at me, with much more warmth than Geoff Warwick. "Delighted to meet you, Miss Wilson," he said. "I've heard a great deal about you."

I smiled back. He was a bit above my height, dark haired, vaguely handsome, vaguely recognizable. "Please," I said, shaking his hand, "it's Kate. I'm sorry, have we met before? You look so familiar."

Silence fell with an almost audible *plop!* into the center of the box. I looked back at Julian with a questioning expression.

Julian cleared his throat. "Arthur has been a good friend of mine since childhood."

I saw, distantly, that the chandelier outside the box was rising, that the house lights were dimming. It all took place with agonizing slowness, as though the whole world had slipped into a lower gear somehow.

"Oh," I said. "I see." I looked again at Mr. Haverton and knew exactly where I'd seen that face before: in a sepia photograph, with a straw boater clasping his head.

Haverton. *Hamilton.*

"You must be Florence's brother," I went on. "I'm so honored to meet you, Mr. Haverton. Julian speaks of you so fondly." I felt intuitively the slow relaxing of Julian's body next to me; his hand slipped behind my back, supporting me.

"You must call me Arthur," Florence Hamilton's brother told me. "I hope very much to have the pleasure of your friendship."

"Of course," I said. "Of course."

A few more people entered the box, laughing uproariously, stumbling around in search of their chairs. "I should think it's time to take our seats," Julian said. His eyes rested heavily on Geoff Warwick, who shrugged and sat down again.

Julian took my hand and led me to our chairs at the front of the box. We sat down in the near darkness, and I withdrew my hand and put it in my lap, atop my program.

"DON'T BE ANGRY," HE SAID QUIETLY. "I hadn't any idea he'd be here. Warwick invited him deliberately. Stomach flu, my aunt Fanny."

We were standing together in a far corner of the Belmont Room, the Opera Guild patrons' lounge, where the heavy hitters congregated during intermission. Geoff had triumphantly dragged Arthur Haverton—Hamilton—to the bar, leaving Julian alone to face my wrath.

"You should have told me about him," I said, equally low. "You should have trusted me."

"I *do* trust you, Kate. Of course I do. I didn't want to cause you any pain, that's all. I . . ."

"Florence's brother. Living right here in Manhattan. *One* of you. Tell me, were you planning on introducing us at all?" I kept my voice even, determined not to make a public scene. "Ever? Or just hoping we'd never run into each other?"

"I was planning on it, eventually. It was a difficult subject to introduce."

"So you let Geoff ambush me. Did you see the look on his face? Triumphant."

"I'm sorry for that." He tried to fix me with his eyes. "Darling, have some champagne. Try to relax."

"I am perfectly relaxed. And I'll stick with water, thanks." I put the glass to my lips. Around us, the giddy chorus of chatter rose and fell; a trill of laughter carried across the room, too amusing for words.

"Thank you," he said, after a moment. "Thank you for behaving so beautifully. You're an angel. You were perfectly gracious, far more than any of us deserved."

"I thought Arthur took it well."

"Well, he'd had the chance to prepare. Darling, I was wrong. I ought to have told you long ago."

"You seem to think you can just protect me from everything. That I need to be cosseted and . . . and *kept* from things, like a child. I mean, what else are you hiding from me? What else?"

He looked at me a long time, and was just opening his mouth to reply when Paul Banner slapped his back from behind.

"Laurence!" he bellowed, spilling a few drops of Scotch from the glass in his other hand. "You asshole, you! Savior of Wall Street, huh?"

"Mr. Banner." Julian shifted to stand by my side. "What a pleasure. You know Miss Wilson, of course. My fiancée." He said it with emphasis, and his hand slipped into mine. I let it stay this time.

"Katie!" Banner leaned forward to plant a kiss on my cheek, only just missing my mouth when I turned my head away at the last instant. "Of course I know Katie! Talk about a dark fucking horse, huh? Little did we know what you had up your sleeve last Christmas! Hey, we always said we'd give you the opportunity of lifetime at Sterling Bates! Huh?"

"Well, except when you fired me, of course."

"Yeah." His face fell into contrite lines. "Sorry about that. That fucking bitch Alicia had us convinced—don't know how—but I see you landed on your feet, anyway!" He looked between the two of us.

Julian spoke coldly. "I consider the good fortune to be entirely on my side."

I turned to Julian. "Honey, I think I see someone I know over there. Why don't you two have a little chat and catch up? I'll see you back at the box in a bit." I lifted his hand and gave it a tiny kiss, just for Banner's benefit, and then pulled away to drift off to the bar.

"Holy shit, she's turned into a knockout, huh?" I heard Banner roar drunkenly behind me.

I spotted Geoff and Arthur, pulled up to the bar like horses at the trough, and sidled in between them. "Hello, gentlemen," I said. "Julian's busy with his networking again. Tell me, Arthur, how did you like the first act?"

"Oh, I've always adored La Fleming," he said, with enthusiasm. "I saw her several years ago in the new *Figaro* production. She had us all in her palm. Magnificent."

"And you, Geoff?" I looked at Warwick. "*Traviata* fan?"

He took a long drink of what looked like whiskey before answering. "You know, to be honest, Kate," he drawled, "I just come to these things for the spectacle."

22.

We didn't arrive home until nearly one o'clock. After the gala performance had come the gala dinner, and it had gone on and on with endless speeches and mutual congratulating until I wanted to stand up and scream. The only thing keeping me at the table was the knowledge that if I left to get a breath of air, Julian would follow me. And I wasn't quite ready for that yet.

Instead, I chatted with Arthur Hamilton, mostly about Julian. "Oh, he was always getting up to something," Arthur said, smiling. "He was particularly useful during house parties; his parents held a great many of them, and he engineered pranks of quite astonishing complexity. My sister was always his willing accomplice, of course."

"And his parents?" I asked. "I often think of them. How they must have missed him."

He took off his glasses and squinted at me thoughtfully while he wiped them clean. "I understand they took his departure for New York very hard," he replied with care. "A better man and woman I've never known."

"I'm so sorry. I imagine you miss your own family, as well."

"More than I can say. My sister . . . but of course you've heard about her. An extraordinary woman. Her spirit, her dash, her relentless originality. That finely tuned moral pitch I admired so deeply. And her virtue, of course: nothing like the sort of vulgar woman one finds today, endemic even—or perhaps especially—among the better classes, in every obscene bar and restaurant across the city. How I miss her." He finished on a sigh.

Had he meant to be cruel? His expression was artless, reminiscent. "I expect so," I said at last. "So much has changed. Yours was a different time."

"You can't imagine how different it was. The concept of honor *meant* something then; one's *word* meant something. There was a permanence to things, a kind of sweet immutability. Now it's all quite blown to pieces, of course, this handsome little civilization we'd built for ourselves. Quite beyond recall. Beyond redemption, I should say." He tossed back the last of his Scotch, in a way that made me think he did it often. "Ah! Dancing at last. May I have the honor, Kate?"

"Of course." I rose and danced with him, and then Julian claimed me and we danced silently until, at last, I looked up into his furrowed face and said: "Would you please take me home, now?"

He nodded, sent off a quick message to the driver, and in a few minutes Eric was bustling us into the rear seat for the voiceless drive back to Julian's townhouse.

"Let's go upstairs," I said, when we walked into the entrance hall.

Julian turned to the bodyguard. "Eric, that's all for tonight, thanks."

I led him up the stairs to our room, listening to his heavy tread behind me as we climbed the steps. Once inside, he closed the door behind us and regarded me with a wary expression.

"Okay," I said. "We need to talk. I mean, you really can't go on like this."

"Like what, exactly?"

"This obsessive secrecy of yours! Not letting me know Arthur Hamilton is alive and well? I'm not a child, Julian. I can handle things. I handled *you*, for God's sake!"

"Darling," he said, "you can't deny that every time the subject of Flora comes up, you turn into a virago of raging jealousy . . ."

"Oh please! That's a *massive* exaggeration!"

"It's like walking on eggshells . . ."

"No, it's not! Okay, I'm a bit insecure about it, but you're *historically linked* with her, for God's sake! Open any book on war poetry and there you are, mooning over her!"

"The *devil* take that poem," he hissed.

I drove on. "Julian and Florence, the great tragic First World War romance. I'm amazed they haven't made a freaking *movie* about it! Do you have any idea how *annoying* that is?"

"It shouldn't be. You know the truth."

"Well, I'm sorry, it *is* annoying. But I'm not raging with jealousy, I'm *not*, and it's just unfair to say I am!" I narrowed my eyes. "In fact, it's *projecting*, because *you're* the one who would probably pull a shotgun on the poor schmuck who took my virginity. If I even dared to tell you his *name*!"

"Don't be ridiculous." He tugged his bow tie apart with a single ruthless wrench. "I'd bloody well settle the matter with my bare hands."

I threw up my hands. "Oh, good *grief*! And *I'm* the jealous one? Anyway, Arthur isn't even the point. He's just a symptom of this . . . this whole attitude of yours, that I can't be trusted with my own safety."

"Rubbish. I've merely taken reasonable precautions . . ."

"Reasonable! I can't take a freaking breath of fresh air anymore without bodyguards! You treat me exactly like a *doll*, Julian. You dress me, you accessorize me, you keep me under a glass dome! And then you take me out to play with when you're in the mood, or else to show off to your rich friends . . ."

"To *play* with!"

"It's true! It's so humiliating! And you don't tell me a damned thing about anything. I know you're hiding things from me, things from your past."

"I do not," he said tightly, "treat you like a doll."

"Yes. You. *Do*. Look at me! This . . . this dress, and this stupid necklace!"

How amusing, a part of my brain observed. *She's coming completely apart.*

"I'm on display, Julian! Like I don't have a brain or even a soul of my own. Like I'm one of those fancy little debutantes you used to flirt with. You probably wish I was!"

"Kate, what's gotten into you? You're talking complete rot!" He strode across the room to the dressing hall, where he jerked off his tuxedo jacket and hung it up with a crash of the polished wood hangers. *"Debutantes,"* he muttered.

"I'm not talking rot! I'm telling the truth! It's what I *feel*!"

"Well, you're wrong! A *doll*, for God's sake, as though that weren't exactly . . ."

"Don't tell me I'm wrong! You, with all your lies and secrets . . ."

"*Lies!*" He whipped around.

"You admitted it yourself! You lied to me about the reason we were in Lyme. About your arm. And there's such a thing as lies of omission, and God knows you're the master of that! You and your freaking *boxes*! That shoe-store brain of yours!" I waved my hand at his head. "I just keep waiting for the next one to drop. Maybe you've got Florence herself stashed in an apartment around the corner. Maybe that's why you're never in my bed in the morning. You might be in hers, for all I know!"

Oh, there's a good one, my brain applauded.

"Have you gone completely *mad*?" he exploded. "Like Flora at her damned unreasonable worst, which God knows I've . . ."

"Well, I'm beginning to see her point! My God, facing the prospect of marriage to you, of being locked like a bird in a gilded cage! Nothing to look forward to but a good fuck once in a while!"

Silence spread between us. Julian went still, one shoe in his hand, poised in the half-shadowed doorway to the dressing hall without a hint of expression. A curl of hair gave way and dropped like a sickle against his forehead.

Well, Kate. You've said some stupid things in your life, but this just about takes the freaking prize.

"A good fuck," he repeated at last. "That's all this is to you? A good *fuck*?"

I wanted to look away from him, from the accusation in his voice and the curious light glowing incandescent in his eyes, but I couldn't be that cowardly. "I'm no aristocrat, Julian," I shot back. "I'm not an *ingénue*. I'm not even a damned iconic peace activist. I'm an American, and I'm modern and red-blooded and independent and . . . and *vulgar*, I guess. That's the word Arthur used. But at least you have a real woman in your bed, Julian, and not some cold little bitch who would lift up her skirts when you were ready and push you back off when . . ."

"Well, damn it, Kate," he growled, "if a good *fuck* is all you're after . . ."

I took a wary step back, but he was far too quick for me. In the instant it might take for a predator to snatch a rabbit, he'd lifted me bodily, hoisted my legs up around him, kissing me, pushing me inexorably backward. We thumped against the wall and with one hand he ripped my ten-thousand-dollar dress down the middle, his mouth never leaving mine, rigid and unforgiving.

I tried to turn my head away, but his grip was too firm, and suddenly, shockingly, I was more aroused than I'd ever been in my life. I started clawing at him, popping the buttons on his shirt, tearing it from his shoulders, biting and gasping and begging. I fumbled with his waistband, unfastening it somehow, and then I was up in the air, his teeth on my breast, my head thrown back. I heard him groan my name raggedly, felt the muscles of his arms flex around me, and I clutched at his beautiful lion's head and was wholly lost.

HE SAID NOTHING AFTERWARD. I could hear him heave for air behind me, but all I could see was the polished wood of the bureau beneath my face, the jewelry and objects scattered across it; all I could feel was the hot dampness of his skin pressed against mine and the pulsing aftershocks of a singularly explosive orgasm.

"Holy crap," I muttered, trying to summon my wits.

His arms disappeared from my peripheral vision, and I felt the agony of separation. An instant later he returned; something silky draped across my shoulders, and then I heard the bedroom door open and close.

That broke through the swirling eddies around me. I straightened achingly and turned around. My dressing gown slipped from my back to the ground; I snatched it up and shoved my arms into it and went to the bathroom.

My face gazed back from the mirror. A stranger's face: coldly, objectively, I saw the beauty in it, which I'd never done before. I saw how the large silver eyes fit expressively into the elfin bones, almost childlike; how the pale velvet skin sloped down from the wide cheekbones to the graceful chin. How the dark hair tumbled down around the shoulders, half hiding the rivière of rubies along the delicate ridges of the collarbone. I looked like a whore. An elegant, expensive whore.

I closed and belted the dressing gown and put my hair back in an elastic. I fumbled at the clasp of the necklace, and finally left it there around the base of my throat.

I FOUND HIM in the piano room, seated in darkness on the bench before the instrument, his elbows propped on the closed keyboard and his head in his hands. He didn't even look up when I entered.

He'd slipped his undershirt back on; his tuxedo pants had never, strictly speaking, made it off. I could see, in the faint light from the hall, the way his broad white-clad shoulders tapered down to his lean waist, disappearing into the blackness of his trousers: that mesmerizing physical beauty of his, which he carried off so gracefully, so unconsciously.

The heavy silence in the room pressed into my flesh, an unbearable weight, until at last I padded over the knotted floorboards to stand behind him. Gently I placed my hands on his shoulders. "Will you play for me?" I asked, soft as a whisper.

"Kate, I . . ."

"Please?" I urged.

My hands rose and fell under the heave of his sigh. "What would you like to hear?"

I hesitated. "The C-sharp minor. The nocturne."

Silently he drew up the keyboard cover and rested his fingers on the keys. I bent my head, brushing my lips against his hair, and then he began to play, aching desolation, elusive joy, yearning on yearning. My fingers hovered for an instant longer at his shoulders, but I forced them down again, crossing my arms behind my back.

When he was finished, when the last note had dissolved into emptiness, his hands dropped on either side of him, gripping the bench. I sat down, facing the opposite way, and twisted my fingers together in my lap.

"Whenever you play that," I said, "I always think of that first night. My first night in your arms. I don't know why. So many beautiful nights together, but that one . . . I was so desperate for you. I needed the certainty, the honesty, everything else stripped away, just *us*. And you *knew*. God bless you, you *knew*. That look on your face, the way you touched me. The things you said. You understood what I meant. And it was so perfect, Julian. As though I became a new person in that moment."

"Kate." His voice held an edge of despair.

"I'm so sorry. Darling Julian. I said the most awful things, and I didn't mean any of them. You . . ."

"Don't," he said, staring at the piano keys. "Don't. I should be begging your pardon." A sigh shuddered through his torso. "I treated you like . . . I used you . . ." He didn't have the words, of course. He didn't have the vocabulary to describe it to me.

"Look." I hitched up one knee to rest beside his leg. "You may or may not have noticed I enjoyed that, Julian. I *wanted* you, just like that, just ferocious and beautiful. It was . . . catharsis. It was amazing. Do it again sometime."

He didn't respond. I tried to catch his expression, the half of it facing in my direction, but the room was too dark.

"Besides," I continued, "I goaded you into it. I struck out like a child, instead of discussing things reasonably. I disproved my whole point, which is really annoying. I don't like to lose arguments. But I lost that one, okay? Yes, I've been a jealous idiot about Florence Hamilton. Yes, I know you've forgiven me for my own past. Or I don't know, maybe you haven't. Maybe it's just sitting there like a canker on your British brain somewhere, being pointedly ignored. Anyway, the point is, *mea culpa*. I overreacted."

"I wish, for once," he said, and I realized he was still angry, "you would just trust me, Kate. I have reasons for my actions. I'm not being arbitrary."

"Well, if you would, like, *tell me what they are*, for example, then maybe we wouldn't be having this argument. You're the one who won't trust *me*."

"Not for the same reasons. I happen to know it's better for you, vital for you, if you don't know certain things."

"Oh, please," I groaned. "Julian, either you're a paranoid obsessive, or else you're still caught in that ridiculous Edwardian mind-set, seeing women as children, not to be taken seriously . . ."

An exasperated bark. "Priceless. Did you learn that at university? Some bloody history seminar?"

I looked down at my fingers. "All right. Fine. But either way, it can't go on."

He turned at last: pale, beaten, his golden hair strewn about his forehead. "What do you mean by that?"

I gathered my courage. "That I'm ready to pack my bags and head back to Lyme until all this has blown over."

He jerked, as if he'd grasped a live wire. "You'd *leave me*?"

"Not leave *you*. Never that. Leave *here*."

My words seemed to echo about the room. I felt his blank stare absorb me, grasping for comprehension. "Kate, you wouldn't," he said at last. "You *can't*."

"I can't stay, Julian. I can't bear seeing you like this. Burdened, tormented. Treating me like a child who can't fight her own battles. I want the Julian who trusts me, who opens his heart to me." My voice strained against the rising lump in my throat. "The one who laughs when he makes love to me. Who keeps nothing back."

He opened and closed his mouth.

"Look," I said. "*That's* what I mean. Holding back. And I keep thinking to myself, when will he finally tell me everything? Trust me enough? Because I've laid myself so *bare*, Julian. I'm so open and vulnerable to you. You can just destroy me with a single breath."

"Oh God, Kate." His right leg swung lithely over the piano bench, straddling it; his arms bound around me with harrowing strength. "I'd kill myself first."

"I'm ambitious, Julian," I said fiercely, into his shoulder. "Greedy. I want to be the one who knows you best. I want to have that all to myself. I want *you*. I *demand* you. Let me share this thing with you, whatever it is; let me *help* you."

"Kate, I . . ."

"No, wait. You trust me with everything else, everything you shouldn't. Keys, passwords, bank accounts, alarm codes, credit cards, your entire life. So why not this?"

"I've trusted you with my past, Kate."

"But not all of it. Not the unpleasant parts, the uncomfortable parts. Not whatever it is that's bothering you now."

"My heart. Every last atom of *that*."

I turned my head inward and kissed it, right over the breastbone. "You're trying to disarm me, aren't you? You know I can't resist that."

"I'm just trying to make you understand," he said, "you already have everything you want. You own me, Kate." He reached back and found my hands and brought them before him, kissing each palm. "Right there, in the hollow of your hand. Even if I lose my head and . . . *take* you . . . like some sort of animal . . ."

I took hold of his wrists and drew his hands behind my neck. "Stop that. Stop it now. This is the twenty-first century, Julian Ashford, and you're allowed to have raucous sex with the woman you love without feeling guilty afterward."

"I was angry. I lost control. I might have hurt you."

"You would *never* have hurt me. If I'd said no, instead of jumping on you like a cat in heat, you would have stopped. I know you, Julian, and you would have stopped."

"Would I?" he asked bitterly.

I glanced upward at the ceiling. "Yes, you would. Self-control is what you *do*, Julian. It's what holds you together. And that's a wonderful thing.

This discipline, this ability of yours to keep everything in check, to meet everyone else's needs before your own. Always trying to do the right thing, holding yourself to some impossible standard. *Torturing* yourself with it. But you *do* know you can let that go with me, okay? You don't have to be noble; you can be selfish with me. I *want* you to. It's what I'm here for, what I was put on this earth for. To give you a *break* once in a while, you poor weary man, with all the world's expectations on your shoulders since you were born, for God's sake."

"But not to be a *beast*, Kate . . ."

"Hush." I brushed my fingers against his lips and moved them to cup his cheek. "You have so much passion. You feel things so deeply. Look at you, my God! It's all there, burning in your eyes, all that love and loyalty and *fervor*. Your barbarian streak, you called it once. I know you think it frightens me, that it *should* frighten me, but it doesn't. It's the core of who you are, and it's precious to me."

He closed his eyes. "Kate, you'll break me, you damned uncanny creature. You're merciless."

"Oh, Julian. You really don't know, do you? How compelling you are, how absurdly *sexy*, even and especially when you're angry." I moved forward to murmur in his ear. "I can't ever resist you. I want you now, again; did you know that? I can't help it. One look from those eyes and I'm melting for you . . . Are you *laughing* at me?"

His chest was shaking.

"You'd better not be *laughing* at me, Ashford."

"Kate," he gasped, "Kate, you're killing me. I don't know whether I'm laughing or weeping. You've gutted me tonight."

I slipped my hands down along his back to rest at his waist and laid myself against his chest for a moment, feeling my body move with the steady rhythm of his breathing. His arms went around me lightly, almost tentatively, as though he were afraid of crushing me. "So tell me about Arthur Hamilton," I said. "I'll be good. Reasonable. No jealous rages."

"You've no idea, do you, how terribly *precious* you are to me. How deeply it pains me to give you even the smallest amount of uneasiness."

"But that's it. Why should the existence of Arthur Hamilton make me uneasy?" I asked, deliberately disingenuous.

He looked back at me, uncertain, until at last I eased out of his arms and went to sit on the sofa; I needed to be away from his touch and his scent for a moment, just to speak clearly. "Julian, I was angry, of course. I didn't appreciate getting ambushed back there, having to dig so deep to keep my composure. For poor Arthur's sake, first of all. And to pay Geoff back by staying as calm as I possibly could."

"You were extraordinary, darling. And you're entirely right. I should have told you about him. I'm sorry about that."

"Can you understand, though? I'm not *like* the women you used to know, Julian. I'm used to being independent, in total charge of my life. And suddenly nothing's in my control anymore. I mean, what kind of job can I get now? Just people wanting favors from you. I can't go back on the Street anymore. I don't know what I'm going to do."

He came to me then, swiftly, kneeling before me and taking my hands. "*I'm* in your control, Kate. You have only to ask, and I'll give it to you. Anything at all."

"*You.* That's all I want. Just you. No rubies, no designer dresses, no bodyguard. Just you, *all* of you. Lying in the grass with me, with the sun in your hair. It's all I'll ever ask from you." I wound my fingers through his.

"Beloved," he said brokenly. I slid down from the sofa and buried myself in the loving mass of him. "Forgive me. For this, and for the rest of it."

I looked up at his face, at the harsh shadows under his cheekbones cast by the single lamp. "Actually," I said, "I think Geoff's the one who really needs to pay, here."

"Oh, he will," Julian said darkly.

I sat back and took his hands in mine; some instinct made me look down at them. "Oh my God! What happened?"

He glanced down at the red raw skin on the knuckles of his right hand. "Nothing."

"You *punched* someone!" I said accusingly, looking back up at his face, over which the shutters had abruptly slammed tight. "When did this happen?"

No answer.

I narrowed my eyes. "Fine," I said, and took his hand to drag him back down the hall to our room.

"Oh, bloody hell," he said when he saw the small blue first-aid kit. "It's not a *wound,* Kate."

I said nothing, only opened the case and took out the alcohol swabs.

"I survived the Western bloody Front without this rubbish," he grumbled, wincing manfully. "The most unsanitary conditions imaginable."

"It was Banner, wasn't it?" I tossed the swab into the wastebasket and uncapped the Neosporin.

"We exchanged a few words," Julian said, "by which I conveyed to him my displeasure at his insulting manner of address."

"Defending my honor, were you?" The corner of my mouth turned up; I bent my head over his hand to hide it.

"The trouble with the modern era," he said, "or one of them, is that boorish idiots like Banner are allowed to run amok, insulting other men's wives . . ."

"I'm not your wife. And he *was* pretty drunk."

"Men who can't hold their liquor shouldn't drink. And you *are* my wife, as far as I'm concerned. Oh, not a *Band-Aid,* Kate!"

"SpongeBob or Hello Kitty?"

He glared.

"Kidding. Just humor me for tonight, okay? You can take it off in the morning before anyone sees you." I began removing the tabs.

"Kate," he sighed, "I think I've done a reasonable job of conforming to the conventions of this world. I've made adjustments, I've modernized, I've adapted. But one thing I refuse to concede is my right to punch the lights out of any man who dares to insult you. Not because you're helpless; God knows you're not. But because no man can stand by idly and see his idol defamed."

I gave his hand a last pat and looked up, hoping he wouldn't notice the sheen in my eyes. "Well, I guess I can live with that. Just try not to hurt yourself, okay?"

A faint snort. "Men haven't the least idea how to fight properly anymore. No sport in it at all."

"So what did Banner do when you hit him?"

A smirk hovered, for just an instant, around his generous mouth. "Begged your pardon." He reached out and cupped my chin. "Am I forgiven yet?"

"The trouble with you, Ashford," I said, taking the hand and weaving my fingers inside it, "is that you make it so freaking hard to stay mad at you. So, before I melt completely, can you at least tell me the full story, please? What's Arthur Hamilton doing in your life?"

Julian shrugged. "He walked into our offices one morning, right after we started up. It was just Geoff and me and a back-office assistant at that point, and Geoff quite literally fell out of his chair. It was a cheap second-hand chair, you understand," he explained. "He hadn't any financial-markets experience, of course, so we took him on in a sort of marketing role, just to give the poor blighter a job."

"Had he just, you know, *arrived*?"

"More or less. Among his papers were directions on how to find us."

"That is just so weird. I mean, how is this *happening*?"

"Believe me, I'd give my left arm to find out." Julian drew me into the armchair with him and tucked me against his chest. "In Arthur's case, I wonder whether it wasn't more a curse than a blessing. He wasn't a born soldier, you know. A bit windy, to be perfectly candid; his letters always bristled with a palpably false cheerfulness. The powers that be rather wisely assigned him staff duties, behind the lines in Amiens, but it didn't last, unfortunately; he transferred to battlefield command just a few weeks after my own disappearance. I daresay he was fairly miserable, leading his men over the top."

"But isn't he glad to be alive now?"

He began to stroke my hair. "I'm not at all sure he is. It's not easy, you know, being lifted away from everything one knows, even in the middle of a hellish war. It's damnably disorienting. One's got to find something to live for. I often feel he hasn't really joined this world, this modern world; he misses Flora, for one thing. She was his mainstay, fighting his battles for him and all that. Now he hardly knows what to do with himself. We try to bring him out, buck him up. He leans particularly hard on Geoff, shares an office with him. Poor devil." He shook his head. "It's as though he left his soul behind him. Forgot to bring it along."

The silence closed back around us for a moment, lighter now; I felt his hand move in my hair, his steady heartbeat under my ear, and no longer felt like a doll or a caged bird or a whore.

Just myself.

"If I married you tomorrow," I said, "would you tell me?"

"No."

"When, then?"

"In the fullness of time, beloved. You'll know everything. My only task is to protect you until it arrives."

"Freaking paranoid."

"Afraid so. Can you live with *that*?"

"I have to. I can't live without *you*."

"Then"—his voice dropped down to a low whisper—"you'll stay here with me? No more talk of packing your bags?"

I bit my lip. "It's not fair, Julian. You say you're mine, you'll do as I ask, but I end up with nothing, don't I? You win. Again."

"Kate, Kate." His arms tightened. "Don't, sweetheart. On my honor, it's all for you. If you *knew*. If . . ." He cut himself short, then went on, more evenly, "When it's all over, I'll devote myself to your every whim, I swear it. No law whatever but yours."

"That's not what I want from you."

"Please, beloved." His voice turned beguiling in my ear. "Say you'll stay. You know I'm useless without you. Give me just a little more time; that's all I ask. Have faith in me." He skimmed his fingers along the length of my arm to clasp my hand, and I closed my eyes, fighting him. "Please, Kate. My only beloved." He kissed my fingers. "Say it quickly, because the sight of you in that robe makes my head spin, and I'm not certain how much longer I can remain reasonably coherent."

The breath went out of me in a snort of laughter. "Fine. You win. One week."

"One *week*?"

"You have one more week to figure this thing out. If I don't get answers, I'm going back to Connecticut."

"One week." He frowned.

"You can come up and visit," I said. "I'd let you in."

"Thanks bloody much."

"And I'd take Eric," I added, though his frown only deepened at that. "Please, Julian. Just promise me no more secrets."

"I'm sorry," he breathed into the skin of my throat. "For tonight, and for all I've asked you to bear, you lovely noble thing."

My eyelids sank down. "The *secrets*, Julian."

He paused, his lips just shy of my mouth.

"Oh, all right. You still have a week. As long as it's nothing to do with this."

"This?"

I waggled my finger between his chest and mine. "You know. This *thing* between us."

"Ah." He smiled against my lips. "You must be talking about *love*, Kate."

"Mmm-hmm."

His low chuckle rippled the air. "Sweetheart. Then I'll say it enough for both of us. I love you, Kate." He kissed my lips. "I love you." He kissed the hollow behind my ear. "I love you." He bent and kissed my bare shoulder. "I love you." He picked me up in his arms and laid me reverently on the bed. "I love you, minx. Though you're the devil of an amount of trouble."

I curled my hands about his face. "That's why you love me, though."

"Beyond all bloody reason." And he eased off my robe and made love to me, thorough and tender, with the dim lamplight slanting over his skin and only the gleaming red rubies between us.

"So THERE'S ANOTHER REASON," I whispered, as we lay tangled in the darkness.

"Another reason for what, darling?" he said, sleepy-voiced.

"Another reason I was a wee bit emotional tonight."

"Were you? I hadn't noticed."

"Um," I said.

"Ah. An interesting sound, that. I wonder what it means." His hand stroked along my arm, up and down, as if he were calming a skittish horse.

"It means . . ." I swallowed, gathering courage.

"Yes?"

"It means I'm pregnant."

Amiens

Julian knocked on my door at exactly five minutes to seven.

"Come in." I set down my newspaper and rose from the bed.

"I'm so sorry to be late," he said, entering in a gust of male energy. "These colonels do go on."

"That's all right," I choked. My voice had dried up. This was my last chance; I had one final desperate card to play.

"Have you had a pleasant day? Found lunch and so on?" He glanced at the fire, simmering feebly in its tiny wrought-iron surround, and stepped to the coal scuttle.

"Yes. I went out to that place you took me for breakfast yesterday. The Chat d'Or. Then I did a little shopping." I watched him straighten from the fireplace and turn to face me. I twirled for him. "It was nice to change out of my travel dress."

"It's lovely." He paused, putting both his hands behind his back. "I'm sorry to have abandoned you all day. I realize it must be rather dull for you. Rather strange. Not your own time."

"Dull? Not a bit. It's like walking into a history book. The cathedral, all sandbagged. Everybody in uniform. All the signboards and things. It's amazing. I . . ." The cheerfulness rang false. My gaze slid down to the unfinished floorboards beneath my shoes, to the corner of a threadbare rug fraying next to my toes.

I heard Julian's feet shift, creaking the floor; his throat cleared into the silence. "Perhaps . . . would you perhaps like to have dinner? We might run down to the Chat, or else . . . I believe there's another café, near the station . . ."

I looked back up at the meandering glow cast across his face from the candle on my bedside table. The electricity had gone out an hour ago, with abrupt finality. "We don't need to go out. I've brought a few things back from the shops. Wine and cheese and bread. Unless you'd rather . . ."

"No, no. That sounds lovely. A sort of picnic."

"Yes, exactly." My hands came together in front of me, tangling at the tips. *Now. It must be now.* "Do you mind . . . do you mind if we talk for a moment first? There's something more I want to tell you, and since I've been sitting here working up the courage, I might as well do it now."

"Of course."

The room had only one chair, skinny and wooden, its worn rush seat unraveling precariously. I motioned Julian into it, and then eased down on the edge of the bed. "Um, I'm not quite sure how to begin."

He leaned forward in his chair, setting his forearms on his knees, clasping his hands together, and smiled. "Kate, I believe you."

"I know. I know you do. But this involves you as well as me, and it's . . . it may be hard for you to understand. To accept. You said . . ." The words jumbled together in my mouth. I closed my eyes and gathered myself, forced my thoughts into the logical train I'd spent the afternoon rehearsing. "You said you had the feeling we've met before. That's not exactly true, but it's not exactly false, either."

"What do you mean? When did we meet?"

"You asked me my last name before. I told you I couldn't tell you, because you wouldn't believe me. Possibly you still won't."

"Why wouldn't I believe *that*? After everything else?"

"Because my name is Kate Ashford. And I'm your wife."

His face, so open and ardent, seemed to freeze in place like a death mask.

"Julian, listen to me. You're not going to be killed in that raid tomorrow night. You'll be transported through time, like I was, into the end of the twentieth century. Where you'll meet me, eventually, in New York City."

"You." The word fell between us.

"Me." I couldn't stop the tears then: they welled around the edges of my eyeballs. "For some . . . *unfathomable* reason, you'll fall in love with me, and I with you. And I never told you that. I never told you I loved you, because it frightened me; I somehow thought that would jinx it all, because you—your love—were all too good to be true. And because I couldn't say it as well as you, couldn't put the right words together. Which was so stupid of me, so cruel, when you were always so generous that way."

I slid my thumbs under my eyes and gathered the ragged ends of my courage. "So I'll tell you now. I'll tell you everything. I love the sound of your voice and hearing you play the piano for me in the evenings. I love the silly little verses you write and leave on my pillow in the morning. I love your brilliance and your kindness, the way you can slaughter fools on Wall Street and then weep at the opera the same evening. I love those old moccasin slippers you wear around the house, when it's just us. I love the way you hold me in your arms at night and call me your little minx, even though it's probably really sexist somehow, and the expression on your face when you . . . when we . . ." My voice stumbled. I turned away, to the wall, where a small cheap painting of a Madonna regarded us beatifically from the faded wallpaper. "I know I'm nothing but a stranger to you now. But you're everything to me. You're my life. Just to have you near me, even the *you* that doesn't know me, is like heaven to me."

I heard his silence with dread, unable to move my eyes. The rapid heavy thump of footsteps broke into the stillness between us, crossing the hallway just outside the door before receding up the stairs.

"Do you still believe me?" I said, looking back at last.

"I . . . I don't know. I suppose I must. I believed the rest, didn't I?" He shook his head and stared down at his hands. "I've been fighting the most unreasonable jealousy of this man, this unknown husband of yours. The luckiest damned chap in the world. And he's me?" He looked up. *"Me?"*

His eyes stretched wide, the brows slanting upward, almost pleading. I held his gaze for an elastic second, and then rose to cross the room, where my coat hung on a hook near the door. I drew my BlackBerry from the pocket where I'd kept it safe, all last week, slogging through England, across the Channel to France, down the railway line to Amiens. I turned it on. The startup music chimed into the candlelight, absurdly anachronistic. "Can I show you something?" I handed it to him. "Here. It's my telephone."

He gazed at the object in his hands. "Telephone?" he said numbly.

"Yes. I told you about these last night, remember? You can carry them around with you, take pictures with them." I reached over and scrolled through the menus before his astonished stare. "Look. Here we are sailing last summer. The marina guy took that one." Our bodies sprang bright and sharp into the dim old-fashioned room, standing on the deck of Julian's cutter, my arms wrapped around his waist, his arm enclosing my shoulder. His laughing face was half-turned to mine, as if he'd just given me a kiss; he rarely missed an opportunity for that. I wore a short strapless beach dress, my skin gleaming in the sunshine, and the smile on my face was so wide and delighted I nearly wept. Happy Kate. All-unknowing Kate.

The phone began to shake in his hands. "I'm sorry." I tried to pull it back from him. "That was too sudden. I didn't mean to . . ."

"No." He held on firmly. "You look beautiful."

"I was happy. So happy." My voice wavered.

"Is there more?"

"Um, yes." I reached over and scrolled for him. "Here you are, lying on the grass at the cottage. I think I'd caught you napping. Oh, gosh. That's the beach. You don't need to see that. My stupid bikini. Sorry, all the girls wear those."

"Good God."

"I could show you your . . . your messages. You were always so funny and tender and . . ."

"You speak," he said, looking up, "in the past tense."

"I told you I was a widow."

"I'm . . . I'm dead?"

"Yes." I sat down on the bed. "That's why I'm here. To save you. To keep you from that raid tomorrow, from being transported to my time. Because you'll die."

"*Die?* But I thought . . . but *how?*"

"We were only just married. You went off to . . . to find me, to rescue me, and then they took you away and they . . ." I swallowed. "They killed you."

"*What?* Who? Why?"

"It doesn't matter. It's too complicated to explain. But do you *see* now? Do you see why it's so important that you avoid that raid tomorrow? Take no chances at all?"

He didn't answer. A profound quiet settled into the room. I couldn't imagine his thoughts: reeling, no doubt, as mine once had. He sat there, with my BlackBerry still in his uncomprehending fingers, saying nothing at all, and I let him be. It seemed enough that I had this present moment with him at all. He existed, his living self, a few feet away: his beating heart, his flickering brain, his long clean limbs still whole beneath the unknown layers of his clothing.

At last I heard him clear his throat. "Is that your wedding ring?"

I looked down at my hands. "Yes."

"May I see it?"

I hadn't expected that. I fumbled with the ring, trying to remove it, but my swollen flesh clung stubbornly to the metal. "I'm sorry," I said, "I haven't tried to take it off yet." I glanced at the candle on the nightstand and reached to take a bit of fallen wax from the pewter holder; I rubbed it into my finger until it softened, and at last the slender band gave reluctantly away. I placed it in his palm.

He looked at it closely, clinically. "I can't quite make out the engraving."

"There's engraving?"

He stood up and went to the window, and rolled my ring in his fingers until the inside was exposed to the dim rain-washed light from the glass. The color deepened and spread along his cheekbones. He looked back at me. "Where did you get this?" he demanded.

"You gave it to me, when we were married. You put it on my finger yourself."

He said nothing. He studied me a moment longer, and then went back to the chair and sat down and took my left hand. "Allow me," he said, and slid the ring back on my finger and kissed it and placed my hand back in my lap.

"Do you believe me now?"

"Yes," he whispered back.

"What does it say?"

"You can see for yourself, if you like."

I looked down at my hand. "No. I couldn't."

"Why not?"

"I don't know. I suppose because even though you're sitting there, the same man, I'm still grieving. For the Julian Ashford I left behind. The one who knows me, who loves me. The one who . . ." I stopped.

"The one who what?"

I fled to the window, staring out at the darkening street outside, at the unfamiliar shapes and the faint gleam of the wet cobblestones below, reflecting the light from the nearby houses.

The one who would take me in his arms right now.

I didn't hear his footsteps as he approached. His hand, when it touched my elbow, made me startle and whirl around.

"I'm sorry," he said gravely, looking down at me, his face shadowed by the arriving twilight. "I didn't mean to frighten you."

He was so close, so real. Alive. Just alive. "Please," I said.

"Kate. Brave, beautiful Kate. You've come all this way for *me*?"

"Yes." I looked down at my shoes. I couldn't bear the sight of his face: Julian and not-Julian, agonizing dissonance.

"To give up any hope of our meeting again one day?"

"I had to. I couldn't just let you die. Die, and leave me forever?" I shook my head. "At least this way you have a chance. At least here you're still alive."

"My God," he said, "what an extraordinary girl you are. What a lucky chap I was. Or will be, I suppose."

"Don't say that. You *can't* go. You'll be killed."

"But what will happen to you, if I never go forward to your time?"

I looked back out the window. "I don't know. I don't . . . I didn't really think about that. I just had to do something. You were dead. I couldn't just *accept* that. I had to do *something*." I frowned, trying to think things through. It had all seemed so simple, so obvious: keep Julian away from his doomed future. But was it? What could I change, without changing everything? My life, Julian's life. The lives of complete strangers, probably, who had nothing to do with any of this. Did I have that right?

He picked up my left hand. His thumb and forefinger found the ring on my fourth finger and massaged it gently.

"Would you still be my wife?"

I replied without thinking. "Yes, of course. Always."

His hand began to ease its way up my arm. "And that, I suppose, makes me your husband."

I turned. "What? No! I didn't mean . . . I wasn't asking . . ."

"No, you weren't. But *I* am." His face edged closer to mine. "Rather awkwardly, I suppose, and without nearly so much eloquence as you deserve."

The blood spread through my body, hot and relentless. "Julian, that's just . . . That's not why I'm here. I don't expect you to . . . to sacrifice yourself . . ."

"*Sacrifice?* Kate, how can I look at you, so lovely and so brave, so perfectly captivating, and not want to be the man you married?"

"Julian, you met me two days ago."

"But I'm the same man, aren't I, who *will* fall in love with you one day?"

"Well, yes. But that doesn't mean . . . doesn't . . ." His hand had drawn up to brush my cheek, and my thoughts evaporated. "Oh, don't. Don't do this to me."

"Do what?"

"Seduce me. It's not fair. I can't help saying yes."

He laughed. "Is that what I'm doing?"

"Just by standing in the same room. You always did."

"Did I?" he asked in wonder, as though he couldn't quite believe it, couldn't quite believe his own power. His fingers stroked again, testing me.

"Stop. Please stop. It's not fair. I'm *his*."

"Aren't we the same man, though?"

"But you haven't fallen in love with me yet. You haven't married me yet."

"According to this ring," he said, touching it again, "I have."

I went still under his finger. "What do you mean?"

"I mean if you want me, Kate, I'm yours."

"Don't say that. Don't."

He took each of my hands in his own. "Kate, the past thirty-six hours have been like a dream to me: an extraordinary, luminous dream. A beautiful woman approaches me in the rain, and then falls exhausted into my arms. Every moment I spend with her, I'm more intrigued, more enchanted by her. She's utterly original, different from any other woman I've ever known. So fine and faithful and candid. Vibrant with natural grace. The most exquisite contrast imaginable to . . ." He paused delicately. "And then, by some improbable miracle, she tells me she loves me, she belongs to me, she's sacrificed everything to save my life. And she bears a ring that tells me how to love her."

"What, exactly, is engraved on this ring?"

"Ah, you'll see," he said, drawing me close to him. His voice became a breath against my temple. "Can you possibly wonder, Kate, why I feel as though I should die to lose you? To hurt you?"

"That's impossible."

"I've never been more sincere in my life." His head bent; he lifted my hands and kissed them, one by one. "Dearest Kate. What will happen to you tomorrow, when my pass expires and I go back up the line?"

"I . . . I'm not sure. I guess I'll have to find a way back to my time, if that's possible. Or else make my way here, somehow."

"Stay with me here. Be my wife."

He said it quietly, hardly more than a whisper; at first I didn't think I'd heard him properly, that my brain had rearranged the words to suit its own private longing. My lips wavered, trying to form some question or objection, some reasonable thought.

He reached out and drew his thumb along my jaw. "Kate, please. I want you to stay here, to let me take care of you. To marry you, or rather to honor the marriage already between us."

"You can't mean that."

"I mean it passionately."

"You hardly know me!"

"Ah, but that doesn't matter, does it? I *will* know you. I'll love you. And I have the luxurious confidence of knowing that for a certainty." He eased me back into his arms, against his chest. "Stay with me, Kate. Stay here. Be my wife. After the war . . ."

"Julian, the war won't end for years. There's a battle coming this summer, a complete disaster. Even if you avoid this thing tomorrow, you're going to be slaughtered at some point. I'm saving you from one death, only to leave you to worse."

"Stay with me. Please stay. I'll find a way. After all, what's waiting for you in your own time?"

I looked up at last. "Either way, I lose you."

"At least here we have a chance."

It was true. I'd rather stay here, hoping he'd survive, than find a way back to my own century and face a long bleak future with no hope at all. Wasn't that, really, the reason I'd come here at all? To lure Julian back to me, because I couldn't bear to live in a world without him? I gazed at his face, trying to examine it all logically, trying to work past the dawning recognition of my own ignobility, but he stood so close, his scent and his touch, and I couldn't focus on anything else.

His lips brushed against mine, a question.

I gave up then. I had no more resistance. It had always been like that for me, with him; he burnt me to a cinder just looking at me. I brought my hands up around his neck and kissed him back, savoring the touch of his lips, the familiar taste of him, exactly the same as I knew it, marking him *mine*. I felt tears well in my eyes, spilling onto my cheeks; he felt them too, and drew away. "I'm sorry," I said. "I didn't think I'd ever do this again."

His eyes wandered over me in amazement, in disbelief; his hands came up to clasp my face, brushing my tears with his thumbs. And then he kissed me in earnest, in true honest passion, not quite so skillfully as I remembered, but with such fervor my brain spun. "Wait," I said, "stop. Stop. Before I . . ."

"I'm sorry," he gasped out. "Do you not want . . . I'll stop, if you want . . ."

"Oh God. No. Don't stop." I reached out and unbuckled his belt, unbuttoned his khaki wool tunic, his shirt, until he stood before me, quivering, his pale apricot skin gleaming in the dusky candlelight. "Is it all right?" I whispered.

"It's all right." He took my left hand and pressed it to his lips. "Mrs. Ashford." He said it just as he once had, or would do; the sound sent a shiver all the length of my body. He turned me around and began to undo the long row of buttons, his breath on my nape and his fingers trembling against my spine, until my legs nearly gave way beneath me. The dress loosened and slipped downward, pooling about my feet; one by one I slid the straps of my bra—suddenly so strange and modern—over my shoulders and reached back to unhook the clasp. I turned to face him.

The look on his face was priceless: so exactly like a boy in a candy store. I laughed. "You're just saying all this to get me in bed, aren't you?"

"I should tell you something," he murmured, dragging his eyes upward. "Or perhaps you already know it. You see, I haven't the faintest idea how to proceed, at the moment."

"That's all right." I took his hands into mine. "I'll show you everything."

23.

His hand went still on my arm.

"Julian?"

"*What* did you say?" His voice was an asthmatic strangle.

"Um, I'm pregnant."

"You're . . ."

"Pregnant. Yes."

He shot upward. "But that's impossible!"

"Well, no, it's not. I sort of . . . I messed up, Julian. I don't know *what* happened. I . . . I forgot to start the new pill cycle, and . . ."

"For God's *sake*, Kate!" he burst out. "You *what*?"

"I forgot, all right? I'm sorry. It was right after Newport. I didn't even realize it until a couple of weeks ago. I know I should have said something, but you had enough going on, I didn't want to worry you." I sat up and met his eyes. "I was just praying . . ."

I don't know what I'd been expecting from him. A bit of shock, of course. Disbelief. And then rueful acceptance, perhaps. Sorting through it all, figuring it out together. A part of me had even been thinking he might be glad, that he'd been secretly hoping for this so I'd push the wedding forward. I certainly wasn't prepared for the expression of undiluted horror on his face.

"Oh my God," I said.

He ran both hands through his hair, looking wild. "You *can't* be pregnant! How the devil can you be pregnant? You *told* me, Kate, you *promised* me!"

"I'm *sorry*! I screwed up, okay?"

"You screwed *up*? That's *all*?"

"Don't be an ass, Julian! I said I'm sorry! Don't you think I'm a little more devastated than you are? I mean, it's *my* body. It's my *life* that's being turned upside down here!"

He didn't seem to hear me. He sprang off the bed and paced sinuously to the window. "For God's *sake*, Kate! I thought we were *safe*!"

"Well, if you were so goddamn worried about it, you could have bought yourself a box of freaking condoms, you know!" I scrabbled for my robe, down on the floor next to the bed, and wrapped it around me.

"If I'd known you were simply going to forget about something so bloody important, I would have! My God! I'd never even have touched you to begin with!" he exploded, into the windowpane.

"How dare you! How *dare* you!" I tried to shout, but my larynx was so paralyzed with rage, it came out little better than a hiss.

He wrenched around.

I went on, forcing the words from my dry throat. "Do you think I *wanted* this to happen? For God's *sake*! I am *pregnant* with your *baby* and all you can think about is your own damned *convenience*? You can just go to *hell*, Julian Ashford!"

In the next instant, he stood before me; his arms crushed me into his chest. I tried for an instant to struggle, but it was like pushing against a stone wall. A stone wall during an earthquake, that is: he was trembling violently. "Forgive me, Kate," he said hoarsely. "Good God. I should be horsewhipped. Forgive me. It's all right. It's just the shock. Forgive me, darling, please."

"Julian, don't." My voice muffled against his skin. "I saw your *face*! You were horrified!"

"Just . . ." He drew breath. "Just at *myself*, Kate!"

"Whatever." I pushed off again, and this time his arms gave way and I went to curl up in the armchair in the corner. The fight in me had vaporized; I'd argued with him so much tonight. I was exhausted, my nerves blunted. "Look," I said, tucking my feet up, "I didn't mean to freak you out so much. I just always figured *you* would be the one pushing for kids, and *I* would be the one wanting to wait, and you would be . . . well, maybe even *happy* about it."

"*Kate.*" The word whispered through the air. I felt his footsteps approach me, saw his pale skin blur along the line of my vision as he knelt before me. "Beloved. I don't know how I could say such things, blame you for something so patently my fault." He reached out and drew my hands into his own and bent his face into them. "You *must* forgive me, Kate, because I can't forgive myself."

"Please stop shaking. You're scaring me."

"I'm sorry. I'm sorry." He looked up at my face; the nightlight in the corner glowed behind him, so I couldn't read his expression. "Are you sure, darling? You're quite sure? There's no possibility of mistake? Have you seen a doctor?"

"Julian," I said, "you don't need a doctor for that anymore." I slid from the chair and went to the bathroom and took the wand out of the drawer.

Still blue.

I came back into the bedroom. He was sitting on the edge of the bed now, staring thoughtfully at his hands. I leaned over the nightstand to turn on the lamp and handed the evidence to him. "See that blue line?" I pointed to the screen, which shook in his hands, and sighed. "Our baby."

"Our baby," he repeated, staring at it for a long time, without blinking. I sat down next to him and let the silence fill in around us, the reality of it absorb into our pores, easing from shock into acceptance.

"That was probably why I was such a nut earlier," I said. "Hormones. Just think, only seven or eight more months of that."

At last he took a deep breath and turned to me. "I'm sorry, Kate. I've failed you, haven't I? I'm so terribly sorry."

"You've failed *me*? Julian, I forgot to take the stupid pills! It was *my* fault." I paused. "Well, that, and on top of everything else you probably have a sperm count in the gazillions or something. That would just be *like* you."

He looked up at the ceiling, scarlet.

"But the point is," I continued, "I took it on. You trusted me, and I screwed up. That's why I was so mad when you called me on it. Because you were right."

His arms went around me. "Don't talk rubbish. I was wrong, entirely wrong. You're blameless, darling. I left it all on your shoulders, went on my merry way, never gave it another thought, never so much as reminded you. It was unforgivable."

I leaned into him, craving the warmth of his body. "So we'll deal with this? We'll figure it out together? Because I have to say, right up front, I can't give it up."

"Give it *up*?" His body stiffened.

"I thought about it for just a split second, and . . . well, it's *your* baby, Julian, *ours*, and I . . . how can I not love a baby of yours? We *created* it. It's *us*."

"Kate, Kate! I'd never ask . . . I'd never even *think* it. Oh, Kate." His hands ran in rapid strokes along my back.

I went on huskily. "And now that it's here, I . . . when I think about *that*, about a baby, *our* baby, I'm filled with such . . . I just want to *keep* it, this little piece of you. Is that okay? Can you live with that? Becoming a father so soon?"

"Live with it?" I was hauled up against him again, even more tightly than before. "What I can't live with," he said in my ear, "is that I've done this to you, made you the mother of my child, without having insisted, *insisted*, on making you my wife first. I've been living in a dream, thinking the mere promise of marriage, of feeling it in my heart, was enough. Tomorrow," he said, with conviction. "Tomorrow. We go down to City Hall tomorrow."

"Oh, God!" I jumped back. "Julian, you don't need to do *that*! You don't have to marry me out of *duty*!"

"Duty?" He looked astounded. "*Duty?* Sweetheart, how *long* have I been begging you to marry me? For months!"

"Only a *few* months."

"For months," he said, gathering my face between his hands. "I *want* children with you, Kate. I want *this* child with you. Did you think I didn't?"

"But your face, when I told you . . ."

He bent forward and kissed me, tender little kisses, all around my face. "Beloved, it's the most precious gift you could offer me. Only I wasn't daring to hope for it yet, before I'd properly married you, and with all the other worries so foremost in my mind."

"You and your buttery tongue. Telling me what I want to hear."

He smiled dimly. "And I was just thinking, a while ago"—he cupped my breast—"I was imagining things. That perhaps it was the lighting . . ."

I looked down. "Oh my God. Are they getting bigger?"

"Only to a minute observer," he said, kissing each one. "Are you feeling ill yet?"

"Well, I thought I was feeling kind of sick in the car, on the way to the opera tonight, but I think that was just nerves."

"You will soon."

I looked at him quizzically. "What do you know about it?"

"Trust me. Now come to bed, darling. It's frightfully late; you're exhausted." He pulled me backward, into the pillows, and drew the thick down comforter over us both. "Don't worry about anything. I'll sort it all out. I'll take such care of you, I promise."

I yawned. "Listen to you. You'd probably have the baby for me, if you could. What am I going to do with you?" His arms closed around me, snug and secure, and I felt a fleeting desire to rebel against the protectiveness of the gesture.

Then I laughed.

"What is it?"

"Just thinking. You at Lamaze class."

"Christ."

"Oh, lighten up. It'll be good for you. Helping me breathe. Cutting the cord. I'll bet you fifty bucks you're one of those dads who faints on the delivery room floor."

I thought he'd laugh at that, but he didn't. Instead he sighed, a deep heave of his chest, and said quietly, "Kate, that's the least of my worries."

"Damn it," I said, pounding my fist into my pillow. "What does it *take*, Ashford?"

Julian came out of the bathroom in a white undershirt and boxer briefs, brushing his teeth. "Whah?" he said, frowning through his toothbrush.

"I tell you I'm having our *baby*, and you *still* can't be there in the bed when I wake up? I mean, what do I have to *do*?"

He laughed and disappeared back into the bathroom. I heard the brief hiss of the faucet, and then he returned and climbed atop the covers and drew me into his arms, smelling sweetly of toothpaste and shaving cream. "Better?" he asked.

"Better," I said, "but not exactly what I had in mind. What time is it?"

"Nine o'clock. I waited as long as I could. We have to get downtown to the Marriage Bureau."

"But it's Sunday."

"I made a few calls."

I laid my head on his shoulder. "Of course you did."

"Kate," he said, "there's a twenty-four-hour waiting period. We'll get the license today, and be married tomorrow by a city clerk, if that's all right. I can put in a call to the mayor, if you'd like something more splashy, but I insist on its taking place tomorrow. If you'll have me."

"Oh please. If I'll have you."

"You're remarkably acquiescent."

"Julian," I said, "I'm pregnant. I'm at your mercy. My parents would *die*."

He groaned into my hair. "Oh, Lord, Kate. Your parents. I hadn't even thought . . . Christ. I'll make it right, sweetheart. I shan't *rest* until . . ." His voice seemed to trip over itself; he stroked my arm for a moment, and went on. "I want to apologize again for the way I behaved last night. To have given you even an instant's distress, at such a moment . . ." He shook his head. "I can't think about it without shame."

"For goodness' sake, Julian. You're so hard on yourself. It wasn't my shining hour either, after all."

"Rubbish. You were quite right to bite my head off. I deserved it. In any case," he said, leaning over to kiss my temple with determined cheerfulness, "now the shock's worn off, I'm as pleased as Punch. You can't string me along any longer. I shall have you as my wedded wife at last, and by the end of spring, my dearest Mrs. Ashford, we'll have our own little family. You don't suppose it might be twins, do you?"

"Bite your tongue."

He didn't answer, only shifted around me, settling himself lower, and put his hand with great delicacy on my belly.

"Go ahead," I said. "It's probably only about the size of a thumbnail."

He lay there for a moment, watching his hand.

"You're going to be a wonderful father, you know. The best ever." I stroked his tawny hair, letting the images form at last. "I can picture it."

"Can you?" He bent over and kissed the hollow of my stomach, and turned his cheek to rest tenderly against me.

"You know," I said, swirling the fine hair around his temple, "the deadline still holds, wedding or not. One week."

"Don't worry," he whispered. "Everything will be cleared up before that."

IT WAS ALL SURPRISINGLY EASY. Once I'd showered and dressed, Julian drove us to the Marriage Bureau downtown, leaving Eric behind so as not to draw undue attention that might land us in the gossip columns tomorrow morning. Nothing says celebrity like a dark-suited bodyguard shadowing your footsteps.

"I want to know what your papers say," I said, grabbing the manila file folder as we curved around the FDR.

He smiled. "Go ahead. You've a right to know whom you're marrying."

"Julian Laurence—you've gone with no middle name all this time?"

He shrugged.

"Date of birth, March thirtieth, 1975. And are you actually thirty-three?"

"Yes. Well, technically I'm a hundred and thirteen, I suppose. I was born in 1895." He laughed ruefully. "Truly robbing the cradle, aren't I?"

"Letch. I'm sorry I missed your birthday, though," I said.

"My fault, chasing you off like a damned fool. At least I haven't missed yours."

"Don't worry about it. I hate my birthday. How would you like to have been born on Halloween? It's just creepy." I looked back down at the passport in my lap. "Place of birth, London. Well, that's good. Supposedly the best lies are the ones that stick close to the truth." I started laughing. "Oh my God. Is that your passport photo?"

"Give me that." He snatched it back.

"Well, now I feel better. If the photo booth can mess up *your* face, then there's some excuse for this horror show." I held up my own passport.

He glanced over and smiled.

"You see? That's what you're marrying. Are you sure you want to go through with this?"

We parked the car in a garage a block away from the Marriage Bureau. I handed him a Yankees cap as he came around the other side to help me out. "You'd better go incognito, Goldilocks," I said, "unless you want another call from that Page Six reporter."

"Good idea," he said, putting it on his head.

"Hold on." I reached up and folded the brim for him, then stood back critically. "You still look too ridiculously handsome, of course, but that's just my cross to bear."

He took my hand. "Come along. Let's get this done."

For once, I had to appreciate the VIP treatment. Someone was waiting at a side door to usher us through the empty building to a small office, where a clerk helped us fill out the forms and checked our documents.

"Good God," Julian said mildly, looking again at my passport, "is that really you? Or merely a deranged body double?"

"I know, right?" I sighed. "I overslept and forgot the elastic for my hair."

"Overslept? Are you quite serious?"

"I'm marrying a comedian," I informed the clerk.

In twenty minutes we were out the door, marriage license in hand. Julian checked his watch. "Should we find some lunch?"

We wandered over to South Street Seaport and ate hot dogs on a bench along the pier. "It's nice to be alone," I said, leaning back against the railing. "No bodyguard. No helpful friends and family."

"It makes me anxious, frankly," he said.

"What? Why?"

"Because I'm trying to protect you against a threat I don't even understand. It's nerve-racking."

I put down my hot dog. "Nerve-racking?"

"You're pregnant, and we're getting married," he said. "Everything's coming together."

"Look, I'm sorry. Rushing you into this was the last thing I wanted."

"That's not what I meant."

"Well, what *did* you mean? Second thoughts?" The smell of the hot dog wound around my nostrils, heavy and sickening.

"Of course not." He let out a long breath. "I'm sorry, darling. This is a happy moment, isn't it? The State of New York has given me official permission to marry the woman I adore, the woman who carries my child. And in a matter of twenty-four hours, she'll belong to me forever. Are you all right?"

"Ugh. It's just the hot dog." I pushed it away a few inches.

"Oh, hell. Here, darling. You're going to be ill." He took his half-finished drink cup and emptied the contents into a sidewalk drain next to the bench. "Take this." He held it in front of me.

"Julian, I'm not going to throw up . . . oh God."

When I'd finished, he tossed the cup into a trash can and came back to wipe the damp hair from my forehead. "All right, darling?"

"Ugh. I thought it was supposed to be *morning* sickness."

"It can happen at any time."

"This is so humiliating." I paused. "How do you know so much about it?"

"Common knowledge." He stood up and held out his hand. "Shall we walk a moment? It might help."

I took his hand and walked beside him, feeling strangely downcast. It was a cool morning, thick clouds scudding across the sky, a hint of approaching autumn riding the air, and the broad river walk stretched empty of the tourists and office workers ordinarily crowding the pavement. On my right, the water eddied into New York Harbor, scattered with tugboats and trawlers, all business. A Circle Line ferry was making its way upriver, the bow railing dense with sightseers craning for a clear camera angle of the Brooklyn Bridge.

"Let's talk about the wedding tomorrow," Julian said. "Would you like to do it alone, or should we invite a few friends?"

"Oh, alone. Just the two of us."

"We'll need a witness," he reminded me.

"Eric? No, forget that. It should be someone we know." I gazed ahead at the massive stone pediments rising mightily from the water and took an odd sense of comfort from the familiar shapes of the twin Gothic arches. *Hello, Brooklyn Bridge. I am planning my wedding.*

"I don't suppose you'd consider Geoff?"

I frowned. "I'd rather not."

"I'd ask Arthur," Julian said, "but I suppose it's rather tactless."

"Well, in a way. But in another way, it's sort of fitting. Almost tact*ful*. Otherwise we're stuck with Charlie."

He laughed. His hand squeezed mine, solid and reassuring. "We could do worse. I rather like the chap."

"I'll call him up. I think classes have started by now, but he'd be more than happy to ditch. We could have them both. Arthur and Charlie. Your side, my side."

Julian leaned over and pressed a kiss against my hair. "And afterward? I thought perhaps we might have a dinner to celebrate. Your family might be able to join us. Michelle and Samantha, of course. And I was thinking I might ask Hollander to come down from Boston."

"Oh! Wow. That's a wonderful idea. I'd love to meet him."

"He'd love to meet you. Let's make it all a surprise, shall we? We won't tell them it's a wedding dinner; we can announce it there. I'll get Allegra started on the details straightaway."

His phone rang over the last words; he took it out of his pocket and looked at the screen. "Christ," he said, "I don't believe it."

He fitted the Bluetooth in his ear. "Laurence," he said. "Yes, that's true . . . Yes, I did . . . I'm afraid I'm not at liberty to say. Clearly, it's valid for sixty days . . . Yes, look, Miss Martinez, I realize you've a job to do, but I ask, as a personal favor, you forbear . . . If you could at least leave the names out of it, and leave it as a blind item, I give you my word we'll release any statement to you first. Yes, for twenty-four hours. Yes, I appreciate it. Thank you." He pulled the Bluetooth out of his ear, muttering.

"I take it our cover's blown?" I asked.

He shoved the phone in his pocket and scowled into the pavement. "Wide open."

24.

"It's not so bad," I said. "And it's Monday. The Sunday paper has much more circulation."

"It's bad enough," Julian said. "Anyone with the faintest connection to us won't have any trouble deciphering it."

I yawned and leaned back on the pillows. "It's not the end of the world. Besides, I thought we were trying to attract attention."

"Not on my wedding day."

I looked back at the paper on my lap.

WHICH hunky hedgie may be taking time off from rescuing Wall Street to make things official with his toothsome fiancée? The love-struck pair, who've been photographed together all over town in recent weeks, were spotted after hours yesterday at the downtown Manhattan Marriage Bureau, picking up a license . . .

"You never told me I was toothsome," I accused him.

He grinned and set a knee down on the bed, leaning over to kiss me. "Absolutely the most toothsome woman I've ever met."

"Mmm. You're pretty toothsome yourself." I ran my fingertips along his shoulder.

He reached up to squeeze my hand. "Alas, I've a million things to do at the moment, pulling this thing off. Can I get you anything else? How are you feeling?"

"Perfect. Thanks for breakfast," I added, holding up the scone and coffee he'd brought me with the *Post*. "Oh, wait." I looked at the cup and frowned. "Decaf, right?"

He looked aghast. "Oh, hell. I didn't think of that. I'll run out for another."

"Please don't. You're not my errand boy. I'll grab one after my appointment." I looked at the clock. It was half past seven; Julian, as always, had risen early, this time to fetch the newspaper and assess the damage. "What time should I be ready?"

"We're due downtown at noon. I'll pick up Arthur on my way—he's in Sutton Place—and you can bring Charlie."

I swung my legs out of bed, and found myself hit by a dizzying rush of nausea. "Oh my God," I groaned, and staggered to the bathroom.

Julian came right behind me, holding my hair away from my face. "Better?" he asked, when I'd finished.

"I'll live."

He handed me a damp washcloth. "Poor Kate," he said remorsefully. "Look what I've done to you."

"Like I said, I'll live." I wiped my face and hung the washcloth on a towel rack. "Besides," I added, slanting him a look, "I wouldn't give up a single night with you. Not even if I knew which one had done the deed."

He smiled then, wanly. "Eric's downstairs, when you're ready to go out. I'll be back by ten. Can you be ready to go at eleven-thirty?"

"I think I can manage it." I reached up to caress his cheek. "Julian, are we really getting married today?"

His grin illuminated the room. "Yes, Mrs. Ashford." He hoisted me up to plant a kiss on my lips. "Depend on it."

JULIAN HAD WANTED TO COME to my doctor's appointment this morning, but I'd convinced him his time was better spent elsewhere. "She's not going to do a scan or anything," I said, "just give me a quick once-over and give me the list of dos and don'ts."

The truth was, I wanted to keep things low-key. People would notice the two of us walking into the ob-gyn office together: Julian was so recognizable now, and I couldn't take a chance that my parents would get word of the pregnancy before I told them.

I'd been lucky to get the appointment at all, or else I was just naïve about the power of money and celebrity in arranging things like last-minute before-hours doctor appointments. My doctor did regard me with more respect than before. I apologized about the missed appointment, joked about its consequences—*I'll never miss another one, I promise!*—and she brushed it all off without the usual smug resentment.

"Now," she said, "I have to ask you: are you happy about this?" She gave me a meaningful look.

Oh. Like, did I want to keep the baby. "Well," I said, voice as firm as I could manage, "it was definitely a surprise, but now that we're used to it, yes. We *are* happy." I felt myself begin to shake. We were going to have a baby. Kate and Julian, *parents.*

I stumbled out of the office somewhat dazed, wishing I'd asked Julian to come along after all. Eric had been waiting outside; I wondered what he was thinking. If he was thinking. He didn't talk much.

"I think I'd like to stop for some coffee on the way home," I told him, in a scratchy voice, and he nodded his impassive nod and escorted me to Starbucks.

I ordered a decaf vanilla latte and asked Eric, as I always did, if I could get him something. He declined, as he always did. I picked up my drink and sat down at a table and began to look through all the materials the doctor had given me. Apparently I would be having my first ultrasound at nine weeks, blood tests, urine tests, no alcohol, no caffeine, no Advil, no tuna, no liver, no soft cheese, no medium-rare, no sushi, no freaking nothing. Between the forbidden foods and the ones that were making my stomach churn, it looked like I'd be living on charred steak and crackers for the next seven and a half months.

"Oh my God! Kate Wilson! What a coincidence."

I looked up into the smirking face of Alicia Boxer.

It wasn't quite the same face as before. The CNBC perp walk had aged her a good five or ten years. The smirk was more subdued now, the skin slackened; the lines around her eyes had dug in to stay, though her forehead bore the preternatural smoothness of a thorough Botoxing. She carried a copy of today's *New York Post* under her arm.

"Alicia?" I asked, in disbelief.

"Can I join you?"

I considered her for a second or two. Eric stepped forward and raised his eyebrows at me. As in, *You want I should break her kneecaps, Miss W?*

"Wow," she said, "is that your bodyguard?"

"Yeah." I stuffed the papers back into my handbag. "So. Have a seat."

She set down her coffee and settled into the chair next to me. "So, like I said, big freaking coincidence." She patted her newspaper. "That was you, right? You and Julian?"

I opened my mouth to deny it and realized there was no point. "Maybe," I said, taking a lazy drink of coffee.

"I have to hand it to you. You won. I mean, I totally underestimated you. Now my life's a fucking ruin, and you're marrying a billionaire." She shrugged. "Nice work."

"Alicia, I didn't mean for that to happen. Ruining your life."

"It's what I would have done."

"Well, I'm not you."

She laughed. "No. No, you're not. So I guess there is a God up there, handing out justice and whatever. Peggy Sue takes it all." She drank her coffee and stared down at the paper for a moment. "So when's the wedding?"

"Sorry. Top secret."

"Is it true love?"

"The truest."

"Wow." She sat back and looked at me, her face cocked to one side like a parrot's. "You know, I'm digging deep here, and I actually think I'm kind of happy for you. Weird."

"Well, you know, I never did anything to deserve your little vendetta. I wasn't plotting with Banner, or trying to steal your clients, or any of that."

"Yeah, well, I probably knew that," she said, "but I was just pissed. Maybe I still am. Anyway, I've got to go. My apartment's got a showing this afternoon, and my shit's still lying around."

"Wait a second," I said. "I mean, I don't want to sound . . . I don't know, I guess I'm trying to say that if there's something I can do to help . . ."

"What, like clerk for my trial?" she sneered. "That's kind of ironic, right?"

"Look, I didn't mean to come off like that. Just, you know, if something comes up, something I can help you with."

She looked at me disbelievingly. I couldn't blame her; I didn't quite believe the words coming out of my mouth either. But the firing, the frame-up, all seemed so distant now, and petty. I felt sorry for her, trapped in that calculating mind of hers, keeping such uneasy company with the pinprick of goodness trying to leak out through the murk. Maybe I could help her somehow. I'd been so wildly fortunate; I had Julian's love, Julian's child inside me. Surely I had to find a way to do some sort of good in the world, to balance out the cosmic scales somehow. Well, putting it that way, a *lot* of good. Redeeming Alicia's soul should just about cover it.

"Yeah, whatever." Her eyes rolled. "I'll let you know."

I opened my mouth to say good-bye, and a question flashed across my brain. "You know, Alicia. Something's kind of bugged me about this whole thing. I don't know why. What exactly did you have on that Southfield trader, to get him to go along with you? To go against Julian?"

"Oh, Warwick? He approached *me*. Called me up the week after that ChemoDerma meeting. Would you believe it?"

"Warwick? *Geoff* Warwick? I thought . . ."

"Oh, that poor schmuck trader that took the fall? No way. It was Geoff Warwick who was behind it all, *chica*. The one giving the orders. I'd watch my back, if I were you. He is one wily fox, and *he*"—she rose up from her chair and gathered her newspaper—"doesn't like *you* one bit." She giggled, as if something amusing had just occurred to her. "You know, for a nice girl from Wisconsin, you have a way of making enemies." A wink. "Any-whoodles. See you around."

I sat there with my mouth slack and my pulse thudding in my neck. Geoff Warwick? Geoff Warwick was behind this?

I knew he didn't like me much, but *ruin* me? He'd actually sought out Alicia and plotted my downfall with her, nearly bringing down himself and Julian in the bargain, a risk he had to know he'd be taking.

Well, assuming she was telling the truth. But—and granted, I didn't have the world's most devious strategic brain here—I couldn't think of a reason why she'd lie. Except troublemaking in the abstract, and Alicia, troublemaker though she was, still needed an angle. She wasn't a total psychopath.

I looked down numbly at my watch. Nearly ten o'clock now, which meant I'd better head back to the house and get myself ready.

For my wedding.

I swallowed down the panic and got up, drinking the latte for comfort, and feeling Eric's presence with a certain amount of gratitude.

We passed quickly over the few blocks back to Julian's house. My brain spun in crazy circles, trying to put the pieces together. Geoff, calling up Alicia and planning the whole scam, after only a brief meeting at Christmastime. What had caused such an instant, visceral dislike? And Geoff, sending me Hollander's book in May, after my relationship with Julian resumed. Why? Why did he hate me so much? Why didn't he want us together?

My thoughts were so confused, so intense, that when I literally ran into Geoff Warwick on the steps of the townhouse, I thought for an instant I'd imagined him.

"Geoff! I'm sorry," I said, stepping back. "I wasn't watching."

"Sorry," he mumbled, white-faced, looking as distracted as I was.

"You were meeting with Julian, I take it?" I shifted my latte cup to my other hand. I felt Eric withdraw discreetly behind me, a few paces away.

"Yes. I wanted to convey my congratulations." The word fairly dripped with irony.

"Look," I said, "can you at least try to be happy for us? We *are* in love. You're supposed to be his friend."

"And yet," he said quietly, a trace of his native accent staining the words, "I'm reduced to having my wife point out the wedding news from the gossip columns."

"We haven't even told my parents yet, Geoff. It's supposed to be a surprise. You know, fun."

"There are reasons why I ought to have been informed."

"Oh, stop it," I said. "I *know*, Geoff. I know you planned that scheme with Alicia. I know you sent me the book. You're probably the one who's had me followed, had my things searched. You've had Julian in knots with worry, and why? Why do you dislike me so much? I'm a nice person, I really am. I'd do anything to make him happy. I could care less about his money; I wish it were at the bottom of the ocean, I really do."

He looked at me a long time. "I don't dislike *who* you are," he said. "I dislike *what* you are."

"Oh yes," I said. "I'd forgotten you were a paid-up member of the Florence Hamilton worship society. Well, I'm sorry I'm not her. I'm just me, Kate Wilson from Wisconsin, and I love Julian, and for some insane reason he loves me too. And we make each other happy. So I'm sorry to have to tell you this, Geoff, but you're just going to have to deal with it."

His face might have been carved from granite, for all the impression my words made: even the crash of a taxi's indignant horn a few yards away caused no more than a flinch of his right eye. After a brief cold moment, he turned to walk down the steps, passing Eric without a glance.

"Wait a second," I called after him.

He paused, tilting his head in my direction, one polished shoe on the sidewalk.

"I really am sorry about everything. I'm sure she was a wonderful person. I wish . . . I wish I could thank her," I said. "For giving him to me."

His expression turned odd, quizzical. "Flora's the least of it," he said, shaking his head, and he turned and walked away.

Well, it had been worth a try. What was that old saying?

Keep your friends close, and your enemies closer.

25.

Julian drove himself to the wedding in the Maserati, picking up Arthur Hamilton along the way; his driver took me down in the black sedan, with Eric in the front seat and Charlie in the back next to me.

"So what am I, your fucking bridesmaid?" he said, settling back in his seat. He was hugely enjoying his importance in our lives, and for the life of me I couldn't quite figure out how he'd earned it.

"No swearing at my wedding, okay?"

"Why the fuck not? Kidding," he said hastily, seeing my face. He sucked in his lips, evidently trying to think of something appropriate to say. "You look nice," he offered at last.

"Thanks." I looked down at my outfit, a bone-colored knee-length sheath, closely fitted, with a graceful ballet neckline: not quite white, but not quite beige. Very civil ceremony.

His face split into a grin. "So you must be knocked up, right? Hence the rush?"

"*Jeez,* Charlie," I hissed, feeling my cheeks erupt.

His smile vanished. "Dude, for real? That was just a joke. Wow." He looked warily at my midsection, like he expected a baby to explode from it at any second. "That is one fucking *stud* you're marrying."

"Um, Charlie? No swearing?"

"Sorry, dude."

"And that's a *secret*, okay? Seriously classified information."

"Locked in the vault, dude. Thrown the key away." He went quiet for a moment, and then: "So can I be the godfather?"

"No freaking way."

Instead of driving to the Marriage Bureau, the building we'd visited yesterday, we pulled up alongside the dirty white walls of the City Hall building, right next to a side door on Broadway. The car had barely rocked to a halt before Eric swung open the door and bundled us inside. Someone was waiting there to escort us, an eager-looking suit who clearly wasn't just an ordinary city clerk. He led us to the elevator bank and upstairs to a plush waiting area.

"Mr. Laurence is inside already," he told me, nodding at the door; he walked us up to it and turned the knob.

A large high-ceilinged room opened around me, an office of some kind, containing a gleaming antique desk with a pair of chairs arranged before it, like supplicants at an altar. Julian stood near a tall triple-sash window, talking to Arthur Hamilton and a man who looked vaguely familiar. Where had I seen that profile before?

All three men turned when we entered the room, but Julian lured my attention, dressed impeccably in a sober well-tailored navy suit and white shirt, his hair collecting the light, his smile stinging my eyes with its radiance. He stepped forward and held out his hand; the fingers, when I clasped them, curled tightly around mine.

"Ah, there's the blushing bride now," said the other man, and recognition burst across my brain at the sound of his voice. "Shall we begin?"

The ceremony was short and simple, no soaring rhetorical flourishes. Just the plain familiar vows, read out by the mayor of New York City and repeated by the two of us with sincerity and conviction: *I, Julian, take you, Kate* and *I, Kate, take you, Julian;* and *with this ring I thee wed;* and *by the power vested in me by the State of New York,* and we were married.

He bent his head and kissed me on the lips, and then lifted my hand and kissed the plain platinum band that nestled there, atop the circle of diamonds he'd given me in May. I hadn't even thought about rings, but one had appeared in my hand when I was supposed to do my part, and now it rested on the fourth finger of Julian's left hand, gleaming gold. I looked at the ring, and then I looked up at the firm elegant lines of my husband's face, at his green-blue eyes and the curve of his smile, and I realized this hadn't been a superfluous formality at all.

"You're mine." I smiled. "My husband."

"God help you," he whispered back, with a little wink.

Then we turned to Charlie and Arthur and received their congratulations.

"Dude, that was awesome," said Charlie, looking, in fact, awed. "No flowers and shi . . . *stuff.* Just the basics. Powerful, dude. Powerful."

I turned to Arthur Hamilton. "Thank you. Thank you for coming here, for being a part of this."

His eyes were wet. "The honor is all mine," he said.

No flying rice, no crowd of adoring relatives waited for us outside. Just an ordinary bustling Manhattan sidewalk to cross, with Julian's driver, holding open the rear door of the black Cadillac, on the other side of it. Eric swept us both inside, and the last thing I saw as we drove away, with Julian's warm hand woven through my own, was Arthur Hamilton's face, all the false joy washed out of it, leaving only an expression of profound elemental misery.

WHEN WE ARRIVED BACK at the townhouse, Julian, who had been subdued and reflective in the car, hoisted me into his arms.

"What?" I exclaimed, grabbing wildly for my right shoe, which nearly fell off with the force of the upward swing.

"Carrying you over the threshold, darling. It's traditional." He swept me up the front steps, past Eric, and into the entrance hall. "At last," he murmured, kissing me, hard and fierce and short; then he set me down on the old marble tiles.

"At *last?*" I laughed. "You've known me since December."

He kept me within the circle of his arms, studying me seriously, as though I were some sort of exotic animal he couldn't quite decide what to do with.

"So, husband." I eased my arms around his waist. "What's on the agenda? How much time before our guests arrive?"

His fingers massaged my back. "Not much, I'm afraid."

"Then I suppose I should go upstairs and change."

"Hmm. And you'll want to pack, of course."

I frowned. "Pack?"

His lips moved toward my ear. "There's an airplane waiting for us, after dinner. Have you forgotten our honeymoon?" Something about his voice made the word sound deeply dissolute.

"Honeymoon? Where are we going?"

"I'm afraid I can't tell you that. Now go upstairs."

I drew back in his arms. "Aren't you coming?"

"I'm already packed."

"But . . ." I fingered his lapel and cast up what I hoped was a seductive look from beneath my eyelashes. "I might need help with my zipper."

He smiled and leaned down to kiss me, his lips slow and suggestive. I felt his hands move along my back and draw down the zipper of my dress. "There," he whispered.

"You're outrageous."

"Be patient, darling," he said.

Something in his expression, in the tone of his voice, made me draw back again and peer closely at his face. "What is it? What's wrong?"

"Nothing's wrong. Everything's just as it should be. As it was meant to be."

"But you look *sad*," I said. "Oh, Julian. What's wrong?"

He smiled again, but it was as though he pushed it out of his mouth by sheer force. "Kate," he said, his voice tender, "my beautiful Kate. Katherine Ashford." His hands glided up my sides to rest on my shoulders. "My wife. My bride. The mother of my precious child. Let me make something perfectly clear. I have never in my life felt so happy as the moment, a short while ago, when you walked into that room and married me."

"Oh." I couldn't bear the beauty of his face, the strange severity in his eyes; my own cast down, studying the subtle pattern of his pale blue necktie.

"Listen to me, Kate," he continued, taking my chin. "Please look at me. There isn't a word to describe my happiness. I can only say this: whatever I am, wherever I am, I am your husband. Always, that truth lies between us. Do you understand?"

"Yes."

I thought he would kiss me then, but he didn't. He only grazed my lip with his thumb once, twice.

"Now go upstairs and pack," he said huskily. "Before our guests arrive."

I nodded and stepped away to hurry up the stairs. When I reached the landing, I looked down to see him staring after me, his expression anything but joyful.

"OH," I SAID, pausing at the archway into the living room half an hour later, "you must be Dr. Hollander!"

The gray-haired man on the sofa stood up and unfolded himself to a broad enormous height. "And you," he said, holding out his hand, "must be Kate Ashford. Even more beautiful, I must say, than Julian described."

I went over and reached for both his hands. "So he's told you! I thought we were surprising everyone." I leaned forward to kiss both his cheeks. "I'm so pleased to meet you, Dr. Hollander. I know it sounds like a cliché, but I really do feel as though I know you already. Please, please sit down. Can I offer you something?"

He gestured to the coffee table, on which a drink of some amber liquid—Scotch, probably—tumbled around the ice in a plain lowball glass. "Julian's already seen to it, thanks. Of course he had to tell me; I don't usually travel except for compelling reasons."

I sank down on the sofa next to him. "I have dozens of questions to ask you, but I'll spare you for now." My reaction had surprised even me; the instant I saw him, I'd known who it must be, and delight poured through my body. Maybe it was his looks: not handsome, exactly, but friendly and open, with crinkling dark eyes and an air of genteel distraction. He must have been sixty or seventy years old, and six foot five at least. And he was the world's leading expert on my new husband. I smiled at him. "Before anything else, I want to thank you for being such a good friend to Julian over the years. When I think of how hard it must have been for him, in those early years, without anyone at all to talk to, I just . . . Well, it must have been terrible. And then you came along. Thank goodness."

He blinked at me. "Dear me. How kind of you. And all these years I've felt it to be the other way around, you see. To have the very subject of my study walk into my office one day. A historian's impossible fantasy, come to life."

"So where is he?" I glanced around the room with a frown. "He hasn't abandoned you, has he?"

"Oh no. He had a phone call, just a moment ago." He cocked his head toward the pocket doors to the library, which were closed tight.

"Oh. Sorry about that. He does it to me all the time. Savior of Wall Street." I rolled my eyes, just to show how unimpressed I was.

Hollander scowled. *Ruddy old Marxist,* Julian had said. "He should have let it all go to the dogs, as far as I'm concerned."

"All right, now," I said. "You're talking to an investment banker here. Well, former investment banker. A total capitalist pig, anyway. I can't wait until we're close enough friends to have some knock-down drag-out arguments about it."

He started laughing. "Ah, Mrs. Ashford, I'm beginning to see Julian's point. One so rarely encounters a beautiful woman who also happens to be good company."

I wagged my finger at him. "Oh wow. A smooth one. I'll have to watch myself. But it's Kate, please. Only Julian calls me Mrs. Ashford."

He chuckled and took a drink of his whiskey.

Something else occurred to me. "We were so worried last summer, when you disappeared. I hope everything's okay now?"

"Oh, perfectly fine, thank you," he said, so brightly I knew he was lying. "Just a last-minute research project. A request from a particular . . . friend of mine."

"Oh, really? What kind of project? Out in the field somewhere?"

"In a manner of speaking," he said, as the doorbell rang.

"Oh! If you'll just excuse me a second. My whole family's flying in. Oh wait—don't forget, the wedding's a surprise. And his last name is Laurence, as far as they know."

"You haven't told them?" he asked me in astonishment, as I rose from the sofa.

"Like they would even *believe* me!" I tossed over my shoulder.

WE DROVE TO THE RESTAURANT in two separate cars. Julian took Dr. Hollander in the Maserati, with Samantha and Michelle squashed sideways in what passed for the back seat. Julian's driver, with Eric up front, chauffeured the rest of us in an Escalade.

We arrived a few minutes late. Geoff and Carla were already waiting at the bar with Arthur Hamilton. None of them looked happy, although Carla was at least making an effort at a grin. "Hello, Kate!" she exclaimed with a meaningful wink, as she leaned in for an air kiss.

Another man stepped forward from the bar, his round face pink with all the delight missing from the expressions of the others. "Mrs. Laurence!" He thrust his hand forward. "Can't tell you how glad I am to meet you, all proper and official-like. Andrew Paulson."

"Sergeant Paulson!" My hand was being pumped up and down like a jackhammer. "Julian didn't tell me you were coming! What a wonderful surprise!"

He was beaming so broadly, I'd never have connected him with the downcast figure on Park Avenue last May if he hadn't introduced himself. "Wouldn't miss it, Mrs. L. Wouldn't miss it. Couldn't be happier to see that boy settled."

"Boy?" asked my mother, over my shoulder.

"Mr. Paulson is an old friend of mine, Mrs. Wilson, from England. Just moved over a few months ago," Julian said. I glanced again at Paulson's face; I guessed he wasn't much older than Julian now, though they must originally have been born at least a dozen years apart.

"I see," Mom said, in a tone I recognized from my teenage years, meaning *not quite buying it, honey.*

The maitre d' led us all down the hall to a private room upstairs. A round table had been set up in the middle, with a snowy white tablecloth and glasses of champagne at every place setting, still fizzling. Each plate, I saw, had a name card in front of it; Julian was urging everyone forward to sit down, the consummate host. At the last moment, he turned to me with a sweet smile, almost wistful, and squeezed my hand. "All right, darling?"

I nodded. "Perfect."

"How are you feeling?"

"Pretty normal, for the moment. As long as they don't serve any hot dogs."

He lifted my hand and kissed it. "Let me know if you need to dash out."

He led me to my seat and pulled out my chair, then moved to the one next to it and picked up his champagne glass. The table fell silent and looked up at him expectantly. Samantha wore an enormous grin.

"Ladies," he began, returning her smile, moving on to the others, "gentlemen. All our dear friends and family. As you've no doubt guessed by now, judging from the expressions I see around me, Kate and I have asked you here tonight for a special dinner indeed."

"Hear, hear!" burst out my father. For God's sake.

"Early this afternoon," Julian said, "Kate did me the very great honor of becoming my wife, in a small civil ceremony at City Hall."

The table erupted into cheers and applause. From most of them, at least; Arthur stared down at his plate, and Geoff wore an expression of sclerotic hostility.

Julian waited for the enthusiasm to die down, a smile teasing the side of his mouth. "Of course, we're deeply sorry we couldn't ask all of you to attend, but after some reflection we decided that, rather than endure a long engagement under public scrutiny, we wanted the legal ceremony to be performed as soon as possible, to be followed, at some point in the next few months, by a more traditional wedding, which I sincerely hope will put me back in good graces with Kate's mother and friends."

"Hear, hear!" called out my mother.

"In any case," Julian went on, twinkling at her, "I'd like you to join me in toasting my new bride, my beloved Kate. To her health and happiness, which I shall devote my life to undertaking."

My blush, by this point, had reached every last node of my body, and when Julian lifted up my hand and kissed it in front of everybody, I thought I might disintegrate. But the faces around me, with the exception of Geoff and poor Arthur, were so radiant with delight—even Carla, who had enough estrogen in her to appreciate a romantic moment, even someone else's—that the confusion began to recede. Julian sat down, still holding my hand, and I scanned the eyes fastened so eagerly upon me.

With sudden confidence, I released my husband's hand and reached for my own glass. "Excuse me," I said, standing up, "I think it's my turn."

Silence, close and expectant. I felt Julian's warmth next to my arm, the coolness of the glass under my fingers, and gathered courage. "I'd just like to thank everyone for coming this evening. Having all of you here to share my joy—*our* joy—makes it all the more precious to me. So, to all of you," I said, raising my glass and turning to Julian, "and to you, Julian, to your own health and happiness, which I very much hope to share with you for all the rest of our life together."

I sat down hard, to a chorus of cheers and *hear, hear*s, and took a drink of my champagne, which turned out to be ginger ale. He'd thought of everything. I felt a weight on my knee: Julian's hand, squeezing gently. I looked sideways with a wan smile, unable to say anything more.

Then the toasts began in earnest, mingling with an appetizer course whisked in by an army of waiters. Some sort of asparagus dish; I sniffed delicately to test my reaction, and found no swirl of nausea curling my belly. So far, so good.

Charlie, who'd already had a glass or two of Julian's single-malt Scotch before leaving the townhouse, began a rambling toast in his usual style, which I hoped my parents weren't following. My own mind was already beginning to drift: to the plane that supposedly sat waiting for us, to the honeymoon ahead. Where we might be going, how long we might stay. In the midst of this meditation, I happened to glance over at Arthur Hamilton.

He was staring at me, directly at me, and his expression was neither pleased nor sad nor wistful nor tormented. It was cold. Stone cold. Like he was staring down a tennis opponent at a championship match. Like he'd just been told I'd killed his favorite cat.

Like I'd just married his beloved sister's fiancé.

The entrée had that instant been placed before me, an elegant rack of lamb in a pool of minted butter. I looked down at it and felt the contents of my stomach heave drunkenly back and forth. "Excuse me," I whispered to Julian.

He looked at me in concern.

"Lamb," I said. "I'll be back in a minute."

He started to rise.

"No, no. I'm okay. Stay here. They'll worry."

I slipped from my chair and out of the room, just as Charlie was winding up with some hilarious and probably grossly embarrassing anecdote. "Bathroom?" I begged a waiter, as he came up the stairs in front of me.

"Basement," he said, in heavily accented English, "to the right at the end of the hall."

I flew down the stairs, to the main level and then down to the basement, where I could hear the clatter of the pots and pans in the kitchen. Down the hall to the right. I looked frantically in front of me and saw a signboard painted with a female silhouette.

I made it just in time, emptying asparagus and ginger ale into the toilet until it seemed like the lining of my stomach had been stripped out as well. "You," I muttered, straightening at last and catching my breath, "had better be a really cute baby. Because this is getting old *fast*."

I opened up the stall door and staggered to the sink, one of those stylish bowl-above-the-counter models. A neat stack of linen towels sat by the basin; I took one off the top and wet it with some cool water from the faucet and looked up into the mirror to wipe my forehead.

Arthur Hamilton's face stared back at me, from just above my right shoulder.

I wanted to scream, but my vocal cords had locked. I whipped around instead.

"Come with me," he said.

"Where?" I gasped out.

"Out of here."

I made a lunge for the door, but he grabbed my arm and shoved something into my belly. A gun.

I don't think I'd ever even seen a real gun up close. Just stared uneasily, once or twice, at the pieces hanging on the hips of the NYPD, wondering what it would be like to hold one, fire one. They'd always looked a bit scary to me. Hard, lethal. Not something I really wanted around me.

"You wouldn't use that," I whispered. "You wouldn't do that. It would kill Julian. He's your friend."

Arthur said nothing, only nudged me with the gun. Hard. I swallowed, trying to think rationally. "You can't kill me," I said. "You wouldn't do that."

"Open the door slowly," he said. "We're going out the back way."

"No. I won't."

His finger moved, and something clicked. He'd been a soldier, whether or not a good one. He knew how to use a gun. He'd probably even killed someone before. I reached for the door handle and opened it.

"Turn to the right," he said, and I turned to the right, walking down the hallway, hoping I could go slowly enough that Julian would notice the two of us missing, would get suspicious. Would come after me and freaking save me. Wasn't that what he was supposed to do? Because I was way too scared out of my wits at the moment to save myself. I didn't know anything about Arthur Hamilton. Had he just *snapped*? Was he going to take me out into the street and shoot me there?

Buy time, I thought. Buy time. "Where are you taking me?" I asked, trying to turn around, but the gun shoved into my kidneys.

"Open the door," he said, and I opened the door.

It was a service entrance, rising up the stairs to the street level. "Up," Arthur said, and I started climbing the stairs, feeling the curl of panic now, the evening air cool and damp on my skin, the smell of cooking food making my stomach roil.

I heard some kind of commotion behind me, inside the basement, and called out, "I'm here! On the stairs!"

The gun shoved hard against my back, knocking me to my knees. "Don't do that again!" Arthur hissed. "Now *up*! Now!" Another shove, and I scrambled up the rest of the stairs and through a gap in the railing to the sidewalk.

A car hummed by the curve; not one of ours. I cast about, looking for the Escalade, and saw it, a few storefronts down. Eric and the driver were both reading magazines. I reached up to wave, but Arthur grabbed my arm and wrenched it backward, shoving me toward the back door of the car. He flung the door open and pushed me in and followed, and the car took off with a screech.

I pressed down on the window button, to no avail; it must have had the safety lock on. "Help!" I screamed at the driver, "he's kidnapping me!"

The man didn't flinch.

I whipped my head around, staring back at the restaurant, and at that instant two figures burst onto the sidewalk. One of them was Julian; I could see his hair gleam under the streetlamp. "Julian!" I screamed out, not that he could hear me. He stopped, looking up and down the street, and spotted our car. He started sprinting after us, legs pumping like pistons, chest bursting through his crisp white shirt. I reached for the door handle, desperate, but it was locked, and Arthur's fist came down on my hand.

"Calm down," he said, in a hard cold voice. "You won't get hurt unless you do something foolish. You have my word."

"Your *word*?" I turned back to the rear window, and saw that Julian had given up chasing us and was now running back to the Escalade; we wheeled around the corner, onto Park Avenue, and by some cosmic blast of bad luck the lights had just turned green as far as I could see, all the way up to 125th Street and beyond.

We raced steadily up Park Avenue, through the seventies and the eighties, ambitious limestone Candela façades rippling past my eyes, before the lights turned red again at Ninety-third Street. I forced myself to calm down, to think rationally. Arthur was obviously sick, despondent, not a murderer. Talk him off the ledge. Make him see reason.

"Arthur," I said. "I understand, I really do. I can't even imagine how hard it's been for you, losing your sister. A much better woman than I am. When I see what she accomplished, what she *was . . .*" I twisted the bracelets on my right wrist. "Of course you're upset. Of course you are."

"He loved her," Arthur said. "You don't understand. He loved her. They were perfect for one another. You should have seen them together: the match of the age."

Each word he spoke, with laser precision, penetrated my brain with its own specific sensation of pain. "Of course," I said. "Of course." Keep him talking. Distract him. The car rumbled uneasily below my legs, eager to be back in motion.

"I don't mean to be cruel. You're a nice girl. Pretty, in your way. But Flora! We all worshipped her, Julian and Geoffrey and I."

"I know. Julian"—I swallowed—"speaks of her with such warmth, such regret."

Keep him happy. Just keep him happy.

"He loved her so," Arthur said wistfully. "And she loved him, of course. How could she not? As beautiful as he is. His character, his noble soul. His spotless purity. A star, glowing above us all. There's no one like him in this world. No honor, no decency, no *fidelity*. How I wish we had never been brought here. How I wish . . ."

"You love him," I said, almost inaudibly, turning my head to read, with dawning astonishment and pity, the expression on his face. "You love him, don't you?"

"Of course I do. Who doesn't?"

"I mean you're *in* love with him, aren't you?"

He snapped his face to mine, and I lost him. "*In* love with him! *In* love with him! You *sordid* woman, with your commonplace vulgar mind! I loved him, I love him, with a pure love, a noble love, something as foreign to you as the age in which we were bred. And his love for her! To think he would dishonor that love, betray it, with the vile sensuous *fleshly* passion he feels for you, into which you've corrupted him!"

"You," I said, "are seriously sick." The headlamps of a passing taxi shadowed across his face, and something connected in my brain. "You. It was you following me around. You at the Starbucks that night. No wonder Julian let you . . ."

The crosstown light turned amber, and I felt the car poise upward, ready to take off at the green.

A screech of tires ripped through the air behind us. We both turned to see a sleek dark car whip around the center island from Ninety-second Street. Julian's Maserati.

The lights turned green, and Arthur's driver punched the accelerator, throwing us both back against the seat. I grabbed my seat belt and snapped it in. *Don't,* I begged Julian. *Don't race us. Just call the police. Don't risk yourself. Please. Please.*

Our car was fast, but the Maserati was built for speed. Within a block it was alongside us, then pushing ahead, trying to force us over. I saw there were two figures inside: who was with him? The passenger glanced back at us; I couldn't see his face in the shadows. I leaned forward, pressing against the window glass, trying desperately to peer through.

My window began rolling down, exposing my skin to the outside air, and then I felt something cold and hard press against my right temple, turning my guts to water. Instantly the Maserati slowed down, backing off. It dropped behind us, at a close but respectful distance, and I tried to turn and look around, to glimpse Julian's face, but Arthur snarled, "Don't move. Just sit."

Don't shake. Don't panic. Relax. Think happy. Think Julian holding you, think of his arms, his face, his smell, his kiss. Everything will be okay. You won't die. We haven't even had our wedding night. Can't die without *that*.

We turned right onto Ninety-sixth Street. I wondered if Julian was still following us. We must be going onto the FDR, I thought. Nothing else in that direction.

But we didn't go onto the FDR. We stopped instead on the block between First and Second avenues, and Arthur pulled me out of the car and up the stoop of an ordinary tenement-style walkup building. He pressed a button on the row outside the door, and someone must have been waiting for him, because it buzzed at once and he burst through the door, dragging me with him, just as a shout outside told me Julian and his companion had jumped out of the Maserati and were running after us, into the building.

They just caught the door before it closed, and I heard them running across the bare shabby lobby behind us. Arthur was pulling me up the stairs; I dragged my feet, slowing him down, and tried to look around behind us. He yanked me up on the first landing and spun me around and pressed the gun against my temple, hard.

Geoff. Geoff was the one with Julian. They both froze, staring at us.

I tried to keep my face composed. I didn't want Julian to panic, to do something rash. His eyes locked on mine, ablaze with emotion. *I'm okay*, I mouthed to him. *Okay.*

His head made a tiny motion, perhaps a nod, and his eyes shifted to Arthur. "Put the gun down, Arthur," he said softly. "You've no quarrel with her. It isn't her fault. It's mine."

"No," I squawked.

"Hush, Kate," he said. "Put the gun down, Arthur. Let her go. We'll all sit down and chat. Of course you're upset. Of course you are. Just let her go." He placed his foot casually on the next step up.

"Stop," Arthur said. "I'll shoot her."

Julian stilled.

"You're right," Arthur went on. "It isn't her fault. *She* didn't know my sister. *She* didn't betray her. Betray every principle we once held dear."

"No, she didn't," Julian said. "So let her go. Let her go, and I'll come with you. We'll sort it all out."

"No!" I said. "Julian, *no*! Don't go with him."

Nobody noticed me. Julian and Arthur stared at each other, like dogs in a ring, sizing one another up. Geoff stood there quietly, impassively, a bystander. *Do something*, I thought. *They're your friends, for God's sake.*

"Let her go," Julian said, in his coaxing voice, the one I could never resist. "I'll come with you. Willingly. No trouble."

"Julian, no," I whispered. "Don't be an idiot."

Silence hollowed out the stairwell. I heard a pair of thumps from somewhere upstairs, then another; a baby's cry echoed faintly, fretfully, through the walls. *Won't somebody come*, I thought, agonized. *Won't somebody hear something, see something, call the police.*

"Very well," Arthur said. "Have I your word of honor?"

"My word of honor." Julian's shoulders eased. "Let her go, without any harm, and I'll go with you. Wherever you want. We can sort it all out."

Arthur made an impatient gesture with his hand. "Your gun, please. Slowly."

"He doesn't *have* a gun," I said.

Julian didn't seem to hear me; he only regarded Arthur for a few seconds, opaque and thorough, eyes narrowed. Then, without any change in expression, he drew open his suit jacket and reached inside. His hand, when it emerged, held a small dark object that caught the light from the bare hallway bulb with a dull gleam.

He began walking up the steps toward us. "Oh my *God*! You had a *gun* on you?" I said.

He didn't reply, didn't even look at me. His eyes remained locked with Arthur's.

"Slowly," Arthur repeated. "Your word of honor, remember."

Julian stopped two steps below us, his face a perfect mask, but I could see the steady rise and fall of his chest, slightly faster than usual, and the quick tick of his pulse at his throat. He placed the gun in Arthur's empty left hand and backed down three steps, precise and measured, one foot resting watchfully on the step above.

Arthur shoved the gun in his left outside pocket and looked over at Geoff. "Well, Geoffrey?" he asked brusquely. "Give me a hand?"

And Geoff, the Judas, the filthy betraying mongrel, walked up the stairs, past Julian, and took me by the arm. "Come along. I'll walk you outside."

"You bastard," I hissed. "How can you do this to him?"

He looked at me coldly and didn't answer, only pulled me down the steps with him. I kicked out, trying to break his grip, but his arms only tightened around mine, until he was practically carrying me.

"Julian, no!" I said, as we passed him on the stairs. "This is ridiculous! He'll try to kill you! He's nuts!"

He paused. His hand reached out to my cheek. "Trust me, Kate," he said. "Go home. Wait for me. Promise you'll wait. I'll be back, I swear it. Promise you'll wait. *Don't go anywhere.*"

"He'll kill you!" Geoff was dragging me to the bottom of the steps, like the strongman in some stupid action movie. "He's crazy, Julian!"

Geoff dragged me to the corner of the lobby and turned around, locking me in his arms. I kicked and struggled, fighting him.

Arthur was saying something to Julian; Julian nodded and turned around, walking down the stairs. Arthur followed him, the gun lowered now.

"Where are you taking him?"

"Where he should have been all along," Arthur muttered.

Julian walked by me without even a glance; Geoff jerked me behind them, through the doors and onto the sidewalk. Cars drove by; no one noticed us. This was New York, after all. Weird stuff happened. You just pretended you didn't see it.

Arthur opened the rear door of his car with a cordial air, and motioned Julian inside. My husband started to climb in, and then seemed to remember me; he turned his head over his shoulder and looked at me intently. Then he ducked into the car, his golden head disappearing from view, and Arthur followed him and slammed the door shut.

I turned to Geoff. "You asshole! You freaking asshole! *I love him!*"

"Not as much as he loves you," he said angrily. "*A Blighty one*," he added, in a harsh mutter. He let me go, so suddenly I stumbled to my knees, and strode across the sidewalk to Arthur's car, where he flung open the front passenger seat and jumped inside. The car leapt ahead, and something flew at me from Geoff's window, before the black mass accelerated down the block toward the river and the FDR Drive.

I stared after them, not quite believing it. Then I looked down at the sidewalk to see what Geoff had thrown me.

A set of car keys. For the Maserati.

26.

I thought for an instant about following them. I had Julian's car, after all. It was more than a match for Arthur's sedan.

But I'd already lost the taillights in the traffic, and Manhattan crawled with anonymous black sedans, ferrying the affluent around town. And what did I know about car chases, anyway? I'd get lost somewhere in the South Bronx in a hundred-thousand-dollar sports car, and what use would I be then?

Trust me, Julian had said. Go home. Wait for me.

I bent down to pick up the car keys. My fingers had gone numb; my whole body teetered on the brink of shock. What had happened? Was it a dream? I'd just gotten married, the happiest day of my life; Julian had kissed these lips, these fingers; we were supposed to be leaving for our honeymoon.

Now Julian was gone. Driven away in a black sedan with a man who quite possibly wanted to kill him.

Nausea coiled around me; I placed my hand over my belly. Our baby. Julian's baby. I went around to the driver's side and got in and started the engine. The seat, my God, the seat was still warm. Julian's warmth.

I thrust down the clutch and put the car in gear and merged into traffic, crossing First Avenue, which went uptown, and then turning down York. I cruised without even thinking, stopping automatically at the red lights, my brain just shutting down. Shutting everything out.

Somewhere in the Seventies my hands began to shake. I pulled over to the curb. *Trust me. Trust me. Go home. Wait for me.*

Julian, I can't. I can't just *wait*. Wait for how long? What if you never come back? The shaking intensified, crawling up my arms to my torso.

Okay, think. Be calm. Stop panicking. Think this through. Every problem has a solution. Who might know where they'd gone?

The answer came quickly: Hollander. The world's leading expert on Julian Ashford. I pulled away from the curb and drove back across the avenues to Park, turned onto Julian's street, and pulled into the garage, where I left the keys in the ignition for the attendant and hurried across the street to Julian's house. Our house.

Eric stood on the steps, with his cell phone glued to his ear. He saw me and hung up and went forward to grab me by the arms. "Mrs. Laurence! What happened?"

"Everything's okay," I said brightly. "Mr. Haverton . . . got sick downstairs. I was just helping him back to his apartment. I'm so sorry you all were worried. Is everyone inside?"

His eyes narrowed. "Where's Mr. Laurence?"

"Mr. Laurence thought it might be best to take him to the ER. They're there now." The lies ran easily off my tongue. One thing I knew for certain: I couldn't tell anyone other than Hollander what had happened, at least for now. Because what would happen if everyone knew the truth?

Eric knew I was lying; I could see it in his face. They probably taught that kind of thing in bodyguard school. But he just nodded and opened the door for me. "Everyone's inside," he told me. "I'll be waiting here."

"Thanks, Eric. I'll let you know if we need you."

"You do that, Mrs. L."

The living room was full of our dinner guests, and they all looked up when I walked in. "Honey!" Mom called out, and ran toward me. "What happened? Julian and Geoff just got up and ran out the door, and the next thing . . ."

"Oh, everything's fine!" I said. "So sorry to worry you. Arthur just got completely sick on his way to the bathroom. Vomiting blood and everything. Horrible. Like a *House* episode. So instead of waiting for an ambulance, I just jumped in the car with him to Lenox Hill and called up Julian. Of course he freaked." I laughed. "Anyway, they're all there right now, waiting for a doctor to see him. Total drama."

"Blimey," said Paulson.

"Oh, dear," Mom said, studying me. "Are you going to miss your flight?"

"No, Mom. It's a private jet. They'll wait. We can't just go off on our honeymoon with poor Arthur . . ." My voice caught, not on purpose.

"Wow," Charlie said. "Wish I'd seen it. Vomiting blood. Awesome. Hope he's okay."

"Yeah, apparently it's more common than you think. Stomach bug." I yawned.

"Would you like us to stay with you, honey?" my mom asked.

"Stay with me? Aren't you staying here anyway?"

"No, we're flying back tonight," my father said. "Work tomorrow."

"Oh, of course. I'm sorry. Kind of forgot it was a Monday."

Kyle snorted. "Yeah, well, we're not all married to billionaires, you know."

I rolled my eyes valiantly, unable to form the words to respond.

"We'll get going, then, honey," Mom said. "But congratulations. We're just so happy. And as soon as you get back from your honeymoon, I want to start planning your real wedding. Home in Wisconsin. I can't wait to show off that son-in-law of mine." She leaned forward and hugged me.

"Yeah." I forced back the tears as I returned her hug. "I'll bet he can't wait to be shown off."

Everyone passed by with hugs and good-byes and congratulations, and somehow I kept my composure, kept the panic from rising up into my face. "Is everything all right, Mrs. L?" asked Andrew Paulson, as he leaned in against my cheek.

"Not exactly," I said, in a low murmur, smiling brightly. "But I'm sure it will all work out."

"Goes without saying, of course, if you need anything . . ." He pressed my hand.

"Of course. I know. Thank you."

Dr. Hollander came last, probably by design. He'd been watching me closely throughout; I'd felt his eyes, needle sharp against my face. Now he came up, just as Charlie disappeared around the corner to the entrance hall, and took my hands. "My dear," he began.

"Wait," I hissed. "Don't go yet."

I moved into the hall and waved good-bye at Charlie and Michelle, who were laughing together, walking out the door. "Bye!" I called. "I'll e-mail!"

"Yeah, yeah!" Charlie guffawed. "Like you'll have any fucking time for e-mail!" He shut the door behind them.

I turned to Hollander. "You've got to help me," I said, and burst at last into tears.

THE SOBS DIDN'T LAST LONG. I gathered myself, seeing Hollander's panicked expression, remembering Eric stood just outside the door, and wiped the tears away with swift, impatient fists.

"Come into the library," I managed, taking the professor's hand and dragging him with me.

"What is it? What's wrong?"

"They've got him. Geoff and Arthur. They took Julian with them. I was just the bait, to get Julian out of there, to get him to go along with them. They had a gun, Professor! They'll kill him! You've got to help me!"

He dropped my hand and halted, there in the center of the library rug. "Kidnapped him? Kidnapped Julian?"

"Yes!" I said, agonized. "Took him away in a black sedan, toward the FDR! Where would they be taking him? What's going on?"

Hollander lowered his tall frame on the library sofa, his blue irises surrounded by the shocked whites of his eyes. His head sank into his hands. "It's my fault," he whispered. "I couldn't let it lie. My God. What have I done?"

"What do you mean? Where have they taken him?"

He looked up at me. "Is it about Miss Hamilton? Is that what this was about?"

"Yes," I said, pacing across the room to stare down at the small paved garden in the rear. "But it's more than that. Arthur's gone crazy. It's like he's been at a slow simmer, all these years, and the wedding just . . . and Geoff's gone with him . . . Oh my God! Maybe they've killed him already! Dumped his body in the river!" I jumped up, thinking of Julian's face, still and cold and bloody. Bobbing in the river. Gone. Dead.

"Calm down!" Hollander said sharply. "They wouldn't kill him, I'm sure of it. They were the best of friends. *Are* the best of friends. There's no question of killing."

"How do you know? He was crazy, Professor. Crazy! Talking about vile lust and . . ." I shook my head. "He loves Julian, Professor. Maybe he's even *in* love with him; I don't know. I don't even think *he* knows."

Hollander rose to his feet with an impatient fling of his hand. "No, no. You're mistaking him, projecting your modern ideas onto his. The sentimental convention of the time encouraged affectionate, even passionate friendship. Of course he loves Julian; he idolized him. Surely you didn't suggest to him . . ."

"I guess I did. But it wouldn't have made any difference. He just hates the modern world, the people in it. I think he was sort of living vicariously through Flora before, basking in Julian's feelings for her, and it's like Julian's rejected *him* now." I thought of Arthur's expression on the stairs, the arctic hatred in his eyes. "I think he wants him dead."

He shot me a contemptuous look. "Or himself. I suppose you're aware that Arthur Hamilton had himself transferred to a front-line unit shortly after Julian's disappearance. Suicide, in effect."

"So what does that mean? He's going to try to finish the job? Make Julian watch? But why would *Geoff* go along with that?"

Hollander put his fingers to his temples and began rubbing as he paced the room. "Not sure. Not sure. Where would he take them? Where would they go?" He snapped his fingers and turned to me. "The airplane. For your honeymoon."

"Oh no!" I jumped up. "But I don't know where it was heading. I don't even know which airport. No, wait," I said, thinking, "probably Teterboro, right? That's where all the private planes take off from. Or Westchester. I can call NetJets, right? I'm his wife. They'll tell me." I went to Julian's desk. "Allegra made the arrangements, I'm sure, but maybe he's at least got the account information here somewhere." I flung open drawers, looking for something, anything.

"Try the computer."

"Good idea." I reached for Julian's laptop, flipped it open, pressed the power button. This was good. This was doing something. I knew all about doing something, about keeping busy to stave off panic. Just one small task at a time. Stay focused.

Julian's MacBook booted up in four rapid seconds and then paused to ask me for a password. I knew where Julian kept them. He'd shown me early on, in case I needed to find something, trusting me with heartbreaking thoroughness. I went to the bookshelf and found his worn dog-eared copy of Graham and Dodd's *Security Analysis* and lifted the back flap. Tucked inside was a list of passwords, one for each month.

The MacBook made a satisfied noise and unfolded the desktop for me. Julian kept it tidy, no loose files. I clicked on the e-mail icon and without the smallest tinge of conscience entered "NetJets" in the search field.

Bingo. He, or Allegra, had made the reservation yesterday evening; the confirmation lay before me, account number and flight code and everything. Taking off from Teterboro Airport, expected time of departure 10 p.m.

I checked my watch. Ten-fifteen. Where was my phone? "Shoot," I said, turning to Hollander. "Did anyone bring my handbag back from the restaurant?"

"Your *handbag*?" As if he'd never heard the word in his life.

"Of course you don't know. I'll ask Eric." I got up and crossed through the living room, but before I reached the door I saw my black satin hand-bag hanging by its chain from the newel post at the bottom of the stairs. Something, at least, where it should be.

I drew out my BlackBerry, ran back to the library, and dialed the Net-Jets number. "Hello." I put on my calm professional voice, gave them the account number. "This is Mr. Laurence's office. I just wanted to verify his flight departed on time."

"Just a moment, please," answered a friendly female customer-service voice, balanced exquisitely between intimacy and courtesy: the voice of someone who knew just how much her company's clients were ponying up to ride its airplanes.

I tapped my fingers against the desk, waiting, watching Hollander. He stared back, without blinking, his forehead furrowed with deep anxious lines. I tried to smile. I was feeling a little better. I was doing something now; I was finding my husband.

The voice reappeared in my ear. "Thank you for holding. Yes, I have a departure confirmation for that flight, leaving Teterboro at nine fifty-eight p.m."

I let out my breath in a gust of relief. Or anxiety: I wasn't quite sure whether this was good news or bad. But at least I knew they'd taken him somewhere and not just killed him outright. "Thank you. Oh yes, and one more thing. Mr. Laurence indicated he was considering a last-minute change of destination. Can you confirm whether the flight was headed for"—I looked back at the computer screen—"Marrakech?" I choked at the word. I'd never have guessed Morocco.

"Just a moment, please." Hold music. I chewed my lip ferociously, trying not to imagine myself cruising over the Atlantic with Julian in a private airplane. The voice, mercifully, returned before my will broke down. "Thank you for holding. No, according to the final flight plan, the destination was changed to Manchester Airport in England."

"Manchester, England. As I thought. Thank you so much." I hung up the phone and looked at Hollander. "So? Manchester?"

"Southfield," he said, staring at the floor. "They're going to Southfield."

For a moment, the word confused me. Julian's firm was headquartered only a few blocks away, in a wide limestone townhouse on Sixty-third Street, a discreet brass plaque engraved *Southfield Associates* affixed to the right of the door: a site of abomination, probably, to Hollander. And then understanding burst upon me. "*Southfield?* Do you mean Julian's family estate?"

He looked back up at me and made a helpless shrug of his shoulders. "It couldn't be anything else."

"But why Southfield? What does that have to do with Florence Hamilton?"

He sat down on the edge of the desk and folded his arms. "If you'd read my book," he said, dry and professorial, "you'd know that, according to her last will and testament, she requested the honor of burial on the Southfield estate. She had maintained a friendship with the eventual heirs, and they acquiesced. One doesn't refuse Florence Hamilton, even after her death."

"The nerve. Julian must have been furious when he found that out."

"Yes, that was the greatest surprise of all, for me. Finding out the truth of the Hamilton affair. She'd done such a thorough job, you see, of constructing her narrative."

"Yeah, okay. But why would Arthur and Geoff take Julian there? You don't think . . ." A shaft of coldness split my heart. "You don't think they meant to kill him and bury him with her . . ."

Hollander's eyes went wide; he jumped away from the desk. "Surely not. Arthur might be unhinged, but Geoff's as sound as a nut."

"Yeah, well, he hates me," I said.

"But he doesn't hate Julian."

"Did he love Florence?"

"Possibly," he said. "I've never quite been able to establish it. There is some hint, some hint of a flirtation, in a surviving letter, but my general impression . . ."

"Whatever." I waved that away. "We've got to fly there. We've got to stop whatever it is they're planning for him. Because whatever it is, it can't be good."

"Stop them? Stop them how?"

"Well, call the police! Break in on them! You know, *stop* them!"

Hollander leaned back and pressed his hands on his forehead. "No, no! No police! Think what would happen. Think!"

"Look," I said, "all I know is that my husband, the man I love, is being taken to someone's grave by two men with guns. And I am damned well going to try and stop them."

"How? We've got to get there in time. There aren't many flights to Manchester, and we're too late for them all. By the time we arrive, it will be over."

"No!" I exclaimed, striking my fist on the desk. "I won't accept that! I can't just sit back and hope they're just going to have a *chat*! I can't just hope Julian figures out how to save himself. It's two against one, for God's sake!"

Don't panic. Don't panic. Think.

"We'd have to take a private plane," Hollander said. "We'd never make it. It's all gone to pieces. All my fault."

"Don't do that. Don't tell me it *can't* be done. Tell me how it *can*."

Trust me. Go home. Wait for me.

But I couldn't just wait for him. Wait for him to be killed? Wait for my life to be over? I pressed my hand against my belly; a surge of energy filled me.

Private plane. No problem. I was a billionaire now, right? Could I use Julian's NetJets account? Would they take another reservation when Julian himself was supposedly on a flight already? How did the whole thing work? Would they let his wife take another plane on the same account?

Wait a minute, though. I didn't need to, did I?

"Hold on," I said to Hollander, and ran out of the library and up two flights of stairs to the small office on the third floor. My things from the apartment had been left there two weeks ago, in neat white moving boxes, all labeled with a black Sharpie. Clothes. Shoes. Bedding. Towels. Photos. File boxes.

I tore open the box containing my files. Where was it? I'd just dropped the envelope in the miscellaneous folder, hadn't I? Not knowing what else to do with it. After all, I hadn't ever planned on using it.

I found the red hanging folder marked *Misc Stuff* and drew it out and opened it. I saw the envelope straightaway: the one Julian had handed to me that first night, the night of the MoMA benefit.

With a Marquis JetCard inside.

Amiens

We lay quietly for a long while afterward. I thought perhaps he was drifting to sleep, but the tips of his fingers continued to run up and down my arm, rippling the skin pleasurably. It disturbed me, almost, how this earlier Julian had the same gestures, the same loving caresses, as the one I knew. The two separate images in my mind were beginning to blur and merge together.

"Julian," I said at last, "I've been an idiot, haven't I?"

His fingers halted just above my elbow. "Oh, Kate. Have I . . . My God, I hope . . ."

"No, *no*! Not about this. This was beautiful, wonderful." I let out a breath of laughter. "Julian. As if I could ever regret *this*. No, it's the whole *mission*. All this time I've been trying to convince you not to go on the raid. Not to go to my time. But that's the safest place for you, isn't it?"

"But I'm going to be killed there. You said so yourself."

"But you're probably just as likely to be killed here. And much sooner. So what I ought to do, what I should have done from the beginning if I'd really thought it through—if I hadn't been so selfish, wanting to keep you with me—is let you go, and tell you everything." I rolled over and spread my hands over his chest. "Tell you what to do, to keep them from killing you."

"*No!* No, Kate."

"No? But it's easy, Julian. I can tell you exactly how the time thing works, so you'll know . . ."

"Hush, sweetheart. I'm not going. I can't leave my company. My family, my home. You."

"Oh please. What possible use will you be, getting blown up by a shell in the next few months?"

"And what kind of man would I be, walking away from it? Abandoning my men, my fellow officers, for some comfortable future? Leaving you stranded here, utterly alone in the world?"

I pressed my fingers into his skin. "Please, just listen! I can *save* you!"

"Kate, my charming goose, have a little faith in me." He laid his hands on mine, trapping them against him, and smiled in perfect confidence. "You've done the right thing, coming here to warn me. I'll lead the raid along a different route. I'll start at a different time, avoid this magical time-travel window of yours. I won't leave you here."

I searched his face: his head propped against the dull metal rails of the bed frame, his hair ruffled about his forehead. "You're just so sure of yourself, aren't you? Infallible Julian. So positive you're doing the right thing. That you can manage everything."

"In this case, I can, Kate. I know it." His smile grew tender, and he lifted his hand to brush against my cheek. "Leave you here by yourself? Wait for years to see you again? I'd never do that."

"Julian, you're like . . . like a puppy with a new toy. This is serious."

"I'm perfectly serious. You're the one vacillating. First you want me to stay, now you want me to go."

"I'm just trying to figure out what's best. What's even possible." I paused in frustration. "At least let me tell you, in case you change your mind . . ."

His finger pressed against my lips. "I won't. Trust me, Kate."

"Julian, you pigheaded . . ." I kissed his skin and breathed in his scent, still himself somehow, and yet laced with something unfamiliar— a different soap, probably. And his chest, nearly hairless now, perfectly smooth, but rounded with that lean well-used muscle I knew and loved: the shape of it so exactly right, curving so gracefully into his broad shoulders. "Trusting you is what got us into this mess in the first place."

He laughed at that. "Sweet Kate. You can't win this, you know. I know where my duty lies, and I shan't be swayed by your pleading."

I frowned up at him, prepared to argue, and then the nausea, never fully absent, waved through my belly like a warning.

How could I send Julian away, into the future, from his own child, his single legacy? And yet what would happen to me, to the baby inside me, if I didn't? Would it no longer exist? How could I do that, take even a *chance* of doing that? Lines of conjecture began to collide in my head, scattering, until I couldn't tell them apart. Nothing I could do would make everything all right again, would it? I'd already done too much, interfered too much. I'd acted in terror, in cowardice, unable to face a world without Julian, unwilling to examine the consequences of what I was doing; now, through the flotsam of broken logic, I could no longer see a certain path to redemption.

He went on cheerfully, not even noticing. "No, I'll stay here, instead. Fight for old Blighty. Worship my alluring new bride. A fine life."

I swallowed. "What about going on Staff? That's much safer, isn't it? And you could do it, with your connections."

"*Staff?* You're *joking*, Kate. Let another officer fight in my place?"

I returned his look steadily, and he rolled his eyes. "Oh, Kate, *really.*" He moved like a cat, flipping me over and poising above me, beautiful as an archangel in the frail candlelight. "Look here, my foolish darling," he said, between kisses, "did I ever tell you, in this future life of ours, that you worry altogether too much?"

"Julian, stop. Really. You have to listen . . . We have to figure this out, find the best possible option . . ."

"Enough talking. I shan't change my mind." He moved down my chin to my neck, his lips soft and inquisitive against my skin. "Darling girl. Haven't you done enough already? Disturbed the mysteries of the universe and whatnot? Let's hang up our time-traveling hats, shall we? *You* settle for life as my adored wife, as Mrs. Julian Ashford . . . how absolutely smashing that sounds, dearest"—he bent down greedily to my breasts— "and *I* shall do my very best . . . Good *Lord*, darling, you're so awfully delicious, I should like to feast on you forever . . ."

"Julian, be serious!"

"What's that? Yes, and *I* shall endeavor, as I said, not to get hit by something in the meantime. Everything will work out splendidly."

My fingers curled into his hair, feeling its texture with wonder, finer and silkier than the crisp waves I remembered with such clarity. I closed my eyes. "You silly boy. You'll get yourself killed, for no reason, and you *know* it. You're only trying to placate me, the way you always do."

"Oh, you're far too pessimistic." He raised his head at last and grinned at me. "I might simply be injured, you know. Sent home with a Blighty one."

"What's that?"

"A Blighty one. A lucky wound. Losing a finger, perhaps, or mucking up your knee. Gets you sent back home to Blighty, to England, without being too much nuisance."

"Losing a *finger*? That's *lucky*?"

"Luckier than being killed."

"All right. A Blighty one. Get a Blighty one." I smiled, despite myself. "Only no pretty nurses."

"I wouldn't even notice," he said virtuously.

"Ha. They'll notice *you*."

"A jealous disposition, have you?" He kissed the tip of my nose.

"It isn't easy, being married to the most devastatingly handsome man on the face of the earth."

He threw back his head and laughed. "Such sweet rot. What a delightful little wife you are."

"*Little wife?*" I groaned. "Good grief, Julian. You Neanderthal. I'm going to have to *train* you, aren't I? On top of everything else."

He settled his arms on either side of me, thick and warm, enclosing us. "You mustn't worry, Kate. All this—it can't be for nothing. No merciful God would allow it."

"I hope so," I said, capitulating, because I really had no choice; because I was held fast by the thick moral knots in which I'd tangled myself; because his beloved face was just inches away, golden and glowing and irresistible, making me believe in him against all reason. "Since I don't want this to be the last time we lie together like this."

"It won't, darling," he assured me, running his hand languorously—the damned precocious prodigy—down my neck and chest to circle my breast. "Thank you. I . . . I never dreamed such a thing was possible."

"Oh, come on. I've seen your reading material. *Fanny Hill,* for the love of God. You know a thing or two."

He blushed deeply. "I don't mean the mechanics of it, darling. I mean *this.* The closeness, the feel of you. The joy of it." He tucked his face into the curve of my throat. "Do you feel it too?"

"Julian," I whispered, "I can't even begin to describe it. I never could."

He kissed me, a long heavy kiss, and then raised his head and gazed at me, his thumbs smoothing the hair at my temples. "Would you really send me away from you, into the future, just to keep me off the battlefield? Knowing you'd never see me again?"

"Yes. Yes! I'd tell you exactly . . ."

"No." He laughed. "You splendid thing. I'm not going anywhere. I shall keep you and your love next to me, my dearest Kate, my wife, my *wife*; what a gorgeous, marvelous word; I'd like to shout it from the ramparts . . . Sweetheart, what's wrong?"

"Oh, good *grief,*" I muttered.

"What is it?"

I scooted out of bed and made it to the washstand just in time to heave into the bowl. He was behind me in an instant. "Kate, my God!"

"No, I'm fine," I said, shaking, burning. I felt the coarse wool blanket settle around my shoulders, Julian's arms guiding me to the edge of the bed.

"Sit. Let me get you some water." He poured out a glass from the open Perrier bottle on the nightstand. "Here."

I took a sip, just to please him, but my stomach recoiled. "Maybe in a moment."

"Darling, what's *wrong* with you? I'll go mad!"

"I'm fine, really! It's nothing, it's just a little illness, these old-fashioned germs . . ." I turned to him. "See? Better already."

He grasped my arms and looked into my face. "You're not telling me the truth, are you?"

I gathered the ends of the blanket and bent my head. My hair fell forward in long dark waves, shielding me from the penetration of his gaze; I could see his fingers surrounding my elbows, curving into the wool. "No," I said.

"But you won't tell me what's wrong, either, will you?"

"No."

He took me by the shoulders and dragged me back into the thin pillows at the head of the bed. The blanket slid downward, exposing my skin. "Will you let me guess?"

"No."

"Is it an illness?"

I paused miserably. "No."

"Something you ate?"

Another pause. "No."

"Oh, Kate," he said. We were silent a long moment, listening to the creaking of the house, the odd thump from some other room. The coals gasped from the fireplace, nearly exhausted; I felt the chill air on my bare arms and the damp glow of Julian's body against mine. His hand slipped to rest above my navel. "Tell me one thing: did I know?"

My voice cracked. "Yes."

"We'll be married," he said, "on my next leave. I'll get a pass as soon as

I can. Not that I don't consider you already my wife, but I want no question of it, no question at all, if something *should* happen to me."

I nodded. How could I argue anymore?

"My parents will look after you," he went on, settling the blankets around us with one agile arm. "You can't stay here in France; it's too dangerous."

"Your parents. I don't even know your parents. They'll think I'm . . . some American hussy, *trapping* you . . ."

"I'll tell them, in no uncertain terms, who you are. And they'll adore you. My father particularly. You're exactly the sort of woman he likes." He kissed my temple.

I shifted to face him, small and fragile in the hard circle of his arms. The candle flickered behind him, casting restless shadows along the side of his head. "How can you have so much faith in me?" I whispered. "I show up on your doorstep, claiming to be your wife, pregnant, for God's sake, and you don't even *question* me?"

"I did question you. Thoroughly." He kissed me again, to demonstrate his thoroughness.

"But a *baby*, Julian. I could be trying to pin it on you. You! The most eligible bachelor in England, probably." My voice strained along the walls of my throat. "Aren't you afraid this is all some elaborate trick?"

"Kate," he said, urging my head to his shoulder, "if you were going to trick me into owning a child that wasn't mine, don't you think you'd have come up with something a little more plausible than *time travel*?"

"But it hardly seems fair. Until an hour or so ago, you were a blushing virgin. You . . ."

I stopped. My words echoed back in my ears.

A virgin.

Yes, he'd confessed, that long-ago day in the library. *Once. During the war.*

"Julian," I said, against his shoulder, hearing my own voice from a great distance, "what was that inscription, on the ring?"

"Do you want to read it?"

"Yes. Very much." I couldn't move. He took my hand, eased the ring off my finger, reached for the sputtering candle behind him.

I bent over the band. The letters, in tiny elegant script, were difficult to read at first. I had to squint and turn the inside to the wavering light, and even then I could only just make out the words.

By this ring, you shall know her.

A chill crept upward from my fingers, spreading up my limbs and into my chest. He'd known. For God's sake, he'd *known.*

This had already happened; all of it. I'd already been here. Julian, my Julian, my modern Julian, had lain in this bed with me. Had known me long before that December morning at Sterling Bates, when he'd stared at me so searchingly, fumbled for words at the sight of me. Scraps began whirling through my head: things he'd said that seemed strange at the time. His paranoia about my safety. That odd sadness, after our wedding ceremony. The empty waiting closets. The way he'd fallen in love with me, the work of an instant.

"Kate," I heard him say, "are you all right? Can you read it?"

I looked up at his beautiful young face, gilded by the candlelight, so earnest and concerned and guileless. The walls of the tiny room seemed to press around us, wrapping our bodies in faded fleur-de-lis against the lonely future outside, the disastrous century ahead. "Yes," I said.

"You see? It's all right. I wanted this." He set the candle back on the nightstand and slid the ring back on my finger and kissed it. His lips burnt my numb skin. "Obviously I wanted to be sure I would recognize you when you came back for me. So it's quite all right. I'm supposed to stay behind with you. I'm supposed to marry you, darling." His voice was low and confident. He kissed my hand again, and then my lips. A coal popped in the fireplace, interrupting the even hiss.

"Of course. Of course you are." I reached my hand around the back of his neck, the skin unexpectedly tender beneath my fingers. Of course he would see it that way. It would never occur to Julian—past and future—

that he couldn't change his fate, that everything he did in the way of warnings and vigilance was simply a part of the pattern already woven for him.

But for me, it all became clear in an instant. Julian had heard my warning before, lived all this before, and it hadn't done any good. The very act of trying to avoid the time transport would make it inevitable, and anything I might try to say to him, even now, *would already be accounted for* in that ordained sequence.

All of it—our meeting, our beautiful summer, our marriage, his death— was already going to happen, and I couldn't do anything about it. The mistakes I'd made were irrevocable, had always been irrevocable.

I'd failed, before I'd even begun.

27.

We took off from Teterboro at twelve minutes past midnight, Dr. Hollander and I.

The NetJets folks hadn't given me too much trouble. Julian had already activated the account in my name, the very day after he'd bought it for me, with typical self-assurance. A JetCard represented the bottom rung of ownership, so I'd had to pay an enormous extra fee. Well, it sounded enormous to me, but then I'd remembered such an amount was now just a rounding error, and I'd whipped out that black credit card Julian had given me all those months ago. I didn't mind making *this* charge.

"You should sleep," said Hollander, staring at me with an expression I couldn't quite read. Troubled? Resigned?

"I can't. I can't sleep until I know he's safe."

He didn't reply. I leaned my head back against the butter-soft leather of the seat and looked at the ceiling, at the long row of dimmed cabin lights. Corporate luxury, the sleek sterile quiet kind, its familiar feel rushing back to me in the beiges and blues of my earlier life.

"It's bad, isn't it?" I said. "You think they're going to kill him."

"No," he said, too swiftly.

"Well, we should consider it, shouldn't we?" I said dispassionately, raising my head. If I'd learned one thing in the past few years, working at an investment bank, it was how to solve a complex problem. Break it down into manageable chunks. Analyze each one. Then put it all back together and deal with it. "Look, I see maybe three potential scenarios here. First, that Arthur and Geoff just want to talk to him. Maybe talk him out of the marriage. Show him Florence's grave, whatever. Now, that one's easy. He can talk his way out of that. He'll be on the next plane home."

"Very well. I agree, more or less. And the next?"

"The next is that they don't plan to kill him, but Arthur snaps. And then everything depends on Geoff. Which way he swings. So, possibility of a bad result."

"And the third?"

"That they do mean to kill him."

"I really don't think that's likely."

"But it's still possible, and it's the worst potential outcome. So that's what we need to focus on. I mean, what do we do? How do we stop them?"

"We can't," he said. "I haven't the faintest idea how to fight someone."

"We can bring the police with us."

"What, and have them ask questions?" His tone was scathing.

"Well, yeah!" I exploded. "I'd much rather have the whole thing exposed than Julian dead, for God's sake."

"It can't be exposed! It can't! You don't understand."

"No, I don't understand. I don't understand any of it. How they all came to be here. Why. It's ridiculous. It's freaky. And now it's possibly going to get Julian killed, if I can't find a way to stop it."

He shrugged helplessly and set his elbows on the table between us. "I wish I could think of a way," he said, his voice fragile, strained.

"What if he's dead already? What if he's already dead when we get there? What if . . . oh God!" I straightened in my seat, something dawning on me. "Professor, it's all my fault, don't you see? If he'd never met me, never married me . . ."

It all tumbled down around me. I'd just been dealing with the facts until now, the facts and the possible solutions, not wanting to think too deeply about causes. The what-ifs. The reasons why. Perhaps because I knew I was at the root of it. If Julian had never met me, we'd never have become lovers. Never conceived a baby. Never gotten married. Never sent poor Arthur Hamilton over the edge.

"It's all my fault," I said. "And if he dies, it's because of me." I put my head down into my hands. "I've got to stop it. I can't live with that. I'll just die."

"No, no," he said, in a gentle voice. "Poor dear. It's not your fault. You fell in love. You made him happy. It's not a crime. *You* can't help Hamilton's mental state."

I lifted my head and looked at him. "I'm pregnant. Did you know that? We're having a baby. It's why we got married so suddenly."

The color leached from his face. "I'd no idea! My God!" He stopped, blinking, turning the idea over in his mind. He spoke in an awed whisper. "Julian Ashford's child. My God. I never thought . . ."

"Well, it's true. We just found out for sure on Saturday." I looked out the window at the unremitting black of the nighttime sky passing swiftly by, merging with the dark sea below. "He insisted on marrying me right away. He already felt guilty, not having done it already."

"Yes, well," Hollander said, rousing himself, "he would."

"He'd make such a great father, if only he had the chance. Can't you see it?" I laughed weakly. "Julian Ashford, soccer dad. Coaching Little League or whatever. He'd be good at it. So we've got to figure this out, Professor. This baby has to know its father."

The pain pressed around my brain. How could I live without him? No more Julian in my life? It wasn't possible; it couldn't be done. It couldn't even be imagined.

Hollander regarded me steadily. "Tell me something, Kate. How far would you be willing to go, if Julian were in fact in mortal danger?"

"I'd give my life. I know that sounds corny or whatever, but it's true. Tell me right now to put a gun to my head and blow my brains out and Julian would somehow be safe, and I know for a fact I'd do it."

"Even though you'd destroy his child?"

I hesitated. "But at least he'd have a chance at other children, wouldn't he?"

"But he wouldn't want you to, would he?"

"He wouldn't want me to do it, period. Baby or no baby. But what are we talking about, exactly?" I asked, narrowing my eyes at him.

He sat in quietude, running his finger in broad circles along the lacquered surface of the table. "One of the great mysteries of this whole affair," he said, "is, of course, the question of how these men arrived here, in the present time, in the first place."

"Well, sure. I'd love to know how. Why. I mean, I still just struggle with believing in it to begin with."

He turned his palms up and stared at them. "I believe I can answer that."

I straightened in shock, not quite certain I'd heard him correctly. "You can? Seriously? Why didn't you *say* something? When did you figure it out?"

"I've known, in fact, for some time."

"For *real*?" I leaned toward him, curving my fingers around the edge of the table between us. "So what is it? Wormholes or something? Some sort of cosmic event?"

"No." He looked up at me, his eyes apologetic. "I'm afraid it's just me."

The cabin lights seemed to dim, briefly, then recover. I sat in bemused stillness, listening to the faint whine threading through the drone of the engines.

"You," I said at last.

"Yes. Just me."

"What do you mean, just you? How can you . . . *do* that? Why?" I shook my head, disoriented, feeling as if I were watching the scene from a distance.

"The *why* is easy enough. Because I'm a historian. Because I study the most fascinating subjects, these extraordinary men caught up in this most tragic of wars. As for the *how*"—he shrugged—"I can't say at all for certain. It just . . . happens."

"Just happens. Just *happens*. This isn't a joke, is it? I mean, how can one human being, like, *teleport* another to a different time? How would you even know you could? I mean, this is insane! *Insane!*"

He sat back in his seat. His gaze slipped past me, dark and pensive; his chest rose and fell in an agitated rhythm under the soft brown tweed of his jacket. "It was in 1996," he said at last. "I'd just published my third book, and was nearly finished with the Ashford biography. A few loose ends to tie up." He reached over to the catering tray and picked up a ham sandwich, fingering it. "I took rooms in Amiens, which was more or less the center of British activity on the Western Front. From there I explored the territory, often on foot, sometimes hiring a car to take me about. Have you ever visited the battlefields?"

"No. I did see some war graveyards while I was on the Eurostar to London. Just little squares, filled with headstones."

"The Calais-Paris line," Hollander said, "runs more or less along the old Western Front for much of its length. At the time of the war, you could walk the trenches all the way from Switzerland to the English Channel. It's quite well mapped. I used to spend hours with my charts and diagrams, walking along various lines of advance and retreat, seeing how the battle lay on the land, on the actual hills and slopes and valleys."

"Wow," I said, when he paused. "So you did that for Julian's movements?"

"I was fascinated by the last few days of his life. He sent an odd letter home to his mother the evening before he went on that fateful patrol. He refers first to Florence, not in so many words, of course. *I hope soon to introduce you to the daughter you've always wanted for me,* he wrote. And then, *I am certain now of God's own hand in my fate, and I place my faith in His mercy.* As though he knew he were about to die that night. Which was uncharacteristic of him, you understand; he always had this jaunty faith in his own ability to survive the war."

"Did you ask him about it?" I said, just as the airplane hit a bump, making my teeth clatter together.

"Yes, and he agreed with my assessment. But that, of course, came later. At this point, I'd no idea of ever meeting Julian Ashford in the flesh. My God! The absurdity of it. No, but I'd come to know him well. His letters, his poems. I knew his mind, I thought. And so one morning, I set out from Amiens to track his movements on the night in question, to perhaps discover the exact spot where he fell."

"Did you find it?" My lips felt dry, cracking; I ran my tongue along them, watched Hollander's deep-lined face.

"I suppose I did. For I stood there, meditating most intently for the longest time, conjuring up his face, trying to picture what that last instant had been like. And then I heard the strangest sound. A long, loud whine. Exactly like you'd suppose an incoming shell to sound. And then the most horrific bang. I cowered, closing my eyes, covering my head. And when I opened them, a man in khaki lay at my feet."

"Julian." I let out my breath. "So it was *you*. You . . . you *brought* him here. Into the present with you. My God. My God. You saved him."

"I was shocked, of course. I thought I was dreaming. I thought perhaps he was dead. But he was breathing, though unconscious, and of course I had to do something. I ran to the nearest farmhouse to call for an ambulance; I asked them for clothing. I told them it was a stranger, some damned fool who'd been doing a reenactment—they get them all the time, these fanatics—and I thought perhaps he'd had a seizure."

"Did you know it was Julian?"

"I realized it had to be. I knew his face, of course. And he had his tags around his neck, as well. I slipped those off before the ambulance arrived. Once they'd taken him away, I realized the magnitude of what had just happened. I went back to Amiens, made inquiries. There's a place in Paris where you can get handsome forgeries made. I made up a pack for him, did the best I could."

"I'm amazed you had the presence of mind."

"I was in shock. Only later did I have the chance to think it all through. During the crisis, one simply acts."

"I know." I rose unsteadily from my seat and went to the catering tray to find a drink. Diet Coke. I needed something fizzy, something to cut through the fog in my brain. Screw the caffeine for now.

"And then, of course, he came to see me in Boston, a year or so later.

Having no idea, of course, that it was I who saved him. I'd stayed away until then, of course, though I tried to find out what he was doing. But if I'd approached him, I'd have to tell him I was the one who'd brought him over. And then he might ask . . ."

"Might ask what?"

"To be sent back."

"You could do that?"

"I believe so." He bit his lip. "I know so."

"And let me guess. You saw how lonely he was, and brought back Geoff to keep him company. And then Arthur Hamilton."

"Hamilton was quite difficult. I didn't have the right location for him; it took years of trying. I brought a few others, men I'd admired in the pages of history, who'd been reported missing but their bodies never found. There were a great, great many of those, you know, and I thought, well, why not save them, if I could? A direct hit from a shell doesn't leave much evidence behind."

"But how?" I burst out. "How does it work? You just sit there thinking about it, and it happens?"

He shrugged. "I don't know. No, not exactly like that. Certain elements have to be in place, it seems. I have to be standing in precisely the spot where that person existed at the point of crisis, for example. That's without question."

"Point of crisis?"

"The point at which that person disappears from the historical record," he said impatiently. "Secondly, I must have, upon my person, some personal artifact. In Julian's case, quite without premeditation, I had his last letter home. The family had loaned it to me, in the course of my research. In the case of the others, I had gone out seeking such items, thinking that might be part of the key."

"And what else? It can't just be that."

"Well, I suspect there might be some question of emotional connection. The person must have an emotional connection to the modern period."

"But what connection could Julian possibly have to 1996?"

"Perhaps because you were alive."

"But he didn't even know me!"

"He *would* know you. If time is really as flexible as this, as circular, then it wouldn't perhaps matter whether he'd met you or not."

I sat back, absorbing this. "Have you discussed this with anyone? A physics professor? Because you can't just go around ripping holes through the freaking space-time continuum, all by yourself. Like you've got some voodoo power, like the Force or whatever."

He went quiet for a long moment. "I can't explain it. I don't know what it is. Why I should have it; how I acquired it. Whether I'm the only one. But there it is."

There it is. So simple, so impossibly intricate: a stone thrown into a shoreless pond, the ripples radiating out into infinity. Infinite consequences; infinite possibilities. "Let me ask you something," I said. "If I wanted to go back to 1916, and prevent Julian from ever being on that patrol, he might stay where he was? *When* he was, I mean?"

"I don't know. That's an interesting question."

"What do you mean?"

"Why, whether you can change the history of it. We know, don't we, he *did* come forward to our time. So is it possible for you to go back and change that? It's a great risk, to you and him."

"But if he dies now," I said, "wouldn't it be a chance worth taking?"

"I don't know. I don't know. What are the ethics? *Are* there ethics? I don't know. The mere flutter of a hummingbird's wings . . ."

"Would you do it for me, though? If we land in Manchester, and find out they've killed him, would you do it? Would you send me back?"

He took a bite of his sandwich and chewed patiently. "What would you do there?"

"I'd find him. Try to change his plans."

"You realize," he said, swallowing, "that Julian disappeared near the end of March 1916, and that shortly more than three months later his company went over the top on the first day of the Somme. The captain that day, Julian's replacement, was killed."

"But he'd have a chance, wouldn't he? I could tell him, warn him. I could guide him through the rest of the war."

"A chance. A merest chance," he said. "And then, only if it worked. Only if you could, in fact, change history. Or whether some cosmic force would prevent you."

"It's worth it," I said recklessly. "Don't you see, I can't do *nothing*. I can't just let him die. You saved him once; surely I can do the same. I have to, after all. It's my fault he's in danger in the first place."

Hollander sighed and stared out the window. In the last few minutes, a pale blue glow had spread out over the horizon, as the airplane hurtled toward the approaching dawn. I slipped my wristwatch over my fingers and spun the hands around five times. "It's nine o'clock, British time," I said. "They'll be landing soon. If not already."

He turned to me. "Very well. If it all goes badly, if they've . . ." His throat worked; he shook his head. "Then I'll do it. But you must be ready. You'll appear at Southfield in 1916; you'll have to find clothes, food, shelter. Make your way to France. You'll need money."

I looked at my wrists. "No problem," I said, taking off the triple gold bangle around my wrist, one of the few of Julian's jewelry gifts I regularly wore. "And my earrings. They must add up to several ounces, at least. I can change it for local currency when I'm there. Gold's always gold."

"What about your necklace?" Hollander nodded at my throat.

"My necklace?" I put my hand to my collar and looked down. "Oh. When did that get there? He must have . . . when I went upstairs to freshen up for dinner . . ."

In fact, I'd gone upstairs to vomit. Julian stood there in the bedroom when I came out, looking concerned. "I'm okay," I'd said. "Just the usual."

He'd put his arms around me and held me for a minute or two, not saying anything. "I hope you're not standing there feeling guilty," I'd whispered into his chest. "I'm the luckiest woman in the world, carrying our baby."

"Kate. You beggar me sometimes, do you know that?" He'd turned me around in his arms and slipped something around my neck, clasping it with nimble fingers before I could object. "A wedding gift. You're not allowed to say no." Then he'd turned me back around and started kissing me, not with the usual tantalizing deliberation, but as if his life depended on it.

So until this exact second, I'd forgotten it was even there.

I fingered it now, large round pearls the size of gobstoppers, black alternating with white. "I can't sell these. They were his wedding present."

"I'd take them with you, though," Hollander said practically, "just in case. Put them in your pocket."

I fumbled with the clasp; my fingers were trembling too violently, and in the end I had to ask the professor for help.

I took them over to the closet, where I'd hung my raincoat, in case of typical English weather, and slipped the pearls into the inside pocket.

Hollander cleared his throat. "As I said, you'll have to make your way to France. I'd suggest the Folkestone crossing; the passage from Dover may be quicker, but possibly more dangerous. U-boats, you see. If we were in my office, with all my research notes, I could tell you which ships to avoid."

I nodded and sat back down in my seat.

"I *can* tell you exactly where to find him in France," the professor went on. "He spent the previous few days before his patrol on a seventy-two-hour pass to Amiens, in order to meet with some of the divisional heads about new tactics. Arthur helped him to arrange it all. He'd been after them with memoranda for months, you see, trying to change . . ." He shook his head. "I don't suppose that matters. In any case, early the first morning, he attended matins at Amiens cathedral. That's well established, with an exact timeframe. You could wait for him outside." A frown passed across his face.

"Matins? What's that?"

He roused himself. "The early morning service in the Catholic liturgy."

"Julian's *Catholic*?"

"He converted in the weeks before he disappeared. You didn't know that?"

"No. I didn't." Another unopened box. I stared down at my Diet Coke, counting the bubbles.

Hollander fell silent. I lifted my head and watched him, watched his fading blue eyes stare out of his round heavy-jowled face, all of it weighed down as though the struggle against gravity were becoming too much to bear. Why him? *How* him? How could this ordinary mortal have that kind of extraordinary power?

"Professor," I said at last, leaning forward and taking his hand, where it lay limp on the table, "we have about two hours left before we land. You're going to need to tell me everything you know. Just in case."

SOUTHFIELD LAY SIXTY MILES to the southwest of Manchester, and as each precious yard spun out from the tires of our rental car, it became harder and harder to force down the panic. Julian's plane would have landed two hours earlier, I knew. Plenty of time for Geoff or Arthur to drag him to Florence Hamilton's grave; plenty of time for all kinds of scenarios, each one more unimaginable than the last.

I forced my brain to concentrate on other things, immediate things, like remembering to stay on the left-hand side of the road. How to go around a roundabout without getting killed. How to convert kilometers per hour into miles.

Not that *that* mattered much. I pushed the little tin-box Fiat to its limit, and we still weren't going much faster than the tractors harvesting the fields on either side of us.

"Your husband's a billionaire," grumbled Hollander, "and you couldn't rent a car faster than this one?"

"It was the only one they had left. We landed late, remember? All the morning flights had taken the good ones. Besides," I added, throwing the gearshift back into third in an attempt to bring more power to the failing wheels, "you're the freaking tree-hugging Marxist around here. I'm all for Maseratis."

I was trying to joke, but in reality I was terrified: each lost second put Julian closer to his fate. Farther, possibly, away from me. I didn't want to have to go back to 1916 to save him. I wanted to be in time, to save him now, to stay with him here.

Unlike many of the grand English country estates, Southfield hadn't been transferred to the National Trust at some point during the long mid-century of 90 percent tax burdens. The Ashford family still spent much of the year there, not quite in the same style as Julian's day, with its foxhunts and house parties and eleven full-time gardeners, but still resident. Not open to the public. Which presented a problem, because it meant there were no helpful signposts along the roadways to tell us where to go.

At least I had Hollander, who'd visited the place several times while researching his book. It had been an admiring biography from the beginning, and so the family had taken him up with enthusiasm, sharing papers and showing him around the estate. "The cemetery is a bit off the beaten path," he told me. "You have to know where it is."

"We can do that? Just walk onto the estate and wander over to the cemetery?"

"Walking rights are fiercely defended around here; besides, who would know?" Hollander shrugged. "The house is a good mile or so away, and at the moment it's only the dowager in residence. Her son likes to spend his time in London, shagging models, as they say." His tone didn't convey any particular disapproval.

"And the son is what? Julian's cousin?"

"Distant. Here's the turnoff." He pointed to a small drive on the left.

"Seriously?" I swung the ungainly Fiat onto the track.

"It's not the main drive, just one of the estate access roads."

408 / BEATRIZ WILLIAMS

"Jeez," I muttered, concentrating on not getting the car stuck in one of the enormous potholes cratering the surface of the drive. "I guess you know it pretty well."

"My dear girl," he said, "I've spent most of my life researching your husband and his contemporaries."

I shook my head in wonder. It looked like the area had seen a fair amount of rain recently: mud slipped under the Fiat's tires, slowing us down, and the newly stubbled fields on either side of us lay tired and wet and brown. "These are all part of the home farm," Hollander said absently, "the land the estate farms for itself, as opposed to letting it out to tenants. Coming up at the end of the drive is the start of the parkland."

I peered ahead and saw a stand of trees, the leaves still lush and green, huddled around a hillside. A few drops of rain splashed down on the windshield; I pressed the wiper button once, whisking them away. "It had better not storm," I said.

We bumped along as fast as I dared in the mud and potholes, with our ridiculously underpowered car. I should have stood my ground at the car rental place, I realized. I wasn't used to this billionaire thing yet; I could have demanded better. I could have made some irate phone calls, flashed my obsidian credit card, demanded a Range Rover. Bought a freaking Range Rover, for God's sake. What was I thinking? Julian's life was at stake.

"How do we know they came this way?" I demanded. "Shouldn't there be tire tracks?"

"They might have taken another access road. Come up the other side of the estate." He was peering ahead too, looking for some sign of human activity.

I swiped the windshield again. A few sheep crouched in the field to my right, stirring anxiously. Was it going to storm? "How much longer? I can't see anything, just the trees."

"I don't know. It's been years," he snapped. "A few hundred yards, maybe. Then it's a good half-mile walk through the park."

"And no one's going to see us?"

"I don't know! I don't know the conditions anymore! Maybe a game-keeper, who knows?"

I shut my mouth and kept driving, until we came to the end of the track and parked the car next to the fence and jumped out. I checked my watch. Nearly two o'clock. "Where do we go? Hurry!" I urged him, slipping in the thin layer of mud. The rain began to patter lightly on my coat, turning more earnest. I looked up at the shifting iron-gray sky, mottled with threatening clouds, and turned up my collar. Just all I freaking needed: British weather.

I spied a stile along one side of the fence and slipped down the muddy track toward it, hearing Hollander grunt along behind me. "Come on," I said, holding out my hand to help him cross. His tall awkward body lurched over the rungs, narrowly avoiding disaster, just as I felt a gust of wind spray my cheek with stinging rain. "I think we're going to get nailed," I said. "We've got to hurry."

A footpath wandered out from the stile, and we scrambled along it, following the slope of the hill toward the trees. "The edge of the lake is just on the other side," Hollander said, breathing with effort, "and the cemetery is laid out near the shore, between the ledge and the water. You can't see it right away, because of the overhang."

"Are you okay?" I asked, trying not to panic; he'd winded himself, just walking up the hill at three miles an hour. My own muscles were ready to burst with energy and adrenaline. All that running with Julian, all that training. I wanted to sprint, to fly.

"Fine, fine. Go on ahead. I'll be right there," he said.

"I can't leave you . . ."

"I'll be fine!" he puffed. "Just find him!" He gestured impatiently, brushing me away.

"Okay. I'll run ahead and see what's up. I'll yell if I see anything."

I didn't know what to expect. It seemed like a lonely chance they'd come this way. We'd just speculated, Hollander and I, based on the fact that Julian's plane had landed in Manchester.

And what the hell would we do if we saw them? *Trust me,* Julian had said. *Go home. Wait for me.* He'd be furious with me now. If he were still alive.

I sprang forward into a jog, sliding over the rocks and muddy bits in the footpath, past shivering trees flinging off droplets into my hair. My raincoat flapped wildly in the strengthening draft, and I slipped my hand into my pocket to secure the pearls inside.

I crested the hill and dropped down to a walk, scanning the ground below me. The slope dropped away to a ledge, along which the footpath stretched until it dipped down through a shallower portion to the grassy lakeshore at the bottom.

Where was the cemetery? I wondered, confused. I could only see the lake, rimmed by trees and meadow grass, gray and fitful under the uncertain skies. I tripped down the footpath at a jog, drawing close to the ledge, and abruptly it came into view, perhaps a quarter-mile to my right, hunched up against the shelter of the ledge: a few short rows of plain marble tombstones, surrounded by a waist-high white fence.

It was empty. The air whooshed out of me. Relief not to see Julian's dead body in a heap at the bottom of some grave marker; alarm now, that we'd been wrong, that they hadn't come this way after all. Now what did we do?

I fingered the BlackBerry in my coat pocket. I'd sent several e-mails to Julian, even a phone call, but nothing had come back. The phone hadn't even rung, just gone straight to voice mail. Probably he'd left it in the restaurant, or Arthur had taken it. I drew mine out anyway and tapped in another message.

Where are you? Getting desperate. My fingers hovered for an instant, and then I added, *I love you.* Send. I put the phone back in my pocket and looked again toward the cemetery.

Three figures now moved warily among the tombstones.

The breath seized up in my chest. I couldn't see their faces, couldn't even discern hair color in the murky cluttered air, but I knew who they were. I could hear their voices, raised in argument, carried directly to my ears by the wind off the lake.

I wanted to run, to fly to them, but my muscles had frozen into horrified immobility. What were they doing? What were they saying? One of them was backing up, hands raised, palms outward. Was that a flash of gold in his hair? I couldn't tell. "Julian!" I croaked out, but the wind, blowing in my face, swallowed my words whole.

Then another one raised his arm, pointing it, something dark and gleaming in his hand. Julian—was it Julian?—started slowly toward him, hands still forward, coaxing. "No!" I heard myself scream.

They couldn't hear me, of course, not with that wind in my face, but then the man with the gun glanced in my direction. He stilled for an instant, and then he turned and ran into the trees.

"Wait!" I yelled, but the other two were already after him, running out of sight toward the lake, hidden by the branches and leaves.

I scrambled down the ledge, not bothering to take the footpath down the easier way. Pebbles skittered out from under my sneakers, slick with rain. I jumped down the last few rocks, landing heavily on my feet, and started running toward the cemetery.

Julian's ancestors had chosen this spot well. It was high enough to overlook the lake, and sheltered from the aging effects of the weather by the ledge behind it and the surrounding trees. I hardly felt the rising storm at all now. My feet beat against the turf, the damp sparse shaded grass, until I reached the burial plot and spun around.

Nobody. Just a dingy white fence, looking as though it could use a coat of paint, and the tombstones laid out in a grid, with gravel tracks that badly needed raking; each grave looked identical to the others, words chiseled at the top in plain Roman lettering, names and dates and Latin tags that meant nothing to me.

I looked toward the trees, trying to discern which direction they'd run, and at that second an unmistakable sound cracked along the wind.

"No!" I screamed, and then I heard another one.

The sensation of cold trickled down my spine, as though someone were pouring ice water onto the back of my neck. Stay calm, I thought. I felt my brain begin to float upward, detaching, trying to see the situation objectively. Just another problem to solve.

"Kate?"

I started and looked around. "Who's there?"

"Up here. Did you find anything?" It was Hollander, of course, standing at the top of the ledge and looking down anxiously.

"No one's here," I heard myself say, "but I think I just heard gunshots from the woods. I'm heading over to check it out." Why didn't I sound panicked?

"Good God. Wait. I'll be right down." ·

He turned to the right, to follow the path, and I scanned the area around me, the grassy lakeshore with its stands of birch and chestnut and English oak, all rustling erratically in the rain-dashed wind, smelling of cool damp earth. Where had they gone?

Something moved in the trees. I gasped reflexively and looked hard, straining my eyeballs. Was it just the storm? I walked closer, each step deliberate, my heart starting up a steady quick rhythm against my ribs.

There it was again! A flash of muted color, just for an instant, at the base of a large mature chestnut. "Who's there?" I demanded.

No answer.

"It's Kate," I called out. "Where's Julian?"

A figure stepped away from the tree, a slight brown-haired figure, wearing a tweed jacket over chinos, collar turned up protectively against his neck. Arthur Hamilton.

"Kate?" I heard Hollander call from behind me.

"Arthur." I stepped nearer. "Arthur, it's me. Kate. How are you? Can you tell me where Julian is?"

He shrugged. His hands were shoved in his pockets, moving around restlessly.

"Arthur, you can tell me. I won't be angry. You've had a difficult time."

"Bad show," he muttered. "Very bad show."

"Yeah, I'm sure," I said, ignoring the frantic ringing in my ears, the rising panic. "Very bad. So where's Julian, huh? Where's Geoff?"

I was only fifteen feet away now. I could see the expression on his face: dazed, wondering, a little cross maybe. He had a small cut below one eye, beginning to swell, and a dark splash of a stain marring the weave of his jacket, just below the upturned collar.

"Come on, Arthur," I said. "You can tell me. Let's sit down."

He shook his head. "The boathouse. All dead," he told me. "Bad show."

"No," I said, "they're not all dead. You didn't kill them, did you?"

"Geoff. I couldn't manage it. Never could. Geoff did it."

"Geoff did what?" I begged. "He couldn't shoot Julian. He didn't. Tell me he didn't."

"So it's good night, sweet prince," Arthur said, staring at the ground. "At last. Flights of angels . . . all that . . . rubbish."

"Oh no," I said. "Oh no."

"I loved him," Arthur said. He looked up at me. "The rest is silence," he added, and pulled a gun out of his pocket.

"Oh no," I repeated.

He raised it to his mouth and fired.

I CRUSHED MY HANDS over my head and whipped around and ran back toward the cemetery, toward the ledge, running into Hollander. "They did it! They killed him! Geoff shot him! Shot Julian!"

"Oh God," he cried, shutting his eyes. "Oh God!"

"He just shot himself! Right there behind me! His *brains . . .*"

"Who?"

"Arthur Hamilton! So do it, Professor. Do it *now*! Send me back! Please, I can't stand it!"

"Oh God!" he cried again.

I grabbed his shoulders. "Do it now! Before I pick up that gun and shoot *myself*!"

His eyes snapped open and he stared at me.

"Do it!" I screamed. I fell to my knees at his feet and bent my head.

I felt his hands on my shoulders, gripping me, and the wind and rain lashed at me, hard, in one long unbroken gust. "*Do it!*" I screamed again, and the air emptied out of my ears, and I was tumbling, tumbling endlessly through a frozen void, and then I woke up to the steady beat of a March rain streaming on my face.

Amiens

I never slept that night. How could I waste a single minute of my final night with Julian? I couldn't have slept, even if I'd wanted to. Every nerve vibrated, as though a magnetic current looped continuously through my body.

I hadn't told him. What would have been the use? He wasn't going to change his plans, decline his duty as an officer, renounce his every principle. Better to let him go on thinking he could trick fate, foil divine will; that by shifting the time of his raid or by some other petty adjustment, he could avoid Hollander's reach. That he could stay in this century, return to me, marry me, and be a father to our child. A beautiful dream; why not let him hold on to it until the end?

I could scarcely move in that narrow bed. I lay pressed against his drowsy flesh, cheek to toe, and watched him sleep, gazing at his dear familiar face in the faint light from the moon outside the thinly curtained window. This man-child version of Julian: part soldier, part schoolboy, and yet with everything I loved about him already inside.

Had I ever come to terms with his beauty? Not really; it had only become entwined, in my mind, with the beauty of himself, with his quintessence. The Julian I loved. And I realized I couldn't let him stay here, to be killed at the Somme or at Passchendaele or some meaningless night raid, like the one he was about to undertake. He had twelve certain years of life ahead, including one perfect summer; he'd done so much good with them. All those Southfield investors, all those endowments and retirements assured. Sterling Bates saved from bankruptcy, livelihoods made safe by the sheer force of his personality and his ingenuity and his example. A baby he'd conceived with me, who would live on after him, or rather before him; a baby I'd love with all the strength in my body, a baby I'd raise to worship the memory of its golden father.

Any and all of those things far outweighed my own selfish need for a little more time with him, stolen from fate.

At one point, well after midnight, he stirred, some part of his unconscious mind fumbling with the unfamiliarity of another body in the bed with him. He opened his eyes sleepily, a bit confused, terribly boyish, and looked across at my face on the pillow. "Kate," he breathed.

I reached out and placed my hand on his cheek, and I kissed him. I kissed him with every bit of that tenderness, that passion I felt for him, and then I made love to him. I had the advantage; I knew exactly what he loved, what made him cry out with pleasure. All those endless beautiful hours of practice, and I used them well. I brought him shuddering to completion, almost outside himself with the strength of his release, and then I held him to my breast, soaking him into my skin, whispering to him how eternally I desired him, adored him, loved him.

So he wouldn't need to hear it from me later. He'd know.

When dawn broke, he awoke again, and this time he took me in his arms and possessed me with an exuberant male confidence—a man of the world already!—that made me smile, before I went mindless with anguished bliss, gripping the robust curve of his shoulders and marveling at him.

No, I didn't waste a moment. Not even an instant.

He rose reluctantly, pressing kisses all over my body, in all those newly discovered places, murmuring words of wonder and love and gratitude. He washed and dressed in the numbing air; I helped him with the buttons, straightened his tie. Then I made myself ready while he went back to his own room to shave and gather his things. It didn't take long, and when I was dressed I sat down and wrote a few lines on a piece of paper, though I knew it would make no difference, though I had no right even to try.

When I finished, I slipped down the hall to his room and rapped on the worn wooden door. It opened at once.

"Darling." He tucked me into his arms, his cheek damp and sleek against my temple. "My train leaves in half an hour. Will you come to the station with me?"

"Of course," I said. I pressed my nose into his neck and inhaled deeply.

"I'll remember everything. I'll change the time of the raid, and I'll be careful. No wild risks. I'll return to you, safe and whole. I won't fail you, I promise."

"Of course you won't, my love. Of course you won't."

He sat us both down on the bed in a creak of old springs, turning me around so my back rested against his chest. "You must go back to England, where it's safer. I'll be due for a week's leave in another month or two. We'll be married then—legally, I mean; you're already my wife—and you can live at Southfield with my parents. Our child will be born there. I'll write straightaway and start preparing them. Darling, don't be worried," he said, kissing my hair. "You look so frightfully glum. You mustn't. Everything will work out perfectly. I've someone to live for now. Two of you." He let one hand slip downward.

I covered his hand with mine. "I'm the luckiest woman in the world. To have found you. Your loving, open heart. You hardly know me, and you've taken me in, accepted every word I've told you. Given me this perfect night, when I thought I'd never hold you again."

He chuckled against me. "Darling, the honor was entirely mine." His arm twisted; he checked his watch and sighed. "It's time."

He took my hand and slung his pack over the other shoulder, and then he led me out the door and down the stairs and into the deserted street. The last of the rain had blown away in the night, and a clean new sun backlit the attic rooftops in palest gold. A few streets away, the cathedral bells tolled dolefully through the air, calling the faithful to matins, the same service at which I'd found Julian two days ago. His hand squeezed mine; he was thinking the same thing.

"Only two days," he said, "and I feel reborn."

"You're insane," I laughed. "You trusting fool. Of course I'm a complete imposter, trying to land you as my husband, trying to pass off this baby as yours. I mean, really. A *time traveler*. You'll believe anything, won't you?"

"As long as it comes from your lips," he said, laughing too.

We made it to the station with a few minutes to spare. I spotted Geoff Warwick down at the other end of the platform, alone; he gazed at me with angry contempt and looked away. "That man," I said, "just doesn't like me."

"Don't mind him. He'll come around."

"No, he won't."

"Now," he said, firm and officerlike, turning to face me, the brim of his cap casting a diagonal shadow across his face. "First of all, no sadness. We'll be together soon. I'll write as often as I can. I'll send something for you to live on as well, until everything's all legal and proper and so on. What are your immediate plans?"

"I suppose I'll stay in Amiens a day or two, to make sure things went as planned. Could you send me a postcard or something, and let me know? Because I'll worry."

"Of course. I'll send one first thing. You'll stay on at rue des Augustins?"

"Yes. And then I suppose I'll go back to England. As you suggested."

"Right-ho. Now, darling," he said, drawing an envelope out of his note-book, "I must insist on your taking this, to help with your passage and doctors and whatnot. I haven't anything larger at the moment, but I'll write to my bankers . . ."

"No! Please don't. I've got all the money I need right now; you practically draped me with jewelry that last day. Look at this." I eased the pearls halfway out of their pocket. The morning light caught the curves with a low gleam. "Your wedding gift."

"Good God!"

"Yes, you're very generous. Far too good to me."

"Oh, you married me for my money, did you?"

"Of course. What else?"

He pressed the envelope into my hands. "Take it anyway, darling. Please. For my own peace of mind, if nothing else."

"Julian, I can't. Last night . . ."

His face went pink. "Was my wedding night, as far as I'm concerned. And husbands and wives don't keep accounts with one another."

A clean brisk *snap* inside me, nearly painless.

"Take it." He closed my hands around the envelope. "Please."

"All right," I said reluctantly, "but only if you'll take this." I drew the folded paper out of my pocket.

"What is it?"

"Just in case. In case it happens, after all."

He shook his head. "It won't, Kate. I shan't leave you."

"Please? Just humor me?"

A steam whistle sounded, long and lonely, beckoning.

"There's me," he said.

"Please." I reached forward to slip the note into his pocket.

"Darling." He smiled. "Very well, then. Write to me whenever you can. Let me know how you're feeling, what you're doing. I'll be thinking of you, every moment. I shall fight like mad for the earliest possible leave."

I nodded. "I'll write. Every day." I could hear the engine now, loud and immense, pulling into the station. Its great black mass slid alongside us, hissing steam, filling our noses with the damp dirty smell of coal smoke.

"And your direction, of course, so I can write back. Love letters, perhaps some rubbishy poetry if you're exceptionally unlucky."

I nodded, not quite able to speak.

He placed his hand under my chin, his other arm around my waist. "One more," he said, and bent his head down to mine.

"I love you, Julian Ashford. Just remember that, okay? It's important."

He pressed his forehead against mine. "And I love you, Kate Ashford."

"No, you don't. Not yet."

The train jerked to a stop with one last heave of steam, rousing the platform into motion: men getting on, men getting off, a swarm of uniforms through the drifting clouds. A few nurses here and there, blue skirts and white aprons and short capes.

"You're wrong," he said. "I do love you."

"No, you don't. But you will."

He grinned. "Well, that we can agree on. Good-bye, darling. Be safe. You'll hear from me soon."

"Good-bye, my love. My own dear love."

He kissed my hand and let it go.

"God bless you," I whispered. He nodded, and stared at me hard, and then he wheeled around and pushed through the crowd to the train, without looking back. I searched the windows desperately as the cars began to pull away, but in the tangle of identical khaki arms and capped heads, he had become invisible.

THE CRAMPING STARTED IN THE EVENING, and by morning I had lost the baby.

Julian's postcard never arrived.

28.

A week later, I stood at the quayside in Le Havre, surrounded by more khaki soldiers and more blue-and-white nurses and the salty-wet smell of a busy harbor. The whole world seemed to be in one uniform or another.

I wasn't quite sure how I'd managed to get there; the past few days had passed in a nightmare blur. Somehow I had existed, had put food into my mouth, had dressed and breathed and even slept a few meager hours.

Had found my note to Julian, tucked back inside the pocket of my jacket by his confident fingers, probably while he was distracting me with that last kiss.

Had gone to the steamship offices, a full four days after Julian left— just to be sure, just to be absolutely positive he was gone—and booked a second-class berth to New York City, knowing I couldn't stay in France, knowing I couldn't go to Julian's family, knowing that America was my home, whatever century it was.

Had dropped off a letter at the post office, which I'd written during the journey to Le Havre, laboring over each word, not certain I should write it at all:

Please don't grieve for Julian. He has been delivered from this horror to a different time and place, alive and well, where he has grown into every early promise, as fine and honorable a man as ever walked this earth; where his only sadness is the knowledge of your own sorrow; where, above all, he is loved, as no man ever was, by

Kate Ashford

I'd addressed the envelope to Viscountess Chesterton, Southfield, England.

I'd spent a day wondering, quite objectively, whether I should just kill myself. I mean, here I was, stranded in the middle of the First World War, with nothing but Spanish flu, hyperinflation, and Hitler to look forward to. What was the point in existing, if Julian was gone, if our baby was gone? If everything and everyone I knew and loved didn't even exist yet? Oh, there was a chance that Hollander might, out of kindness, try to bring me back, but Julian didn't exist in that world either. I'd be his widow, the tragic Mrs. Laurence, surrounded by physical reminders of him and dying inch by inch. Turning into some reclusive cat lady in my Manhattan townhouse.

Anything but that.

But Julian would have been furious if I'd killed myself. That was just the kind of self-indulgent Hamilton-like behavior he scorned most, exactly the opposite of what he'd loved about me. *He* hadn't thrown himself in the river. He'd gotten on with life. Of course, he knew he'd meet me eventually, but the prospect would have seemed dim and distant in those early years.

So I'd go on existing. I'd try to find a way to be useful, to turn my knowledge into good. Maybe I could spend the twenties on Wall Street, amassing a fortune, and then use it in some sort of relief work during the Depression and the next war. Something to keep my brain busy. Something to live for. Something to make amends for having abandoned Julian's broken body on a fool's errand, for leaving only Hollander and Andrew Paulson to lay him to rest, to keep his vigil.

Right now everything was numb, and for that I was grateful. It was as though I'd grown a thick mucous membrane around myself, so the pain only stung on the surface, not quite penetrating all the layers. *No. More. Julian.* Not even our baby. The thought still bounced off. Not denial, exactly; my brain recognized what had happened. The information just hadn't sunk down to the silent void at my center.

Even now, I didn't really feel of this world. I simply sat, watching the roiling dockyard scene from the peace of a wooden bench, waiting for eleven o'clock to toll out from the clock tower, signaling it was time to board the Cunard *Columbia* and get myself back home to America. I'd flown over the Atlantic by private jet, and now I was returning aboard a small old liner belonging to the previous century, only brought out of mothballs because of the exigencies of wartime. Fitting. But she was a pretty ship, at least. Painted gray for camouflage, but with a hint of winsomeness about her. She'd held the record for fastest crossing in her day, the man in the Cunard office had said proudly. For about a week, anyway, until some German liner took back the honor. I could get my *Titanic* on, do the Kate Winslet thing in the bow some evening after dinner. Try to get myself to feel something other than this alarming numbness.

"Hello, miss?"

The voice cracked against my ears, making me jump.

"Hello, miss? English miss?" It was a little boy, skinny and barefoot, maybe eight years old, looking up at me with a hungry hopeful expression. Was it so terribly obvious I wasn't French? "I take your suitcase, yes? Only ten centimes, miss."

"*Oui, merci.* I'm traveling on the *Columbia.* Do you know it?"

"*Oui,* of course, miss. You follow me, yes?"

The clock tower began sounding out eleven o'clock, and I stood up and handed my tiny suitcase to the boy. I had only a pair of pajamas and a change of clothes, and the pretty dress I'd bought for my last evening with Julian, together with a few odd toiletries I'd found to fill the needs once met by Neutrogena. Not much to build a new life.

The boy slipped his hand into mine and began leading me toward the ship, a couple of hundred yards away. A troop ship had just arrived and disembarked its passengers, and they marched now in loose formation down the pier, singing robust cheerful songs, an endless khaki stream of them, bristling with packs and rifles and helmets. I'd been so focused on Julian, on preserving him somehow, I hadn't had time to appreciate that either: the fact that I was in 1916, watching history unfold.

All these men, these nurses, these townspeople—they were fighting a war. Maybe I should stay, I thought suddenly. Maybe I should join the Red Cross, or some other volunteer organization. Drive ambulances, like Hemingway, or nurse. I could help.

I stopped about fifty yards from the second-class gangplank, where a crowd was beginning to gather in order to board. Women, mostly, some with children. One beautiful boy with flaxen curls, scampering just out of his mother's reach, exactly as I'd always pictured Julian at that age. A few men in civilian clothes, their plain suits almost exotic in the militarized landscape; the only males I'd seen out of uniform for the past two weeks were those conspicuously incapable of war service. So these must be Americans, I realized, returning to New York. The United States wouldn't enter the war for another year.

The little boy turned to me. "Why do we stop, miss?"

"Let me think a moment." I reached up to press my temple. Maybe I *should* stay. Maybe I could be more useful here, at the moment. Certainly busier. I knew a little French; I could learn more.

The little boy tugged at my arm. "Come, miss. They go in the ship. You miss the ship."

"No. Wait. *Attendez, s'il vous plaît.*" I stood there, watching the shifting crowd, the laughing, talking throng of passengers a hundred feet away, inching up the gangway to the ship. America or France? New York or Paris? I couldn't decide. I felt as though I were being ripped apart. A ship's horn sounded in my ears, going on and on, and the little boy stared up at me in wonder, and then the air emptied out of my ears, and I was tumbling through the freezing void again, and then nothing.

COOL AIR, DAMP AND BRINY, brushed my nose; something warm and solid surrounded me. I tried to open my eyes, but my lids felt heavy, lazy, and I gave up.

A voice murmured lovingly in my ear. "I thought I told you to go home and wait for me."

"I couldn't," I whispered back, through cold immobile lips. "I couldn't just wait for you. What if you needed me?"

"So you came running to my rescue," the voice said, infinitely tender, "and I nearly lost you forever." The warm mass moved beneath me, and I heard, more brusquely, away from my ear, "She's coming around, thank God. Is the car ready?"

Some distant words shifted by; I couldn't quite pick them out. "No, on to Paris, I think," the voice continued, deep and rich under my ear. "I think she's well enough. Have Allegra inform the hotel. We should be there in two hours." Then it bent toward me again. "Can you move yet, darling? The car's waiting."

"Car," I said. I struggled again to open my eyes, knowing it was important somehow. This time I succeeded, just barely. Enough to see that it was dark out, dark as midnight, and that the face next to my own, illuminated faintly by a distant streetlamp, was Julian's. "But you're dead," I said hoarsely.

"No, darling," he said, and I felt my hair being pushed back in that familiar gesture of his. "I'm not. I've been searching for you, trying to bring you back, before you went ahead and boarded that blasted ship."

"What?" Sense was beginning to trickle back to me, enough that nothing was making any sense at all. "Julian?"

"Yes, darling. It's me."

"But you're dead. Where am I?"

"Le Havre. You were about to board the *Columbia*, to return to New York. We've got you at last; it took some trying. I take it you never quite made it to the gangplank?"

"No. I was trying to figure out . . . Oh my God. Julian. It's not possible. You're a ghost. Wait a minute. *Which* Julian?"

He laughed. "Darling, haven't I told you? We're the same man."

"Yes, but . . ."

"The older one, darling. If that's all right. The one you married."

"But . . . but Arthur said . . ."

"Hush. I'll tell you everything later."

"But Geoff killed you . . ."

"Clearly, he didn't. Can you move now? Can I carry you to the car?"

"Oh my God," I said again, and burst into tears.

Dimly I felt him gather me to himself, felt him rise up into the air, felt his calm easy stride move us through the night. I sobbed helplessly against his chest, long past the point of being able to control it, to hold in the tears as I'd done on the railway platform. It all came out, every last particle of grief and fear and anguish, seeping into his shirt and the living skin beneath.

We must have reached the car, because I felt myself being swung inside, still carried in his arms; I heard the door slam behind us, and then the sound of another door closing in front.

"All in," Julian said, and the car started moving.

Gradually my sobbing began to lapse; not because I felt it any less, but because my energy was ebbing away. "Shh," I heard him say against my hair. "I know it's a shock, darling. I'm sorry."

"Sorry." I hiccupped. "Don't be *sorry*. You're alive. You're alive. You're *alive*." I kept repeating it, trying to convince myself. It couldn't be a dream: it didn't feel at all like a dream, but it couldn't be real, either.

"I'm alive," he said, "and so are you, thank God, and I love you, darling. Brave, marvelous Kate. I'm alive. My brave darling. My precious wife." He kept murmuring into the tangles of my hair, stroking my arm with his agile fingers, until his sweet words and the motion of the car lulled me into sleep, deep and dreamless.

29.

When I woke, Julian lay beside me in a bed of depthless softness. His left arm encircled me, while his right hand stroked at my temple. "Good morning, beloved," he said.

"You're alive." My voice scraped against my dry throat.

"Yes, darling. Alive. Always was."

I closed my eyes again, concentrating. "You knew. When we met in New York, you knew it was me. *I* was the one who . . . All those years, you were waiting for *me*?"

A soft rumble of laughter rose up from his chest. "After a night like that, darling, don't you think I'd wait forever, if I had to?"

"I thought I'd never see you again."

"No soldier ever had a better send-off."

I turned my face into the pillow. "I love you," I said, muffled.

"Darling, I don't *quite* think I heard you. What was that?"

"I love you."

"Hmm. Still can't quite make it out. You . . . laugh at me? Bluff me? Stuff me?"

I turned my face up and leaned over to his ear. "I love you," I whispered.

"One more time. Just to be certain."

"I love you, Julian Ashford." I smiled and kissed the tip of his nose. "Which you knew already."

His beautiful laugh again, his arm drawing me closer, his lips brushing mine. "Yes, darling. I knew it already. Believe me, I've heard your sweet voice saying those words in my ear for twelve long years. Tormenting me,

428 / BEATRIZ WILLIAMS

stupid ass that I was, arrogantly thinking I could somehow change the course of fate. Leaving my wife and baby behind."

Baby. I sat up, letting the covers fall to my waist and noticing, in passing, someone had taken off my old-fashioned clothes and put me in a pair of beautiful silk pajamas. I hoped it was Julian. "Wait a minute. Where are we, anyway?"

He began laughing again, relieved and delighted, and propped himself up on his elbow, looking at me. His hair tumbled over his forehead. "We're in a suite at the Crillon, darling. In Paris."

"Oh," I said, looking around the room at the dark shadows of the furniture, the gilded carvings on the high ceilings. The curtains were drawn tightly, allowing only a trickle of light from outside, but I could see it was daytime. "What time is it?" I asked.

He looked at his watch. "Eleven o'clock in the morning. Are you hungry? I can ring down for croissants and whatnot."

"How long have we been here?"

"Since I brought you here in the wee hours of the morning, from Le Havre. Are you all right? You look a bit muddled."

"Of course I'm muddled! I . . . hold on. I really need to use the bathroom."

His hand touched my back. "You're all right, aren't you?"

"Yes. Yes. Just . . . you know." My brain was spinning, and the only clear thought I could pin down was an urgent desire to empty my bladder.

"Let me help you up." He eased me out of bed and set me on my feet. "All right?"

"Fine. Yes. I can walk. Over there?" A rhetorical question; the bathroom door stood well ajar and I was already forcing my eviscerated body in that direction, chased by Julian's chuckle.

A luxurious bathroom, of course: enormous, marble and mirrors everywhere, the faint scent of freesia in the air. When I was finished, I splashed some water on my face and stared at my reflection: at the eyes, somewhat puffy, and the flushed sleepy skin. I touched my fingers to my lips, the lips

Julian had just kissed. "It's real," I told myself, and light began to spread, warm and glowing, from my exact center.

I almost expected him to be gone when I opened the door, but he stood there vibrantly by the desk, speaking into a telephone, wearing a white cotton T-shirt and blue ticking-stripe pajama bottoms. He looked up and smiled at me, one eyebrow raised; his arm reached out, and I leapt into it. "Yes, as soon as possible, please," he said into the phone. "Thanks very much." He hung up, wrapped the other arm around me. "Just ordering a little breakfast for you. Feel better?"

"I lost the baby," I heard myself say into his shirt, not at all what I'd planned. The light at my core flickered out.

"Sweetheart." I felt his lips against the top of my head. "Darling, I know. When I changed your clothes . . . I'm so terribly sorry. I . . . are you all right? I thought I should perhaps call a doctor, but you seemed healthy, and I didn't want anyone to wake you . . ."

"No, I'm all right. It was a week ago. The night you left." My eyes stung; I pressed my face against his chest.

"Darling, darling. I'm so sorry. Sit with me." He pulled me down into an enormous wing chair and held me in his lap, close against his chest. The warmth of his body spread across me like a balm: my every bone still ached with the sucking force of passage, as if I'd been stretched to a thread and let go.

"I'm sorry," I said. "I don't know why . . . I'm so happy, so full of joy and relief . . . but I *loved* it, Julian, *our* baby, and . . ."

I felt his left arm tighten around me, heard his voice waver when he spoke. "Oh, darling. I know, I know. I loved it too." His head dipped into my hair. "Poor Kate. What I've done to you. It's my fault entirely, leaving you like that . . ."

"But I knew." I pressed my cheek flat against his chest, sinking myself into him, as though I could penetrate the skin and become part of him. "I let you go. As soon as I saw what you'd had engraved on the ring, I knew. That there was nothing I could do, that it was all going to happen exactly as it had, that I couldn't—I *shouldn't*—try to play God. So I just let you go. It's okay. You had my permission."

His voice sounded deep and resonant next to my ear. "That's no excuse, my love, and I spent twelve years in purgatory for it, waiting for you, not knowing quite when I would find you. Desperate for you, and then realizing, once I'd met you, I'd been a selfish dog after all, and the best thing I could do was to stay away. To try to keep it all from happening."

"Julian, you idiot." I spoke in a whisper, because I was afraid my voice would break if I tried to use it. "Anything would be better than never knowing you."

I felt his fingertips on my cheek, stroking my skin. "You don't understand, Kate. You don't understand. Those first few months, I searched for you, searched for what happened to you. I was desperate, frantic to know you'd survived. Where you'd gone, what you'd done. Obviously you hadn't gone to my parents. I didn't think you'd stay in France, so I started checking steamship records, looking at passenger manifests, not even knowing what name I was looking for. You'd never told me your maiden name, you know, and for all I knew you'd used that. And finally I found a Katherine Ashford listed on the books for the *Columbia*, departing from Le Havre for New York on April 2, 1916." He paused. "Second-class, darling, *really*. I should have thought those pearls would bring in more than that."

"I couldn't sell them. They were your wedding present."

"Kate, why on earth do you *think* I gave them to you? Why on earth do you think I gave you any of it? I know you don't like being draped with flashy jewels, darling. Being dressed up as a doll, as you put it. But I had to make sure you had resources, whatever happened. Resources you could take with you. Just in case."

"Oh."

"Darling, darling," he said. "Don't you see? It's *all* been for you, every bit of it. Southfield, everything. All for you." He kissed me, urgent caressing kisses. "I had to find a way: first to find you, and then to protect you.

I didn't know where the threat would come from. You gave me so little information, and I, arrogant idiot, gave you back the note that might have saved it all. I knew you'd worked on Wall Street, so I started there. I knew I needed wealth, I needed influence, anything to help me fight against whatever the threat might be; I worked like a dog, *willing* that firm into success, so I might have something to offer you, something to protect you, when I found you at last. To expiate for all I'd done to you."

"But it was such a risk! Someone could have figured out . . ."

"Hush." One finger went to my lips. "I bought that cottage a few years ago, thinking it might be just your sort of place; then, as my fortunes rose, I found the townhouse, when I was out walking one Sunday morning. Always, always you were in my thoughts, Kate. And when you came up the drive that day in May, I thought my heart would explode from my chest. You'd come home to me."

"Stop. It's too much. All that, for *me*?"

His hand massaged the curve of my scalp. "Well, we'd need a home, wouldn't we? Then it occurred to me, after you sneaked down to Manhattan in August, that if I made you conspicuous, *us* conspicuous, it might bring our unknown adversary in the open. So I took the risk someone would identify me, connect the dots, in exchange for the hope that we could head off whatever disaster was coming. And then," he said, sliding his hand back out of my hair to brush my cheek with his thumb, "you told me about the baby."

"You were terrified."

"I always knew we were safe, so long as you weren't expecting. Because that was how you'd come to me, in Amiens, carrying a baby. And so I knew, that night when you told me, the crisis was near. Perhaps already arrived."

"But you married me anyway. Knowing that our marriage was part of the package. Giving me that ring, with that inscription."

"Well, that was another matter. I'd damn myself forever if I let you walk this earth, carrying my child, without calling me husband. And as for the ring, I had to make the contingency. I couldn't leave anything to chance. You've no idea, Kate, no *idea* of all the plans and counterplans muddling around in my head. Agonizing about the damned metaphysics of it all: what could be changed, what couldn't. Cause and effect. What was right. Whether it was all simply God's will. I've been half mad."

"I know, I know." I rested my arm across his waist. "I was too. But you didn't need to, after all. You knew where I'd be on April 2, 1916. You knew I'd come to New York. There would be plenty of chances to find me, to bring me back."

"Kate, I didn't know it was bloody *Hollander* doing all that! I didn't know I'd be *able* to bring you back at will. I thought I'd be *dead*. I'd no idea at all, until I found him puking his guts out in the woods at South-field, having just sent you back to 1916. What I did know, for a certainty, was this: the *Columbia* went down to the bottom of the Atlantic on April 4, torpedoed by a German U-boat, with no survivors."

A knock echoed through the room. Julian rose from the chair, slipping me off his lap and into the seat. "Hold on just a moment, darling. There's your breakfast."

My hand went to my mouth. All those people on the quay, those passengers crowding the gangplank. That little boy with the pale curls. All dead.

Julian walked swiftly across the room and opened one of a pair of lou-vered double doors. I thought it led out to the hallway, but instead I glimpsed a sitting room, filled with sunlight and fine gilt furniture. Julian disappeared from view. I heard voices, the clink of metal and china, and then Julian came through again, holding a tray. "Here you are, sweet-heart." He set it down on the table next to the chair and switched on the porcelain lamp. "Coffee? Croissant?"

"I'll get it," I said, rising, still feeling shocked, but he was already pour-ing me a cup from an elegant silver pot. I frowned. He moved stiffly, favoring his right arm. I took an enormous flaky croissant from the basket and picked off the end, not feeling particularly hungry yet. "Just black, thanks," I added. He handed me the cup and I took a sip, closing my eyes at the hot earthy scent.

"Better?" he asked.

I peered up at his anxious face. "Your arm," I said, nodding at it. "Did you hurt it?"

"A little. Sit. Rest. Let me take care of you."

"I'm *fine*, Julian. Really. Just tired. I'm . . . oh, come here. Keep touching me. Sit down with me again. Is it okay? Your arm?"

"Fine." He eased back into the chair and I settled into his lap with a sigh. He leaned his head back, watching me as I balanced my coffee and pastry. "Now do you understand why I was so frantic?" he said, very low. "It wasn't just my getting killed, and you going back. You'd get on that boat afterward and be killed yourself. I didn't even know, back then, *how* you'd transport yourself; I only knew you'd found a way. Thank God I found Hollander afterward, got him to tell me the truth. The relief, the *hope* that flooded me . . . I can't describe it. Realizing you'd only *thought* I was dead, all that time, and I could *save* you. That we might actually both survive all this."

"I'm so sorry. All that trouble I caused. I was just so panicked for you. I heard the shots, and Arthur said . . . he killed himself, Julian, he put a gun into his mouth right in front of me and shot himself . . . And I thought you *must* be dead, he wouldn't have done it otherwise . . ." I reached over and set the coffee cup down on the table and leaned my face into his shirt. I could not get enough of the physical reality of him.

"Kate, that wasn't supposed to happen. Geoffrey and I, we'd planned it out. I knew *someone* wanted to kill me, *would* kill me: that was why you had gone back. And realizing in the end it wasn't some grand conspiracy, that it was only Arthur, we thought we had a chance to stop him. Lure him away—as far away from you as possible—and then try to talk sense into him, to precipitate some sort of crisis that would resolve things. A stupid idea, desperate perhaps; but we couldn't go to the authorities, obviously. Couldn't have him locked up, and yet we couldn't let it drag on forever, waiting for him to pull the trigger on his own. And if I'd known you'd be right there, watching it all . . ."

"But I heard *shots*, Julian. And I tried to follow them, to find you, but instead I ran into Arthur in the middle of his freaking mad scene . . . Oh my God. The poor man."

"I regret it bitterly. You've no idea."

"Regret *what*, exactly?" I lifted my head to examine his shuttered face. "Wait. Hold on. Julian, *why* did Arthur think Geoff had shot you?"

"Well, because he did," he mumbled.

I whipped upward. "Oh my *God*! You were *shot*? *Where*?"

"Just the shoulder. Flesh wound. He was quite careful."

"*Julian!* Where? *Which* shoulder? Why didn't you *say* something?" I leaned back and stared at his chest, not daring to touch him.

"The right." He pointed. "It's nothing, darling. Practically healed."

"But what if he'd hit something else? Your heart? Your lung?"

"He was a sniper, darling. He can point a gun properly."

"Well, an *artery* or something? Bone?"

Silence.

"Oh God." I sank my head down into his chest. The left side. "You've had a doctor look at it, I hope?"

"Of course I have. Treated and released."

"A *little* hurt, you told me. When you were *shot*." I stared at his right shoulder, covered by his white cotton shirt. I could see, now that I was looking, the faint square of a dressing underneath. I reached out and fingered the edge.

"You worry too much, darling. Everything's going to be fine now, I promise."

"Julian. Julian. I can't believe this. And . . . what a . . . Geoff *planned* it with you?" I shook my head, trying to calm my heartbeat, to think. "But he was behind it all, Julian! He sent me the book, had my things searched; he helped Alicia set me up . . ."

"But he didn't, you know. That was Arthur all along."

"It was *Arthur*? But . . . the cell number . . . and Alicia said . . ."

What *had* Alicia said?

"Arthur was hiding behind Geoff, sweetheart. Using his phone, pretending to be him. It was quite easy; they shared an office, as you'll recall."

"Oh please. Is that what Geoff said?"

"Think about it, sweetheart. Geoff would never willingly reveal our secret like that, sending you the book. And he'd certainly not risk Southfield itself."

I couldn't deny *that*. "But why would Arthur pretend to be Geoff?"

Julian shrugged, moving my head up and down. "To deflect my suspicion, I suppose; or perhaps he hadn't the courage to face my reaction, if I found him out."

"And what about Hollander? Was Arthur behind that too?"

"It's all so evident now, isn't it? But right up until the end, I thought we had two problems on our hands: the real threat, the man who was after Hollander and then presumably you, and then the more personal matter of poor old Arthur watching me fall in love with you. It never occurred to me that Arthur was the one hunting down information about you from Hollander. Not his sort of caper at all. And he'd never spoken to me about Amiens, after all; I simply assumed he didn't know what had happened between us, that he mightn't even remember you at all. So I didn't put the two together until Geoff came to me that last morning."

"I remember that. Just when I came home from my appointment."

"Yes. Geoff had had his suspicions already, because of the book, and especially after Arthur's behavior at the opera: he'd insisted on coming along to meet you, betrayed a kind of obsessive mania about it. And then the next day, after I'd rung up Arthur to ask him to witness our marriage ceremony, he'd gone straight to Geoff, half-mad already with panic, with a sense of the last pillars of his world coming down. Arthur confessed the rest of it—all he'd done to keep watch on you, to chase you away, the whole deception with Sterling Bates—and asked for Geoff's help in stopping our marriage. By force, if necessary."

His words shifted in my brain, forming and re-forming, refusing to assemble into this alien image of Geoff as ally, as stalwart. I pictured instead his angry face, heavy with resentment. "And you trusted Geoff's version of events?" I said at last.

"Kate," he said, "there are two people on this earth I trust absolutely. You, and Geoffrey Warwick."

"In that order, I hope."

"Jealous little minx. Yes, in that order, if you like." He reached over with his left arm to the table and grasped my coffee cup. "Here, eat your croissant. Have some more coffee. You must be famished."

I sipped obediently, nibbled at the pastry. "But still. To let him shoot you, after everything . . . my God . . ."

"Well, we hadn't much choice. We let Arthur take me to Southfield, to the cemetery. I tried to explain things, to tell him I still honored Florence's memory. To show him her grave, to make it forcibly clear that she was gone, that the old world itself was gone, that it was time to face reality and move on. Closure, I suppose, to use your modern word. But it only maddened him further. He took the gun out, threatened me. I tried to take it away, but he took off running. As you saw, I suppose." He shook his head. "If only I'd *seen* you on that damned ledge . . ."

"I tried to yell, but the wind was blowing in my face. You never heard me."

"That's it, isn't it? Every possible element was lined up against us." He rubbed his forehead. "Geoff and I chased him as far as the old boathouse and cornered him, there with that damned gun in his hands, exactly the situation we'd hoped to avoid. But he couldn't do it."

"Couldn't do what?"

"Couldn't shoot me."

"Of course he couldn't. He . . ." I drained the last of my coffee and set the cup back on the table. "He cared too much."

"So he gave the gun to Geoff and told him to do it. Took the other gun from his coat pocket and put it to Geoff's head. Tried to shoot him afterward, too, but missed." He shook his head. "Though it was practically point-blank, the poor bugger."

I shut my eyes. "Those two shots. You were lying there, bleeding, hurt . . ."

"Darling, Geoff *had* to do it. We'd even discussed it beforehand, the possibility of deliberately injuring me; a sort of preemptive strike, you see, to make Arthur realize it wasn't worth bloodshed. Geoff didn't like the idea, but I'm jolly glad we had at least some degree of preparation when Arthur forced his hand . . ."

My eyes shot back open. "A Blighty one! Oh God! *That's* what he meant, when you all drove away together! Only I didn't understand it, back then."

"The right shoulder, we'd decided, since I'd already switched to my left hand." He waggled it helpfully before me.

"You crazy *idiot*. How can you plan for your own shooting?"

"Darling, what else could we do? We had to get him away from you. Had to find some way to resolve things without harming him, without bringing in anyone else, without having to keep him under private lock and key the entire rest of his miserable life. The madman in the attic."

"And you were willing to stake your own life on that chance?"

Julian shrugged his left shoulder beneath me. "It was our last hope for the poor chap." His arm traced along my back. "And in saving ourselves, we failed him."

"It wasn't your *fault*, Julian. *He* did it." I spoke urgently. "My God, you did all you could for him, you gave him every chance. I saw his face. He *wanted* to die; he wanted an excuse. Don't you *dare* take this on. There was never any perfect solution, Julian. Things are just messy sometimes."

"I *told* Geoff to run after him, but he was worried about me, the fool . . ."

"Oh, Julian." I covered my eyes, forced the tears back. "Risking yourself like that. Hurting yourself."

"It doesn't matter, Kate; nothing at all matters to me, next to your safety. I'd have . . ." He stopped, stroking my hair. "Well, you know all that. You'd already made the greater sacrifice, the bravest thing any human being could do, sending yourself back."

"That wasn't brave. I had no choice; I didn't even stop to think."

"And that wasn't brave?"

"No. The hardest part came later. Standing at the station, letting you go."

His hand stilled, wrapped inside my hair. "Do you see, darling"—his voice was low, dark—"do you see why I never needed the words? You'd already shown me. Told me, too, bless you, but that wasn't necessary at all. I'd *seen* your love. Been awed by it, humbled by it. Wondered how I could ever hope to deserve it."

"Julian." I reached up, and his hand found mine, lacing our fingers together, so I could feel the unfamiliar hardness of his wedding ring pressing into my skin. "They're such small words," I said, "when I love you so much. So infinitely. Like I'm just *made* of that one pure element. How could I simply say *I love you*? It wasn't *enough*." I paused. "And then you always said it so much better than I could. Whenever I tried, it all came up so short."

"I don't know. That was a splendid effort, just now. Most effective."

"Well, I'll write it down. Read it back to you every day." *Every day.* The words echoed beautifully in my head. I tightened my fingers through his. "I'm so sorry for all this."

"*Sorry?* Sorry for what? For loving me? For following me to the ends of the earth, without a second thought?" He drew me against him. His hand traced delicately along my spine. I felt my muscles uncoil, felt the flat crushed sensation dissolve, bit by bit, into quiescence.

At last I felt a chuckle vibrate between us. "What?" I asked.

"I was just thinking of that night in the cottage. You can't imagine how I felt, holding you in my arms again, after all that time. All that longing, those sleepless nights, recalling every last detail of our night in Amiens."

I turned and nuzzled his shirt. "Well, that was your fault. Spending twelve years as a *monk*, for God's sake. I mean, I was only thirteen years old or so when Hollander brought you back. I'd never have known."

"Katherine Ashford," Julian said, in shocked tones. He pushed me upward to face him. "Are you suggesting I should have *cheated* on you?"

"Well, it was a long time to go without sex. I mean, it wouldn't technically have been cheating. I didn't even know you existed."

"Kate, exactly how was I supposed to let myself *look* at another woman, knowing you were alive in the world somewhere, waiting to be found? Break faith with you, just for *sex*?" He sounded deeply exasperated.

"Twelve years is a long time. And there are plenty of beautiful women dying to get into bed with you, Julian. I think I would have understood."

"I hope you're being facetious. One of your cheeky little remarks."

"I wouldn't want to think about it," I said, fixing on his chest. "I wouldn't want to think about you with anyone else. But . . . well, it would have evened the score, right?"

"That was different. You didn't know me. You weren't married to me."

"You weren't married to me, either."

"Yes, I was. In my heart. Didn't I place that ring back on your finger with my own hands? Seal it with my own lips?" He tilted my head back to meet his eyes. "Kate, beloved, all I wanted—those long, wretched years—was my wife back. My Kate. Nothing else would do. No one else was *you*. When I walked into that conference room and realized who you were . . ."

"After twelve years? With one little glance?"

"Well, I wasn't *absolutely* certain," he said, "but I jolly well wanted to find out. So I made my excuses, found my way to your desk. And there you were, with your hair back in that damned elastic, with the light catching the silver in those extraordinary eyes of yours, and I knew. I knew it was you."

"I didn't know what to think. The great Julian Laurence, *hitting* on me." I laughed and rubbed my nose into his collar. The warm scent released a kaleidoscope of memories; I turned my head and looked past the curve of his arm to the wide bed with its carved headboard and its rumpled sheets. "But you know, you could have told me," I said. "You could have warned me not to go back. That you'd already met me, and it wouldn't work."

"As if *that* would have stopped you! Kate, you thought I was dead. *I* thought I'd be dead already, if you'd gone back. And I knew you'd willingly sacrifice yourself for even the smallest hope of saving me, my brave darling. That you'd discover how to go back anyway, just to try, because you love me far, far more than I deserve." He pressed a long hard kiss against my hair. "So I couldn't afford to give you even the *idea* you could go back after me. Not the smallest hint. That way, even if I couldn't save myself in the end, I could at least save you."

"Always thinking you could handle things for me."

"Perhaps I've learned my lesson, then."

I looked back up at him. "I'm not holding my breath. Once a male chauvinist . . ."

"I am *not* a male chauvinist!" He looked shocked, and then his face softened. "Only protective of you. That I can't help. And I won't apologize for. You're my *life*, darling. I can't possibly do without you." He paused a moment. "But perhaps you're right. Perhaps I ought to have told you more. I've made so many mistakes, sweetheart, and you've paid for them all, haven't you?"

"For God's sake, Julian. How can you say that? You're the one who had yourself *shot* for me!"

"Darling, a mere winging, I promise."

"Let me see it."

"Later. It's nothing."

"Stoic freaking idiot." I smiled and took his face between my palms and kissed him, again and again: his nose, his forehead, his eyelids, the hair at his temples, the soft unshaven scratch of his cheeks. A man's face now: tiny lines about his eyes, skin fitting snugly about the bones. Twelve years of life, of change, and I'd missed them all. "Darling, faithful, irreplaceable idiot," I said, into his lips. A contented noise rose from his chest; I felt his hands close around my back and rise up slowly until they cupped the ball of my head. I reached back, remembering something, and brought his left hand in front of me. "You're wearing your ring."

"Of course I am. Why wouldn't I? I'm your lawfully married husband. At bloody last, I might add."

I circled it with my fingers, watched the light gleam around the slim golden surface. "I'm just not used to it yet, that's all." I looked up at him and smiled. "It looks wonderful on you."

"Feels a little odd, still. But I rather like it, all the same."

"*Still?* How long has it been, anyway? What day is it?"

"Today? October tenth, I think. I had to spend a night or two in ruddy hospital . . ."

"Good *grief,* Julian . . ."

". . . while Geoff sorted out poor Arthur's affairs, and then it was down to Le Havre with Hollander before we finally found you." He slipped out from under me and went to the pair of enormous windows along the side of the room, speaking as he walked. "We were focusing on the area where the gangway would have been, but without success. So we started moving outward in concentric circles . . ." He drew open the curtains, letting the bright Parisian morning tumble into the room. "There, that's better. Bloody mausoleum. Of course we could only try in the dead of night, when we wouldn't be much seen. We came all week. I would have kept trying forever if I had to." He drew open the curtains on the other window and turned to face me with a broad grin on his face. "And at last, there you were, so alive and unutterably beautiful. And I have never felt more joy in my life, darling. Now come here. I want to show you something."

I rose from the chair and went to stand before him. He reached out for me with his left arm; the right one he held rather stiffly at his side. "Don't you have a sling or something?" I asked suspiciously.

"Yes. I'll put it back on later."

"No. *Now*. I'm not taking any chances with that shoulder. I'll bet you still have *stitches* in it, don't you?"

He narrowed his eyes at me. "Bossy little minx."

I turned and watched him move across the shadowed room to the bureau. His pajamas hung perfectly beneath his white T-shirt; shamelessly I ogled the lean curve of his bottom as it shifted under the loose cotton, and when he turned back in my direction, a sigh slipped out from my very bones.

"What is it?" he asked, returning to me with the pale blue sling in his hands.

"Just admiring you. Here, let me." I reached for the straps, putting them around his neck and buckling them securely. A smile spread across my lips.

"You're *smiling* at this contraption?"

"I was just thinking. You're going to have to exercise your ingenuity for the next few weeks. Or else remain uncharacteristically submissive."

"Ha." He gathered me up. "Shows how much *you* know of my capabilities."

"You're capable of one-handed push-ups?"

"I'm capable of anything, given the proper incentives."

"Serves you right," I said smugly, closing my eyes against the lovely sensation of his warm cotton-clad chest against my face, "being such a freaking superhero. Arranging your own shooting, for God's sake. Don't you ever do that again, do you hear me?"

I felt him toy with the hair at my back, felt the gentle tugs as he wrapped curls around his finger and unwound them again, just as he used to do. The commonplace gesture seemed now like the greatest luxury in the world.

"You asked me once," he said, after a while, "if I'd wait with you, wake with you, instead of rising at dawn. And I told you all about stand to."

"I enjoyed waking up in your arms just now. Just as heavenly as I'd dreamed."

"What about Amiens?"

"I was awake the whole night. It wasn't the same."

"You didn't sleep the entire night?"

"How could I sleep?" I shrugged. "I thought I'd never see you again."

He didn't say anything, only tightened his left arm around me so hard I could scarcely breathe. "There's another reason," he said at last. "Have you any idea how lovely you look, when you sleep?" His voice slipped into a lyric cadence, as if he were reciting poetry. "The flush of your skin. The long beautiful angle of your cheekbones, just so. The way your eyes tilt up, ever so slightly, at the corners. Your hair, tumbling madly over the pillows, or else spread across my chest, dark and soft. That wide mouth of yours, pink and round, the lips just parted. All last summer, I'd wake at dawn as I always did, every sense alert, and instead of the mud walls of an officer's dugout I'd find *you*, heavenly vision, lying in my arms like an angel. I couldn't bear it. If I'd woken you, I should have wept with it."

"That's all right. Tears are okay."

"Mmm." He turned me around and pulled me back against his chest, his left arm slung about my waist. "Look out the window, darling."

"It's beautiful." The view cast southeastward, across the Place de la Concorde to the Tuileries, with the bright mass of the Louvre perched at the end. We were several stories above the ground: the grand mansard rooftops, luminous in the midday sun, spread around us in a wild irregular pattern of boulevards and squares and parks. Off to the right, the Seine glittered provocatively between the buildings, and a memory drifted past me, of trudging across the Pont Neuf three years ago with Michelle and Samantha, arguing about whether we should squander our money on a cup of coffee each at a sidewalk café that afternoon. The quintessential

Parisian experience, of course, but a budget buster for Let's Go travelers like us.

"A much nicer view than the youth hostel I stayed at last time," I said. "In the Marais somewhere, I think."

His laugh rustled near my ear. "I should hope so. We'll go out this afternoon, sweetheart, and do a little shopping for you. Find you something to wear."

"A toothbrush might be nice."

"And tonight I'll take you to dinner. The finest table in Paris. Make you splendidly tipsy on champagne and Burgundy and, oh, perhaps a little Muscat with dessert. And then whatever you like. Dancing, theater. A boat along the river, all to ourselves. Paris is at your feet, darling. The world's at your feet." He bent his head and kissed my neck. "*I'm* at your feet."

"The most important part."

He laughed aloud. "Kate, don't you see? We're perfectly free now. We can do whatever you want, my love. Anything at all, anywhere. I'll give you *such* a honeymoon. Just name the place."

I leaned my head into the hollow beneath his chin and sighed. "I can't think. Just somewhere we can be private. I'd like . . . let me see . . . a piano, so you can play for me in the evenings. I've missed that. And a beach, where we can lie together and watch the palm trees sway."

We stood quietly for a moment, staring out the window.

"What is it?" I turned toward him and looked up to see his brow knit together in long worried lines. "Spit it out, Ashford."

"Well," he said carefully, "I expect we should find a doctor for you first. Make sure it's all right."

I lowered my head. "I should be okay in a few days, I guess. I was only seven weeks along. I'll need . . . a new prescription, of course, and . . ."

"And the rest of it?" His hand began to drift against my back, long gentle strokes.

I couldn't speak without sobbing, so I remained quiet for a moment longer, letting his warmth, his stroking hand, absorb the pain for me. "I loved it so much," I said at last. "I don't know what happened, if it was the grief of seeing you go, or just exhaustion, or if . . . if going back in time . . . killed it. But I loved it so much. It was all I had left of you. Your son, your daughter maybe. Now I'll never know . . . And I never even thought . . . I never thought about babies before . . ."

"Don't blame yourself. It's my fault, if anything."

I stood there against him for the longest time, trying to understand how the joy and the grief could coexist together in my heart. He went silent, stroking my back with his uncanny patience, not crowding me with words. Waiting for me to speak first.

"You'd make an amazing father." I kept my voice even with some effort. "I wanted so much to give you that."

He let my words hang there for a moment. "Perhaps," he said, "when you're ready, we might try again."

I put my arms around his waist.

"Maybe not just yet," I said, "but sometime."

Epilogue

Somewhere in the Cook Islands

Halloween 2008

Though the sun burned overhead, the white sand felt cool and powdery beneath my legs, protected since daybreak by the lazy fronds of the palm tree against which I was leaning.

Julian's head rested in my lap; his body lay stretched out perpendicular to mine, long and lean, his navy blue swimming trunks topped by a white linen shirt against the sun. No sling today; I'd let him take it off at last.

We were talking about his father. "I so wish I could have met him," I said, looping Julian's hair around my fingers, the sun-lightened strands like corn silk on my skin. "I mean, he obviously did a great job of raising you."

"He'd have loved you," Julian said, his eyes closed with contentment. "You're exactly his sort of woman. Funny, opinionated, natural. He despised affectation."

"What did he think of Miss Hamilton?"

Julian opened one eye. "Didn't like her. It was one of the few things my parents fought about."

"I think I like him even more."

Julian closed the eye again. "I picture the two of you, sometimes. How proud I should be, presenting you as my bride. You two getting on famously."

"Stop. You'll make me cry."

He reached up and found my hand and caressed my thumb, saying nothing. I gazed down adoringly at his face. A relaxed face now, its great burden of care finally removed. I hadn't realized how much it had affected him, this fear for me, this certain knowledge that some crisis was coming that he might be powerless to avert. And now that I'd survived it, that he'd rescued me from the fate he'd always feared for me, his soul had taken on the peace of the fully redeemed. It had made for an epic honeymoon.

"Recite me something," I said, after a while.

"What would you like to hear?"

"Something romantic. One of those old story poems."

He smiled, and without opening his eyes, began "The Highwayman." He was no fool. He knew that by the time he got to the second *I'll come to thee by moonlight, though Hell should bar the way,* he stood pretty good odds of getting laid.

Today was no exception.

So it was only some time later, brushing the sand from my skin, he remarked, "You know, there's one poem you've never asked for."

"Which one's that?" I turned over onto his chest, being careful to stay on his left side, and pressed little kisses into his sunlit flesh, into the neat pink scar to the right of his collarbone. "Mmm. You taste delicious. That coconut massage oil."

"Mine."

I looked up at his chin. "Julian, it's a wonderful poem. But I really don't need to hear about your insatiable longing for another woman's beauty. Particularly Florence Hamilton's."

"What's Flora got to do with it?"

"Well, she was the one who had it published. Obviously you sent it to her," I said, trying to sound casual. "Unless there's someone else I don't know about." I picked up his hand from the sand and began licking the fingertips with great concentration.

"Kate Ashford," he burst out, struggling to rise, "do you mean to say that after all this time, you still think "Overseas" was an ode to Florence bloody Hamilton?"

I sat up and stared at him. "Wasn't it?"

"Don't you know when that poem was written?"

"Well, I just assumed . . ."

"Kate," he said, "I scribbled "Overseas" into my notebook on the train, going up the line from Amiens, the morning after the most astonishing night of my life, having just fallen desperately and irrevocably in love. Haven't you even listened to it? *Her beauty, glowing through the rain . . .* That was *you,* idiot love. Outside the cathedral."

"Oh."

"I did, after all," he said, his voice gentling, "promise you rubbishy poetry. Even if Flora saw fit to snatch it for herself, when my kit was returned home."

"So," I said, "when I was sitting there in my AP Lit exam, writing that stupid essay, analyzing those lines . . ."

"You were writing about yourself, yes."

I began to laugh. "Well, you might have *told* me, you know." I grabbed his hands and put them around my naked waist and kissed him long and deep. "You adorable man. What am I going to do with you?"

"I daresay," he murmured, returning the kiss, "if you simply continue on as you are, forever and ever, I should be very happy indeed."

"Forever and ever? Never getting older? Never having, for example, birthdays?"

He dipped his head down and snorted into the skin of my shoulder. "As to that, darling . . . and, in passing, have I mentioned how much I adore this unspeakably alluring neck of yours?" He kissed around the base of it with tender little bites, taking his time. "But as I said, in the matter of birthdays, I'm shocked you have so little faith in me."

"You did tell me, once, you needed reminding."

"Not for the first one, I should hope."

"Ohhh, I see. So that *was* my birthday present, this morning? I wondered."

"Kate, my love," he laughed, bearing me down in the sand with him, "you get *that* present all the time."

"And always deeply appreciated." I began kissing my way downward.

"Kate, you're distracting me. I'm trying to work up to something here; I need my wits about me."

I propped myself up. "Julian, seriously, I don't need a present. I was only kidding, to see if you remembered. I mean, you've given me this entire magical honeymoon, to say nothing of buying up half the rue du Faubourg, waiting for your stitches to heal . . ."

"You enjoyed that, darling. Admit it." He tweaked my nose affectionately.

I conceded. "Okay, a little. I sort of needed the clothes, after all. And it's easier now. Knowing you'd met me before. That I was in your thoughts, all those years, while you were running Southfield. That I did help, in a way."

"*Help?* For heaven's sake, sweetheart, it wouldn't have existed without you. So no more tedious rubbish about spending a little money now and again. You're my properly legal wife now, thank God, and I take great pleasure in exercising my husbandly right to buy you whatever I jolly well please."

I opened my mouth, but he placed his finger over it.

"That being said, darling, I'm not so thick I'd give you exactly what you didn't want, just in order to please my own vanity. You'll be happy to know I spent nothing at all on your birthday present. Not a single centime." He beamed at me virtuously.

"Really?"

"Indeed. In fact, you might well say it's something that already belongs to you." He pulled himself upward and reached one long arm toward the picnic basket.

"What, a ham sandwich?" I inquired.

"Ye of little faith." He flipped open the lid and fished inside. "It's two things, really. The first is rather practical. I nicked it from the hotel manager in Paris." He handed me a yellow legal pad and a pen.

"Very nice, Julian. I could use one of these."

"Sweetheart. It's for your business plan."

"My business plan?"

"Mmm." His arm curled around me. "You said something, in the middle of some argument or another, back in Manhattan, about how you couldn't just go back to work anymore, because of me. The rather long shadow I've apparently cast. And I realized you're quite right."

"Julian, it's not your *fault*. And it's all so silly now, after what we've been through. Unimportant."

"For now, perhaps. But once we're back home, settled into our lives, you'll want something more." He paused for a single self-deprecating chuckle. "All those years, my darling, I thought it was enough I'd built a fortune to lay at your feet. I pictured selling off Southfield, being able to sweep my sweet Kate into a life of idle luxury. Rather proud of myself, I was. And then I found you at last, and it began to penetrate—through the swirling mists of adoration, you understand—that my beloved has rather a fierce streak of independence underneath her quiet exterior. That she wouldn't quite be content as my—what was it?—*arm candy*?"

"That didn't come through in those two days in France, when you claimed to have fallen in love with me?"

"Have a little pity, Kate. I was but a young pup then, overcome by your beauty, without a clue to the modern female mind. But I know you better now, darling. You want to accomplish things, your own things, and you won't be happy without it."

"But I don't even know where to start."

"I daresay you'll think of something. Because I don't want any more rubbish about dolls and gilded cages and bloody *chauvinists* . . ."

"I didn't mean that, Julian. You know I didn't."

"Then let me prove it to you. You can do anything you want, sweetheart. Bookstore. Café. Start your own fund, if you like. Even a—what were your words?—a pansy philanthropic foundation, I believe. We've all the resources you need."

"You'd seed me?"

A tender smile touched the edges of his mouth. "Darling, this fortune of ours—*ours*, Kate—isn't meant to cage you, to limit you. It's to set you free, sweetheart. Free to do whatever it is that makes you happy, that fulfills you."

"And what about you?"

"What *about* me?" He shrugged. "I'll be busy enough helping sort out that damned fiasco back home. Or else rescuing Hollander from his latest folly, God rot him. I shall simply cheer you on from the sidelines."

"Oh, really?" I reached out with one toe and poked his leg. "And how long is *that* going to last, do you think? I know you, Julian, and you won't be able to help yourself." I bent closer. "And you know what? That's fine. I can't do it without you, you know. I'll be counting on your help. Your advice."

"Be careful, darling. Invite me in, and I might try to manage everything for you. Interfere remorselessly. Protect you from every vicissitude."

"Oh, I'm learning how to deal with you. Keep you at bay with a few well-timed shrewish remarks." I looked back down at the yellow pad. Blank. An open promise. Whatever I'd been expecting, it hadn't been this. "Thank you. I'm overwhelmed. This is . . . this is the most amazing gift. And a little misleading, you know." I looked back up. "It's going to be pretty expensive, in the end."

"Oh, you'll make us a handsome profit on it, I've no doubt." He rubbed my chin with his thumb and smiled broadly. "And now for your second gift, which is rather more in the sentimental line."

"Am I going to cry?" I set the legal pad down in the sand.

"I should jolly well hope so." He reached back in the basket. "Ah! Here you are. Only twelve and a half years late. Beastly old postal service."

I stared down at the envelope in my hands. "What's this?"

"You're supposed to open it, darling. I daresay it will all become clear."

I turned it over. It was addressed, in a lopsided black scrawl, to Mrs. Katherine Ashford, 29 rue des Augustins, Amiens. I turned my eyes back to Julian's face. "Oh God. How did you . . . ?"

"I kept it in the pocket of my tunic, darling. I meant to post it once I returned to the trenches. In my ever-damned arrogance."

It wasn't sealed. I lifted the flap with shaking fingers and drew out the folded paper inside. It felt crisp and new, only a single sharp crease across the middle. "Didn't you ever open it?" I said.

"No. I always thought I'd wait for you to do that. Ah, there it is." He reached over to collect me. "What a weepy female you've become."

"Sorry," I whispered. I unfolded the letter; a smaller sheet slipped out, the left side slightly ragged.

"I made a clean copy for you, from the notebook. Ironically enough," he drawled, "my everlasting fame, as you put it, comes from a mere first draft."

I held up the paper. "Overseas," he'd scrawled at the top, and the fourteen lines followed, spare and evocative, the ending now devastatingly clear: "*. . . in this shadowed hour/The vision guards my faith, while overseas/Her heart beats mine, defeats eternity.*"

"Your poem," he said.

I nodded. There was no point in trying to say anything. I turned back to the enclosed letter.

He cleared his throat. "It's not long. I was in a hurry."

I read it through twice, and then the poem. I put the one sheet back in the other and folded it up again and slipped it back in the envelope.

"Was that all right?" he asked.

I nodded and turned and let him ease us down into the sand.

"Happy birthday."

"A year ago," I said, a long silent moment later, "I didn't even know you. Didn't even know this much love existed in the world. Isn't that funny?" I spread my fingers out on his chest, watched the slow rise and fall of his breath. "Charlie and a couple of the other analysts took me out for my birthday. My twenty-fifth. Kind of a big deal. We went to this Tex-Mex bar in Tribeca and did tequila shots."

Julian snorted.

"I did *not* do that many," I said defensively. "I'm not much of a partier. But I *was* kind of hungover the next day."

"Poor darling."

"Anyway, that was my last birthday. Now here I am."

"Here you are. No tequila shots, I'm afraid."

"No. Thank God. Just you." I turned over in his arms and lifted myself, so I could stroke his cheeks with my hands. "Thank you. Darling Julian. The most wonderful birthday presents in the world. Both of them." I lowered my head and kissed him.

"Mmm. You're quite welcome."

"You know, you're very good at all this. At love. At marriage. The whole husband thing."

He grinned. "It's my life's work, after all."

I kissed the tip of his chin. "When we get back, I'm going to take *such* good care of you."

"You already do."

"I'll get up early and make you pancakes." I kissed a trail down the underside of his chin to the hollow of his throat.

"Oh, ha bloody *ha*. I'll believe *that* when I see it. Ow!"

I'd just pinched his side.

"Maybe just on Sundays." I followed with a tickle. "And bubble baths."

"*Bubble* baths? Oh . . . for God's . . . *sake*," he managed, between gasps of laughter.

"Back rubs. With that yummy coconut oil."

"That's . . . more . . . like it. Kate, *stop* it . . . little *minx* . . ." He writhed helplessly.

I coiled my body and leaned into his ear. "Beat you to the water."

I took off running, a dead sprint, powder flying from my feet. Ahead, beyond a hundred sloping yards of clean pale sand, the lagoon glowed aquamarine under a white sun.

He timed it all perfectly, as he always did, snaking his left arm around my waist and hauling me down with him just as the wavelets hit my thighs. The crystal water splintered above us; his sunlit body wrapped around mine; our wet laughing heads bobbed up together.

Tempting the gods.

Acknowledgments

So many people—knowingly and unknowingly—contributed to the publication of *Overseas*, it hardly seems fair that I only have space to single out a few.

I'm forever grateful that my search for a literary agent began and ended with the incomparable Alexandra Machinist, who plucked me from the slush pile in one whirlwind week, and whose faith in my writing makes everything possible.

My warmest thanks belong to Rachel Kahan, Lauren Kaplan, and all the wonderful team at Putnam, both for their reckless enthusiasm for *Overseas* and for their expert advice and guidance in turning the manuscript into a book people might actually want to read.

While I spent most of my professional life on the fringes of Wall Street, I turned to my dear friends Anne and David Juge for specifics on the structure of investment banks and capital markets divisions in particular. I'm deeply grateful for their perspective and their support; any dramatic license or outright error is, of course, entirely my doing.

I owe more than I can say to Sydney and Caroline Williams, who have supported and encouraged my writing career at every stage, and who show me every day how to be a better spouse, a better parent, and a better person.

To my parents, who gave me such a solid literary foundation; to Jana Lauderbaugh, who provided shrewd advice on the initial draft; and to my sister, who cheered each step along the journey: this book is as much yours as mine.

The love and loyalty of my family gave me the courage to attempt the lunatic challenge of writing a novel for publication. To my four precious children, and to my beloved husband, Sydney, I can only offer my heartfelt thanks and my promise that, next time, I'll try not to stay up writing past four a.m. on a school night.

I owe a final debt to a young history professor whose name I no longer recall, though I can conjure her face and Dorothy Hamill haircut like a photograph in my brain. As a junior in college, I took her seminar course on turn-of-the-century Europe and the First World War, which shocked me into awareness of a generation of brilliant young men who'd charged from the trenches of the Western Front into oblivion. In creating the character of Julian Ashford, I borrowed biographical details from a number of these historical figures. Students of the period will recognize, among others, a dollop of Roland Leighton, a hint of Rupert Brooke, and pieces of Julian Grenfell, who lent my fictional Julian both his Christian name and his birthdate (the latter, I swear, by coincidence). But Ashford's habits and personality are completely his own. He leapt from my brain onto the page, and I hope he does some lonely bit of justice to the men who, in dying, gave him life.

About the Author

A graduate of Stanford University with an MBA from Columbia University, Beatriz Williams spent several years advising senior executives on communications and corporate strategy before turning to the more productive pursuit of writing novels. She lives with her husband and four young children near the Connecticut shore, where she divides her time between writing and laundry.